"YOU CAN NEVER MAKE IT,
THROUGH THIS LIFE ALONE."
-MEONIAL

THE

JOURNEY

OF

CELESTRA.©

THE HYBRIDS OF APROPON RAR SERIES©

BOOK ONE

The Journey of Celestra

Written and Illustrated By: §K Palser

Edition 4
2001 – 2019

Available for sale via Amazon.com/ Barnes&Nobles.com/

BISAC: Fiction / Fairy Tales, Folk Tales, Legends & Mythology

ISBN-13: 978-0692701430

ISBN-10: 0692701435

INDEX

Acknowledgments

This series, is quite a story within itself. The first book began back in 2001, the night before 9/11. After that awful day in history, I started writing this story. The first medium was a Palm IIIe and then later on a Palm Zire 72. During smoke breaks, gigs or parties where I was able to slip away to write… somehow, this story grew larger than ever expected. For many years, this *'tail'* has remained sealed away, hidden from the public's eye.

To see these characters traveling together experiencing pain, challenges and happiness, will always be one of the greatest gifts in my life. To thank all the people involved in creating this series would certainly take an extra five hundred pages. No man is an island, and I am certainly no exception. Your best real-life professors, are the ones who leave an imprint; those who have shocked your soul, into life.

These are the people I care for the most. The fly by personalities, set afire with passion, who come in hot, yet leave you with a lifetime of smoldering lessons, well after the wick has burnt out.
Some of these wonderful folks might be reading this book right now, so sincerely I say with love: 'Thank you for being.'
This all wouldn't exist without you.
The last dedication is to Tarmax & Uniqua: You may be gone from this world, but never forgotten. Trinity hybrids and their masters, will always leave a deep mark on the world, they have left behind. Sometimes, the mark left within our hearts is deeper.

So, with that, I welcome you now, to the lands of Apropon Rar.

APROPON RAR

The Central North East

Celestra's Journey

Preface

I hear phantom footsteps behind my paws. I tell myself, *Keep running. You have to now!* My feet move like the wind, and my head races.

Pushing too fast around a bend, I fall straight to the ground. Skidding into the dirt, my shoulder hits a tree root. Fatigue sets in quickly. Panting relentlessly, my heartbeat becomes deafening. I cannot catch my breath. Rising slowly, I try to gain composure. Self-doubt starts to fill my mind. *Have I gone past the point of no return? What was there to go back to anyway?*

Why did I allow myself to be tricked like this?

Like a chump, I chased my master's scent trail without thinking of the consequences. It's obvious that the sun is setting soon. *I really need a positive sign, or I'm going to break.*

Staring up at the treetops, I try once more to feel Uniqua's energy. Nothing comes to focus and only tears well up in my eyes. Instead of breaking down, I growl out loudly in frustration. This is no time for fear.

Looking down at my blood matted fur, I cannot recall the last time I stopped to clean up. My ears fall flat in disapproval. This recent upheaval has left me feeling weightless. I fight the present sadness as hard as I can. *It is just not possible until daylight to make it back to my den.* Bothered heavily over this wasted day, I must admit, I am lost on what to do.

Looking closer at my scars, these lines of pink skin made my heart sink. These were permanent reminders on how I could have made better decisions. I must cease this madness. I have to stop and rest tonight.

It's been four years since my master Uniqua disappeared. He was basically, my only guardian. Absolutely nothing has been the same without him.

Honestly, all I want is a real conversation, a deep mind to chat with, or the rub of a face with pure intentions. What can a panther do in these times of uncertainty and chaos? I've been on my own for so long, things just seem routine now. Day in and day out, it is always the same, just a broken ring of existence.

I try hard to let these thoughts pass without entertaining them. It is time to attend to the most important issue. Exactly where I am. Finding shelter is necessary, if the night is coming. Scanning the area, the environment feels strange. A restless feeling comes over me, yet stronger than before.

I shake my body and happily watch the dust and twigs fly off. Licking my paws carefully, the muck falls from my claws. My front pads, worn and calloused, still carry an air of feline femininity. Any animal around *my* territory knows better than to mess with Celestra, the white panther. If they tried, they would end up with a poor night's rest mending their wounds.

I laugh at myself. My pride might be stronger than my body it seems. I'm still hurting from my last meal yesterday. That buck may have been tasty, but he put up a hell of a fight. An antler managed to pierce my chest during the struggle.

Concentrating on my goal, I find a new trail up ahead. My whiskers perked at the change in the air. As I walked, memories quickly flash through my mind. Uniqua hated when I would daydream. Tonight, these thoughts sadly, were my only companion.

I began to remember, how the local animals would make fun of me as a cub in Fictine Forest. They would call me a freak, but when I was flying straight for them with claws extended, their tune quickly changed. *So what if I was born different?* My master would often reassure me by calling me "unique". It always worked to stop the tears. Certainly, fitting seeing his name was Uniqua. He was bothered many never said his name right. If one studies the cherished Native American language, his name becomes quite easy to speak correctly.

The Ancients gave him this name when he was just a small cub in a meditation. Uniqua always seemed so proud telling the story. I felt honored just to hear it. Mind you, this happened quite often. It still made me smile none the less.

One thing that always seemed constant, was my master. He made me happy like no other. A true friend in a world of lost souls.

For many years, Uniqua and I, explored the lands around our territory. Every new thing I would find, he had a reason for its existence.

He taught me what animals to stalk, what streams to drink from, and where to go during a storm. Also, I received the education on how to hunt alone successfully in the woods.

Despite the local animal life calling me a freak, Uniqua always said my differences were gifts, and they were simply jealous. As I grew older, it became obvious, he told me this to stop me from moping around.

He taught me that my wings were a huge advantage over the local wolves while hunting. Yet my white fur would remain a real bother while stalking prey. This was my life challenge to overcome. I happily worked on maintaining my low profile. I learned how to strive for the right to live free, and how to claim a stake in the land. Thank the stars for Uniqua. Without parental guidance, he was all I had.

Bothered with all these distracting thoughts, I shake my head one more time. I would rather be sleeping when the darker creatures come out to play.

Walking quietly, I made note this forest looked different from my home back down south. It held a warming light, much like a cluster of fireflies. I smell the air again and tried to find something familiar. Slowly, a curious but friendly feeling lifted my heart; there was no desire to send it away.

Still cautious, I approach a large bush to further inspect the strange scent. My whiskers stand straight out and twitch with the twilight sounds of the forest. Out of nowhere, odors of burning wood and herbs tickle my nose. I sneeze. This surely is not the territory of another animal I've ever known. Alone and a bit nervous, I start to panic. *Oh Uniqua, where are you?*

Turning around, I inspect the dense brush again.

My instincts told me to remain still, yet my mind was screaming to run away and to run fast.

In the distance, I heard rustling… Something *was* here. My heart started to race. There is no room for mistakes. Not now and certainly not in my present condition.

Chapter One

Panther's Company

Celestra's growl of concern broke the unnatural silence. Another branch snaps in the background. She is positive something was here. Instantly leaping to her feet, her hackles rise. Teeth bare and jowls pulled tightly back, she stands with her paws ready to attack.

Celestra refuses to move a muscle. Even in her present condition, she's ready for a fight. With her face now an inch from the ground, whiskers fully extended, a laugh trickles out from the thick leaves. The dry dirt scatters like down feathers as Celestra prepares for battle. There is no other choice but wait and see, what stirs in the bramble hidden behind the darkness.

Before Celestra could blink an eye, or watch the dust settle, something large quickly jumps on top of her. With its bulk firmly pinning her down, she tries to tear through its hide, but with no success. Feeling one of her front canines giving way, she lets go. "Who are you and what do you want with me!" Comically, the creature stands upright and bows in front of her. Perplexed at its bi-pedal movement, she stays tense watching its every move.

Noticing that Celestra was nervous, the dragon spoke softly to her, "Well hello there… little panther. How nice of you to drop by. I will not hurt you in any way… so please relax. I want to spend some time with you. Please walk with me."

Celestra swallows her fear. Her instincts tell her two different things: One is to trust the dragon and walk with him. The other was to make a run for it whenever she could. *If this is his idea of being friendly, I don't want to see him angry.*

Celestra decided to keep walking. With all this activity her head was spinning. Trying to focus on the present moment, she uses Uniqua's training to remain calm. *Dragon or no dragon, no living creature is without its faults. There will always be a moment they drop their guard.*

She wonders if he was from a rogue group that managed to live past the Draconian war. Uniqua taught her that not a single dragon survived the wrath of the humans. Yet oddly, here there was one walking and talking with her alive, and well.

The dragon's cheery energy bothered Celestra. It made her feel terribly vulnerable. *Dragons have superior minds, or this one is just playing with his food, before he eats it.* The dragon affectionately turns down and looks to Celestra, "You know, the stars should have led you here a long time ago." Confused, Celestra responds, "I'm not quite sure what you mean, *dragon*."

"Please, call me Drako; I prefer that to such a *generic* name." Celestra turns her head and rolls her eyes. "Sure *Drako*. Just to let you know, I do not travel outside of my territory often. Today is just a fluke. If I wasn't so exhausted, I would still be trying to fight you." The dragon laughs loudly as he claps his hands. His bi-pedal movement made her nervous. It reminded her of those terrible humans. She lowers herself a bit while walking out of concern.

Drako starts to laugh quietly, "oh my….

A warrior who's forgotten her real land and her real lineage. This is so very sad."

"What do you mean Drako? How would you know *my* past? I have never met you before today." She snarls and becomes increasingly defensive. Drako will not have such an outburst in his presence. He speaks:

"I say such things because I *know* what you really are. *You*, on the other hand, have no clue. My friends will be able to show you soon enough..."

Celestra was now growing tired of this nonsense. "I don't think any of this is funny...*Drako*. I have no known lineage and *no* existing family. I am a weird white panther with wings who was raised by a bear. My parents abandoned me at birth and this is all I know. Besides, why should I bother daydreaming of my bloodline when there are better things to do.

- Like making sure I have food to eat and a place to sleep at night."

Drako slowly bends down his neck, and looks deeply into her eyes. Celestra stops short terrified, lets the dragon speak. "Why would it be bad little one to have a desire to know your heritage? I believe it will show you what to actually fight for and what to protect." Celestra's heart skips a beat thinking Drako wanted to take a bite out of her. Thankfully, she was mistaken. Overly stressed, the poor white panther has had enough. It was obvious in her body language.

"Where are we going? It's taking a lot out of me to not run off or fight you. I'm not a fan of temporary acquaintances." Drako looks to Celestra with a toothy grin. "Well, we're going to where you will rest and learn how to appreciate your gifts. I notice you are quite wounded. Also, worry little about this 'acquaintance' issue. Changing minds are friend or foe, depending on the circumstance. By adhering to trepidation, true happiness can never be achieved." Celestra finally having enough, growls at Drako with an attitude, "Why are you being so nice to me?" You know *nothing* about me dragon! I *could* be a threat you know..."

Drako smiles, and shakes his head at Celestra, "Ah. This is where you are wrong little panther. I have known of your kind for a long time. Your species' survival is key, to all of our existence here on Gaia."

Drako gestures straight ahead with his claw. "Come now and let's head out to meet my friends. Who knows, maybe you'll even learn a thing or two about that key I see dangling around your neck." She quickly turns to Drako with a nasty look. Softly she growls in discontent. Celestra knows no history of her silver key. *My parents left it with me before they ran off. At least, that's what Uniqua said.* She decides to say nothing about it. With everything going on, why make it harder for herself.

Watching the night curl around them all, Celestra wonders why Drako knows so much about her. This was not comforting. He looks at Celestra and motions for her to come forward,

"Let me carry you and we will fly to our next destination." Celestra huffs loudly and snarls. She refuses to move an inch.

"Well actually *Drako*, I am perfectly capable of flying myself. I do *have* my own wings..."

Drako sighs and decides to show up this snotty little panther. "That may be, but can you keep wingtip with *this*?"

Lifting up one great wing, Drako flaps down, and creates a rush of hard wind. Celestra flipping over, ends up crushing her feathers badly. Fur awry, wings mangled, she raises her head with one eye closed. "I suppose you're right when you put it that way. Fine, let's fly." Drako grabs the nape of her neck in his mouth, and carries her away. The night air was cool and refreshing through her badly matted fur. The little panther tries to stay awake, but passes out rather quickly in the dragon's large mouth.

Chapter Two

Dragons Run from the Dawn

Celestra woke up on the ground a bit dazed. Looking up, she saw a blazing fire surrounded by grey mossy boulders. Her instincts told her to be wary of the red burning devil in front of her. Yet she found it hard to deny the warmth it gave off. Celestra saw large flat stones placed around the pit, but further out. This was all in the center of a circular clearing, with uprooted trees lining the outer perimeter.

Within the darkness, every now and then, she would see tails thrashing back and forth. There seemed to be three. Peering north out through the cracks of the forest, Celestra could make out large mountains and what appeared to be a wide winding river.

Feeling intimidated, she knew to keep her wits. Celestra might have gained some strength, back while sleeping during the flight, but had little idea where they were. Frustrated, she rests her head back down. A soft hopeless sigh blows out from her nose. Turning around she sees one of the dragons throw a huge log onto the pit. As the fire grows larger, Celestra can make out Drako and two other bi-pedal dragons. They seemed to know each other well. It was obvious by their body language. Staying quiet, Celestra pretends to be asleep, so she could study them further.

Drako was a dark maroon colored dragon. The horns on his head were tightly spiraled in brown with hints of gold. Small spikes started at his tail tip and then gradually became longer further up his back. The ones at the base of his head were quite impressive. Next to him, was a very smooth and streamline dragon, in a beautiful dark blue. It appeared to be a female. She had very guarded energy. Celestra doesn't work well with reclusive personalities.

The third one was a stout and portly dark green dragon, with very stubby arms and legs. His claws were short, but looked incredibly strong. His spikes were wide and appeared to be rock hard.

His deep and familiar laugh warmed Celestra inside. *This one reminds me of Uniqua… Soft and warm laughter usually points to a strong and ferocious soul.* Overall, Celestra can see that these dragons were not out to harm her… yet.

Drako carried a large cauldron of steaming liquid and a bowl towards Celestra. She quickly laid still and breathe slowly to look like she was sleeping. As he poured it, he looked her over with a half-tilted smile. To wake her out of this youthful display, he blows hot air at her face. Celestra twitched and backed away from him instantly giving up. Drako leaned down and looks her in the eyes, holding her chin in his claws. "I knew you were awake, little one. Remember we dragons may seem absent-minded and carefree, but we are *quite* perceptive. Never mistake our kindness for weakness."

What Celestra was taught about dragons didn't seem to add up. They are playful jesters and highly intelligent, not barbaric meat-eating monsters. How would Drako know these herbs for healing if he wasn't provided a proper education? Celestra thinks, *so why were they all waiting for me? What else do they know about my past?*

Looking over to her far left, the other two dragons were calling out to Drako to introduce his new companion. He turns to Celestra and brings the bowl towards the fire. With his elbow, he nudges her along to follow. "Well little warrior, let's go meet your new 'acquaintances'. It is best not to keep my friends waiting."

Drako and Celestra walk over to the others. Celestra cannot help but be mesmerized by the flames as they crackle in front of her. *I'm not used to seeing it contained like this. The bright embers dance and flicker yet remain in the stone circle without spreading. So brilliant, yet so frightening.* She notices quickly, that Drako is pointing to the blue dragon. She looks up from the flames and tries to pay attention.

He starts the introduction. "This beautiful creature over here is Lastra. She is a dragon of the water and air. You see, Lastra has webbed toes. These help her move at great speeds while using very little energy. Her tail is long and slender with a tall fin that runs down her spine. This acts like a rudder allowing for sharp changes in maneuvering."

Celestra interrupts, "What are those long whiskers coming out of her face? I didn't know that dragons could have whiskers." Drako sees the look of insult on Lastra's face and tries to explain. "Little warrior, those aren't whiskers, they're *feelers*, almost the same. They let her keep her balance when upside down." Lastra folds her arms quite offended, "You are quite strange yourself *dear*. Gaia's panthers do not have wings. So, either you are a freak of nature, or a hybrid."

Celestra looks back at the blue dragon and snorts. "Not really sure what a hybrid is... *Lastra*. All I know is when I was younger, these wings just popped out of my back when I was running away from a wolf pack. My master Uniqua told me it was just a stroke of luck. He spoke nothing about this 'hybrid' thing before. Am I *not* just a panther? Can't a panther *have* wings?"

"Well, I'm sure they can if dragons can have *whiskers*." Lastra blurts out angrily. Drako cuts them both off and moves over to introduce Celestra to the stout dragon. He throws a disappointed look towards Lastra to cut it out.

Pointing over to the large dark green dragon, he smiles warmly at Celestra. "This is Partune. Our battle-ram. He's our scaly wall of strength. Even the strongest slab of steel couldn't puncture that hide. If he's charging at an enemy at full speed, there is no chance they would be living afterward."

A jolly laugh rolls out from Partune's mouth, as he holds his stomach. "Hello there little one. It's nice to meet you. It seems you have an interesting birthmark there on your forehead, that *dark* star."

Celestra tilted her head in confusion. She wondered why her unique physique was such a topic of conversation amongst these dragons. They all smiled and winked at each other as if they were hiding something.

Drako comes to Celestra's side and offers her a drink out of that small wooden bowl from earlier. The steam rises up and reaches her nose. Pungent and sour, she is revolted by its smell. She backs up with a horrid look on her face.

Drako offended growls out, "What's wrong? Can't drink something that smells a bit *foul*? This will tend to your wounds and your tattered fur. Drink it. It's really not that bad." Apprehensively Celestra laps up the terrible liquid and tries to ignore the taste.

Almost immediately, her stomach rejects it. She gags a few times. Clearing her throat in between coughs, she attempts to settle down. "What *exactly*...did I just drink? You know, to remember for other times ahead of me..."

Drako happily tells her, "Gotu Kola, Nettles, Echinacea and Pau d'arco. This should help your deep wounds heal and prevent infection."

Celestra grimacing over the taste shakes out her head, "I let my wounds heal naturally. Noticeably faster than other animals in my territory. I guess it's just one of my gifts." Drako looked deeper at the dark star on Celestra's forehead, while scratching his chin. "You're stronger than I thought. This is something to consider. Your wounds are so deep you should be at death's doorstep, not talking back with snappy retorts. Let's just say the tonic will help you further along then, all right?"

"I must say it's a bit bothersome being in the dark like this. What do you mean I'm stronger than you thought?"

Out of nowhere, something disturbs the dragons. They quickly turn away from Celestra and her confusion. All are staring at the sun rising in the distance. Drako apparently very concerned turns to face the other dragons. "Lastra, Partune, we must start to move. Greggils will be crawling here shortly, and our hides will not be decorating their castle walls anytime soon."

Ignored and upset, Celestra turns to look at the sun as well. *What the heck are Greggils? ...Must be strong to frighten dragons away.*

Turning back, she sees Drako walking towards her. Partune kicks out the fire and Lastra helps remove their presence from the area. Drako picks Celestra up by the nape of her neck and quickly flies off with the other two dragons. There was no conversation this time. Before the cold air soothed her to sleep, Celestra memorizes their location.

Traveling this high was wonderful. Celestra only flew a few meters from the ground while hunting. High flying wasn't something she chose to explore. Earlier while sleeping in Drako's mouth, she couldn't experience this joy. Looking at the dragons in flight was also a special moment for her. Especially Lastra who flew so gracefully it denounced all the rigid thoughts placed on dragon flight. It's hard to imagine those old nasty stories about dragons holding any validity. All she thought prior was quickly becoming a fairy tale.

In front of her, was her entire territory behind them, fading into the distance. Directly below, she could see rolling green hills. Some had jagged and steep cliffs which hid caves amongst thick brush and trees. Most creatures cannot see during this time of day, unless they were predators. Celestra wondered why these dragons were being so secretive. *Was there something stronger out there that could even scare dragons? Maybe these 'greggils' they spoke of earlier...*

In flight, Drako points to a large cave. They start to descend and make a great landing. He places Celestra onto the ground and leads her into the cave with the others. Darkness is once more upon them inside. Drako quickly blew out a huge blast of fire to light a pile of logs. Instantly the room lit up. Celestra saw this was another common meeting ground for the dragons. *There must be many of these places. I shall remember this.* Before Celestra could settle down the three dragons began expressing their present concerns. One of them brought up Roden forest towards the west. She also heard them say that they were on the edge of the Tressdresua Hills. Finally, Celestra knew where they were.

Apparently, greggils stole Roden forest away from these creatures called the Carthines. Drako was talking to Partune about other recent disappearances as the two dragons grunted in displeasure. *These greggils sound terrifying. I hope we never come across one.*

Lastra walks forward with a sad look. "Don't forget my whelp and mate went missing four years ago as well Drako. Still to this day we have no idea where they went." As tears fall from her green eyes, Partune growls out in anger. He thrashes the wall with his claws removing a large chunk. Dust falls from the ceiling along with some small stones. "I hate those barbaric creatures. They destroy everything, feel terrible about it and then rebuild it all only to destroy it again. I hate to say it but they're just overgrown hairless apes."

Slowly Celestra is beginning to understand the irony between dragons and these 'greggils'. Walking out of the cave, she stares wildly out into the sky for answers to all this madness.

The wind gently moves her fur and brings about a small memory. Mouth agape, she recalls something disturbing.

She remembers a strange situation when she was a young cub. Walking out into a clearing, two pale bipedal creatures were playing. She knew that these were human children from

Uniqua's lessons. She tried to walk away quietly but they spotted her. Instantly, they started to run in her direction and very fast. For some time, they kept on chasing Celestra. These awful things were quite relentless.

The longhaired one managed to corner Celestra. Just as she was about to scratch its arm, the other one jumped in front and blocked it. It took the blow from her claws.

After the two ran off, Celestra headed straight for her forest. *Greggils and humans must be one in the same.* She understands this now and can understand why adult humans must be ten times worse.

Drako walks over to Celestra and pats her head. "Little warrior, I've been so rude by not asking your name." She responds, "Celestra. That's what my caretaker Uniqua always called me." Partune looks over at them quickly at the mention of her name. Drako too smiled, hearing it spoken aloud.

"May I ask what kind of creature your teacher was?" Celestra stares at the morning sun and puffs her white chest out. Her silver key bounces off her neck. "Earlier if you recall Drako, I said he was a bear. My teacher was a great big brown and white bear. His name was Uniqua and for quite some time he was my master and my only friend. He taught me everything I know and I'm very grateful for his dedication." Drako still eyeing Partune, looks back to Celestra.

"...Well you speak very highly of him. I must admit, it would be a pleasure to meet him someday..."

She turns away in sorrow towards the horizon.

Celestra thinks of the day he disappeared. It grew deathly quiet around her. They all felt her deep heartache and sadness. Drako softly asks Celestra, "You lost him little warrior, didn't you? I'm so sorry." They see this fierce little panther had some scars deeper than her skin after all.

Drako and Celestra stare out into the morning skyline, in each other's quiet company. He eventually decides to break the silence and speaks.

"We will move soon to the dragon city, Drondia. We will find the hybrid mystic, Avalo Ryu, as he is trained for what comes next. He knows much more about your species than all of us combined. Let's take a small catnap before the journey. I'm flying with an extra couple of pounds after all." The group laughs and they all start to wind-down.

Drako kicks the fire back a bit and the embers glow a deep red. Celestra was in a better mood as the three dragons tucked in around her. This made her feel like she belonged somewhere. They were all starting to feel like companions. Tears welled up in her blue eyes. This feeling was so strange that she wanted to run away from it. For now, though, she'll accept the affection and the tears on her muzzle as they all fall asleep.

Later that night they all wake up and stretch out in similar fashions. Celestra closely examines her surroundings again to make sure she wasn't moved while sleeping. She wants to wander out for a while and goes to tell the others. *It's so hard to accept that these creatures being perfect strangers are this willing to help me, but why though? Why?*

Exploring this new environment, she sees many unfamiliar things. So much is quickly changing that it is impossible for Celestra to get a grip on what is actually reality. Trying to find north, she can see in the distance those same mountains again and can tell they are closer now. The first star of the night is shining down from the sky. She can see the river in the distance is very wide and deep. *There is probably some great fish in there. It's been a while since I have had the chance to dine on such enriching food.*

Walking a bit more, she ponders these new acquaintances. *Why do I trust these dragons? Why have I grown attached to them as if they are my friends? Maybe it's because my heart tells me to trust. It's strange; I feel like I have known them forever.* Yet doubt gets the better of her. She pushes a rock off the cliff and sighs. As she watches it fall below, Drako walks up from behind and blows her over, with a puff of hot air, like last night.

Ruffled fur and dazed in mentality, she turns to look back at him. "What was... *That* for?" Drako smiles at her with a sly look, "That's for doubting us. *Greggils* doubt. Gaia's creatures trust." Celestra gets Drako's point. She nods still uncomfortable from the jolting moment. Maybe her unguarded energy gave her away. Being alone for so long her social graces were non-existent.

I really do wish to find out more about my heritage, as well as my past..., but what I already know, seems good enough for me. Well, it used to be anyway.

Drako and Celestra go to retrieve the others to set out on their journey. Once all together again, they start making travel plans. With Partune being so bulky, Drako explains he will not fly the entire way. He will meet someone halfway instead and complete the journey on the ground. "The *rest of you*; we will need to keep vigilant for all 'night time greggil' activities."

No one argues, and they set forth.

Celestra realizes there really is no real way she could run away from these creatures. Even if she wanted to leave, they are much too massive for her to take on. Besides, no harm has come to her. Why be hasty and lose the chance to make a run for it later.

Drako turns to Celestra and sees her discomfort. *This kitty has a hard time hiding her inner thoughts.* Scratching his chin, he smirks at her obvious dilemma. *There must be a way to help her understand that she is in good company. She must get to the city. Then she will know the truth.* Turning back to the other dragons, Drako winks at them. They smile softly back. He nudges Celestra with his chin. "I'm curious. Do you think that we are holding you captive here?"

Celestra rudely snaps back, "Well Drako actually it should be obvious that if I wanted to leave I couldn't. All of you dragons are about four times the size of me. There are three of you as well. Besides, you have already shown your strength. I will decide not to fight and lose my hide."

Drako concerned tries to word their intentions honestly, so Celestra would ease up. "I did not bring you here to make you feel like a prisoner Celestra. We are leading you to where you will learn your lineage."

Celestra turns to look at Drako, finally without fear.

"So, I am *really* not going to be held against my will?" Drako feeling her relax, hopes in time she will change her tune. "No. If you desire to leave at any time, you may. We are only here to help you." She can feel her body relaxing. The freedom to leave as she wishes helps her regain some confidence. Her shoulders drop and she raises her body. "Well, if that is the case, I guess I should say thank you. For clearing that up that is. It was bothering me."

Celestra sees Drako smile and nods at the others. Maybe they really are here to help.

Within an instant, Drako picks up Celestra and can notice the change in her attitude. She is beginning to trust him. This brings a big toothy grin to the dragon's face. She sneaks a smile out herself in return but tries to hide it from the others.

Lastra, Partune, and Drako fly with Celestra straight to the dragon city. In the back of Celestra's mind, she realized something has gone missing: A silver ring from her past. Instantly within Drako's mouth, she wriggles upset at the possibility she may have lost it. Drako with a mouth full of fur said, "Stop moving or you'll knock me out of flight!" Celestra grunts out of frustration. Realizing her irresponsibility, she tries to calm down. *Shame*, she thinks, *I've traveled far. Who knows if I'll ever find it? My master gave me that talisman.*

Celestra knows Drako's right. Grumbling under her breath, there is nothing she can do about the ring now. The cool night air ends up soothing her into a deep sleep. Thoughts of the last day jumble together in her dreams wildly. Drako can feel her twitch in her dream state as they all fly. *She's such a tortured creature. She needs time to heal despite what she says. She needs to believe in the good things that life has to offer. - Such a sad little hybrid. No sense of companionship is left within her.*

Chapter Three

The Griffin and the Raven

Partune said his goodbyes and heads off on his journey. Looking for a proper landing spot, he feels his wings almost give up. Quickly circling downward, he sets his heavy rump to the ground and takes a deep breath. Lying backward, he stares at the sky. He wriggles his toes but, cannot see his feet past his stomach. Realizing his weight is becoming more of a problem these days, he sighs while poking at his belly. *I've let city living make me soft again.* Grunting in disgust, he shakes off the cold winds from flight. Sniffing the air, he scans the perimeter. It seems safe enough for him to continue.

Walking along, Partune spots a river that comes up to a small bank. "About four wings in length. This is the place he told me to meet him." Partune dips his toes in the cool water nervously. He watches the fast stream trill past his claws. These times in Apropon Rar seem rather imbalanced. Not like those peaceful days playing in the hills outside Drondia City. Thinking about how strange everything has been lately, makes him shutter. *There is such a dark veil over us all. It's even penetrated the strong elements of nature. This stream feels all wrong.* Partune senses these changes in the world around him and feels a bit helpless. A shiver shoots down his spine, but he quickly sends it away. He knows fixing this darkness will take many lifetimes.

Turning back to the sky, Partune remembers the 'task at hand'. Allowing whelp'ish fears to take over will get him nowhere. He picks up his head and growls out loudly calling for his companion. He sits back down and awaits his arrival in a pensive state.

Partune is reminded that one voice can make a difference if it's carried to the right ear. His deep growl penetrated the entire area for miles. Anything sleeping surely wasn't any longer.

He finally hears something familiar in the distance. After few moments, a gigantic lion-like creature swoops above him and skids down into the bank. Partune wags his tail almost like a dog and smiles widely seeing his old friend after so long. The griffin, watching his friend dance in such a whelp'ish display, cannot help but smile. Raspier was studying abroad and this is his first time back in the south.

"My Old Friend, how was your flight?" Partune joyfully spits out. Raspier tired from evading settlements, rolls his eyes at his excited friend. "Well, it would have been better if we did not have all these greggils out tonight." Partune displeased with the news, shakes his head low, "What are they doing out this late? Not liking this old friend, not liking it at all."

The two decide to head over to a close meeting den with an underground cave. It should be within an old tree very close to their location. No need of anyone listening in, if they weren't invited. They must remain secretive and careful.

The entrance to the den is within the center of an ancient oak tree. There were brown ribs of dirty tan and black around the base. Large tuffs of grass shot out from in between the roots. Time has been hard on this large land watcher. Exaggerated growths curl in and out of the opening. In the moonlight, it looks like a wooden snake charred from a fire. It's not only a beautiful work of art, but a great place to meet in bad territory.

Raspier walking forward slips easily into the opening of the tree with his lean physique. With Partune's weight, the opening of the tree just holds onto him, preventing him from passing through. Frustrated, Raspier pulls hard on Partune's legs to free him. With a huge popping sound, Partune flies into the den. Pounds of ancient untouched dust floats about, as they both roll back into the cave from the force.

Raspier gingerly shakes the rubble from his fur and feathers, a bit stupefied his friend has gained so much weight. "Partune, you need to tend to that belly of yours... Walking, is the best form of exercise. Why not try more of that." He pauses to put his spectacles back on his beak. "...Then you'd be able to fly with the others, and like here, not have to be uncorked like a bottle of old grulo."

Partune instead of listening just grumbled quietly. He is very aware of his weight issue. There is no need in making him feel worse.

Griffin's think they're so smart... Partune smirks at him with narrow eyes.

There is no way around Raspier's bold comments. Nor a point in staying mad when he means well, he is just direct. Partune is quite the opposite.

Straightening up and clearing off the last of the dust from his scales, Partune looks over to his snarky friend. "Raspier, more important than my weight here, we need to let Drako and Lastra know about the greggils before they are spotted. If they see them up there, a hunt will be put into action immediately." Raspier sits down and scratches his fur and feathered head. With one eye closed and head cocked to the side, you can hear a soft 'hmm' as he ponders. Small down feathers spiral outward and dance down to the floor as he pulls away from his blue claw.

"Partune I will get a message to them by order of the ravens. While studying abroad, I managed to make a messenger pact with them."

Raspier turns around and places his haunches slowly to the dirt floor in front of the opening. Curling his tail to the left side of his body, he inches forward to position his head. Sticking his blue beak out into the darkness, he only shows the very tip of it into the moonlight. Eyes beady and glistening, he slips out some more from the den to check what's around. It may be quiet in this part of Apropon Rar, but to be safe he checks for activity. Raspier heard how careless Partune was in calling out to him earlier. *Greggils know the call of a dragon. He should be more cautious.* Motionless, Raspier waits for some sort of natural cue before calling out to the ravens. Positioning his head high, he lets out an ear bleeding shrill. Raspier's call will alert any raven in the local ten miles at that decibel. Thankfully, most greggils will think it was just a hawk.

Partune had already shoved dry leaves and two local field mice in his ears, to protect himself from the sound. After the rant was finished, he placed the frightened rodents back down, thanking them for use of their soft fur as earplugs. In a silly attempt to show disapproval, the mice snort and walk away with tails high. Partune watched the mice intently, as laughter softens his face, watching them scurry away. Raspier confidently turns around and stares at Partune's strange moment. Ignoring it with a head flick, he speaks. "I'm sure a messenger will come soon."

Despite the awkward commotion, the two relax and catch up for a while. Time sneaks by as these gentle giants take refuge in the magick of friendship. Partune sees his friend is aware of the darkness and it comforts him a little bit inside. Talking about old school stories and calamities, Raspier and Partune forget for a while just where they were. The great mother watched two of her children laugh and share in delights for a small amount of time. This comfort was broken abruptly when a little black raven crashes into the cave.

Partune was startled, and slammed his head into the ceiling. Biting his tongue, he yelps out of pain. Jumping like a rabbit, he opens his eyes to see Raspier and the raven talking. Raspier turns and shakes his head at Partune.

Turning back to the raven, he finishes the message for Drako and the others. "Please find Drako and the rest to tell them the news. They are flying towards Drondia's southern entrance." The raven caws in return to Raspier.

Feeling confident in the way he explained himself, Raspier continues, "Good, I know it's a hard feat to accomplish, but you can do it quickly. Tell them what you see on the way and what the greggils are doing." The raven caws out a few more times and nods its beak at him. Raspier pleased with his messenger, sends him off. "Good luck little fellow, may you fly steadfast to your destination." The raven flies out of the meeting den to Partune's left side.

Raspier looks out the door and then back at his hurting friend. Partune was still tending to his swollen tongue. Raspier sticks out his fluffy chest and speaks, "Splendid thing birds. They are always there when you need them. Know what I mean there Partune?" Raspier had no clue that wonderful bird just left him a stinky token on his shoulder. Partune didn't want to ruin his moment but he couldn't help but laugh. "Yes, splendid creatures." Partune mocks him while some drool falls from his mouth.

DRONDIA CITY

Land of the Free Dragons

Chapter Four

Drondia the City of Dragons

Drako, Lastra, and Celestra are almost in the city. They're exhausted but continue to push on. The cool night air ruffles Celestra's fur. She is quickly growing fond of this. Her eyes, however, were not too pleased with the strong blowing winds. Tears continue to cloud her vision and she squints harder. Trying to see the lands below was almost impossible.

Down on the ground, all life is sleeping waiting for the dawn. Drako snorts in disgust as he sees greggils setting up camp in the distance. He motions to Lastra to reach a higher altitude and tells Celestra to close her eyes. They shoot up about ten dragon lengths, rapidly into the clouds. The air is so thin, Celestra begins to pass out but tries hard to remain conscious. She was not born with air sacks like dragons after all.

Drako tells them that if greggils are below, something unpleasant may come of this journey. It will be an act of stealth and timing if they escape their vision. One sense greggils have very well.

Celestra shutters over the thought of a greggil skinning her alive. *That's right at the top of my list next to being tackled by a dragon four times my size.* At that moment, she saw a little black bird flying incredibly fast from behind. Celestra motions to Drako with the little consciousness she has left, of its presence.

Drako turns to look and smiles. With her nape in his mouth, he decides to let Lastra speak for him. All hope the bird comes with good news. Lastra and the bird discuss what the greggils were doing. "Are they all right?" She said. The raven looks up with beady black eyes and caws out that they are fine. Relieved

Lastra lets out a sigh, "Well thank you for bravery. It will not go unnoticed. I'm glad that Partune and Raspier are okay."

Feeling successful, the bird flies back to Partune and Raspier. Travel would be easier if it wasn't a full moon. The last thing this little crow wanted was to lose his life to a night eagle.

"This doesn't seem very promising. All this greggil activity going on at night makes me uneasy." Drako says with a mouth full of fur. Lastra response: "Well, maybe they're just expanding a territory, and there is nothing more to it." He turns and gazes at the moon, "Let's hope Lastra. Let's hope so."

The two of them fly quietly for the rest of the way as Celestra fights to stay awake. She can sense a romantic bond between these two dragons. It's possible Drako and Lastra were old flames. She laughs quietly at the thought of dragon love. *So... dragons have hearts after all.*

They approach a great wall of stone surrounded by thick trees. The scent in the air is similar to when she met Drako; however, the light was much brighter. This seemed to be cloaking magick. Uniqua taught her about this but she has never seen it before.

The wall looked like an old forest yet she knew better. Flying over it Celestra felt a warm sensation throughout her entire body. Then to her surprise, she sees a huge community of dragons, creatures and a lavish civilization. Her eyes widen with wild curiosity.

Drako and Lastra, happy to see the city, finally perk up and bury their previous emotional disturbance. Slowly they land and drop to the ground exhausted. Before either of them could catch their breath, a massive black dragon greeted them. One of his eyes was scratched out and a thick scar kept it closed. Celestra looking to the others saw that they both recognized him, so she relaxed a bit.

This dragon was indeed impressive. The kind of creature you would not want to upset. He introduces himself quite promptly, "I welcome you both back to Drondia. Please come with me and I will get you the update on all the present act-." Cutting himself off, as if he was startled by a ghost of some sorts, he bends down his long wrinkly neck to look at Celestra with his last good eye, "By the first dragon's scale; a hybrid! Where did you find this little legend?" Celestra smiles to be polite but is still dazed from the high altitude during the flight. *I still don't understand what is so special about me, or what a hybrid is, but I'm sure my questions will be answered later.* She thinks while waiting for the three dragons to include her in the conversation.

The large black one-eyed dragon turns to Celestra finally and smiles. His teeth were quite impressive and Celestra leaned back a bit. "I am Garsa Yean the leader of this free dragon city. I see my friends here have brought you to the right place. Please, feel free to stay as long as you like, and know that much will be learned from your stay here." Garsa Yean motions over to two yellow and gold looking dragons with large wings to approach. They were carrying long staves that held clear crystals. Celestra seeing these weapons knew not to object to his wishes. Garsa points, "These dragons will lead you to your quarters, where you will rest and relax. Enjoy the finer life little hybrid. I'm sure this is quite different from how you lived before."

Drako pulls Garsa to the side and explains what the raven told Lastra, where Partune and Raspier were and his spin on what the greggils were doing in the dark night. Garsa seemed displeased but oddly calm. Lastra nudged Celestra forward with her sleek head, to distract her from paying attention to Drako and Garsa. Instead, she pushes her to follow the yellow dragons to their quarters. The two of them were looking forward to resting. *There is so much to discover here,* Celestra thinks. *I could be amused for quite some time. I'll sneak off and explore later on.*

Drako tells Lastra and Celestra he would meet up with them later with an update and wanders off with Garsa. The ladies continued walking with the guards towards their quarters. Celestra inspects this bustling community of creatures. She couldn't have ever pictured anything like this before. Wide-eyed, whiskers perked, she gazed out at all the wonder.

Celestra being raised completely in nature had no concept of a city. This was something completely different and new for her. This is a way of living above nature, or maybe it was a way of defying the great mother. She could not make up her mind right away. *Frankly, I cannot really find the right expression in words for what this feels like, but it's wonderfully exciting.* She thinks how Uniqua would have loved to see this for himself. That is if he didn't already know of this city. Uniqua was infamous for withholding information. This seems like something he would hide from her. He knew her mind would easily wander and daydream. Shaking her head back and forth, Celestra smiles softy laughing, *you still get me every time Uniqua. Very funny old bear.*

Reaching the quarters with the guards, Celestra sees that the rooms were beautiful and ever so large. Tapestries and jewels were in every available space, Gold covered everything that it could be attached to. Fresh flowers and plants grew in personal gardens inside and running water was streaming through each room. One of the guards approached Celestra and put his finger on her forehead, "Maybe I'll do better on my mating dance tonight with this little lucky charm." Laughing, the guard begins to walk away disregarding his action as being rude in Celestra's eyes. "Thanks, little fuzzy one, hope tonight goes better with your star charm. That beautiful dragoness surely will approve of me now." Fur puffed out and pride shot down, she snorts and starts to clean herself to calm her nerves, "Well I guess some dragons are just plain gruff after all..." Lastra soaking in the cool waters of the bathing pool smiles at Celestra. She motions for Celestra to approach to sit and relax, "Why do you think you have that star on your forehead little panther?" Celestra again frustrated with all these strange comments about her physique rolls her eyes at Lastra. "I don't know really. My master told me one day the truth of my lineage would be told to me. That's all I know."

Lastra moving to the edge of the bathing pool smiles and points out the door, "Well for starters, you saw how that guard put his finger on it for good luck?" Celestra thinks before speaking yet her tail was still swaying back and forth. "Yes, but I thought he was just being rude." Lastra finding this all a bit funny chuckles, "Well, ever heard of the horned beasts before? You know unicorns?" Celestra's ears perk forward and she became curious. "No, but what do they have to do with me?" Lastra swam backward in the pool and squirted out some water from her mouth. "Ah", Lastra said, "This is a wonderful creature. They can heal any wound, and pierce any material with the same horn." Celestra confused looks at Lastra, "A horn? But I have no horn. I'm a feline."

Lastra turning onto her back floats in the water looking up at the ceiling. "Well, *that* star holds the same magical power that a *unicorn horn* has. Besides don't you think it's odd you have wings? You are a panther *after* all. How could a panther have *wings*, right?" Lastra folds her arms as she finishes. Thinking, Celestra realizes that Lastra is right. Obviously, she is no ordinary creature despite how Uniqua trained her to feel and act. He may have done this to ensure a true heart and an unbiased way of thinking. Uniqua never gave into Celestra. She had to fight her whole way to the top; a mighty feat indeed. Uniqua was a strong paw with a soft heart.

Celestra missing him allows a single tear to fall from her eye. She craved his wisdom and his hard love. *Now it seems I must make my own way Uniqua; with or with you.* Celestra remembers her master telling her about how one day she will learn of her true powers. Uniqua made sure to tell her that others in the future would show her this special magick. "My master taught me never to grow reliant on that kind of power, for no true warrior needs anything more than their instincts and a fast paw full of claws." As Celestra states this she pushes out her soft white chest and the silver key bounces off of it forward. Lastra chuckles, "Yes that is a true warrior but you possess much greater powers than a paw full of claws, as you say."

Opening her eyes, she stares at Lastra just utterly confused. Dragons really speak way over her head and it continuously bothers her. "Why can't any of you tell me what I am straight out? You all speak in riddles and it's very frustrating." Lastra leans her head on her arm hanging out of the pool and looks at Celestra with a smile, "Well that now is the truth, Celestra; and to answer your question straight, I don't think so. Dragons are about growth; we do not spell things out." They both yawn and curl up for a small nap. All this talk of riddles and horned beasts has made Celestra weary. She is growing tired of dragon speak. For now, she can rest feeling secure in the fact that this city may hold the secret to her past and maybe the secrets to what her future will be.

Chapter Five

Let Sleeping Cats Dream

Celestra falls asleep quickly. Colors and vivid pictures start to form inside her mind disrupting her snoozing serenity. Right before the sharp cliff of sleep, she sees a black paw. Similar to her own but definitely from a male's body and it hands her a silver dragon ring. It looks like the one she lost recently. Hearing a dragon growl she looked up and was startled by what she saw. It was no panther at all actually, this ring bearer turned into a strong dragon! A smile ever so strange curls around his muzzle. He jets off, leaving her with the ring. Before he turned away, she noticed a white star upon his forehead. It reminded Celestra of her own star. What does this all mean? This dream fades away to the sound of heavy feet running; whispering, 'The dragon and the unicorn; firstborn kit...' repeatedly over and over, until it's was barely audible.

Celestra was obviously scratching and growling in her sleep. Lastra noticed this and moved towards her concerned. Before she could even ask Celestra what the issue was she jumps up and begins to look for this mysterious ring bearer. "Where did that dragon go?!" she said running around with fur all awry. Lastra looking quite confused grabs the nape of Celestra's neck. Shaking her softly she snaps her out of it. "What dragon dear?" Lastra asks putting her back down. Celestra was still waking up and looks at her terribly confused. "Oh, I must've been dreaming. I saw this black panther paw giving me that ring I lost, but when I looked up again, he changed into a dragon and ran away muttering something." Lastra smiles and nudges Celestra with her head soothingly. "Little Celestra, I think you may have had a visitor. Who knows; maybe another hybrid is trying to find you…"

Lastra walking towards the window sticks her long neck out the diamond opening. Looking around for Drako, or even a sign of Partune and Raspier, she sees the empty gold cobblestone roads of the city. Bothered that she ends up becoming a babysitter to her newfound fuzzy friend, she realizes it's simply in her nature. *After all, I am a good mother. Besides, I deserve the rest.* Pulling in her neck Lastra turns back in towards the room. "Celestra, I think we should send a guard to locate Partune and his friend, what do you think?" Celestra ponders this and swats at a bug crawling around on the floor, "I think they'll be alright, but let the guards know they are still traveling mostly on foot. If it gets too late, we can arrange to send out a search party." Lastra saw Celestra liked being included in decisions and figured it would help her calm down. "Good thinking Celestra. I like that idea. Besides, those twisted greggils are out there. No need to endanger more of our kind." Celestra motions to a guard outside their door to come in and talk with them. She explains the urgency of locating them before sunrise. A search party will be the last resort. The guard agrees and sets off to find Drako and Garsa to tell them of the idea.

Chapter Six

Charging Towards the City

Partune and Raspier are much closer to the greggils than before and are presently spying on their affairs in the dark. They study them carefully and make a detailed report. Nothing can be trusted with the darkness looming. In this area, no greggil communities are settled and nature remains the queen of the land. The trees were dense with overgrowth. Morning glory vines choked out much of the grasses. Small critters and deer loved this tender natural hiding place.

Their presence greatly disturbs both these travelers on their journey to the city. "They seem to be building some sort of castle over there." Partune whispers. Raspier turns his head while walking, "Why in this wood? There are neither roads nor trails to lead more of them here. That seems to be their usual plan when they build." Partune looking further out notices it's not like other greggil designs, "Maybe it's possible this isn't a homestead and it's for storage purposes? What do you think Raspier? Are they up to something again?" Raspier nibbling at an itch picks his head up, "Either way we'd better not be seen or our hides will be the payment." This, they finally agreed on. They try to find the best route back to the city while studying what the greggils were doing. Observing from a distance will prove valuable to the leader at Drondia. They can also keep themselves out of their crossbow sights and live to tell the tale.

Where the greggils had cleared the trees away, the ground was now prepared for building. Large stones were in a pile on one side of the clearing. Crossing over a thick patch of wood, Partune and Raspier slip by unnoticed. They see a large group of male greggils building as fast as they can. Many would twitch at the crack of their master's whip. "Faster scrubs!" the leader snaps out, "We need this castle done in eight and ten moon cycles!" All the greggils pushed on with their build yet none were enjoying their work. They were obviously hungry and very dehydrated. Still, they continue their job for this devilish greggil. Both Partune and Raspier shiver over this abuse. Thankfully, the great mother decided against bringing them into the world as one of them.

Raspier sneers at how the lord relaxes by a makeshift fence. "He's not even lifting one hand to help those men. What a barbaric overlord." Partune nods agreeing. Quietly continuing past this slave party, they notice an unusually large horse with what seems to be a white star on its forehead. Tied to a post, the horse seemed to be distressed as well watching the crew. Something told Partune that this horse was far from ordinary. Apparently, it was a very sentient animal. He makes an assumption this is certainly a hybrid. *That star looks too familiar.* Still, it appears unaware of its own enslavement. He carries an air of innocence Partune could not ignore.

The large black charger, almost twenty-two hands high, seems to watch this greggil leaders' every move. It patiently waits for when he can rest without him near. This must be his master. Partune looks at the horse a little closer while Raspier begs him to move on. Partune waves down his friend and continues watching. Raspier highly frustrated now scratches the earth with his claws. Small down feathers twist to the ground, as Raspier shakes his head in discomfort.

Partune ignoring Raspier turns back to the horse. He notices that his energy doesn't match that of a horse at all. It is more of a hybrids for certain. His senses never fail him. Judging whether to act upon this will be hard, let alone risky. Yet something tells him that he needs to help this poor animal. He carefully plots out a map in his head knowing the terrain so well. *If this horse ends up noticing us, I will leave behind a common Draconian writing all animals can more or less understand. If he makes it to the city, I'll be thankful I didn't just walk off.* Raspier turns to see Partune bent down drawing in the dirt. Tapping him with his beak, he pushes them to move further on; sunrise draws near.

Maybe I'll get a sign. Partune grumbles under his breath, "This is why I hate most greggils; they will even enslave their own kind as well as wild creatures." Sadly, at that very moment in time, a small stick cracks beneath Partune's feet. The large black horse turns to see what made the noise with ears perked forward. Both Partune and Raspier freeze instantly. Raspier fluffs out his head feathers beaming in utter anger at Partune. The horse leans his head out and speaks to the night air. "Hello? Is someone out there?" Both Raspier and Partune pray no greggil was paying attention so that they can continue unharmed. Partune wants to say something to the horse but knows he cannot. Instead, he leaves the directions as planned on the ground hoping the horse is what he *appears* to be. The map entails the way to the dragon city, Drondia. Partune sides with Raspier finally and they both leave quickly.

Raspier hisses, "Why did you do that all for a common horse? Those greggils may find it." Partune disturbed how selfish his friend is acting looks at him with concern, "He needed our help and he was no horse Raspier. Did you see the star on his forehead? This could be one of those surrogate-raised hybrids who have no knowledge of their true genetics. We studied them in the academy I'm sure you remember. We must always help a hybrid out no matter the cost." Raspier obviously bothered about this unneeded reminder decides to keep his cool. "We must hurry now for light approaches very soon. As we travel, you will tell me *why* you feel *this* creature is a hybrid. Let's just do it further away from these greggils please."

The horse flicks his ears at the sound from before. There was something touching the ground and leaving marks in the dry autumn dirt. Quietly, the black charger slowly chews the rope keeping him restrained. Watching the men pile and cut the rock, he maintains a low profile in order to walk over to where those weird creatures were. Studying the marks on the ground, he realizes it was a map. The horse gazes at this and beams with excitement. This simple black horse always felt he was destined for something greater. He knew this from his heart. "Thank you great beyond, I knew you would eventually show me a sign. I just hope this is what I've been looking for, and it's not just some cheap trick."

While Lord Cannor was driving the other greggils, the horse remained pensive to leave. He has been kept standing there by rope unable to explore his surroundings; a slave. Finally, this unnatural life can fade away. With courage, this proud black charger can explore what is out there past the fences and the barns. Not completely confident about leaving his present situation or trusting if these creatures were actually helping at all, the horse slowly approaches the ground sniffing. Reading it he notices oddly it makes sense to him. "It's a map of this place called 'Drondia, the Dragon City'. Never went to a dragon city before. Quite frankly, I've never been anywhere by myself at all."

Knowing how relentless Lord Cannor is, the steed was certain he would seek his whereabouts. *I should leave no trace of this at all.* Gently rubbing out the writing, he covers it with leaves and twigs to hide its existence. Looking back at the only human master he has ever known, a part of him wishes to stay. Yet his instincts tell him to run fast and far away.

When he was a young foal with his mother, she used to tell him a story about a horse that broke free of his stable and his tale in the wild. As this indecision rolls around in his head, he recalls the "Tale of Yaster":

"Yaster was bored and tired of his farm life. Nothing ever changed nor was out of the ordinary. This monotony soon became too much to bear. The wild and untamed nature inside him told him to escape for freedom, to be the one responsible for his own life.

Upon leaving his quaint lifestyle on the farm, he encountered many challenges not common to his previous way of life. Animals were not trustworthy, there were now carnivorous creatures out to make him their next meal and he had no fence to protect him. There was also the constant threat of starvation and thirst without a stable hand. He was on his own now and it was up to him to make sure his needs were fulfilled.

One day when Yaster was walking along a hillside, a mountain lion approached him slowly eyeing him for a tasty meal. Due to his domestication, he couldn't sense as well as other prey creatures and didn't realize that he was being stalked. The lion drew closer, paying full attention to his every move. Claws drawn and head low, the lion pounced for its meal. Yaster heard the lion and turned thankfully just at the right moment. The lion was frustrated and advanced closer in full force now. With Yaster's hoofs flaring in the air, he returns a powerful blow to the lion's skull and it falls to the ground stunned. Running away, he pants in fear with the whites of his eyes glaring. Not paying attention to where he was, Yaster fails to see a cliff in front of him. Running at full speed he skids right before the cliff, yet it wasn't enough to stop him. Now falling very fast, he begs the higher powers to help him to survive this ordeal.

Yaster notices he wasn't falling as fast as before. There was a strange drag behind him. Opening his eyes, he sees tangled up wings. Amazed that this miracle happened, he quickly goes against his domestic instincts telling him to stay panicked. Instead, he extends his neck outward to slow his fall, pulls in his front legs, and extends his new wings. Safely he slows down into a glide and sees the entire range he was roaming. Happiness welled up in the young horse's heart and now he understood what his master had provided for him all along. Now, he will happily provide that for himself. Now independent, Yaster realized he could never return to his old life. He has lived to see another day and learned to trust his true instincts. He has returned to the wild."

"The moral of the story is what Tarmax?" he remembers his mother saying. Ears flicking and eyes rolling around, a young Tarmax spits out, "Uh, never get caught with your wings tangled?" His mother laughs and shakes her head, "No, not at all Tarmax. The moral is – 'When life offers you a challenge, your mind should bend like grass to solve it.' Therefore, you must change for what the moment calls for my little foal. Only, expect change to stay the same."

A spark of courage took light inside him and now Tarmax saw what his mother meant by the story. He thinks to himself for a moment. *Thank you, mother, you were wise beyond your years for a common horse.*

Galloping as fast as he can, Tarmax runs for freedom. With the directions safely nestled inside his mind's eye, he evades Cannor to get to this so-called Dragon City. "There will be creatures there that'll help me find my way, I'm sure of it. I just wish I knew why I feel so compelled to go. I never really trusted anything like this before, at least that is before my mother was taken away. Well, I guess destiny seems to knock at barn doors in the oddest of fashions. Either way, I'm going."

Chapter Seven

The Warrior's New Etiquette

Up north in Drondia, Lastra walks with Celestra into the main hall in the city. As expected like all of the other rooms, jewels and lavish decorations showed the dragons' style and taste. Lastra and Celestra were walking to the inner hall for supper. Curious at what dragon royalty eats, Celestra quickly scampers to the entrance to the room. However, Lastra grabbed her before she could run in. "Have patience now Celestra. You're not a warrior on the plains in here." Lastra instructs Celestra while pointing her finger at some unknown dot on the ceiling. Celestra loses interest quickly. *There is so much to learn; a bit embarrassing.* Sticking her head out from around the gigantic doorway she examines the spacious quarters. Filled with unknown foods and delicacies, her small size became more apparent around these dragons. Everything was so large.

She thinks back to her plains and all those rough battles. Each day was lived with little sleep and savage emotions. There was no time to enjoy anything. Celestra almost found it hard to picture this comfortable life her new reality. Such negative reinforcement on a constant basis truly has stunted her growth in many ways. She's a trained warrior after all, not royalty. Yet all these creatures coming into the room seemed calm, passive and honest. Celestra will study them here at this large table while they're distracted by food. *No creature can mask his or her true intentions while eating.* Celestra sees everyone sit down and get ready for the meal.

On the table sat a tray with a large bovine-like creature baked with vegetables. Fruits were surrounding the platter and all of it smelled heavenly. Star-shaped bread adorned each place setting as well. Celestra felt like a newborn cub being brought to the river for the first time. The table was so large they let her sit on a tall footstool to reach up to it. With all this food, her mouth watered, and eyes glistened with hunger. After a brief silence, a small prayer was spoken before the meal and then they all dug in. Celestra at that point did not hold back.

There were the three dragons Celestra had not met yet at the other side of the table, and two were eyeing her from across it. One seemed irked by her presence as if she should have been eating on the floor. *Not like I would care anyway. That's how I always eat. I had to kill my meals and they certainly were never served to me.* She rips a chunk from a leg on her plate and chews loudly to upset them further.

The third one was very intriguing. Definitely male, but sent out a whirlwind of energy and refused to make any eye contact. This puzzled her greatly. Five horns circled out from the back of his skull like a mane, then four larger ones from the top of his head. He had a very long and slender snout with a short center horn protruding out. His claws were extra-long and precisely sharpened. Every scale seemed to carry its own vibration as if each one was its own private sun.

A small blue dragon pops his head through the door. This was obviously a juvenile. He looks directly at this strange dragon and winks. Without looking at the little whelp, he gracefully raises a single claw and spins it in a circle. Instantly a small doll appeared above the whelp's head and fell into his claws. Giddy he received what he had asked for the whelp runs away to play.

Now, this dragon had an allure of mystery to him! Celestra stops staring at him and tries to finish her meal. She sees him smile at her from the corner of her eye. *Tricky things these dragons*, Celestra thinks, *really though. It's getting quite silly.*

Lastra was speaking with another dragon about her concern for Partune. They continue gossiping while the one, who had sneered at Celestra, stayed very quiet. Drako and Garsa were planning some sort of journey to find out what the greggils were doing. As per usual, Celestra just observes her surroundings.

While trying to pick up a large cup in front of her, Celestra feels a tickle on her forehead. She intuitively looks to the mystical dragon ever so slowly and sees he's smiling. A loud cackle rings inside Celestra's head and makes her whole-body twitch. She loses grip on the cup and it starts to slip. As it drops to the floor, everyone stops to see what happened.

Garsa looks to that same dragon with a bothered look. "Avalo Ryu! Why on earth are you bothering our new guest with your antics? She isn't trained yet; you will only frighten her." He laughs aloud this time and offers Celestra an apology, "Sorry hybrid, I was just testing your abilities." Befuddled and embarrassed, she attempts to settle this discreetly to avoid more eyes on her. "Well, no harm was done. I can't drink from these cups anyway. I have no thumbs you know..." They all laugh a little and continue eating disregarding the moment completely.

Not Trained Yet? She thinks while chewing some meat. A piece falls from her mouth to the plate. *What training is Garsa talking about?* Then it hits her hard. *Could this Avalo Ryu be the one who will help me learn what I really am?*

Avalo turns to Celestra, "You're very right little kitty."

Celestra's eyes widen and her hair stands on end. It feels like thousands of butterflies are bouncing around in her stomach. Avalo continues to talk but through his mind. *Little panther you are one of many that need to come together. It's written within the prophecy. That tickle you feel inside, is your inner consciousness starting to open up.* Avalo nods his head at her and winks. He then goes back to talking with Garsa and the rest while eating. Celestra stopped chewing for a few moments and blankly stared out into nothing.

She sits straight up obviously moved. Her hackles stiffened and her heart throbbed fast. *This must be the thrill of adventure that's perking up my whiskers. Oh Uniqua, if you could only see me now.*

Staring out at the city, Celestra's face softens and a large smile widened across her face. *You know* she thinks; *I believe this is going to be a grand story to tell my future kin someday.*

Chapter Eight

Ripples of Horns

The sun has been up for an hour and Tarmax the horse has almost given up on finding the city. He has been following the map he saw earlier those strange creatures left behind. Thinking about them further, quite frankly they looked like dragons. His mother would tell him stories about them. *Strange to see one alive. I thought they were only fairy tales.* Going north just as the map said he came to the end of a small forest.

Stopping to eat some tasty plants, he sighed and relaxed. This lack of tension was unusual for him. Looking far ahead Tarmax can see brighter lights in the distance. This was the end of the forest and if he remembered the map correctly, there were only grasslands to cover until the city. This was the beginning of his new life as a wild animal. Standing at proper attention, Tarmax felt tall. Like a champion horse should. He neighed loudly stomping his hooves onto the ground. Running at full speed, he plowed through the soft earth. Branches whipped him in the head as he flew through the forest, but he didn't care. He was free.

Tears of joy ran down his face as he let out another loud neigh. Once at the mouth of the forest, he stopped to try to catch his breath. Thinking about his mother and how she would scold him for running off too far, a pang of longing hit his heart. "Mother I can return to the wild. You'll see."

Tarmax hears the caw of a raven above his head. Looking up at its direction, the bird jumps up and down on a branch above. It points straight ahead with one of its wings. Tarmax looks and sees the shimmer of a small pond and the white light of the sun bouncing off it. He turns to the raven and smiles. "Why thank you little bird. That looks like it was on that map!" Looking towards the opening of the forest the horse experiences something new. Throwing his head back and bucking he screams, "I will no longer be domestic! I will be *free!*" With that, he cuts loose and bolts out of the opening of the forest like a grassglider across the plains.

Suddenly his mind wanders as he starts to lose control. A deep booming voice inside his head says, *Tarmax, you are the darkness I need...Come home to me...* Terrified he neighs and gallops faster. Then the voice fades as quickly as it came. Tarmax skids short, shaking his head and stumbles to the ground. He decides to rest, seeing he has reached the pond. "I haven't run that fast and free in my entire life! What a feeling! Still, I wonder what that voice was..." Taking in a big drink of water, he closes his eyes and tries to get steady. "This doesn't taste anything like my barn water. It's actually full of flavor!"

Drinking much too fast, he swats his tail in pain and starts to feel queasy. He remembered when his mother scolded him for doing that. Back then, all he knew was his mother and that barn. That was all he wanted to know. He stared into the pool and watched the ripples disappear slowly. Lowering his head, he sighs again. "Mother, if you could only see me now. This is so silly, what am I doing? Why would these creatures want to help me? I'm just a dumb horse. They're just collecting a meal like in those human stories you would tell me. What will I do about Lord Cannor? He may be mean, but that man protected me from everything. Mother, I have failed you." He sniffles out in misery.

A tear falls to the pond and his reflection is lost in the movement. At that moment, a great bear turns around to look at the horse gazing into the water. He was tracking his scent through the forest for some time. Glaring with hunger, he stares at the plump muscular horse as a five-course meal. Without knowing, Tarmax turns around to face this beast running for him at full speed. Just like Yaster from his mother's story, he is faced with survival or death. Shuttering now in the presence of this large predator he can't help but feel worse. Yet something within his instincts tells him that it will turn out just fine.

The bear slowly approaches and growls low. Its massive size becomes ever more intimidating to Tarmax, yet he holds his ground. Knowing if he stays still, the bear won't charge. *If I can just hold on right up until he jumps, he will fall into the water and I can escape. I'll hop to the side and hopefully survive.*

The bear finally leaps as Tarmax jumps to the right. It cries out in pain and drops into the pond violently. He threw his hooves up waiting for it to come at him but instead it just shivered. *Why is he not attacking me? Is he hurt from the jump?* Then Tarmax sees blood swirling in the calming ripples of the water. Confused, he looks at the bear and tries to find where it was coming from. It was obviously too weak to leave the pond. As Tarmax stares at the bear, something trickles down his nose and slips into his mouth. Naturally, he laps it up. "Blood; am I bleeding too?" However, watching the bear slowly drown, he figured differently.

Parched from the ordeal, he goes to drink some of the red shimmering water. Something inside of him liked the taste of blood. It invigorated his soul. This was concerning. Standing back away from the water, he looks down into the pond. A reflection is settling into focus, but different from what he was used to. As a stern wind blows his mane, he sees that two long shadows were clearly into focus above his head. *Are those horns? Where did they come from? Is that how I defended the attack from the bear?* For a moment, he thought back to when he jumped out of the way. He remembers how it cried in pain as he felt a tingle on the top of his head. *What has happened here?* Out of fear, Tarmax knew he had to run and run fast.

Chapter Nine

Companions Rest

Partune and Raspier are almost on the great wall. Yet now Raspier has to help his friend complete the flight. The landscape has that healthy glow that always lifts their spirits. This becomes a great help to them both.

The plant life that circled the city grew lush from the barrier and many animals appreciated it. Dragons have an important part in keeping balance on Gaia. Repairing all the mistakes the greggils make is surely a difficult responsibility, yet this was their forced duty. Partune takes much of this on too deeply sometimes and Raspier knows it. Unfortunately, Partune also likes to comfort his pains with over-eating and heavy drinking. He's noticed Partune has overdone this while he was away.

Raspier was suffering trying to keep his friend high enough in the air. They fly through the clouds appearing as if they were drunk. "You really need to lose weight Partune, this is ridiculous", Raspier said to him grunting. "Oh, shut up Raspier, sometimes your timing is just so off. Shut your big beak, put your fancy feathers to work and get us over that wall!"

The wall is almost within their reach as they see the warm glow of the city. Partune, giving up, pulls away from Raspier's claws and drops into a free-fall. Despite his large and cumbersome body, he falls gracefully and with character. He spreads his wings and readies his arms to hug the earth below. Thankfully his flight sacks save him from descending to hard. Just nearly missing the stones on the city wall, he flies over and safely makes into the city. Raspier gasps in relief and ruffles his head feathers in delight seeing his friend survive the landing.

The city glows with familiar light the both had missed for so long. Warm scents of flora bring their senses back to life. Being out in that untamed world is tedious and straining on the soul. The time of peace is slowly coming to an end and they all felt this deep inside. Partune drops to the soft grasses breathing heavily. Turning onto his back, he flattens out his wings and drops his arms in dead weight. Panting like a dog, no recognizable words seep out just grunts. Raspier cleans his fur and starts to purr to calm his friend, "Just rest now. We're home old friend, just relax. Please lose some weight though…"

A guard came to them with cheerful greetings. They asked where Drako and Lastra were. Directing them to the main hall, the guard walks them to their temporary quarters. He also told them their companions were all in the garden.

Raspier obviously adoring the first-class treatment immediately requests a bottle of grulo and some goblets for them both. Partune chuckles at his dear friend and lets him enjoy his long missed royal treatment. "It's important that I find the other two before I drink in merriment. So, go on and start without me when it gets here." The guards lead Raspier away and Partune walks to find the others. Raspier hollers out to him as he walks away. "Once I get the grulo, I'll be in the secretarial room relaxing if you need me." He smiles.

Chapter Ten

The Ones That Came Before

The group was enjoying a smoke after dinner and chatting. Celestra coughed every time she inhaled the hookah. She was confused why anyone would want to breathe smoke in for fun. Most laughed at her and sold her short. Dragons obviously do not have any issues with smoke.

The atmosphere was inviting and she loved the company. Partune lightened up quickly as well. Walking up to the small gathering, he smiles at them all. "Well, we finally made it here. I'm so glad to be home." Drako smiles and asks for a report.

Drako, Partune, and Garsa sit to discuss the whereabouts of the greggils. Celestra stares at Partune and wonders where his companion was. Asking Lastra if it would be okay to wander around a bit, she goes off in search of him. Just before Celestra heads off, Partune walks over to her and smiles. "I see you are wondering where my friend is? If you go back to our quarters, he's enjoying a bottle of grulo. He's in the secretarial room. Follow the signs." Celestra thanks him and goes on searching for Partune's friend. "Oh, by the way, his name is Raspier. Can't miss that one," Partune laughs.

Celestra bids good day to the others and walked towards the secretarial room. Looking at the signs she panics because she cannot read Draconian. Walking through the city streets lost, fear overcomes her. After some time, she hears a loud cackle and a tail swishing in a doorway up ahead.

She runs faster towards her discovery. Ecstatic that Raspier turned out to be a feline, Celestra runs and calls out his name. "Raspier! It's me! I'm that hybrid they've been talking about!"

His tail disappears and now the mystery continues. Celestra wishes to see a strong sophisticated feline waltz out but instead sees a large hawk head peering out of the doorway. Confused as to where the lion went, she asks the hawk if he was Raspier. He replies, "Why yes little hybrid, I am." Saddened that he's a bird and not a feline, Celestra explains she saw a lion tail just before he had turned and peeked his head out.

Seeing him roll around while cracking up, Celestra notices his body is half-lion and half-hawk. "Are you a hybrid too?" Raspier was still laughing but finally stops to answer her, "No Celestra, I am a griffin." In between giggles of laughter over her confusion, he explains further. "We are not greggils scientific children, but of Gaia's own magick. You are a hybrid because of things you do not understand yet. Griffins are born this way, mate this way, and die this way." He proudly states this with feathers spread and chest puffed out. "Oh, then you are a natural breed, Sir? Beg your pardon but what do you mean Greggils made us? I only recently learned they are hum-"

Raspier replies stopping her rambling, "Yes hybrid, I am. Let me show you something in the history hall within the main wing. This may help you to understand just what you are. I've finished my tasty bottle of Grulo so I can find something else to keep me occupied."

As they approach this section of the estate, Celestra feels her forehead burn with quite a power. It almost made her faint, but she decided to keep it to herself despite the pain.

Inside the hall are rows of gigantic portraits, spaced about three tails apart. Celestra sees a collection of many creatures; dragons, lions, and griffins. Some she is not familiar with. Raspier with claws wide shows her the room, "Celestra, this is the hall of our forefathers. Here you will find many great heroes and heroines." Celestra gazed out at all the paintings and was amazed. She's never seen art like this in her whole life.

"It's so nice to see so much heart into preserving your heritage. I, unfortunately, do not know anything of my own kind."

Raspier looks at her and pulls Celestra down to the other side of the hall. Pointing up to a certain section of the wall, she sees a black panther with strong shoulders and graceful black wings. "He looks like me with that star, but who is he? I must know, Raspier?!" Raspier clears his throat seeing she's involved. "That is your great Grandfather dear, his name was Garlock. His nickname was Nightstream because he was one of the few hybrids that loved to fish at night. Odd past-time I say, but I am no hybrid."

Celestra remembers thinking to herself how she wanted to fish in that river. Tears welled in her blue eyes. Mesmerized in a moment lost to the bitter realities she's come to know, Celestra stretched out her arms and hugs Raspier tightly. He chokes up on his words, seemingly taken by surprise at the gesture. "Raspier, you have no idea what this means to me. For so long I've been the only one like me. No bloodline, no family, no one to teach me my real heritage, just my master Uniqua. This is my full circle, my destiny. I must find another like myself to keep the blood alive."

No matter how hard she tries to stop sobbing and shivering, her body refuses to give in. Raspier looks at Celestra and for a moment ignores how strong she is for such a little panther. "Well Celestra, I think Partune will be the one to thank for that." Celestra stops sobbing for a second and misses the comment Raspier made. "How did you know to take me here, Raspier?"

Now free from Celestra's strong hug, he cleans his feathers. "Well seeing you're a hybrid and I've heard that you're quite ignorant when it comes to your heritage. It just seemed to be the right idea." Celestra licking her paws and cleaning her face looks up for a moment. "Oh, well I see all of this is starting to come together then. Am I really a part of all of this history? It's very exciting, but also very terrifying."

Raspier adjusts his glasses and fogs up the lenses to clean them. "Upon explaining who you are and your story, I realized that you must be the reason we were all called to meet in the first place." Celestra a bit confused, "Why so much trouble over me?"

He chooses not to answer. Smiling, he skips into a bouncy step away from her and he motions to follow him. It's obvious the grulo has loosened him up a bit. Walking now down to the other end of the hall, Celestra sees a painting of an elegant dragon-like creature. Yet something is different about her. She's somewhat similar to a horse yet also a panther. With blue eyes like her own, she saw a black star on her forehead and pride in her stance. Celestra continues to stare and something familiar catches her eyes: a key. It was there hanging around her neck. It was the same key had on. Garlock had a dragon ring on his toe as well. She broke down and cried...

Raspier points with his claw at due north towards the painting of this white dragon hybrid. He starts to tell Celestra about her past, hoping she won't go into another hugging fit, "First off, this is your Grandmother, Garlock's daughter. Her name was Larcatch, a strong and intelligent warrior. You must have acquired that key when you were born to your parents. Sadly, you may have been the only one to survive out of the litter."

Stunned at what he was telling her Celestra, she continues to stare at the beautiful portraits and listens intently to Raspier. "Now Celestra, this beautiful female mated with another hybrid before the Draconian war. They hid in the underground meeting den to bear their litter. The terrible war waged on for years and most hybrids fought bravely defending the city to their deaths, but your grandmother was one of the few who knew how to breed and keep the race going."

Celestra staring with fear and pride turns to Raspier with puffy eyes, "But where do I come into play with all of this, how do you know I'm related to these great creatures?"

Raspier grins and winks at her, "Well that key on your neck told me as soon as I saw you. Without any doubt, you are their kin. Now, to continue, Larcatch knew she had very little time to raise her whelps and cubs, but she defended their innocence strongly. Nothing got in her way, not even her own mate. He was a panther, horse hybrid. His name was Calikon. What a sweet creature, he always did whatever that female wanted, as I was told. Because of that, their young survived. I know this or you wouldn't be sitting here today."

For a moment, Celestra pictured these strong and intelligent relatives upholding the honor of being a hybrid in a world without faith or love. Her loneliness wasn't that important anymore and in actuality, it seemed quite selfish. Celestra was lucky to have such a loving caretaker. She had no real dangers to be wary about due to his strength.

Raspier looks down at her and asks if he could continue. She nods yes, and he clears his throat.

"This portrait is of your father Celestra. He had three siblings; two sisters and a runt brother. Bardone was the only survivor of Larcatch's litter. The star on his head comes from a long line of warriors. Drondia protects these kinds of hybrids with honor.

As well as him being a third level hybrid, Bardone also resembled your great-grandfather more than his other siblings did. Garsa was the one who found him when his army had advanced further past the greggils base. Alone in the den, your grandmother had protected so strongly, Lu'barthrow sat and awaited his mother's return.

Little did Bardone know that while his mother was off investigating a sound in the night, something was watching her. She felt vulnerable and feared the worst. Instantly Larcatch returned and moved her litter to a new den. Unfortunately, after she safely transported the other three, a greggil enslaved dragon thrashed her and her litter down. Bardone had no kin like you.

Poor Bardone was in for a true reality shock, and Garsa was the one to explain it. Now during this whole ordeal, Calikon was missing and was never seen again after that day. No one knows if he chose to fight for the cause or chose to run. Since there was no carcass found, the question remains unanswered still today."

Concerned about his whereabouts, Celestra poked Raspier's brain a bit more, "Well if he lost both his father and mother, what happened to him after that?"

A sigh could be heard escaping Raspier's beak. Some of his feathers fell in front of his beady eyes, as his head got low. "Garsa a young healthy dragon at the time, not yet mated with young, had a drive that was unstoppable. His leader here at Drondia was Tiergon. He warned him to scout out and see what destruction this brainwashed greggil dragon had done. While researching, he came across the bastard just after killing Larcatch and her young. Enraged that he had destroyed such important animals, he challenged his fellow blood brother to a fight.

In all of dragon history, nothing hurts worse than their own kind going off course. He wasn't doing this of his own free will. Garsa was younger but already an adult. He found it impossible to throw the first real blow, but each time he thought of Larcatch and the lost hybrid litter, his claws found the power to attack. Larcatch meant much more to him than a dragon astray.

Teeth noshing into scales, claws ripping through wings, tails slamming down heads; the sound was outright frightening. When two dragons fight, the animosity is inconceivable. Imagine that you have to fight one of your own species. As far as we now know, all those dragons that were warped by the greggils were destroyed in the war. Garsa was full of pain fighting yet keep on for the right of way. His name was Dorcore. The very father of that Dragon you met at dinner. He's the one who was sneering at you in disgust. I have ears everywhere…"

55

"Is that why he doesn't like me?" Celestra looks up through puffy eyes. Looking down at her Raspier chooses his words carefully. "Well, it's a bit more complicated than that little wing. Your father watched these two creatures battle it out for quite some time and prayed that Garsa would be okay. Dorcore, in a last-ditch effort to save his hide dishonestly, tried to befriend him. Just before Garsa was about to land the killing blow conveniently.

Garsa being a good-hearted dragon fell for this trick as he was still very young. Sadly, in turn, Dorcore slashed out his eye. That was all he managed to accomplish before Garsa snapped his neck. Your father saw Garsa in pain bleeding. His heart was deeply hurt. Licking his eye and his wounds was an instinctual urge. Thank god he was a trinity hybrid for his saliva had healing agents. Another thing you will learn in time.

The wounds on Garsa were tended to quick enough so he healed well, despite his lost eye."

Celestra was amazed at all this knowledge. "How do you know all of this history on these animals, Raspier?" Sitting upright his tail sways back and forth. "Well Griffins are responsible for knowledge and the preservation of history, just as much as dragon's dear. Would you like to know more?"

"Yes; everything, please sir." Celestra's tears cease and her tail slowly wags across the floor along with Raspier's. He continues, "Well, your father and Garsa then, went back to the remaining ruins of Drondia and tried to just pick up the pieces. Thankfully, there were a few hybrids that we managed to save. They remained inside the city walls for protection. Many were left for dead, broken from the chaos. Unicorns were one of the main healers and they tried to do their best for the massacre that destroyed most of our population."

Unicorns, Celestra thinks, *those are those creatures Lastra was telling me about.*

Raspier is not about to stop when he finally has an audience for his knowledge. "Your father was raised amongst others of his kind, but he took more to the unicorns as he grew up for whatever reason. As he became fully developed, a hybrid female by the name of Celestaria, found him one day by a river. Times were growing easier for us to roam in our chosen homeland, so these two had the privacy and innocence to build a wonderful relationship. Your father seemed dumbstruck when it came to her. In her feline form, she looked much like you and your coloring. Just like your dragon hybrid grandmother.

In those times, Celestaria and Bardone would change back and forth between creatures. Romping in the sun, playing adolescent games with each other. They preferred to stay in their mountain lion form while together though. He could change between a full panther, a dragon and a horse, as your mother was a winged panther and an anicorn. They fell deeply in love while training to shapeshift, under the watchful eye of Avalo Ryu, The mystical red dragon. He blessed their union as the city was struggling to stay functioning. It was a moment of true joy for most of us, amongst such a terrible time.

Sadly, the war had not yet ended and times of joy were closing down on us all. Garsa and Avalo knew better to let the young hybrids enjoy each other's shortening time in vain. They had never seen any creatures more in love than your parents, Celestra. Sadly, when it came time for your parents to mate, they were about to be discovered.

A greggil guard was spying on the two innocent lovebirds' quietly. He planned to steal them to prevent further breeding. Since they were the only ones known that coupled out of the saved hybrids, they were irreplaceable.

Bardone was softly licking Celestaria's face in the faint rays of the dusk light, as they both purred in delight. Your father said this to her: 'I have never imagined having a beautiful mate such as you, or a love that is this indestructible. My Celestaria, my soul is always yours.' Around them, the tall summer grasses swept back and forth in the dim light of the setting sun.

Bardone decided, in that moment to give his mother's key to Celestaria. She happily accepted it, and looked deeply into his eyes with a soft purr. Walking in circles around each other, they softly growled with anticipation. They embraced for quite some time and mated passionately. Their unshielded energy became so strong, that they became the very beacon of their own destruction. A greggil guard spotted this magical moment and couldn't deny the purity of it. He simply could not kill them. It was as if, Gaia herself, somehow spoke straight into his heart. Crying loudly, another guard overheard him and went to investigate. He stood, confused over his comrades' behavior. Obviously, this greggil, did not have such a soft demeanor. He personally raised the first attack on the two lovers, without hesitation. His bow aimed straight for Celestaria's chest, yet neither of the two hybrids had any idea. He patiently waited, in the low purple and orange light for the chance to unleash his arrow. This death would bring heavy changes for both sides, but only the dragons know this truth. The other guard straightened up, after his breakdown, and took aim alongside them, tears still streaming from his eyes.

The night was so beautiful and so perfect for the two hybrids in love, yet nothing comes without a price. The guards kept position and shook with nervous tension holding their arrows right on their mark.

Bardone's ear twitched when the winds change direction. Then the scent of greggil was all around them. Bardone locates them and immediately orders her to lie flat and not to move. If necessary, as all anicorns' can, she was able to turn into a unicorn and run. Greggils cannot see the horn of a unicorn anyway, so she was to run as fast as she could, far away towards the city. She knew if this came to pass, her heart would be left there behind; behind without her dear soul mate Bardone." Tears begin to well in the young hybrid's eyes.

"Bardone dips down into the grasses and makes sure he's not to be seen. The greggils now frustrated they lost sight of the pair, knew they still had to press on. Their overlord will be displeased if they do not bring back a kill, so they proceeded. Bardone turns into his dragon form and hurls his long tail off to sideswipe the guards. Bardone screams to Celestaria, "Run! Run dear and don't ever look back!" She flees as tears fall endlessly from her eyes. Knowing instinctually this coupling was successful, she's worried of raising them without him. Quickly, she runs to find Garsa and Avalo. There was nothing more Celestaria could do. Her heart would die there with her lover if she chose to stay, as well as their future kin. This was the sad truth.

Just as Bardone suspected, it was an ambush attack. As soon as he stepped out, more greggils came to defend the others. He realized he must stay and fight to protect his mate and the damaged city. It was his time to show the greggils, just what they created.

A huge growl echoed across the lands as Celestaria fell to the ground outside the battered gates of the city. She knew what that call meant. The last bit of her faith died with that scream. Surely, that implied the death of her soul mate. For all anyone knew the greggils took the body away with them. They must have falsely mistaken the hybrid as a dragon to become a stuffed trophy in the lord's hall.

- No one after that day, like his mother and father before him, saw Bardone again."

Celestra was shocked over what her parents had to do to make sure their species continued on. Pain yet again overwhelmed her heart. "Did my mother survive Raspier?"

He shook his head no. "She was able to give birth to you apparently yet she was very young. Mentally scarred from Bardone's death, we deducted that Celestaria passed while giving birth to you; however, no one could find her body. Therefore, the truth about her after this remains unknown. There are many mysteries to your family Celestra. Many unanswered questions exist.

Now back to the story: Garsa arranged for you to have a surrogate family. You were only to know you were a panther and nothing more. Many other hybrids after that agreed to send off their kin the same way. To be protected from the barbaric greggils. You see, greggils have forgotten their own lives are much shorter than hybrids, so placing you all in surrogate families was of the utmost importance.

Most modern greggils were lucky if they lived to be eighty. Hybrids can live well over one hundred years. With so few left to continue the race, there wasn't much to do about it. Outside of our grasp, there was no contact or news if any lived. So, we never knew if there were any of them that survived until you, of course." Raspier stopped and watched her expressions as he collected his own memories of those times… "So *little wing*, are you satisfied now?"

With puffy eyes, fur still wet with salty tears and a heart finally open, the only thing Celestra could say was one thing:

"Yes."

Celestra didn't talk much on the way back to the others and Raspier understood. He curled his wing around her back as they walked, trying to comfort her. She realizes that many brave and heartfelt kin walked this earth before her and now it was her time to carry the torch of survival.

She tells the others she's in dire need of meditation and some personal time. "I'll return shortly. I just need some time to digest all of this new information."

It should almost, be expected, after such a shocking revelation. Celestra thought while smirking. *Finally, after so long, I have a true lineage. I now know my past. Just like*

Uniqua taught me long ago, 'When you have learned of your past Celestra, you will understand how to make your future brighter.'

She walked tall for the first time, proud. Tails swished methodically back and forth, her head high, with a smile proudly beaming, ear to ear. She was Celestra the 'White Hybrid' after all, not Celestra the 'White Panther'. "I am a hybrid. This, I can start to like. At least there's a good reason for these wings."

Softly, she chuckles to herself.

Chapter Eleven

Brother of the Paw

Looking around at this new place, Celestra notices many different kinds of animals. Mostly dragons, some griffins, some odd mammals, yet none other like her. In fact, Celestra saw no other hybrids at all. Remembering what her family had to do in order to survive, raises a terrible thought... *Am I the only one left alive?*

Her face showed deep pain.

Heartache slowed her down again, yet without that innocence she had before. Resisting the urge to give up, she feels a new and enlightening emotion softly emerging. It was not of her own. This alone, drew her closer to an abandoned part of the city.

Ears perked, whiskers extended to full length, the atmosphere around Celestra began to separate from the living city. To her right, there is a pile of older buildings, crumbled and obviously broken down by large cannons. Death loomed everywhere as if spirits seem to overlap the spaces between time and life itself.

There were buildings made of different color brick. They certainly were *not* the nice gold ones from the other parts of the city. The dirt even seemed older, more ancient in comparison.

There was a quaint feeling left behind in these old ruins. Certainly, they were less elaborate and more natural. All was earthy in nature.

Celestra's whiskers sensed something around an old coral-colored building. The original state was definitely peaceful and tender, yet somehow managed to stay alive amongst all this death, destruction and pain. Celestra turns to walk through a very familiar door. Her mind picks up traces of the last moment this building experienced, before its partial destruction.

A loving family was living here, but not one of dragon's blood. Celestra sniffs the ruins, choked with ancient dust and instantly, her hackles rise:

Someone is here. I can sense it.

Stalking like the predator she was trained to be, Celestra blends into the walls and corners, never revealing her location. She hears painful sobbing from the far corner of the room. Within the small bit of light shining down from a cracked roof, there, stood a creature in silhouette.

Celestra can smell this animal is similar to her own genetics. *This must be a hybrid without a doubt. Why is he here alone in the dead part of the city?*

Walking slowly up to it, claws extended for any sort of reaction, Celestra crouches low to the ground without making a sound. Knowing this creature is in distress, she cannot make any assumptions as to what it will do. Remembering a trick Uniqua taught her, Celestra grabbed a small stone with her teeth. Ever so carefully lifting it and turning her head, she throws it across the room. The creature quickly turns to inspect the noise. "Who's out there?!" She does not dare answer.

Staying low to the ground, Celestra can see the curves of this feline. *It has Mountain lion genetics...* Immediately it runs to where the stone fell, and looks around panicked. Gazing on his sleek and taut physique, she cannot deny being attracted to him. In the back of Celestra's mind, she can sense his hybrid gene.

The dark panther growls in disgust. "By teeth, terror, and claws, it's just these old ruins playing tricks on my mind again. Nothing should remove me from my solitude; nothing!" Slashing the wall with an impressively large black paw, Celestra remembered something as the wall crumbles to the ground. *Could this be the black panther in my dream?* Celestra wonders.

Her guard falls for a second. She should have concentrated more on staying in the shadows, but it was already too late. The panther spoke out to her from the other side of the room, "May I ask stranger... What would bring *you* here to such destruction and darkness?" Within seconds the panther jumped right on top of Celestra. Gasping for air as his mouth held her throat; she can only gaze in silent panic.

Jaws tighten around Celestra's larynx, as she growls in retaliation. "Why would such a fluffy little panther *disturb* such ruins if not in search of something? Hmm? Answer me." Due to the darkness, he apparently could not make out her true form. She decided to use this to her advantage. With the front joint of her wing, she quickly extends it outward to knock him in the head, very hard.

Instantly stunned, he stumbles backwards and releases. Her neck now shows his teeth marks, red with blood, bleeding hard. "Who are you to threaten *me*, dark stranger?! Thinking you can take me down so soon, is only foolish on your behalf. Stand your ground now and let me talk with you. I have earned at least this."

Stunned that he was outwitted, the dark panther walks into the light. Surprised at seeing another panther alive, Celestra stares curiously and studies his features. This obviously is making him uncomfortable. "Why do you gaze upon me as if you were the only one?" Celestra snorts at his rude response.

"...Because I was the only one before meeting *you*... *stranger*. Understand I've only been educated recently on my heritage, my breed, my kin, and what this place really is. Before this peaceful and innocent habitat here, I lived off the plains with no family. I killed to live. I killed to eat, and I killed to survive. I had no chef to cook my meals for me. I ate my meat raw - not like these *spoiled* creatures, I see around this weird city. So... What is *your* story, *Sir Solitude*?"

She was met with silence. Then, his growl grew larger, with every moment. To her, it sounded like a feline, who had forgotten how to purr. He approached her slowly. "You talk as if *you* are a *hybrid*!"

Celestra remains quiet. His eyes were turning dark green, widening into shards of yellow and brown. Apparently bothered, he stands taller than her. "I am Lu'barthrow, last living heir to the great Garlock." He proudly stated curling his tail in, while puffing his chest out in pride. Celestra sneers at him and says, "You mean *Nightstream*?" Lu'barthrow stares amazed and backs up, "How do you know his nickname? You are a *mere* panther?" In that moment, Celestra stepped out of the darkness to show her true form. Wings extended fully, chest pushed out in flair, key toggling around her neck, he can only sit there and stare. Stare at the wonder of seeing another hybrid alive. He could not help but stutter.

"What... Is your name... My fellow hybrid?"

Celestra happy the ice is broken gingerly answers. "I am Celestra, the genetic great-granddaughter to Garlock the Nightstream. Pleasure to make your acquaintance, Lu'barthrow. Apparently, we are related somehow."

For the first time, Celestra had to defend her heritage from another hybrid who obviously lost his way. Deep inside, Celestra feels that Drako must have seen her like this, back at her forest. Lu'barthrow circled Celestra slowly, staring at her wildly. "You look just like Garlock, but in white. Do you know who your mother was?"

Celestra closes her eyes and perks her whiskers. "Yes. She was Celestaria. My father was Bardone, the solo walker." A sharp moment of silence hangs over them both. She sees Lu'barthrow's paw curl around his face. His eyes widen, as he slowly sinks down into the ground. "Mother. I never knew I had a *sister*. Why didn't you tell me?!" He cries softly to himself ignoring her presence.

Stunned at this reply, Celestra reaches for his face with her muzzle and lifts it up without hesitation,

"Lu'barthrow… You mean to tell me, you are my… *brother*?"

In that very moment, they both embraced each other as if the world itself had stopped turning. Nothing mattered more to Celestra at this moment, nothing except holding a brother stolen from her, and the world.

Chapter Twelve

The Plague of Greggils

Running from the pond as fast as he could, Tarmax finally reached his next destination on the map. At that moment, he could barely make out the hazy gates of the dragon city, Drondia. Tarmax stared at the gigantic stone wall that kept him outside. He snorts in utter frustration. *The trees are way too high, and there seems to be no way in, except above. Maybe, I can find an opening if I look carefully...*

The same raven from before, is sitting in a tree by the wall to Tarmax's left. Watching this strange looking horse ponder the entrance to the city makes the bird chuckle. Tarmax looks up at the black bird, "What are you laughing at? What's so funny?" The Raven sees the star on his forehead and still continues to laugh. He actually falls out of the tree.

Stomping his hoof in anger, Tarmax apparently put a show on for this feathery onlooker without even trying. Walking over to the raven, he stops and pounds his front hooves straight down hoping to startle him. Nothing; the raven keeps on laughing. "Well then, if I have given you such a good laugh from all of this, do you care to tell me how to get over this wall?" Tarmax waits for an answer as the raven calms down.

Through laughter, the raven retorts, "Caw, Caw." Tarmax shakes his ears quickly and throws his head. "Fly over? Are you mad, little bird? Does it look like I have wings?" Tarmax thrashes his tail back and forth out of anger. "Caw, Caw. Ca'Caw."

Frustrated, Tarmax grinds his teeth. "You are of no help little bird. What do you mean I haven't used them yet? I'm a horse for sun sake. Do you see any wings?"

Thinking back, he remembers the event with the bear. Somehow, he grew horns from his head at the last second. The realization that he's no typical horse, starts to sink in. Tarmax, doubting himself, shakes the thought away. *Horses just don't grow horns spontaniously...*

In that instant, his inner consciousness awakened. "I'm just like Yaster, from my mother's stories!" Tarmax whinnies, and flicks his mane.

"Raven, can you scout out a trail on the wall, so I can climb up for a take-off? I may be able to change form. It's worth a shot." The raven shakes his head yes. It sets off to find a good location. Tarmax happy yet spooked all at the same time, tries to figure out how to spark these mutating abilities out of dormancy. He remembers his forehead became warm when those horns shot out from his head, so this was the first clue. This may take all morning, but Tarmax decided he was not going to give up.

As the raven is inspecting the wall, he sees a greggil walking with a dog. Fearful that the horse may become captured, he flies back quickly. Skidding down into the ground, he tells Tarmax the news, and begs him to do something about his horns. "Hide them, but I just learned I can grow horns, why?" The raven tells him a greggil is coming. Tarmax looks up at the raven and flicks his ears in confusion. "Greggil, what is a greggil?" The raven shakes his head and his beady little eyes shine brightly. "Caw, Caw!" the raven says to him in a panicked state. Tarmax neighs in laughter, back at the raven. "You mean humans, oh that's silly. They wouldn't be bothered with a hor..." Then it hit him.

He wasn't just a horse anymore. Tarmax panics, and feels something warm, retract from his forehead. The dog growls low at Tarmax, fully aware of what type of animal he was. Thankfully, this human only trusts what his eyes can see, and not what his instincts tell him. Many animals, wonder if humans even remember, if they have instincts at all. The human turns and sees Tarmax frantic. "Hey boy, what are you doing out here without a rider? Come with me. We'll find your master."

Tarmax terrified runs for the only opening in front of him. Knowing the human will try to follow, he leads him down a false path, away from the wall. The human running as fast as he can, tries to find the horse, but loses him, in the thick brush. The hound dog tracks him for a while longer, until his master calls him back. The dry leaves cracking under the dogs' feet, were fading in the distance as Tarmax kept running.

"I've never been so afraid of a human before. This is disturbing. They've taken such good care of me up until, I ran away."

Tarmax sighs. "Well, mother, I guess I've broken free of my barn life for good. Your little foal has chosen to be like Yaster the wild one after all."

What a frightening day for Tarmax. So many new and terrifying things keep challenging his narrow view of life. *Am I really not a horse? If I'm no horse, then what on earth am I?* For the first time, Tarmax has to listen to his instincts. Living with humans for so long, he's never really had a need. "This, is the limitations of domestication I imagine. You suffer the same pain as humans."

"So, this is what it's like to be a *wild* creature. Not as much fun as I thought it would be." As soon as he said the word 'wild', something stirred inside of him. At first, he shoved it down and called it nervousness. Then it surfaced again, similar to when he would eat bad grain, left out in the rain for too long. Within an instant, not only did his horns grow back, but also his two front hoofs, now morphed, into feet with three claws.

Stopping dead in his tracks, he begins to understand what his body was trying to accomplish. Bewildered, Tarmax continued to concentrate on this warm electrical feeling. Slowly, the hybrid gene has awoken inside of him. His back legs became dragon legs, dewclaws and all. His tail grew longer, thicker and lost all hair except on the very point. His back arched up into a wonderful curve and wings sprouted from his shoulders. "Raven! Raven, look at me?! I'm a dragon, this is so wonderful! Yet how did this come to be? How could I actually manage to turn into a dragon and have lived as a horse my entire life?"

He thought back to when he was living with Lord Cannor. He was lonely and almost dead inside from the harsh treatment of humans. They weren't kind to him at all. "I was only their property." Tarmax now realized what it truly meant to be alive. His freedoms were stolen as they shaped him to serve humans. Truly, a slave.

A deep burning rage seeps out from Tarmax and it slit his newly shaped eyes. This rage would soon show him a different way to live. He stretches out his wings and lets out his first roar. It echoed all throughout the valley like an earthquake. He finally understood the meaning of true freedom, creation, and independence. Now, the only problem left was for him to get over this damn wall.

Garsa was sitting with Drako at the gate, discussing the future for Celestra, when they hear an ear-piercing roar. Instantly they rise and Garsa stops. "I know that roar anywhere! That's a hybrid!" The very sound, reminded him of Bardone's last call. Shivers creep up his scaly spine, but he shoves them away. For all he knows, he just might be outside the city right now. Yet, rumor has it, that the Darkness is roaming around. Either way, they must go investigate. Garsa and Drako go back to the others and assemble a search party for the unknown soul roaming the gates.

While everyone is getting ready, Lastra looks everywhere for Celestra, yet cannot find her. Disturbed at this, she asks the others if it would be okay to stay behind to wait for Celestra. Garsa looks to Lastra, "Sure, if you feel that would be best." Lastra with worry all over her face nods, "Did you set out any search parties before we arrived in the city?" Garsa shakes his head no. Turning towards the city wall, he laughs. "Yet oddly enough there is someone who has found us instead."

Partune fidgeting with his claws says, "Well, not to startle you guys, but I think I found a hybrid when Raspier and I were spying on the greggils. Tied to a post, this hybrid had no clue.

I felt that my intuition was correct. I waited for a sign to confirm it. Funny enough, a stick cracked beneath my feet, and the horse startled, asked who was out there. I ended up leaving a map, drawn into the dirt of Draconia, where we were standing, hoping the horse hybrid would understand. Apparently hearing that roar, he's found and followed that map. On his travels, who knows. Maybe he even learned how to change into his other forms. Rare, yes. Yet, possible. Hope greggils didn't find the directions. I'm sure he would cover them up anyway…"

- Partune bowed his head, in fear of a scolding.

Garsa stunned, looked sternly at Partune for his brazen act, but realized, Partune is never wrong. "Let's trust your good inner judgment, for the moment. If it was a hybrid, you've certainly saved its hide." Raspier sneers at Partune, but is quickly shot down by Garsa. The two of them need not start old whelp'ish fights, when a hybrid is on the loose.

Garsa's heart lifts a bit, knowing better, then getting lost in the past. He must remain conscious, and in the moment. Yet, there is a growing uncomfortable feeling deep in his core, that this hybrid, may bring more trouble than good. Either way, they must go out and find him. With that, they all head to the gate and set out searching.

Chapter Thirteen

New Life in a Dead City

Lastra calls frantically for Celestra. She has been gone for way too long. Searching the streets of the city, she looks for the white panther in every corner and every turn, but, sees nothing.

Sitting by a fountain, she senses something strong. Easing into her deeper consciousness, she can see a moment frozen in time between a hybrid and a dragon. Somehow, this incident seems burned in the local lands lay lines, deep into the earth. Lastra concentrates harder.

Curling into a ball, she meditates to see if it could help her find Celestra. Within Lastra's drifting, she notices a familiar smell, that strikes her nose.

"Celestra..." she says. "I must find her." Without easing out of her meditation, Lastra stumbles over her resting body and chases the scent. Realizing she could be in trouble, Lastra keeps a strong pace. *There are more than just dark memories in these ruins.*

Celestra and Lu'barthrow are now sitting, talking, ignorant to Lastra's frantic searching. Both are digging deeper into their fragmented memories of their cubhood. Celestra turns to Lu'barthrow and flattens her ears thinking about her mother. "Lu'barthrow, did you remember... mother?"

He sighs, and looks out the broken window of the dwelling. "Of course, she was beautiful. You look very much like her. We were hiding out in this part of the city, since my birth. All because she feared, they would put me into foster care due to the greggil war. My mother was told, this was only for protection. At the last moment, she couldn't bear to do it. So, she ran off, to these ruins, in a dire attempt to save my life from the greggil war. She slipped away from the eyes of all the dragons, to give birth to her second cub. She never told any of them she was leaving, nor told me the truth, that I had a sister. Something I might have wanted to know. Mother, may have hidden everything from me in order to help us survive. We stayed here in the ruins, for quite some time, without any real explanation. I realized slowly, that something wasn't right. Yet moving, might weaken her much faster. We weren't born at the same time Celestra, so this, must have made her sick internally.

Assuming my birth made her this way, I tended to her with care. Also, out of a little guilt. Retrieving food and playing very little, I managed to keep us both alive, off of scraps I would find on the outskirts of the city. She never let me stray too far in fear. they would take me away. So, I wasn't able to grow up with the innocence, that you did. I also cannot deny, it hurt to see other animals of my age, playing while I tended to my duties. Responsibility had crowded my fragile young mind, way before it should have. I grew very bitter of my birth, and the torment I thought it caused my mother.

One day after scrounging up our midday meal, I returned to find she had disappeared. Frightened she had wandered off to die alone; I searched screaming out her name. Days passed and slowly I realized that she was never coming back. Saddened that the only familiar face I've ever known had disappeared, I wandered about the city lost. I became faceless; without a true purpose.

All the creatures I saw were happy and carefree despite having to rebuild their presently crumbling city. Staring at them intently, I wondered what it was like to live amongst these strong-willed individuals. Seeing whelps playing I thought back to my young days where I was helping mother heal. Giddiness overcame my heart to see them so innocent enjoying life, but my own bitterness rose up and ruined the moment. It was no use in denying the truth.

Angered that I was left alone in this way, I wandered to a half-built fountain in the center of the square. Lapping up the water, I was unaware of a large black dragon walking my way. He apparently was equally unaware of me. Painfully, he stepped right on my tail. Yelping out in pain, I turned to yell at the clumsy dragon, "Watch where you're going you big oaf! Someone is sitting here you know!" The dragon obviously embarrassed apologizes and introduced himself. 'Sorry little panther, I didn't see you drinking there. My name is Garsa, who might you be?' I told him my name was Lu'barthrow, and that my mother had disappeared. Explaining why my mother hid me was hard, but he seemed to understand. Talking with someone after such seclusion was calming. Even felt a little more eager to venture out into the living city.

'No worries little one,' he said, 'I know exactly where you can go and you will be very well taken care of.' Garsa said soothingly. 'It's a good thing I did step on you. You could have been out here quite some time by yourself.' I answered back, 'I've felt like I've been by myself for my whole life sir. Why would it hurt to stay this way forever?' Garsa looks at me with a compassionate face, 'Well everyone needs some company every now and then.' After that, I decided to go with Garsa and that's where I felt I went wrong."

Celestra amazed at what her brother had to endure looks up at him, "That's one hell of a story Lu'barthrow; much respect, yet that still doesn't explain why you were hiding in the place of your birth? Why won't you leave?"

Lu'barthrow tips his head slightly to the side and rolls his eyes, "Well after living in the center court with the dragons that ran the city, I can't deny it was refreshing. I liked having my meals prepared for me. Warm baths and having comfortable places to sleep at night, but it never felt right. Avalo Ryu was to become my teacher when I finally became acclimated to the city life. I was never calm surrounded by so many animals. Anxiety attacks surfaced often and would really put me in a bad place. It really limited my ability to learn how to trust.

Being a stray did much more than just rough up my fur and muscles, it destroyed my mind. Having Avalo Ryu as my teacher did not help my issues either. He was very cryptic and would confuse me every chance he got. According to him, he was just testing to see how quick I was.

Others that were taught by him said there was no difference in their training, everyone was treated the same. My personal issue was that I was prideful, young and never learned any social graces. So, in turn, we continuously fought over many things.

Over time, he taught me small techniques like how to sense greggils and how to evade them, the different calls of the master dragons to know what to do in times of crisis. Plants and herbs that help the wounded and what were the ones for poison. Also, meditation and spirit drifting, yet he was wary of showing me how to transform. He never gave an answer as to why, but self-doubt always pointed to me being unable to pull it off.

Time passed as I grew into an adult, yet Avalo still kept me from transforming. I started to become upset over this greatly. Not caring of his reasons, I missed his class that day and went to a secluded area I would meditate infrequently. Fixating on the heat that could change my body, I concentrated for quite some time to transform. In less than a heartbeat, my limbs grew longer and my tail frayed out into hair, my ears elongated and my teeth widened, my back became broader and my paws became hoofs. Ecstatic that I learned how to do this I ran to water to see my reflection wondering what beautiful creature I had become. Instead I saw nothing more than a horse. Depressed, I fell to the ground and sobbed.

Why couldn't I have become something my ancestors could have been proud of? I'm nothing more than a common level hybrid. This is the main reason I am here alone. This is why I came back to these ruins because I am a derelict version of my ancestors. I was told my father was a trinity hybrid and I look much like him, but it all means nothing now.

I assumed Avalo knew that I wasn't anything special. Since that day, I have never returned to Garsa or Avalo and the dragon city. I refused to change as well. It's just too damn depressing to turn into that horse all over again just to feel common. I've let down my species and my father's name. Until you walked into my life, I thought our genetics died with our parents." Lu'barthrow said with heavy sadness.

Celestra begins to realize the true cause of all their pain. Greggils; humans were limiting hybrids to this reclusive training, and protective atmosphere.

"Lu'barthrow, did you ever consider that you really are a 'trinity' hybrid and you just haven't transformed past your horse form?" Lu'barthrow feeling Celestra was mocking him growls low. "No. I'm a level one hybrid. I was just hoping I would change into something my forefathers could have been proud of, but I thought wrong." Celestra convinced this isn't the truth, pries a bit more at Lu'barthrow with the hope of inspiring him. "Are you sure that you don't have a talent or trait left undiscovered? I've learned sometimes reality isn't always what you think. You didn't say that Avalo officially told you..."

"Look, Celestra, there is nothing you can say that can help me feel better or relieve my pain. Don't think it's not appreciated though because it is." Lu'barthrow said cutting Celestra off. She decided to leave it alone due to his delicate feelings and started to explain her own cubhood to him. Maybe she can show Lu'barthrow he wasn't alone in his miseries.

She started at Uniqua and Lu'barthrow listened intently. For the first time, Celestra really opened up to someone. They both did.

Chapter Fourteen

Tarmax Drorsen

Partune, Garsa, Drako, Raspier, and Avalo were approaching the wall of the city. Worried that something could have happened to the hybrid they quickened their pace. "Try to sense where he is and locate his position," Garsa said. Partune runs ahead and checks the surrounding perimeter. While they are searching, Tarmax quite giddy leaps into the air and floats down with his new wings. "Wow..." He thought, "This is fantastic! All of my young life I thought I was just some common black horse, but apparently, I'm this beautiful dragon as well. I wonder if this breed has a name yet." Tarmax thinks as he digs with his new claws. "Well I don't care; I am not a horse, nor a dragon, so I'm a... A drorsen! That's it!"

So many things are swirling inside Tarmax's head that he can barely stay still. Romping like a foal that just learned he had legs, Tarmax explores his transformation innocently. The raven that helped him, hears the other dragons coming. Neither Tarmax, nor the others know how to find each other, so the raven takes matters into his own wings. Flying to where he heard them, the raven locates the group on the outskirts of the wall. The raven caws to catch their attention and Raspier turns to see him. "Hello little raven, how are you doing?" The raven loudly caws at Raspier flapping its wings. Raspier shakes his head as he tries to understand what he's saying. "Okay Raven, one more time I didn't get all of that." The raven explains again, "Caw, caw caw caw." Raspier's head feathers stick straight up and he snorts, "The hybrid? You know where it is. Well, let's go then! Lead the way, my friend."

They all run around towards the other side of the wall. Such a journey during midday is highly dangerous. Finally reaching the hybrid, the group stood astonished at this large odd-looking creature jumping around in front of them. Tarmax was practicing his gliding, yet he continuously lands ungracefully, plodding to the ground like a sack of potatoes. Garsa stares at this large hybrid and is in amazement. "He is very rare indeed. A black hybrid dragon, heavens to claws; I never thought I'd see another one after the death of Bardone."

Partune wriggles joyfully. He knows it's that black charger from days ago. "Wow, he's impressive! Never knew he was a hybrid dragon, he was already a sharp looking horse." Raspier makes a nasty face. He had to admit he was wrong. "Well Partune, your senses override my intellect yet again old friend. Do mind that one day your instincts may mislead you. Always remember it's always better to be safe than sorry."

Partune smiles at Raspier and nods back at him in understanding. Still, Partune knows he uses his instincts, as Raspier uses his mind. When one trusts their inner self, the truth always shines brighter than the illusion. Partune snickers at Raspier but makes sure he cannot hear him.

Drako walks up to the giddy hybrid and studies his strange little dances of joy. The raven watching in the trees begins to laugh at his gawky movements. They resemble more of a horse than a large dragon. "Hello there, we heard your roar from within the city and wondered if you need any assistance?" Tarmax turns to see them and stares in amazement. A bit scared there are dragons in front of him, he steps backward. Then Tarmax remembers he's one now too. Laughing he meets eyes with Garsa and waves hello. Partune walks up to Tarmax and looks at the white star on his forehead. *A true star mark, no natural discolorations. He's a trinity.* "I never imagined you'd get this far. We saw you back at the camp and I knew there was something special about you. We will not hurt you in any way."

Tarmax smiles and tears start to fall from his eyes. He almost quickly forgot he started life as a horse. Crying loudly, he remembers the tribulations that he's endured. The love and protection of his mother, his companions he abandoned and these trails towards the dragon city. "I've never thought my life would turn out this way. I have no idea what to do with this new-found power, let alone master it without training. Mother, you knew more than I. Why didn't you tell me I was this creature? You sheltered me from it, but never thought what it would do to me when and if I transformed. What if I never found this out and I died a plain barn horse?" Sobbing hysterically, he lays on his belly nuzzling the cold dry grasses into his snout. The group backs off and gives him a moment to himself.

Avalo looks at him and feels deeply for the poor animal. *He's so tortured and lost. Let me call him by his real name.* Looking down at Tarmax, Avalo makes sure to catch his gaze before speaking, "Hybrid."

The air almost seemed to silence every soul after Avalo spoke. Never hearing this word before, Tarmax looks up at him puzzled. "What did you say?" Avalo smiles and winks at Tarmax, "You are a hybrid, and there is nothing to fear anymore. You are safe with us. We've been looking for more of your kind to continue the race and here you are a very rare one. You bore the true trinity mark. That small pull inside your heart tells you to remain calm; just trust it." Tarmax calms down for a second and pauses from his present confusion. The tears stop.

He realizes these dragons can help him. Partune trying to aid in calming the new hybrid speaks, "Now what is your name so I may address you respectfully."

"Tarmax" Restraining his urge to keep crying, he attempts to gain back some dignity. "My name is Tarmax. So that is what I am, a *hybrid*? I was calling myself a Drorsen. I figured that was close enough."

Avalo happy the hybrid seems calmer motions for Partune to speak, "Well Tarmax I think that would be fine. Your full name shall be Tarmax Drorsen if you wish. Besides, did you think that life would have left you out here without guides? The raven that you see over there is courtesy of Raspier. He's that griffin you saw in the darkness the first time we met. After much convincing, the raven agreed to follow you. Sometimes those birds are irritating but they do come in handy. Raspier looks over at Partune a bit flustered he used a raven without telling him. Despite trying to hide the emotion, Partune noticed and bowed slightly in embarrassment at his dear friend.

Tarmax looks to the raven and laughs, "So you put me up to this because you knew I would end up doing it out of pride, didn't you? Smart little bird." The raven caws in appreciation. Partune looks over to the others and motions to get back in the city. "I think you've experienced enough oddities for one day Tarmax. How would you like to come into the city finally? You did make it here after all..." Tarmax looked up at Partune and flicked his ears. "That would be great. I could sure enjoy some time to think. Yet, I still do not know how to fly with these things." The group chuckles at his comment. That obviously was the next step.

Chapter Fifteen

Lastra Express

Celestra and Lu'barthrow continue discovering each other's past as the sun rolls across the sky. Within all the excitement and emotional changes, time passed a bit faster than realized. They didn't sense that Lastra was very close to finding them. Running faster now, she feels the death looming over her consciousness. These ruins will always hold such negative memories, from a time when war and famine were ever-present over them all. *Where could she be? I know I sensed a moment there at that fountain, and it leads me into these ruins. Maybe if I keep my senses high, I will find her.*

Celestra is sitting with Lu'barthrow outside the broken-down bungalow enjoying the warmth of the day. Both a bit more in predator mode stay very close to each other. Celestra curls her paw around Lu'barthrow's body to comfort him. Together they clean each other and purr under the warm cloak of the late autumn sunlight.

For the moment, Lu'barthrow knows truly what it feels like to belong and Celestra now knows what having family feels like. Lu'barthrow looks over at his sister with an inquisitive look, "Celestra, so did you ever question where you came from? Or did you just patiently await your heritage to unravel?" Lu'barthrow asks. Celestra tilts her head at Lu'barthrow's question. She never thought she would know her parent's name, let alone that she had a sibling.

Trying to hide her lack of faith Celestra looks up at the waving trees outside the room. "Well as I explained earlier, my master taught me everything he felt I needed to know: All about life, death and everything in between. His story was that I was abandoned at birth and he was told to take care of me. Uniqua said I was very young and weak, and he raised me as best as he could. From your story and what the others told me it makes sense why he hid everything. He had to in order for me to survive. Being that he was such a stubborn bear, he taught more about battle and war, rather than love and creation. Heart matters I learned more in my solo walking. Fighting for the right to know what love was in the first place, is no easy task when love was never around you. It was almost like teaching a creature it has to drink by not letting it reach the actual water. This proved to be a very negative situation for me as time grew on.

Every time I was caught in a battle with the local wolves or the hounds, the only real thing I gained was painful wounds; inside and out. Sure, my fighting skills were top notch, and I could take on entire packs of canines, but I never really understood the point in fighting. One day, after a bad battle with the local wolves over an injured buck, I started to drag my kill back to the den to Uniqua. I may have been ripped up and bleeding, but the reward of bringing home so much meat out-won the pain. I knew Uniqua wouldn't be pleased if I allowed myself to get this injured. He usually just scolded me for it and forced me to eat last. Uniqua often did things like that to teach me to be more careful. I would be hurt by these actions, but never once would I argue with him.

When I finally reached the den, my heart sank. Uniqua was gone. I first thought he had abandoned me like my birth parents, but deep in my heart, I knew something bad had happened to him and it was wrong to slight him in that fashion. There were strange scents all over the den that made my fur stand straight up. Either way, I was alone again; this time, there was no way for me to get out of it. The wolves had no concerns for me other than exterminating me. They wanted the local prey to themselves. The local hounds from the large castles only hunted me for sport, as they were trained. So, I stood there in my forest alone for the first time, this bizarre white panther with wings.

Devouring as much deer as my belly would allow, I sat there after tending to my wounds and tried to cover up the carcass so the wolves wouldn't come and steal it.

Look forward four years. I was jolted awake one morning by my master's scent in the air. Quickly I jumped up and ran out of my den. My keen tracking skills caught a whiff of him trailing away from the den. Following it, I noticed it led out of our territory, and even past the local wolves' territory. I took down a large wounded buck along the way and it had punctured my belly pretty deep. Very similar to that dreadful day my master had vanished. It was not very intelligent wandering out of my territory, this hurt. I certainly didn't have the strength to defend myself if anything large came my way, but the urge to locate my dear master was too strong. I started investigating his scent trail for quite a while until it completely disappeared. As if he went straight up into the clouds. I was now surrounded by a very unfamiliar smell.

I found it incredibly odd that his scent had completely dropped off like that. This is pretty much when Drako found me, exhausted, bleeding, and tired. I only paid attention to the external wounds and never the emotional ones. The one thing that my master taught me was that life is long, and there are no shortcuts to the top. All lessons learned are either from your own mistakes or from watching others make them, it's your choice. Yet the most important factor in life is to know the answers to these three questions. Who are you, where are you going, and what have you done to help the cause? As long as those stay in focus; fate, destiny, and Gaia will always be by your side."

Lu'barthrow just stares at her almost as if, she had something strange hanging from her fur. Uncomfortable with this moment, Celestra awaits a further response. Then, almost as if Lu'barthrow's heart exploded right out of his chest, tears began to fall. "Thank you. For without you, I would have remained alone in this darkness forever. No one ever explained that so well to me before, nor would they have known it was important to me. Your master was a very special creature, you were very lucky to have him." Celestra nodded at Lu'barthrow as the both just eased into a shallow nap. She sat quietly for some time just enjoying this new-found peace. The sun was now quite low in the sky and there were many back at the square looking for her. Celestra tells Lu'barthrow he should come back with her, but he hesitates. Celestra explains things can only be different if you choose yourself for them to be. "This is how I was strong enough to make it this far brother. Walk with me, by my side. Look at the world you threw away through my eyes until you can trust again. Stand tall and be proud of what you are, because no one will do it for you. What do you say?"

Lu'barthrow stares intently into Celestra's eyes with a newfound appreciation. With a strong back, he stands tall, looks up and really feels the cool breeze ruffling his black fur. "I will walk with you Celestra." So together, they walk back to the city, to try to start a new life. Both were brought into this world disorientated and misguided. Hopefully, in turn, they will become just what nature intended.

Lastra's tension builds as she watched the sunset. "These ruins are starting to look all the same. Oh, by first the dragon scale, I won't get anywhere searching this way, I should just go back to that fountain. Besides, that's where that vision popped into my head."

Lastra flies back to the fountain just in time to spot two panthers walking towards the city. Almost tangling up her wings, she stops short an heads into a dive. Swooping down. Lastra picks them both up without a second thought. How many winged white panthers were in this city anyway? Celestra and Lu'barthrow terrified for a second, fights her smooth arms. Celestra however after a few moments realizes it's Lastra. She tells Lu'barthrow to relax because she's a friend. Lastra out of breath speaks, "I was sure you were here little warrior, who's your friend?" She asks inquisitively. "Uh, hello Lastra, nice to see you... What's with the dive bomb pick up; something wrong?"

Lu'barthrow was not pleased in the least over all of this, "Good way to scare us half to death, *dragon*." Lastra sighs and looks down at the two of them. "Sorry about that. There is just so much to tell and very little time to do so in. I've been looking for you all day. There is a new unknown hybrid outside the city walls. The others are out in search of it." Celestra startled tries to look up at Lastra but cannot with her holding her nape. "Lastra, did you just say another *hybrid*? Wow, that is three in one day!" She says cheerfully with eyes squinted and paws tucked into her chest.

Lastra looks at the other panther just before putting them down onto the grasses of the square. Examining him, she can sense his hybrid gene. His facial features are too similar to Bardone for him not to be his offspring. "Pleased to make your acquaintance, your sister has grown on me very much since I've met her, may I ask your name hybrid?"

He feels a bit better from the cool winds of flight answers Lastra. "Lu'barthrow; pleasure is all mine, Lastra. Just wish you were a bit more polite with your arrival back there. Celestra and I were not prepared." Feeling embarrassed, Lastra tilts her head down before speaking. "Yet again, my apologies; I wasn't thinking straight." Well with the three acquainted and settled in one place, they await the return of the others.

Celestra was updating Lastra on how she ended up meeting Lu'barthrow in the city ruins. As she explained, Lastra then remembered the energy still active at the fountain from before. She asks Lu'barthrow if he had any memory of it. Lu'barthrow explained how he met Garsa at that fountain, and his training with Avalo all the way into the reason he ran away. Listening intently as to not offend him, she prepares a small snack for them to tend to their growling bellies. Lu'barthrow touched by

Lastra's kindness, starts to purr. "I must say, Lastra, you are quite the hostess, thank you for your kindness." The water dragon slits her eyes and smiles wide turning to the gates of the city. "Thank you Lu'barthrow. Caring for others is what I do best."

Celestra notices her growing concern for the others. Much time has passed and it's very dangerous outside the city gates. She looks at Lastra. "I wonder what they're dealing with out there. It's almost evening and they're not back yet. Maybe we should go looking for them?" Lastra smiles at Celestra while cooking a small rabbit in a pot over a makeshift fire pit. "Well, one thing I've learned is that staying in one spot makes it easier for others to find you." Celestra winces noting the small jab for wandering off. "Yeah, I know. We'll stay put then."

Chapter Sixteen

First Flight of the Hybrid

The others still with Tarmax were asking him questions about his history. The soft light of the setting sun extends their shadows far across the land. "Tarmax, have you any family?" Garsa asks. "Well, apparently my real family is a mystery to me, but I did have a wonderful mother growing up. She was this beautiful black barn horse, though most of the stables called her common. I think she was brilliant, also very talented."

Drako whispers to Avalo. "Do you think she could be a hybrid as well, protecting her offspring from the greggils? Most hybrids won't change around greggils, even if that is for the rest of their life. Maybe she was too frightened to escape with her baby." Drako concerned scratches his chin. "Did your mother ever have any strange markings on her head, for instance, a two-prong diamond or a star?"

Tarmax flicks his ears in discomfort before speaking. "Well if you're asking if she is my real birth mother the answer is no. She bonded with me when I was very young. According to her story, greggils, as you call them bought me from a fair at a really good price. They told them I would be a strong carthorse or a lead horse for a lord. The latter is what I became. Lord Cannor became my master, and being a young foal, they prepared a segregate mare mother for me. Her foal was sold and they figured I could replace him…"

In that moment, Avalo senses someone inside the city wishes urgently for their return. "Not to interrupt but I will be heading back to see who I can round up. Garsa I can assume you will be fine with this new hybrid here?" Garsa noticing Avalo's concern smiles and allows him to leave. "Indeed Avalo, go on ahead. We'll see you there shortly."

So Tarmax continues once Avalo leaves. "Upon meeting my new owner, and my new mother, fear was the only thing I felt. Yet, I must say, being in that cozy quaint barn was a luxury. Those dirty selling pens of my youth made it easier to make this my new home. Lord Cannor was not the easiest of men to get along with, but he always gave us all the lavish treatment his money could provide.

Top quality grain, fresh hay, beautiful stables and proper cleanup, no corner left undone. Still, he was a very bitter man. Those times growing up with my mother is always what kept me going. She was such a wonderful creature. Over time, we would take long runs inside the training pen, teasing each other. One day she knew her services as a surrogate mother would be finished and the need for her would be as well. I awoke one morning to find that mother had been sold to a local farmer three places out from my stables. Without even thinking about it, I escaped to find her. Panting relentlessly searching each place I hit, terror continued to run rampant through my juvenile veins.

Finally reaching the farm that purchased her, I sniff the air to see where she was being held. 'Ah', I said, 'over there in that pen!' I ran over to it and neighed for her attention. My mother turned around and neighed back out in joy. 'What are you doing here; you should be in your stable dear?' I look at her and rubbed my nose on her shoulder. 'Mother I want to stay with you, why did they get rid of you?' She leaned over the fence and rubbed my muzzle with hers. 'My need was no longer useful Tarmax, no worries now. You are an adult and you need to hold to your responsibilities. Go home dear; I'll always be in your heart.'

Knowing she was always right, I said my goodbyes and went back to Lord Cannor's stable. Not very happy about her decision, I thought about life without her. I also did not consider the serious trouble I was walking back to. Reaching the gate, I whinnied to the guard to let me in. He opened the gate surprised at my return and placed me back into my stall. Lord Cannor was there and quite furious. 'Stupid horse, you escape and then decide to return to these stables? Why do such a thing when you had your chance for freedom?' Grabbing a bit and bridle, he violently put it in my mouth and wrapped the leather around a peg on the wall. 'From now on I will always have you watched.'

I felt terrible realizing I had angered him. For a while, I thought he was worried about me like my mother had done. Yet over time, I learned to Lord Cannor, I was simply property. In no way was I a companion.

Slowly I began to see how nasty this man was. Never really knowing what had made him this way, I was aware now that not all greggils, as you call them were like this. The nice family that had taken my mother in was wonderful. I visited them sometimes to say hello, and romp around with her in their fields. I had learned how to sneak out without anyone catching me.

Lord Cannor seemed to have a terrible situation haunting him inside, and I began studying and investigating just what that was. In the summer once when he rolled up his sleeves, I noticed a row of four tight claw marks scarred on his arm. Unlike a normal animal wound, this seemed to have healed very strangely. It always looked fresh and new. This intrigued me very much, to the point I started to ask the local animals what kind of predator could leave a mark like that; where a scar wouldn't heal. Many creatures just gave me folklore about weird cats with two heads, and snakes with claws. bears that can fly and other ludicrous things.

Soon, I gave up on figuring out the mysterious animal markings and lived my everyday life. Whatever left that mark seemed to hurt him beyond his skin. That was certainly sure." Drako remembers Celestra talking to them briefly in the cliffs just outside Roden Forest about young greggils that chased her. *Could that have been Lord Cannor as a child?*

Raspier looking up at the sky realizes everyone has lost track of time. "Hey, not to interrupt your life story Tarmax, but we really should be making it back to the city. I'm sure Lastra is sick of waiting around for everyone by now."

Garsa agrees with Raspier and they start to return to the dragon city wall. Before the gate, Garsa asks if Tarmax can grow out his wings more. After some trial and error, he manages to accomplish this. Garsa smiles at Tarmax's natural ability to change on his own. "Tarmax, you think you can fly with us over this wall?" He looks at his wings and tries to flap them in a quite undignified manner. The dragons try not to snicker at him. Tarmax looks back at Garsa with a bit of worry. "Uh, I'm not sure really; never tried full out flying yet. I only learned how to become a dragon a few hours ago." Garsa looks at him and smiles. "Well Tarmax now is your chance to. Try to change fully into your dragon form, and we'll start the quick lesson after that."

Tarmax concentrates on the warmth that generated from his head earlier, and the transformation begins. It went much smoother than the previous time. Drako chuckles at the small imperfections Tarmax's change left behind. "What a funny looking dragon." Garsa glares at Drako and then tells Tarmax a few more pointers. "I see you haven't been able to completely change yet. Remember that this will only take time. Your patience is required. Soon you'll make this transformation perfectly. Avalo will teach you more when you're ready." Tarmax notices what he meant by looking at his tail. Tufts of hair still feathered out of at the tip and his horse ears hadn't retracted. "Well is it good enough to fly with?" Garsa still glaring at Drako for his rude comment looks back at Tarmax. "Yes, my hybrid friend, it's more than perfect," Garsa, tells him to tuck his wings under and to fold them in while taking a running jump. "Now curl your front legs in and jump up and flap your wings."

Tarmax does as Garsa instructs and for the first time is hovering briefly in the air. *He is a quick student*, Garsa thinks. "Good, now that you're airborne, tuck your feet under and stretch out your neck. Bend your wings slightly backward as you fly.

Use your tail as the rudder - direct your body where to go. Feel the wind and know it's your fuel to move forward."

Tarmax incredibly happy, follows his instructions and is flying within no time. "Look, guys, I'm really flying, this is great!" Trying not to stifle his eager mind, Garsa gets his attention. "Alright; now that you've had your flying lesson, we can now go back to the city." Now a bit more confident, he lands on the ground feeling accomplished. "Okay; let's go, I think I'm ready now."

Chapter Seventeen

Old Wounds Heal Slow

Avalo had flown up ahead of the others to see if he could locate Lastra and Celestra. Figuring they would be in the main square, he aims straight for it. Avalo hasn't had full-time hybrids in his life since Celestaria and Bardone. Mostly now, he spends his time studying on Hybrid history. Ways to reverse greggils brainwashing over their own kind, the heavens present position and the prophecy of the black dragon. Sorrokine Arou certainly is doing the same up north. "Ah, how I miss that dragon…"

Avalo sighs to himself. Seeing them in the square, he lands and pushes the thoughts far from his mind. He has a duty to uphold now that the hybrids have appeared. No mystic will get anything done with that kind of distraction.

Lastra, Lu'barthrow, and Celestra are greeted by Avalo just as they're waking up after their rest. Lu'barthrow seeing Avalo sneers and snorts in disgust. Banging his tail in discontent, he walks out to the courtyard. He separates to control his anger. Time is hard on deep wounds. "Doesn't forget a thing, does he?" Avalo chuckles quietly. "I haven't seen him in years, and time still hasn't healed him. He has much to learn that young hybrid."

Celestra looks up at Avalo and tries to explain the weight Lu'barthrow had on his shoulders to become something impressive, and majestic. Let alone the grief and personal torment he went through up until he met the dragons.

For a moment, Avalo understood and dropped the cryptic attitude he so fancied. "Wish the rugged little guy would have opened up to me, I could have helped him out of that, but he resisted me out of anger and stubbornness." Celestra watched where Lu'barthrow went off too and feels compelled to help him. "Well, there is always a second chance now to try again. Besides, don't forget I myself, haven't changed yet so we can go through it together, and both of you can assist me. Let me go and talk with him. He is my blood after all. Maybe I can connect with him."

Walking out of the square over to Lu'barthrow, Celestra headbutts his shoulder in affection hoping he would loosen up. Instead, he growls and swats her with his paw. "I know you feel obligated to help in this situation but Avalo and I go way back before I even knew you had whiskers. He can approach me if he wishes; this matter is closed to you and me. There is no comfort in seeing that old dragon after reliving my entire childhood. Mind these years that have passed may be enough time to forgive but certainly not enough time to forget." Celestra snorts back at her brother's stubborn nature but accepts his request. Walking back to the square, she tells Avalo to go talk with him and try to fix this issue before the search party returns. He accepts Lu'barthrow's wishes and goes to talk with him. Lastra and Celestra smile over testosterone's stubborn influence and decide to leave these two alone. The girls tell them they are going to cool off in the bathing pool in their quarters. This should give them a little time to talk in private. It is not their business anyway.

Upon walking to their quarters, Celestra sees small black dots on the moonlit horizon. "Lastra, is that them? I see five creatures; could it be a new dragon?" Confused, she gazes deep into the night sky. "I don't know Celestra, but let's wait and see, they're still a few minutes away." They reach their rooms and decide to relax in the cool waters until they arrive.

Chapter Eighteen

The Hybrid Connection

Tarmax and the rest of them flew over the wall and were almost at the main center court. Every now and then he loses the current and almost falls. Garsa turned and showed him how to make big flaps from his wings to gain back control. Thankful, he turns to the old one-eyed leader and smiles. "Garsa, flying is amazing! But it definitely does take work." Garsa chuckles and remembers the first time he too learned how to fly. "This, as said before, will take some getting used to. You haven't even learned about your air sacks yet." Tarmax huffs out of breath confused. "Air sacks? What...are...air sacks, Garsa?" The black dragon leader laughs and turns to Tarmax pointing to his belly. "Well for starters don't bother talking. You haven't the breath to keep going, Tarmax. When the time comes, these things you will know. Just now for the sake of this situation, keep flying. You'll be fine."

Garsa looks out into the square and sees a black panther talking with Avalo, and almost falls from the sky. Catching himself, he returns to flight and breathes heavy. *For a moment there I could have sworn that was Calikon, yet this still doesn't answer who Avalo is talking with.* Raspier decides to fly up ahead and lands abruptly at their feet. Looking over the young hybrid, he gets the impression Avalo and he knows each other well. To add more distractions into the mix, Raspier walks up and interrupts the pair. "Hello there, sorry to interrupt Avalo, who is this black panther here you're talking to?" Avalo looks intensely straight through Raspier and shouts into his mind, "Go away." Raspier shivers and mutters words of discomfort to where his head feathers puff out.

Obviously, his presence is not required. *Telepathy*, Raspier thinks, *is something I can do without.* Raspier regains his confidence and addresses Avalo coldly. "Fine Avalo, I will pass the orders. I understand you and your *friend here,* are catching up, no need for a *verbal* explanation." Raspier frustrated and insulted, walks back to the others. They will head over to where the ladies are in their quarters. Sometimes he forgets Avalo prefers to speak via the mind. It's a bit too much for Raspier. As far as he is concerned, that practice is very intrusive.

Reaching the others, Raspier explains to Garsa who the panther is, and that Avalo and he need some time to speak. Garsa understands and is feeling better it's not Calikon, as odd as it might have been. "Tarmax, we will prepare a room for you, where you can stay in comfort. Feel free to be whatever you like here, only trusting hearts are inside these walls."

While Garsa shows Tarmax to his room, the rest head over to the ladies and question them about the strange panther taking up most of Avalo's time.

Partune and Raspier reach the room where the girls were resting. Celestra was purring half-awake, content in the cool waters. As usual, Raspier just blurts out his question caring very little in startling either of them, "Celestra you wouldn't have any idea who that cat is talking with Avalo? He seems to make him very uncomfortable. Me as well I might add."

Celestra picking up her sleepy head blinks a few times then stretches with paws extended. "Welcome back. Oh, that panther? He's no panther. That's my brother Lu'barthrow, Raspier. It's a long story that would be better told to you later."

Partune sensing the tension tries to sway the conversation. It's obvious these ladies wish to sleep, not be bullied by Raspier. "Well, glad to have us all together again, right? Amazing huh? Three hybrids are safe within the city right Raspier?" Raspier is obviously not pleased and answers Partune with a snarky attitude, "Humph, correct indeed." Partune looking back towards Celestra ignores Raspier and his crankiness. "Celestra, if you are up to it, maybe we could all sit and chat? I sure this day has been quite heavy on you. There are many new faces to greet and you've already been acquainted with more than enough."

Celestra now cleaning herself has one eye open looking up at Partune. "Sure, it is fine. I am getting used to this commotion slowly." Partune smiles at her. "You're catching up to speed fast little warrior, quite fast." They laugh off the awkward moment and decide to have a social drink to ease the tension. Partune, of course, had no objection to a toast of grulo. Lastra showed signs she would rather have stayed and slept.

Garsa had shown Tarmax his quarters and went off to find the others. He told Tarmax they would find him later after he relaxed and cleaned up.

Inspecting the room, Tarmax notices things aren't really set up well for a horse but would feel more comfortable as his true self. Changing back, he can't seem to lose his wings and decides it really doesn't matter if he keeps them out. Relaxing and soaking in the cool waters, time evades his mind, as he grows somewhat comfortable to his new surroundings. "I wonder what other hybrids I will meet, and if they even look like me. Wow, wouldn't Lord Cannor be mad if he knew I was here, let alone that I am a rare trinity hybrid!" He chuckles over this poor greedy man's misfortune and drifts off to sleep with head on the ground, body still in the water.

Chapter Nineteen

Cannor's Fury

Back by Cannor's castle plot, the men have just finished their twenty-two-hour workload. The new shift was coming in. Due to Tarmax's recently obedient behavior, Lord Cannor stopped having him guarded. There is a good side in Cannor somewhere, despite his offensive temperament. Tarmax had grown on him very much. He turns around to retrieve him to return to his homestead, but only finds a chewed and frayed rope. It's because of situations like this that Lord Cannor is so bitter. Enraged his trusty steed is no longer trustworthy; he grabs another horse from one of the knights, growls out something for them to move and goes out in search of him. Trained in animal tracking, he follows Tarmax's hoof marks in the dirt. "I'll find you horse even if it's the last thing I do today!"

And off he gallops to find the runaway horse, leaving his evening chores undone. Yet this is why he has servants. So, he can leave at his leisure. Freedom is something he takes full advantage of and happily steals it from others.

Chapter Twenty

Three Way Deal

Where we last saw Lu'barthrow and Avalo discussing their past disputes left unsettled, a common ground had developed. "Avalo, so you mean to tell me Garsa didn't really explain my past to you figuring you would sense it? So why didn't you? Was it because you were just messing around with me?" Avalo a bit uncomfortable scratches on the back of his many horned head.

"Well Lu'barthrow, understand you were not considered just a low-level hybrid, you possess much greater capabilities besides transforming. You ran off before I could ever teach them to you." Lu'barthrow sits and ponders this for a moment, in turn making him rethink his question. "Well, then why couldn't you read my thoughts? You still haven't answered me on that."

Avalo a bit embarrassed tries to think of something to say. Lu'barthrow notices this, "Then did I block you from getting inside my head? Is this why you weren't able to understand my past?" Avalo bothered this young hybrid is getting a kick out of him snorts out some smoke. "Do I even need to answer those questions? Frankly, I remember you being able to read my mind very well. If I am correct, this is why you bolted out of the city so quickly. You do not know how to handle this gift, nor behave properly for someone who possesses it."

Lu'barthrow feeling quite embarrassed looks at Avalo in a new light; however, not fully trusting. Silence remains for just a moment, while the two of them drop their guard and stare intently into each other's minds. In almost an instant, Avalo realizes this creature has such grand potential at becoming a mystic. That would mean nothing more to him to pass on his teachings to a hybrid. He never imagined that to be a possibility. Still, his pride, arrogance and undereducated self-esteem issues will need careful attention. It will be a while before this soft-bellied hybrid will become a teacher of the magickal arts.

"Lu'barthrow, how would you like to become my apprentice? Does this sound good to you?" Stupefied this is the first response after the silence Lu'barthrow stutters, "Wh…What?" Avalo tilts his head and spins his claw to form an apple to eat. Crunching it he speaks with a full mouth. "You heard me correctly. Will you become my apprentice Lu'barthrow? Celestra's love and strength is for reproduction, purity, to continue the heritage, yet you bare the timing, couth, and quick-witted skills your grandfather possessed. How about it, old friend…Want to become a mystic?"

Lu'barthrow stunned at Avalo's words, continues to stare with no response. Thinking to himself about the devotion and admiration, he held for his mother, something comes to his mind. *Why was she so protective, and why did she feel so strongly to drive herself into isolation to raise me?* Losing himself in the moment, Avalo gives him some time to think it over while he eats his apple.

Lu'barthrow mulled over these thoughts as Avalo decided to take a short nap. Dragons love to sleep. Some time had passed and Lu'barthrow feels a voice in his head, *Are you, okay brother?* Turning around he sees Celestra grinning at him. "Hello brother; I sensed you from my room, are you okay?"

Lu'barthrow is twisting inside already from Avalo's questions. Now with these new acquaintances and the presence of his estranged sister, who now apparently can read his mind when others cannot leaves him to do only one thing; scream. Echoing throughout the entire city, creatures stop to hear the low growling cry. Avalo jumps up startled and stares panicked at Lu'barthrow. Collapsing to the ground Lu'barthrow pants in relief to vent the frustration. For so long he's kept his poise and never released the torment burning inside. It felt good to *just,* let it go.

Confused, Avalo and Celestra look towards Lu'barthrow wondering if he is all right. Nervous to say anything, or even touch him, they quietly wait for him to make the first move. After a few seconds, he speaks. "Sorry about that, you know it's really hard to hold so much inside without doing a damn thing about it. So, let me get this straight. Avalo, you want me as your apprentice because I possess powers far greater than I can see, and no one can read my mind except my sister. Okay, I guess this will do, we share direct genetics and obviously she would be able to do such a thing...I suppose. Avalo I agree under one condition. That you help me find my mother; I know she is still alive."

Celestra perks her ears forward to see if she heard Lu'barthrow correctly but says nothing. Avalo thinks about the offer that Lu'barthrow made and agrees to help but with his own conditions, "Well upon agreeing to that, here is my half of the bargain. You must help me search out other hybrids to ensure your race will not die." They both agree and shake on it.

Lu'barthrow turns to his sister, "Celestra can you do me a favor? Try not to do that all the time. It really freaks me out, okay? That's the first time I heard someone else speak through my mind." Celestra amused, wags her tail erratically. "Okay Lu'barthrow, you have my word."

She asks him, "Throughout this entire endeavor of meeting you all, finding this city, trusting complete strangers, and now only learning my heritage after thirty years of wondering what the heck I am, don't you think I at least deserve my own request fulfilled as well?" With neither of them planning on Celestra pulling the same stunt, they give up and listen to her standing offer. "I myself continue looking for my master Uniqua. I think he was either drawn away by something unnatural, or someone kidnapped him. It never seemed quite logical for him to vanish like that. It's not in his nature to leave without an explanation, nor without a trace to find him. His scent just plain disappeared as if he was taken into the air."

Lu'barthrow looks to Celestra and starts to think about something. "Sister, would you agree that it was at least four years to this day Uniqua disappeared?" Celestra answers Lu'barthrow without looking up. "Yes, what are you trying to get to? Do you think that mother's disappearance is linked somehow?"

Lu'barthrow looks distracted and tells them he needs to go find someone. They decided not to object. Lu'barthrow thanked them and he ran off quickly into the cool night. Celestra shakes her head and watches Lu'barthrow wander off yet again. "He has some serious hang-ups. Hopefully, we won't have to hear them screamed out like that again." Avalo smiles at Celestra laughing softly, "I guess we'll see Celestra, I guess we'll see."

Chapter Twenty One

Lu'barthrow's Dark Secret

When Lu'barthrow was hiding out with his mother, there was a cart seller on the other side of the city that used to give him food and medicine. This was before he met Garsa and Avalo. His name was Meoneal, an old Saber lion. His breed like Lu'barthrow also was in fear of becoming extinct.

His physical alterations were certainly fascinating. One fang was wooden, apparently carved for him due to the weakness of his original tooth. He had the local carpenter thread the end of the implant to fit correctly. Meoneal must have broken it off while being careless or drunk. It made him feel more alpha, to explain it was lost in a vicious battle.

Meoneal also wore an eye patch, just for the mysterious allure it portrayed. He had two metal tags in his ear left over from when the greggils used him as a slave; he said he kept them in for their style. The real story of what happened to Meoneal while enslaved is still a mystery. Surely, there are many reasons why he keeps it secret. He always has a reason for everything.

Due to his quadrupedal ways, certain things were not as easy for him to accomplish as a medicine man. For a while now, he's had an assistant to take care of the things that needed opposable thumbs. Yewdrone was a purple teen whelp, which patiently waited the day he could become as good as his master. Meoneal took him in when his sight and dexterity started slipping.

Lu'barthrow walking through the market street sees familiar faces and normal routines still preserved. All continue as if time has never passed. Looking around to find his old friend, Lu'barthrow sees some new faces behind the carts. Trinkets, food, mystical supplies, advice; you name it - they sell it.

This is the one area of the city that had the feeling of greggils to it. This was the influence left by the Draconian war. Many different types of creatures and animals congregate here from all over Apropon Rar to barter their services and offer goods.

Turning a corner, he sees the rickety cart with Meoneal snapping at Yewdrone. The young whelp turns quickly to his master's face and apologizes for his clumsy nature. Meoneal examining the mess on the ground growls in displeasure over the raw ingredients he has dropped.

Turning sharply behind his cart, he picks up a bag of dandelion, lobelia, pau d'arco, and yarrow. Holding it carefully in his mouth, he returns to the mortar. Putting the bag inside, he empties the ingredients by grabbing the bottom of the sack. Smelling the strong odor of the herbs tickles his nose. With bag in mouth, he sneezes backward only to fall to the ground. Shaking the dust off Lu'barthrow sees his false tooth has broken off. Yewdrone walks over with a replacement and screws it on. Meoneal gruffs sternly "Thank you, Yew, at least you are good for something."

Chuckling to himself at this symbiotic relationship, Lu'barthrow remembers a time he himself felt like Yewdrone, nervous and pent-up. A small piece of him wishes that whelp would rise up over Meoneal instead of shudder in his presence. Calmly walking over to Meoneal, Lu'barthrow pretends to be a customer knowing his sight is bad. Tapping him on the shoulder, he asks for a ten stone bag of ground up nightshade. Knowing he would question what it was for, Lu'barthrow waited for him to show concern. The amount alone will draw up a second look. Meoneal looks up at him and tilts his head slightly to the side. A low toned growl grumbled out from his throat. "Why would a commoner need so much nightshade if not trying to take the life of another? You must have one strong enemy, my friend."

Meoneal strains to see who is bold enough to ask for such a ridiculous amount of the death herb. Lu'barthrow laughs, "Oh, I don't know; maybe to get inside an old accomplice's head?" Meoneal lifts his eye patch and his stubby tail wags behind him. "Black Paw...how hell are you! It's been so long since I've seen your face. I can barely see now a 'days anyway." Lu'barthrow smiles, as his stress melts away talking with the old cart seller. "Good Meone, Good. So why are you so hard on that little dragon? Cut him some slack huh?"

Meoneal grunting in obvious disagreement looks at Yew trying to grind the herbs with the mortar and pestle. Being much larger now, things are easier for him to do, yet he still has his youthful clumsiness. "He must be at least twice his size by now. What are you feeding that dragon Meone?" Lu'barthrow laughs to lighten the mood further. Meoneal scratches his chin and some fur falls to the ground. "Eich, you know dragons; their body grows before their mind. Wish there was a potion for that problem."

Glaring at his young friend, Meoneal begins to wonder about the real reason for Lu'barthrow's visit. Flipping up his eye patch, he looks at him closely. "Why have you come here; to remind me that I'm old, Black Paw? Any good reason, or are you really here for nightshade?"

Lu'barthrow leans in and whispers to Meoneal so Yewdrone couldn't hear. "Well Meone, I am here for *something* but not anything to get your tooth twisted up over, I am presently seeking assistance with some lost...companions." Meoneal stares into Lu'barthrow's eyes, confused at his choice of words. "*Companions*, since when did you become a team player BP?" Uncomfortable with Meoneal questioning his motives, he stands a bit straighter, "Ah, well it's a long story; just know it involves family quite frankly and nothing more. I am in search of my mother and bartered to get this help by way of the court mystic.

He agreed to do it for me if I... if I find him an apprentice. Not a bad bargain if I say so myself."

Meoneal yet again perplexed at his old friend's situation wonders what really is going on. He is smart enough to figure out that there is more to the story than Lu'barthrow wishes to convey. "Well I never thought you to dance around the dragon royalty before; their interest in you makes me question your blood. You *are* a mere panther after all. Why would Avalo Ryu, the mystic, want *you* to find *him* an apprentice?" Lu'barthrow realizes he said more than he should have. Knowing Meone is usually swayed by compliments, he pours it on thick, "Meone, why wouldn't he want me to find him an apprentice; I was trained by *you* after all?" Smiling at the gesture, he uses his head to push Lu'barthrow to the side of the cart further away from Yewdrone. Yewdrone pays attention despite the crude attempt at privacy.

"If you are truly searching for lost companions the white dragon that leads the corns up north is the best option." He tells Lu'barthrow a bit about her in a faint whisper and the best paths to get there. "You can save the trouble of being sent back by finding a *hybrid* to come along." He states with thick sarcasm. "Good Luck though, as far as we all here in the street have heard, they're completely extinct. She for many years refuses anyone without a living hybrid to enter the city. Otherwise, you would have to know someone with a meeting stone." Looking around Meoneal makes sure no one is listening. "I can at least get you there. You'll have to find your own way in. Come back to me in about an hour, I will have Yew draw you a map if he can ready this potion for the Drexel gang. They're very impatient, and I have one more chance to keep them as repeat customers."

Before he can turn to leave, Meoneal looks at Lu'barthrow. Scratching his chin, he speaks, "Remember Black Paw, this means you owe me ya' know?" Lu'barthrow knows he may be old, but Meoneal never forgets a barter left undone. He thanks Meoneal and heads back to Avalo and Celestra. Meoneal watches him as he leaves. Turning back to Yewdrone, he growls to rush the young dragon into making his potion faster. "If you weren't listening that would have been *finished* by now!" Yewdrone flinches as Meoneal swats his head with his paw.

Lu'barthrow hopes this so-called unicorn dragon will help locate his mother. He smiles that he knows such helpful creatures in such lowly places. Hopefully, this will not create a larger mess in the end. Seeing she only takes in visitors with hybrids is a great convenience. There are three now. Then thinking back to Meoneal, Lu'barthrow is wondering what payment he'll have to give back for this. Meoneal may be an asset, but he's also incredibly deviant. No creature is free of his meddling ways.

He was still curious who this white dragon was. Thinking back to when he was learning with Avalo, a name comes up in his mind. *Ah; it's Sorrokine Arou. That may prove to be a problem actually. If I remember correctly when I asked about her Avalo seemed very upset. Maybe there is a past between the two of them.* Trying to remember anything he overheard back living in the city, nothing comes to mind. All he remembers is that Avalo shudders at the sound of her name. He wonders though what kind of power this white dragon could have. Will it end up helping them find their lost companions? "Mother, I will find you. I know you're still alive."

Chapter Twenty Two

The Trinity Form

Tarmax awakes, still in the water, only to startle himself with his reflection. "Oh, I keep forgetting I have wings! Wish I knew how to pull them back in." He wonders where the others had run off to, and pokes his head out of the room window. A yellow guard is sitting outside the quarters standing post, barely awake. Tarmax humbly nudges the sleeping guard and asks where Drako and the others might have gone to. Obviously, confused by Tarmax's mismatched transformation, the guard shakes his head in confusion, then tells their location. Feeling confident, Tarmax thanks the guard, and heads off with the directions. The yellow dragon watched him walk off content, as a whelp happy in a barrel of gold. "Panthers and horses with wings. Weird times we live in… Great Mother."

Passing many different creatures in this new city, all tickles his curiosity. Staying on course, Tarmax sees the entrance to the main hall. Skidding inside, he stops to see them all talking. Politely Tarmax interrupts. "Hello everyone; woke up from my little nap and just curious what's happening now. Also, you *are* the only creatures I know around here; where else would I go?" Drako smiles and takes Tarmax aside. "We will all be gathering together to figure out what remaining issues exist. Please, Tarmax follow me. There is something I wish to give you." Tarmax obliges and follows Drako into the other wing of the hall. Peering around at the lavish decorations hanging off the walls and the beautiful furniture leaves him to feel a bit in awe. "Never knew what it looked like inside the home of royalty Drako, I only lived *next* to it. It's really magnificent I must say."

Drako laughs at Tarmax and leads him into a room with many old books. Pulling one from the huge shelf, he blows the dust off to read the cover. The title reads, 'Hybrids - The Animal Dakinis'. Giving the book to Tarmax, Drako asks him to change into his dragon form so he's able to read the book. Horses, as we all know, do not have thumbs. "I may need a few moments Drako, still not used to this transformation process yet."

"I noticed that by the presence of your wings. It's alright Tarmax. No need to rush either way." Concentrating the only way, he knows how, Tarmax turns into his dragon form after a few moments. *Still not quite exact yet, but it's good enough to read a book.*

When Tarmax was a young foal, his mother taught him to read common Draconian tongue to ensure his safety no matter where he went. So, this would be no challenge for him. Yet he cannot see very well in this form. His eyes haven't adjusted to the different type of vision, so the words are a bit blurry. Drako looks back over to Tarmax fighting with the book. "This is the historical explanation on hybrids as per dragons. This will show you what you are and what you can do in a language you can understand. I'll leave you for a bit to examine the history and special traits your species possesses." Tarmax thanks him, and tries again to read the book. Before Drako left, however, he handed him a pair of spectacles. "It's very hard to adapt to dragon's vision so quickly." Tarmax places them on right away, and starts reading the book. Drako heart lightens, seeing he has such an eagerness to learn. *That hybrid is heading for greatness...*

As Tarmax reads, he begins to understand why both humans and dragons make such a fuss over hybrids. "Humans created us! By hoof and tail, this is incredible. Humans bread us for their own use. I wonder what this word "lab" means. Also, this word "scientist". I imagine it is some sort of magickal reference. So, we *do* have something to do with that war, I used to hear about in the barn." Reading more into the book, the inner identity he was so scared of, slowly becomes more of his own. He's realizing that Tarmax the barn horse has a real purpose as Tarmax the hybrid. Now those weird moments he had as a young creature make more sense with each passing moment.

Tarmax squinting looks up at the door for a second, "These creatures are really here to help me after all." Slowly, the glasses slide down his muzzle. He places them back with his hand softly. Slowly as he reads on, his star on his head begins to glow without his knowledge. Reading more of the book, he finds a passage about the transformation of hybrids; 'Trinity hybrids were the last stage in the lab's development of the species. Many years of failed attempts brought this tri-animal species to life. These animals can change at will into a different creature due to a mutated gene. By splicing DNA of all three creatures together, a strange side effect happened to the subject's brain. In the frontal cortex, a new fold was created. This controlled the very matter of the animal's body. The scientists noticed when the animal was placed in danger, its forehead would grow incredibly warm. A crude star would begin to form. Many scientists realized these creatures could be quite harmful to the human race, so many were destroyed shortly after escaping their cages.'

As Tarmax reads the new passage intently, electromagnetic currents shiver from his head and spark in the air above him. Not noticing this, he keeps reading. Tarmax starts to lose consciousness. He drops, but the power of his present transformation suspends him in mid-air. The book falls out off his claws. Shards of light shot from his forehead as his mutation took hold of his psyche. Seeing this happen in person was rarer than finding one alive in these times, yet no one was there to witness it. Just Tarmax, the old books, and some dust mites. The air in the room was so charged that dust was floating around him as if held by strings. His mind shut down out of protection. If he was awake for this, he'd surely go insane.

Instead, his instincts kicked into high gear and forced the transformation upon him. Dropping to the floor Tarmax rose dreary and dizzy. Crawling over to a pool in the corner of the room, he looks down at himself. Gigantic black wings were folded neatly on his back. The inside of his wings were blood red. His neck was long, yet had a mane down the entire spine in white. His scales grew larger, blacker and thicker. A sharp curly white horn, spiralled out from his star. His front body was a firm dragon build, but also had the muscles of a well-trained horse. His tail, carried the same white mane down to the tip, with hair feathering out into a whip. Wide spikes trailed in size, order down from the back of his head, to the tip of his spine. His back feet were definitely composed of Dragon. Toes containing sharp claws, dressed with white hair and dewclaws, darted out at each heel joint, facing back towards his rear. He was certainly impressive, and quite large. Tarmax had to bend his neck down, to even fit into the room.

What just happened? Tarmax frightened, thinks to himself. *I guess reading this history book, must have triggered something inside of me. Just like when I changed at the pond and the wall. This is all happening much too quickly for me. I was just an ordinary horse yesterday. Still, I do look impressive! I must find Drako...*

Fumbling for the knob of the library door, Tarmax noticed he was still wearing the reading glasses, but they no longer fit, and were badly bent. Looking around the dim lit room, he went back to the pool of water.

Tarmax can see quite clearly now without the glasses, and he could fixate and sharpen his span of view by choice. His teeth were very large and some protruded out from his jaw. His black horse ears were shorter and more streamlined. His ability to register sounds and tone, had greatly increased. *This has to be that trinity gene I was reading about. I still wonder why I am transforming so quickly; it seems too easy for me...*

Tarmax curious what to do with himself, decides to slip out the door quietly to find Drako. Looking around, he spots him talking to Garsa. Tarmax now understands why the greggils wanted to destroy the hybrids, and has a new urgency to equally protect his kind. Seeing how immense he had become in this form, made him think there may be a reason he was chosen to carry this gene. Maybe this innocence was just the right conditioning, to fuel the preservation of his species. He may have a destiny just like Yaster after all. *Yet will I ever find a mate to continue our race... This trinity gene? I do not see any other hybrids around us, then those we know. I wonder if any are alive, maybe hiding... Or are we all alone, us three?*

Finally getting out of the library door, he walks down the corridor seeing the other up ahead. Deciding not to be conspicuous, he calmly walks up to Drako. Now towering over him, he asks Drako what they were discussing. All of them gasp, falling onto their tails at the sight of Tarmax.

Drako just laughs. Captured in the moment, signs of endearment showed through his scaly face, and beamed into Tarmax. "Well, hello there... It seems I must have chosen the right reading material for you. Oh, and by the way... Where are those reading glasses, eh? If you still need them..." Tarmax chuckles and smoke curls out from his nostrils.

"I don't think I'll need them anymore Drako." The attentive dragon nods his head, as the others slowly get back up from the floor, still amazed, at what's in front of them.

Tarmax looks to Drako, "So I imagine you had an idea about this? Did you know that I would change just by reading about our creation?" Drako rubs his claws on his chest as if he was shining them. "Well, it was a long shot, but learning the truth, can unlock much more than knowledge. It can unlock the inner spirit as a whole. You were already a natural in transformation; it happens easily for you."

Garsa smiles at Drako. He is proud of this future leader of the Drondia. Avalo could learn a thing or two from Drako.

Chapter Twenty Three

The Three Hybrids Unite

Celestra was wondering why it's taking so long for Lu'barthrow to return, and she was beginning to get worried. Avalo tries to keep her busy by talking about future lessons. This still doesn't help her from keeping her mind off of her brother. Avalo is also concerned with his absence, yet knows how he is. Lu'barthrow will do everything at his own pace. There is no controlling that hybrid. "First Celestra, you must understand you are very different from any creature ever produced. Slowly over time, nature adopted your kind as her own. Understand that until that time, your species were thought of as a curse. You possess certain powers other creatures cannot even comprehend. For instance, animals all alike carry the telepathy gene and instinctually use it to communicate, just as well as the deciphering of pheromones. Yet understand that your abilities go way beyond these simple acts.

For instance, telekinetic capabilities, transformations, and reiki are traits basic only to your race. Other creatures must study their whole life to obtain just a small piece of your natural gifts. Some, may never develop them at all.

Your saliva can heal any wound and your claws have a poison that can kill. This engineered gland was created during the production of the hybrid genetics. There are two small sacks behind your eye sockets and nasal canals. They hold the fluid that can heal wounds quickly. The ones behind your claws release poison. Only some carnivorous trinity hybrids developed this. It permeates through the cuticle of the nail bed. Because of the lengthy isolation your race endured, most of these traits must be unlocked, relearned, understood, and mastered."

Celestra starts to digest all this new information. She wonders if this was some of the important history, Lu'barthrow failed to listen to. This would explain so much about his personality.

Turning around, she sees her brother walking over gingerly with a wide toothy grin. "Hey guys, I have a proposition for you. What would you say if I was able to retrieve the white dragon's help in our quest?" Avalo stunned at this statement, tries to understand how Lu'barthrow would be able to obtain *her* attention. Any creature desiring her help, needs to go through ridiculous means to obtain it. "She's not very social with the Drondia community. Most of the time, Sorrokine turns away outsiders who dare enter her realm without a hybrid. The white dragon and her "corns" are incredibly reclusive. When was the last time you saw a unicorn fly above? How did you acquire such services if I may ask?"

Lu'barthrow chuckles deviously that he never told Avalo about his previous teacher, Meoneal. All those mixtures, potions, and medicines that Meoneal taught him were very different from Avalo's boring and tedious lessons. "I have a few friends in high places, but much more who swim the bottom of the barrel. Because of this, they always have shady connections and owe debts. Information and assistance of this caliber is always easy to obtain, that is, if you know where to look for it."

There are not many who've even seen Sorrokine with their own eyes, let alone know where her city is. Avalo curious, is moved to go along with this. He may be able to find out if she is alive and well. So, he starts to ask what necessities will be needed for such an endeavor. Not very comfortable with the idea, he cannot ignore the logic in her assistance.

"The legitimacy of Lu'barthrow's connection is sadly unknown, but it's time to finally go see Sorrokine Arou." The very name makes Avalo shutter in his scales. *It's been so long, and she would be a great asset in the regrouping of the lost hybrids as well. Maybe she herself has disappearances in her northern territory. I've heard stories from Arrow Forest about strange creatures in the darkness. This is right next to her domain.* It has been a long time though since Avalo has seen her; a long time of sadness. Some things may never be undone, never forgiven and never forgotten, as he has learned.

Celestra feeling that this is a wonderful idea starts to purr. Looking over at Avalo however, she second-guesses it. Her pleasant mood fades. He seems quite nervous at the very mention of this white dragon's name. Not looking to stress the matter further, she dismisses the thoughts altogether.

Wondering who had helped him with this information, Avalo decides to ask Lu'barthrow, "So, anyone that *I* would know? Who helped you with this information?" Sensing Avalo's doubt, he tries to walk him through it. "His name is Meoneal; he's a medicine maker of a common barter creed. He has a small cart over on the other side of the city. Meone and I have a history; he taught me basic medicines, and how to be a cat of the streets amongst creatures of bad blood. He even hired an orphan whelp a while ago. Due to Meoneal's age, he is not as able to accomplish his work alone. The whelp is named Yewdrone; nice little dragon, just a little bit nervous and klutzy."

Avalo pays close attention to each word he said, to make sure this bottom feeder, wasn't just using him. Avalo had warned him about that part of the city, many times before, but obviously, Lu'barthrow failed to follow his direction. Many of those cart sellers are quite the backstabbers. He remembers Lu'barthrow did not have the best judgment either.

It seems this may be a good trade-off. This Meoneal character used him for errands and chores, while he taught him the ways of the back-road lifestyle. He thought to himself. *I will have to investigate him later.*

Clearing his throat Avalo turns back to Lu'barthrow with a pleasant face, but held deep concern. "Well you speak of this creature with esteem, so I *have* to trust you for now… However, may I ask what kind of *animal* he is?" Lu'barthrow remembering in an overheard conversation that Avalo doesn't trust most sabers, he walked around the fact with satin-like smoothness. "He's a lion, Avalo."

Seeing this is partly the truth, he hopes Avalo takes the bait. Since he has no ability to read Lu'barthrow's mind, he is at his mercy. Avalo nods his head, and they go out in search of the others to explain these ideas. Lu'barthrow is learning the full extent of his mind's power. *It's nice when no one can read your thoughts. Besides, they should be private. I've earned this at least, over these long bitter years.*

There is no telling what lies ahead, for this wandering group of odd creatures. They're all going to see the fruits of their decisions ripen, whether the result is sour or sweet. As they travel to gather up the others, Lu'barthrow finally understands the severity of his involvement, with them all. There will be many dangers on such a quest. He questions if he will be strong enough to handle such a journey. The black panther thinks as he walks:

The route we need to take to her is on the other side of Apropon Rar, up north before the icy lands of the High King Dragon Deestro. The central territories are ruled by greggils. Maybe if we're lucky, there will be very little contact. I'm not looking forward to seeing their ugly hairless bodies anytime soon. Gaining the courage to speak, he explains the rest of the details. "The map will be ready in a little bit of time. I will go back for it shortly." After this, he stays very quiet. In mind, and in soul.

Shivering at the thought of greggils, he tries to keep steady on the possibility of finding his mother. For himself, as well as his estranged sister. This has become Lu'barthrow's main quest. He knows now, he must always protect her, at all costs. This is his chance to settle the matter of his own self-worth. Walking into the hall, they see Drako, Raspier, Garsa, and Partune standing around an odd gigantic black dragon. Without causing a stir, they say hello to everyone, but can't help but stare at this immense beast.

Celestra and Lu'barthrow are boggled at this new creature. She stares deeply at his broad back, sparkling blue eyes, firm strong jaw, and stark white mane. She has awe written all over her face, and everyone, can see it.

He's so handsome... This doesn't sit well with her. Despite being a hybrid, she was raised a panther. Wouldn't she be attracted to someone who looked like her? Then, as she slowly retraces up to the top of his head, which makes her almost melt, she sees a horn. A long white, spiraling masterpiece, set on his forehead, inside a white star.

Lost in the moment, she realizes this is no dragon. Her actions are incredibly impolite, just staring like a simpleton. Snapping out of it, Celestra instead introduces everyone to her brother Lu'barthrow. They all greet him with wild curiosity, since they thought she was an only cub.

Garsa smiles at Lu'barthrow warmly and nudges him with the back of his claws. He, of course, remembers the hybrid well. "Hello, black panther. We never thought you would come back to us. Glad you decided to in the long run." Lu'barthrow nods to Garsa in appreciation; however, his attention goes back to this highly impressive black and white hybrid.

Being jealous of him in every way, without even knowing his story, is a bit thick-headed, but this is Lu'barthrow. He tries to shake it off by continuing as if the thought never happened. Pushing out his black fuzzy chest to make him look bigger, satisfies his under stroked male ego. He looks back to Garsa trying to make his actions look natural. "Hello Garsa. It's been a while. I had a change of heart, I guess you would say." Chuckling, Celestra asks Drako to introduce this new hybrid to the rest of them. He turns to her and nods at her request.

"Everyone, this is Tarmax."

He looks at all the new faces, but stops, once he sees Celestra. He cannot help but get lost in her eyes. He smirks and snorts into a wide toothy smile. She blushes and turns her head to the side noticing his reaction. Smitten would be the chosen word to describe these two. Tarmax waves his large hand at them all. "Hello there, nice to meet all of you."

Celestra practically squirming out of her fur, interrupts him with a snort. "Ah, well, yes...What was it that we were to do now Garsa?" Garsa affectionately smiles at her, then points to Raspier to tell the good news. "Well it's nice to see you all safe. I've decided to hold a banquet tonight in the ballroom and I hope you all will attend. We will need to discuss a few things before then. Everyone must help to set this up."

Flamboyantly explaining the fancies involved with the banquet, Raspier gets lost within the element of royalty. If you know Raspier, then you know that one of his favorite things to do is organize. Describing up to even the smallest of details, he fails to recognize everyone is losing patience. Feeling quite uncomfortable, Raspier decides to finish. "Did you three have a question to ask one of us, before we all become *side-tracked*?"

Avalo worried about what they would say, holds his claws against his stomach in a tight grip. "Well, Lu'barthrow has agreed to an apprenticeship with me. We have made a bargain to help find their mother Celestaria, as well as Celestra's master Uniqua. We all agree there is a link between them all. The catch is that we've decided to involve Sorrokine Arou."

Avalo shivers at the sound of her name, but continues. "Hopefully, we can convince her to help us in this dilemma. Joining forces could resolve this quickly. So, we were wondering... Who would be up for a quest in the morning?" Everyone grunts at Avalo's statement. They all realize that much grulo would be drank and shared tonight.

If there was to be a journey in the morning, at least one had to obey sobriety.

"Well..." Garsa speaks, "I imagine this can happen, as long as we watch the greggils, as we travel. Our issue with them will not be solved overnight. We already possess a powerful group, and this is a good way to test its strength. If it turns out to be too difficult, we must return to regroup. A trip to the white dragon could end up with our skins warming some Princes' bed, or even worse. There are many issues I'm sure in the north that we can discuss. These disappearances I'm sure are not coincidental. Sorrokine must be aware of the greggils and the looming darkness making the world heavy. We will meet at daybreak. At the northern gate...

Now for this party Raspier was talking about. Let's get ready for a great night!" Raspier less interested now, rolls his eyes at Garsa.

"Whoever is helping me let's go...Now."

Drako overheard Garsa, but his attention mainly was on Lastra. *Would she be up for such a journey?* There will always be a soft spot in his heart for her. Wondering if Sarclaw her lost whelp could be included in the search, Drako eyes Lastra to see if she will speak up about it. He remembers all too well when Sarclaw disappeared. Drieston, Lastra's mate, never really seemed good at heart. Like the overpowered dragons of the greggils back during the Draconian war, he had an obvious darkness to him; that is, except to Lastra.

Lastra loved him dearly. Somehow when they were together, that darkness seemed to fade from him. Drako never recovered from his chance to dance for Lastra. Drieston somehow, slipped in between the two of them very slowly, and broke them apart. As Drako realized Lastra fell much harder for Drieston, he backed off.

Water dragons were quite rare these days. Lastra was special, and deserved the best. Her happiness was all he wished for. If Drieston made her happy, then there was nothing else he could accomplish. Drako hid his emotions from her, ever since.

Watching them together, he never felt Drieston treated her right. Quite frankly Lastra was very blind to Drieston's underlying intentions. Yet in her presence, he was sweet, kind and generous. Drako knew this act, was see-through though. It was all just a play to gain her affections, then to control her in the long run. Something Drako never wanted to see happen to Lastra.

One day, long after they had their first whelp Sarclaw, Lastra was walking back to their dwelling. Pushing open the door, she smiles and calls for Sarclaw. No answer. Calling again and still hearing nothing, Lastra wondered where she could have gone to. Running out back, she saw her toys were where they had been left from earlier. In fact, nothing was moved since Lastra took her trip out to the royal estate.

Hours had past and poor Lastra had not seen Sarclaw or Drieston come back to the dwelling. Crying herself to sleep, she was woken later by Drako softly touching her snout. Both of them tried for a very long time to find Sarclaw and Drieston but without success. Months passed and Garsa then proclaimed them lost. The search party dismantled. There was nothing more they could do. Sarclaw and Drieston just disappeared. Lastra has never been her loving self ever since that day. From that point on, Drako swore to secretly protect her. Still, as time passes, she becomes less of her joyous self and more of a hollow shell, almost as if the darkness has captured her soul too.

This displeases Drako terribly, because, Lastra was so full of life, before their absence. She was also more alive before them as well. *Personally, I still think Drieston had something to do with Sarclaw's disappearance, but I don't know how to tell her that. It's been so long since we talked about those terrible times.*

Turning to Lastra, Drako rubs her neck, and asks her if she wants to help with the banquet set up. Drako too, would rather not think about Sarclaw. Lastra confused by Drako's affectionate gesture, smiles and closes her eyes softly. "Well Drako, that would be nice, since we all know who will be directing the decorating, the more help the better." She giggles softly. Garsa nods his head in acceptance and gets everyone's attention by raising his hands. "We're going to go help with the setup. Let's get what is needed and meet up in the ballroom by the first moon turn. I'm sure Raspier will delegate the duties sufficiently, so I shall retire until then."

Celestra and Lastra volunteered to go into the city for some colorful ribbons, and fancy decorations before it gets too late. Lu'barthrow figured this would be a good way to get out of early preparations, so he willingly accompanied the two of them on their stroll. He wasn't really in the mood to hobnob with the royal family right now. Once a loner they say, usually always a loner. Besides, he'll stop off and get the map from Meoneal.

Lu'barthrow thinks about what he'd say if Meoneal saw him with Lastra and Celestra shopping. Figuring out what to tell the other two was much easier. He was praying on Meoneal's bad sight to let him move freely through the city seller's market.

The three set out and take to the city nightlife. Walking through the bustling streets, Celestra stares in wonder at all the carts and different sellers. Seeing one table with these feathered ties, she asks what their purpose was. The old female dragon smiled at her innocent curiosity. "This is a charm young one. When wrongful magic is intended in your direction, this will ward it off. It is only as strong as the creatures' personal energy level. In your case, I can feel that you wouldn't have anything to worry about. Many shamans wear such a band." Smiling at her kind and informative words, Celestra asks how much the charm would cost.

"For you, little kitty, it will only be five drogs." Turning to Lastra, Celestra asks if there were some extra coins to purchase this charm. Lastra smiles and knows the royal estate has more than enough currency to spare. "Yes, little warrior, I'm sure there's enough. We'll buy it." Handing the coins to the Madame, Lastra helps Celestra tie it onto her tail tip. The dragon behind the cart chuckles at the place she chose to put it. "Unique idea to put that upon your tail, I guess it should match the owner." Celestra blushes and thanks both Lastra and the cart seller. They continue on collecting items for the banquet and try to enjoy the freedom of having their guard down.

Outside these city walls, is a life of struggle they all do not miss, even Celestra, will agree. They should enjoy this evening of celebration, because who knows... In all of their travels when it will come again. Tomorrow, they will start the search party for Celestaria, Uniqua, the white dragon and anyone else missing over these years. These are no simple coincidences.

It seems everyone is ready to take problems head-on, except Lu'barthrow. That hybrid must calculate everything. Living in the moment is sadly just a collection of words to him, and with just cause. He's lived the hardest life out of anyone in this group. He trusts no one, and for good reason.

In the back of Lastra's mind, she starts to think that her whelp might be in the same situation as the others lost. Thinking harder about it, she lags back and lets Celestra find the decorations needed. It's always on Lastra's mind whether anyone can see her pain. Her heart will never rest until she at least knows what happened. Then, Lastra knows, for better or worse, she can move on.

As Lastra watches whelps play in the fading moonlight, that terrible ache inside her heart grows. Never really knowing whether Drieston was responsible for the disappearance of her whelp, she tries to just leave it behind her. It's beginning to consume her, all over again. She tries to gather up the panther hybrids quickly, but with couth:

"Come on now kitties. I think we have what we need for the party. Shall we head back now?" Lu'barthrow realizing they never passed Meon's cart, joyfully agrees. He was thankful he didn't need to lie, so he eagerly tries to carry the items, on his back. Lastra chuckling at his gesture takes all the favors, and puts them in her nap sack. Smiling, she pats him on the head in thanks.

Lu'barthrow caught Lastra's sadness for just a second. He wondered why her eyes were so distant. Did she have secrets just like he did that plagued her mind? In a way, it reminded him of his own sorrow hidden deep inside. Lu'barthrow left it for the winds to decide.

There is more to that dragon that meets the eye... She hides many pains.

Just like me, it seems.

Before Lu'barthrow forgot, he told them both he was going to retrieve the map to the white dragon. They said their goodbyes and went their own way. Picking Celestra up, Lastra flies back to the ballroom, to find the others. For now, she is amongst brethren. Good times are standing high. She will celebrate instead of drowning in her misery.

Lu'barthrow sneaks up to the Medicine cart where Meoneal was yet again yelling at Yewdrone. The Drexel gang was bothering him about how messy their job was. They were displeased at how many days it took to be prepared. Yewdrone was hiding under a cloth in the back of the cart. His purple tail was hanging out shivering. Meoneal was worried as these dragons were not known for kindness. The Drexel Gang were strong players in the Draconian wars, yet never fully acclimated back to calm city life. They lived on the very outskirts of town. The dragon elders, always had their eye on them.

Lu'barthrow worried for his old friend, walks over like a well-trained player of the back roads. "Drexel…Drexel…Where have I heard that name before?" Lu'barthrow arrogantly blurts out. Meoneal looks up and lifts his eye patch. "Black Paw. Ah, yes... How nice, to see you. The Gang and I were just discussing some... politics of the sale." The leader of the gang walks up to Lu'barthrow towering above him. "Who the hell are you ink spot?" Lu'barthrow not frightened at all looks straight back up to him. "Well, I guess you haven't heard? I'm the new liaison for the courts. I was hired by Garsa Yean himself. I make sure transactions are completed peacefully and any issues *I* solve." The leader of the Drexel gang backs up and laughs. "Sure kid. I'm sure. Meoneal, next time, have this right or *we'll* make it ourselves." Meoneal relaxes for a second and winks at Lu'barthrow. "Sure, that's no issue. My assistant will go to bed without dinner for this I assure you." With that, the Drexel gang walks off with their medicinal herbs. "I rarely say this but thank you Black Paw. You've managed to close a very dangerous deal. I did train you well old friend."

Turning to Yewdrone he grabs a metal cup with his mouth and throws it at his face. Yewdrone almost blocked it at the last second but it caught his cheek. "And you! You worthless dragon, I was telling the truth. No Dinner for you! Speed up or starve. That's the deal." Yewdrone sinks low but complies with Meoneal. He had nowhere else to go, so he knew to listen to him. Meoneal gives Lu'barthrow the map and also a few drogs. He was happy for the help. The Drexel gang are no group to mess with. "You take heed outside the city, Black Paw... There are dark things about... Even darker than me."

Lu'barthrow smiles seeing for once this old cat has some heart after all. "Thank you, Meone. I won't forget this. Once I'm back we'll go out and dine on some ladies and grulo together. How about it?" Meoneal smiled an old saber grin, and wagged his stubby tail. "Sounds like a plan pal. Take care." And with that Lu'barthrow heads back to the Royal Estates to deal with this stuffy party.

When Lastra and Celestra arrive, they already see Raspier throwing orders around. Where tables and chairs belong, what color cloth to use on them, and what style of music will be played throughout the night. "Each of you has their own personal job, and we'll have this done in no time if you trust my orders." Occasionally flaring his wings and front feet, he shows where Lastra and Celestra are to put the favors.

Celestra runs and starts to fill vases with water. Ever so carefully she puts tiger lilies in neatly arranged circles. Tarmax still in his trinity form, was told to place the streamers and ribbons around the room. Not fully used to his body structure, he falls down to knock the jug of water from Celestra's paws. Falling to the ground, it soaks her to the bone. "Hey! Watch it you klutz, I'm drenched now." Tarmax sincerely embarrassed, and sorry he knocked it over, goes directly to the stream to refill it. Coming back in, he sees Celestra cleaning her soaked fur. She looks up at Tarmax with the fresh jug of water and smiles. "You didn't have to do that; it's okay. I would have refilled it." Celestra goes to take the jug from Tarmax's hands and thanks him, but upon looking into his eyes, ends up dropping it.

This time it shattered into pieces. Not caring at all about the wet mess, the two are locked in this gaze that the gods themselves couldn't separate. Raspier snaps at the both of them, "What are you doing? Having a staring contest!? Clean that up and get another jug right now!" Both of them shake out of it and start to laugh at each other. Retrieving another jug from the closet, Tarmax fills it again. "I'll try not to look at you, so you can continue your job Celestra." Blushing, she walks over to the next table, trying to gain some composure.

Rushing back to the party, Lu'barthrow walks in to see everyone dashing around quickly to set up the banquet hall. He grumbles. Raspier walks over to him, bothered he was late. "The last chore not started is sweeping the floor. Get to it!" Angered he's already being ordered around, Lu'barthrow huffs under his breath. "That griffin is so bossy and ritzy. Who does he think he is, ordering us around like this? I have paws after all... This isn't very comfortable, without thumbs. Once I'm not needed, I certainly will slip off, quietly."

Lu'barthrow gets cold paws about staying too long. He is not interested in doing chores for the royal southern family. Finishing up, he takes the last bit of dust and sweeps it under the main table, pushing it far under the tablecloth. Raspier is quietly watching him, letting him think he's getting away with it. "Done, there, now I can go." Just as Lu'barthrow was about to leave he turns and walks right into Raspier. Lu'barthrow falls down, while Raspier stood strong and still. Sadly, despite his already nasty mood, he gets more than a beakful of complaints from Raspier. "What kind of sweeping involves *hiding* the dirt? Do that properly or I'll remove you from the banquet list."

Lu'barthrow realizing he can get out of everything by just walking away, he throws the broom down, and crosses his paws. Feathers flying from Raspier's head, he tells Lu'barthrow just what he thinks of his self-centered attitude: "You spoiled little half-breed! Get out! I will not have any freeloading runts ruining our night of celebration!" With that, he picks Lu'barthrow up by his nape, and flings him out the door. Lu'barthrow laughing to himself, realizes that this may come as more of a gift, than a punishment.

Celestra runs to the door and sees Lu'barthrow outside cleaning his fur. Wondering why he was acting so skiddish, she stares back, at the presently frazzled Raspier. "*I guess some habits die hard. Maybe he really didn't want to attend this ball anyway.*" Avalo caught sight of the little argument that Raspier and Lu'barthrow had, and realized almost the same thing Celestra did. *He set that up, that sneaky devil. What are you up to little hybrid? Your pride will be your downfall.*

Lastra is preparing the food with the chefs in the kitchen and tells them exactly the way Raspier had ordered it to be. With all going smoothly, she can now organize the place settings and puts them on the right tables.

Drako finds this group of creatures entertaining. They're all working really well together, except Lu'barthrow. It seems that social graces were not important to him what so ever. *Celestra will be let down, but understanding I'm sure. It's very obvious she has gone through incidents that could have left her the same way. If I remember correctly, she seemed much worse at first when compared to Lu'barthrow's attitude, just not as shady.*

Walking over to Raspier, he tries to explain Lu'barthrow situation. "Raspi, he's never had a group that cared for him. He was always alone. His mother was overbearing and his colleagues were cynical, negative, and smooth backstreet trash. This is a shame because he is a hybrid after all, let alone a descendant of the Garlock line. Try a little harder to see beyond the mask, please?" Raspier feeling bad, goes out to give his apologies, but Lu'barthrow is already gone. Frustrated so much time has been lost, on a straggly hybrid, he drops the issue and goes straight back to work. Some griffins, also, cannot be changed, Drako sees. Raspier and Lu'barthrow, have more in common, than they would like to let on.

Chapter Twenty Four

The Saber's Drool

Lu'barthrow runs to his partner Meone. Finding his cart, he sees Yewdrone mixing a cocktail of herbs together. Nervous, he asks him, "Where is Meone, Yew?" Yew picks up his head, and Lu'barthrow sees a welt under his eye. Knowing all too well why it's there, he asks anyway to make him feel better. "What is that Yew, did you fall?" Embarrassed he has to answer an old student of Meoneal's he explains it different from the true reality. "Uh, I fell on the caldron before. Banged my face..." With a low brow, Lu'barthrow understands why the little whelp refuses to be truthful. "Okay Yew, well do you know where Meone went then?" Yew points to a street adjacent to where they are standing. Leading with his claw he traces a small path off course. At the end of his claw, there seems to be a ragged cloth, over a doorway. "He doesn't like to be disturbed when he visits Cerpiendra. I wouldn't recommend bothering him."

Not caring about his privacy for the moment, he turns to Yewdrone and thanks him. He decides to wait for Meone to exit the room, from a safe distance. Watching the doorway, and the dirty cloth at the entrance, something turns inside his stomach.

Hearing loud growls and laughter, Meone wanders out plastered on grulo, with this drunken lioness. She was so straggly, so underfed, and equally trashed. Both of them biting each other's napes and pawing at privates, they were quite a disturbing sight.

These animals always try to appear poor and helpless, not to earn a step up, but to steal from the ones who earned their way. He sees Meone stumble over to that poor excuse for a living creature, and licks her ear.

Slapping her rear with his paw, she scampers back into the shady room behind the dirty cloth. Seeing Lu'barthrow, he tries to straighten up his facade, and returns to the character, he knows him better as. Not realizing Lu'barthrow watched that whole scene in disgust, he walks up to him greeting in his usual manner. "Hey black paw, what's cooking in the royal palace? Anything worthy of an old friend's humor? Why have you been extra shady lately. Mind you, this makes me think, you've finally learned our ways..."

Not showing his true opinion of his old master, he equally puts up a front and jokes about their prissiness. Meone did not know about his sister, yet Lu'barthrow explains the daily activities forgetting to omit her. "Hey, I never knew you had a sister. Imagine the genetic beauties that would come out of that coupling. Ever consider mating with that bag of meat? I could if you didn't mind. Our offspring could run this town." It's obvious he's still drunk off of the sex as well as the grulo. Lu'barthrow tries not to cringe at his statement, but it's hard.

Meone stops and thinks for a second. "Did you say she was white? How could a common panther be white? You mean tan... Right, Lu'barthrow?"

Knowing to stand his ground, he does not sway with his present mindset, so that he can trick Meone into thinking something different. "No way Meone, she just came out an albino, that's all. Why should I know anything about my sister anyway, I don't even know her, nor that she existed before a few days ago."

Meoneal, despite being drunk, isn't stupid. Much to Lu'barthrow's disliking. "Then, why did you not tell me this before, when I spoke to you last?" Lu'barthrow quickly thinking, spits out a quick retort. "It wasn't on my mind Meone... and does it really matter anyway? Come on now, I care little for these royal fluttery birds you know that." Meoneal growls low under his jowls and starts to back up from Lu'barthrow. "I'm keepin' my eyes on you kid, watch your step. I think you may be up to something, and this is my only warning."

With that said, he turns to Yew, who was pretending not to listen. A fast paw is raised mocking his fear of being hit, and he scampers behind the caldron shuttering. "That's right, you know who owns you... You miserable whelp..." With Meon's head low, claws extended, he refuses to look Lu'barthrow in his eyes. He speaks one last time, to his old pupil. "Here is your last chance to be honest. Not like I ever taught you to be, but Lu'barthrow, if you have nothing more to say to me, then I am finished with you." He swallows a hard lump of fear in his throat. "Goodbye Meoneal...thanks yet again for that map." Meoneal turning around walks low to the ground away from Lu'barthrow. "You need not thank me anymore..."

Slightly frightened Meoneal is now watching him, and kicked out of the ball, Lu'barthrow yet again is all alone. Thankful Meoneal didn't ask more about his sister and his real bloodline, he can at least relax for now. In time, he knows how ruthless that saber is; it won't be a secret for long. The streets will certainly hear of his *albino sister* shortly.

Celestra begins to worry about her brother and a little deeper than what would be expected, but this is Celestra we're talking about. Seeing that the festivities have almost started, she sneaks out to go look for him. Smelling the air, she finds his scent and follows it down to the street vendor part of town. The sweet sensations she felt earlier, seemed to fade into silence. Her instincts kick in, and the warrior unravelled itself from the soft inner nature that was so recently freed. Uniqua's teachings began to repeat in her head. "Never let your guard down in a strange and unknown place, something will remind you why trust is a forgotten kindness."

Realizing she has been letting her emotions get the better of her, Celestra clears her mind. Her survival instincts kick into the wild mode and the huntress was now in full control. Sitting down for a moment to collect her bearings, Celestra smells

Lu'barthrow's scent again, but much fresher. Ears perked, she realizes, she is going to have to pull her wings back into her body, or someone will point her out. A hybrid of her caliber, will draw negative attention. She decides to duck back into an alley. Concentrating on her warm forehead, she imagines her white wings retracting, leaving her a white panther. Instantly by just connecting the thoughts and energy together, her body changed as she wished.

"Wow. That wasn't so hard after all. Avalo was right."

Excited internally, but not exuding it, she walks back out into the street to relocate the scent. Linking up with a cart on the far right, she sees a small whelp quietly separating sage leaves from a branch. The sad and isolated faraway look in his eyes, disturbed her. He seemed like he wanted to know more about life, instead of working that branch. A certain solemn thought escaped her head, and made Celestra start to walk toward the cart. *This is an orphan. A creature stuck in someone else's plans for life.* Tears well in her eyes, but she turns to shield them from view. Running over to a tree, with surrounding bushes, Celestra hides to see what kind of caretaker he has.

Intently cleaning the branches of their leaves, he avidly watches the bend, as if waiting for someone important. Out of the corner of her eye, she sees a saber toothed lion, darting in and out of the shadows. Celestra gets a strange feeling from him. *Could this be that whelp's master? He seems very suspicious. This does not look like supportive company. If I pretend to be a customer, and buy some of that sage from the whelp, I could study this old lion. Maybe even trick him into selling me the whelp for his freedom.*

Before walking up to his cart, she finds a part of the ground that is very dry and dusty. Knowing it would be hard to trust a white panther amongst so many normal looking animals, Celestra rolls around in the tan dirt, until she is covered from head to toe. Looking into a local fountain, she is startled at her appearance. *Geeze, I look like a lioness. This will definitely work.* Walking up very slow, she prepares some low brow humor. Looking over the old saber, she trails her tail high in the air, questioning his masculinity in the typical cat way. His tubby tail toggles back and forth, at the sight of such a creature. Meoneal's eyes follow her every move. Knowing the power of her feline femininity, Celestra slightly purrs, as she gazes over the products on the cart. While the old saber's attention is off of him, Yew, can relax for the moment.

Meoneal excited over such a sight of meat and fur, drools a bit, before talking. "Hello there gorgeous. Would you care to see this wonderful collection of dried lavender, to add to your already beautiful scent?" Blushing in reaction to his sweet words, she realizes he's just coming on to her to make a good sale. "I found your cart by the fresh smell of sage, but what I'm really looking for, is a servant. My bloodline is royalty, and the castle guards are looking for a dishwasher. How much do you want for that... measly whelp?"

Stunned this is her request, Meoneal eyes over Yewdrone. He's terribly frightened overhearing the conversation, yet continues to work diligently, ignoring eye contact. "My name is Garlochia, granddaughter of Drandore. I'm sure you know the bloodline, Saber." Meoneal stutters out a yes, but continues to drool, which is becoming quite a sad sight. Celestra grimaces at his fowl appearance, but smiles in turn. "Good, then you will sell him to me at the price of a pound of sage then. He isn't worth any more than that. Just look at him. He's barely good enough for plucking bugs out of my fur." Yewdrone feeling like a slave, sinks lower into his posture. The saber looks him over again. "Well your highness, I don't know. He's the only help I have. My skills aren't as sharp as they used to be." He says looking at the floor humbly.

Celestra laughs with her head held high, "You? Not sharp? A smart handsome saber? Pish posh, I think you're fooling. I see your brawny muscles and taught chin. Are you not of the dying race of sabers that is slowly becoming rare? The royal courts will always protect your kind. How about this: You provide this measly whelp for the price discussed and we will meet tonight for a royal meeting, one of the fancy kind. By the way, what is your name saber?" Still in shock that this beautiful lioness has taken so much interest in him, Meoneal attempts to talk. "Me? Me?! Um, my name is Meoneal. What was that about later on? If my ears didn't deceive me, I think I like this proposition."

Now too deep into this mess, she realizes this is the same lion Lu'barthrow was talking about. Celestra starts to internally panic, and almost drops her act. Keeping her smooth coolness, she compliments 'his wonderfully strong name'. "You heard me right. A sweet fancy meeting with some court grulo to make sweeter. So, do we have a deal big guy?"

Meoneal looking at Cerpiendra's door, then at Celestra, then at Yewdrone, smiles, with all his might. His fake tooth loosens up a bit from it. "You've got a deal there, Princess!" He violently grabs a chain and puts it around Yewdrone. He orders him to follow her. "Go whelp, where you are ordered. You are no longer a free dragon; not like you were really free before." Meoneal enjoyed the thought of more rapture tonight, His stubby tail wags, as he counts his money. "Until later, my streamline and tender kitty. I will be waiting."

Celestra shakes off the thought, of giving herself up, to this sleazebag, for any amount of time. Walking back to the main court, she figures out what to ask of Garsa to help this situation. Keeping up the facade of this Princess gig, she prods along holding the chain tight in her jaws. Yew, just walks saddened that another comfort is gone, no matter how bad it was. Celestra feels terrible she had to lie to him. Picking up the chain tighter in her mouth, she starts to run on instincts.

Something is watching me, I feel it...

Yewdrone, terrified closes his eyes and prays they're not in danger. Hearing loud paws prod to the ground behind them,

Celestra snaps a circle with the chain. Yewdrone slides under a cart out of harm's way. Terrified, he curls into a ball, shivering.

"You are a liar! Thief! You are stealing that whelp for rocks!" Thinking its Meoneal, she readies for a battle. Turning around, she swipes her paw with claws extended, at the opponents face in a heartbeat's time. Startled, the animal skids back to miss the attack. The dust settles around them both. Celestra is asked her name.

"Give me your name, you yellow bellied royal tramp!" Celestra terrified doesn't answer. "Well, *who* are you?" Lu'barthrow still can't see, so he just states his name. "I am Lu'barthrow, so who are you, *really* now...Princess?" Stunned that she's facing off with her own brother, Celestra waits for a moment to see him through the dust cloud.

Even when the air cleared, Lu'barthrow still didn't recognize her. "Why did you take that old saber's only help? How cruel could you be little miss lioness?"

Realizing she can obtain needed information; she carefully continues with her alter ego. Celestra sees a more precise, mental block will be needed, to tame this beast. She tries to first figure out why Lu'barthrow, wouldn't free the miserable whelp himself in the first place. Adjusting her tactics, she readies for battle.

"I am Garlochia, and why are you calling me a liar peasant panther. Do you know lion royalty when you see it? Meoneal knows my kind, why wouldn't you?" Celestra is frustrated this has developed into a twisted scenario. At least she found Lu'barthrow, and freed a dragon whelp, so all wasn't lost. Not a bad day's work.

"Well *Garlochia*, what's the real reason you took this whelp? What would you need him for anyway?"

Celestra thinks fast. "We at the court have been looking for this whelp and its disclosed information. I was sent knowing I would retrieve him unharmed." Lu'barthrow finally convinced of her role, sits with deep green eyes and listens.

"His mother lost him several years ago and bartered with the court to find him. We got a lead and I was sent to retrieve Yewdrone to save him from slavery."

She knows his full name. Garlochia mustn't be fooling. "Well, I don't think it was right to go fool that old cat, out of his only help, by hitting on him. He had no idea, *Princess*."

Celestra wonders what he sees in that wretched creature, but works her magick nonetheless. "We at the court do not need to give answers. We make orders that you all follow. My father lets me handle this, and I obey his orders." Lu'barthrow angered even more at the courts and royalty, growls in disgust. He lowers his body to the ground as if he is going to attack her full force.

"Now I am finished with them. I knew they were too spoiled to see into normal creatures' lives. Go! Take the whelp and disregard all compassion. Meone was right. You can't trust anyone except yourself." Running off into the ruins, he leaves a trail of dust behind him. She knows where he's headed to. Her main concern is getting Yewdrone back to the courts. Walking over to him, she shakes the dust off from her back and sprawls out her wings. Yewdrone stares wildly at her and gasps. "What...*ARE*... you? Celestra fearing there is no time to waste, quickly turns towards him, "Don't worry little whelp, I'm a hybrid. I'm here to free you from that nasty lion."

Yewdrone still terrified over the ordeal stutters, "But...But... How did you know I wanted to be free?" Celestra feeling terrible she's scared this dragon half to death, speaks soothingly, "It was obvious. You, dear little whelp, did you know once I too was an orphan? I knew no mother or father, but I was taken in by a wonderful wise and considerate teacher. This is why I can stand here strong-willed in front of you now. Now it's your turn to have the same." Tears welled up in Yewdrone's eyes as he reached over for Celestra. Being abandoned at such a young age scarred him, but apparently, he's not alone in feeling it. "Where do you live now, hybrid?" She gladly corrects him, "The name is Celestra; Celestra the white hybrid." Yewdrone looks up at her, "Celestra, what a pretty name." She starts to walk again with him. "Well I really don't have a home to answer your question, I was a wild creature compared to your civilization here. I lived off the land, took what I needed, and protected myself as necessary. Here you all live in communities, which is very alien to me. I am presently staying with Garsa and Avalo in the main courts."

Yewdrone starts to imagine what it would be like if he himself had a family or friends who cared about him. As they walked to the courts, something told him he wouldn't have to wonder anymore. Yewdrone after a bit of time asks, "Do you ever miss the life you left behind Celestra?"

Celestra stares up at the fading night stars in the cloudless sky. "Sometimes little dragon. Before finding the dragons and this city, understand my company only consisted of wild wolves and the creatures I chose for dinner before they died. There were no friends or family after my master disappeared. I realized it was necessary to keep moving, until something gave me a reason to stop. I needed my life to have true meaning." Yewdrone smiling now, seems much more comfortable in her company. Celestra hopes he's young enough to be able to leave these bad times behind him.

Almost at the courts, they see Raspier talking with Drako and Garsa, while drinking the royal grulo. Introducing Yewdrone to Drako and the others, Celestra asks Drako to watch him and show him the same kindness that she was given. Celestra made sure to leave out how she acquired Yewdrone for now.

Making sure Yewdrone's okay, she knows she will have to visit Meoneal later to ensure the deal. If she hadn't come across Lu'barthrow, it would have been possible to slip out in the morning without him knowing. Now Celestra has no choice. She gulps at the hardball forming in her throat.

She understands she will have to tell one of them to ensure she survives. Garsa seemed like the best option. Explaining the situation to him, he tells her in detail now how to handle this without having his thugs find her afterward. "I hate sabers, so back-handed and manipulative; however, you were *very* wrong in what you did. This could be paid back in karma you know? Look Celestra; give him this sack of drogs, wine and this document. It's enough to keep his greed occupied as well as his twisted pleasure."

Garsa writes out a protection letter for his species. Celestra takes both and places them in front of her. "Well Garsa, I realize that manipulating him in order to free Yewdrone was wrong, but I do not believe he would have released him otherwise." Garsa sits on the ground and sets his goblet down on a rock. "Celestra, playing these kinds of godly games are not yours to make. You may have brought more harm to Yewdrone and yourself because of this." Celestra wasn't pleased that Garsa felt she did this in the wrong way. There *was no choice* in her opinion.

"Garsa, he was a slave. Beaten and starved on a regular basis. Yewdrone can now start living a real life. I was raised to trust my instincts. We must bring justice to the wronged."

Garsa irritated with Celestra, tries hard not to knock her off her feet. He has little patience for young stupidity. "Just understand that manipulating anyone at any time for any reason will always be wrong; despite the outcome. Yes, you freed Yewdrone, but still at the cost of someone else's pain." Celestra admits her plan to free Yewdrone might have had some mistakes.

Garsa sighing loudly, picks up his grulo and drank the goblet down before speaking. "Karma, dear little warrior, is brought upon each and every one of us naturally. No one can pretend to delegate it when the Great Mother is watching. *She* deals those blows. The point remains yes, Yewdrone is free. You must go and finish what lies you have started; fully aware karma may turn around and nip you in the tail. Next time you should think before you leap. Okay?" Agreeing with Garsa, she sets out for a moment in solitude. This is something she has done without for quite some time. Garsa watches her as she walks away. *Maybe these hybrids would have been safer with us here, instead of being lost in the great world alone. They're so misguided it's almost dangerous.*

Chapter Twenty Five

The Meditating Intrusion

Gazing at the stars, Celestra sinks down into the cool dry grasses outside the gate. Meditating after such an ordeal, should release her frazzled thoughts. "Ah, there are no buildings, no streets, just nature and my heartbeat." Slowly breathing, she settles deeper into her meditation. Letting time evade her now, Celestra's fully enveloped inside her subconscious mind. Her sacred plains reminded her of who she had to be in order to survive in nature.

Hopefully, this pause can show Celestra how to grow as a hybrid. Within seconds of her reaching the plain, there was already a disturbance. At first, she ignores it; seeing she is meditating in a new location. Her body slowly becomes more acclimated. Yet, she still feels the presence of another. "Hmm, might be someone meditating in the city. Interesting, I can feel their energy. How odd?"

Something was tickling her tail from behind her. She turns to see Tarmax. Stunned he's in her meditation, Celestra doesn't speak a word in order to fully examine the reason for his presence. Watching him move, Celestra notes he's not a figment of her own imagination. He must be sleeping somewhere dreaming this. *Could it be possible that he's meditating and not aware? He was that disturbance I was feeling.*

Little does Celestra know, but Avalo just took Tarmax out on his first inner journey. Somehow naturally, Tarmax slipped into meditation and planed straight to where Celestra was. Avalo studying his breathing, senses that he's not alone in his meditation. Honing in on what the other energy was, took no time at all. It was Celestra.

Questioning why the two of them linked up was the trouble.

Only Garsa knew that shortly, Celestra will need to visit Meoneal. This cat will receive quite a wake-up call, as Gaia watches quietly. She will need more than just her wits.

Avalo was nerved over this dark energy hanging over Celestra. He didn't know why yet, but she will need a bodyguard. Never doubting his instincts, Avalo figured this could be a grand way to bond these two hybrids further along. Oddly they have figured out how to plane together without any of his help.

Knowing that Tarmax isn't fully situated with his new identity, he can let this meditational link guide them both to a better understanding of each other and themselves. Relaxing his mind, he enters the sub-plane on which they have settled, but as a tree. He sees Celestra presently circling Tarmax, obviously questioning if his presence is a good or bad thing. Studying both of their movements, he can see that below all the confusion exists an attraction, but not like that wasn't perceived a while ago. Celestra's curiosity was quite apparent upon meeting Tarmax for the first time. She was abruptly surprised to see this manifestation of Tarmax just as much as he was to see her.

"Celestra? What are you doing in my meditation?"

Annoyed that he has broken into her realm, she bites her tongue and explains. "Tarmax, understand you're actually invading my own meditation, and quite frankly it's a bother. I need to take care of a very touchy situation later with someone and your presence will only slow me down."

Saddened, Tarmax has upset Celestra with his presence, he attempts to better the situation. "Could it be possible it was planned for it to be this way? Maybe we're supposed to be here together like this? Why not see where it goes..." Tarmax hoping his words of persuasion could calm her frayed nerves, ended up being partially successful. Seeing that Celestra was taking to the idea, he himself can settle in this new experience.

She rolls her eyes and starts to walk over to a small pond across the way. Tarmax follows her as she starts to speak. "Well I guess you will need some assistance getting used to existing in this sub-plane, so here is a crash course on planing. First off all of your consciousness remains dormant as your sub-consciousness stands as primary. Secondly, you must remember that any billowing fears that have rested in your subconscious will erect themselves as tangible things here, so don't lose your nerve. They are just reminders of the demons you have to eradicate to further your studies. For instance, that tree appeared shortly after your arrival, so I'm aware that it could be a representation of something inside your subconscious, or a guide to encourage you on your way."

Avalo chuckles to himself at how accurate she is, and grows a deeper respect for this hybrid's simple technique in teaching. Celestra continues, "Also, time is irrelevant here. It will feel like hours when only a few minutes have past. So learning, studying and growing all happens at a hyper-accelerated rate. You can change into whatever form you wish here, and also practice transforming. I've recently learned this from studying the true lineage of what we are. Hybrids…

Meaningful things from your inner consciousness will appear as spoken earlier in many forms, but it's how you interact with them that will produce a positive effect. Upon exiting this sub-plane, it's healthy and equally wise to state or write down what has occurred to ensure it will be remembered later."

Tarmax listens and understands. He will consider completing the writing recommendation, due to his poor memory.

There was a small issue with this.

Learning how to write might be a problem. Only now having hands, over hooves, it's obvious he wasn't taught how to write. He refuses to lose concentration at all costs.

Celestra seeing Tarmax is listening well, she continues, "Okay, first: in our lesson together, go over to that pool of water by your right side. Look deep into its crystal essence to see your form here." Tarmax looks to his side but sees nothing other than grass. Confused as to why she would point to nothing, he stares back undecided on what to do. "Okay, this is what I was saying before. That pool must be derived from your inner mind. Imagine it is there, and it will appear."

Tarmax concentrates and sure enough the pool appears on the right side of him. Smiling, he sees his reflection after a few moments but notices one small change. "I can see everything but my eyes. Why is this Celestra?"

She knows how hard it is for a living creature to let go of the fact their essence can exist in more than one plane. She looks for the right words to explain that eyes are the last thing that materialize. It is the doorway to the soul after all. "The eyes, Tarmax, are the last connection to the reality of meditation; therefore, the very last visual and the very first step to joining subconscious and conscious minds together.

Tarmax, why do you think you can't see your eyes?" He looks deeper into the reflection to notice one thing. He can see Celestra's reflection flawlessly, especially her eyes. She even seems to glow. "I can see you perfectly, but can you see all of me?"

Celestra smiles and touches Tarmax on his head. Instantly a fire burns inside his chest and he gasps for air. A whirlwind of emotions and thoughts collide together in his head, as his body aligns instantly to his surroundings.

Staring deeper into Celestra's eyes, he feels this warm tingle upon his brow. Instantly, without any control, he turns into a black version of Celestra and drops to the ground.

Confused at the transformation, he picks himself up to look into the water again. Seeing what resembles his features, but in feline form brings him to turn to Celestra in amazement. "How did you do that? I look like you, but as myself. Can I do this outside this world?"

Laughing affectionately, she shakes her head no, but deeper inside an attraction is equally burning for that to be true.

Tarmax excited runs around in his new body and admires how easy it is for a panther to move. Jumping and mock stalking everything, he seems so happy to be alive; so carefree.

"Celestra, this world you've shown me is so different, but feels so comfortable. I am falling in love with myself in a new light, and I have many wonderful teachers to thank." Just as he says this, he intuitively looks back to the pool of water again to see his form, glowing eyes and all. "Wow, it feels like an eternity is sitting inside my eyes, yet, time here is standing still. How can this paradox exist?"

Celestra's never heard it phrased quite like that before, so she pauses before she speaks. "Tarmax, imagine everything and nothing at the same rate of existence. Then combine space, all dark matter, and all these paradoxes in between. This makes up the subconscious mind's borders. All dimensions that couldn't be opened before, now open. Theories that lied dormant awaiting the minds approval are now freed and unleashed. Combine them together and it makes up the broad spectrum of understanding energy and matter as we know it. Sound can shape and control matter. The mind conjures up matter, and waves of action become sound. Movement with purpose creates harmony. When harmony, love, and serenity link up with chaos and hate, a balance rings the small strings of the universe. Basically, this is the fundamental workings of the laws of science and spirituality. They cannot exist without each other. Do you understand?"

The very fabric of time and space twirl inside Tarmax's mind. After a few moments, despite a newly growing headache, he thinks he understands what Celestra is explaining.

"You mean to tell me that there are other dimensions, other worlds, other moments that we link up to, yet, cannot see or hear, unless seeking them out directly?   If this is so, then how can most exist in only one dimension their whole life, never knowing about the others?"

Celestra sees this may be a little too much for him right now. It's not likely they will be answered immediately. There are things in this area that she can teach him, but it's obvious that he still had a long way to go.

"Tarmax, why not take what you have learned and let it settle in first. There is much more to discuss and unfortunately, I need to visit Meoneal now. We will continue this when we have the opportunity again. Why not go ask Avalo for some pointers while I'm gone."

Avalo hearing this, chuckles at her statement. *She's quite intelligent this feline. She hides it well…*

Tarmax still rolling around in the soft cool grasses, starts to practice sheathing his claws,

"So, in this realm Celestra, I can remain a panther… is this right?" Celestra smiles warmly at Tarmax and wags her tail to-and-fro, "Yes Tarmax, why do you ask?"

Tarmax lowering his body to the ground, slashes his tail side to side instinctually. "Well I always wanted to know how it felt to rough and tumble like one too!" Puzzled at his statement, Celestra tilts her head at Tarmax, "What do you mean Tar-"

Before she could even finish his name, Tarmax has her pinned on her back. Giving in, Celestra and Tarmax play fight. Nipping and biting each other without a care in the world, Avalo could just smile. They're carrying on like two-month-old cubs. Celestra realizes there is something more to him than she previously perceived. It makes her question how well she knows herself.

Calming down, she wants Tarmax to retain her lesson, instead of fighting like kits. "So, you think you can remember everything I taught you here, Tarmax, minus the play fighting. Fun yes, but this was not intended for the lesson.

Oh, and by the way, maybe it is good you can't transform like this in the outside world, because your jaw is way too strong. It bit through my belly skin. No harm though, Tarmax, all in a good play."

He apologizes for the bite and thinks about all this new information. "Yes, I believe I can remember it. Thank you, really. This has been great!" Celestra smiles and rubs his face. She certainly agrees.

To feel his soft thick fur, brings tears to her eyes. Tarmax feels them fall but says nothing. *Wow! What a lady...*

Saying their goodbyes, both prepare for the chaos that awaits them. Neither have a clue what fate awaits them. The spindle of chaos is letting out its thread slowly.

Avalo sees Tarmax twitch while recovering from his meditation. He left early to watch his progress, in order to help him readjust to waking life. Tarmax opens his eyes and Avalo's red snout is there smiling above him. "Hello Tarmax, see anything worth talking about?" Tarmax still groggy from waking up tells Avalo what he went through.

"Well, Strange thing. Celestra ended up being there in my meditation. We talked about the fabric of time and space. Strange for me really. She was nice enough to give me a crash course on planing. It was very rewarding but awkward."

Avalo listening intently studies Tarmax's interpretation as well as what he saw. He decides against telling him that he was there, watching all along. That might make him feel uncomfortable. It would be better for Avalo to let them think they shared that space alone. Presently, Avalo is more concerned with Celestra alone in the back streets of Drondia at night. All that means is trouble. While the two of them were meditating, he decided to pick her memory and saw what she had done.

What a brazen hybrid. She really didn't think this one through well enough. Good, the whelp is safe, but now to make sure she remains that way.

"Tarmax, follow Celestra. She is heading for a cart seller in the shady part of the city and she might need help if it gets ugly. I know Celestra thinks she's independent, but please follow her. There is no telling what Meoneal will do. Take note that she will look like a lioness without her wings. Try to catch up to her before she changes. Oh, and by the way, be yourself for a change. In your horse form, she won't recognize you right away and you can blend in better." With that, Tarmax changes back into his horse form to run off and find Celestra. Finally, his wings agreed to the transformation.

Avalo chuckles at how these two are reminiscent of Sorrokine and him back in the old times. Those days back when he still had a chance at love and forgiveness.

Chapter Twenty Six

Yewdrone Finds a Family

Raspier, Lastra, Partune, Garsa, Yewdrone, and Drako are sitting by a nice warm fire. The five of them are joking around with the young whelp, trying to figure out his lineage. Partune blurts out, "Well, you are purple. They're not very common around here so, I wonder, if you were from the north."

Yewdrone smiles and drinks some water from a cup they have offered him. The grass glider bone is almost cleaned of its meat as well. "It's so nice to be around other dragons. Something I'm not used to.

A bit about my past: I was told from the care services that took me in that the note attached to me was written in Dortiorn, a language known to come from Gunitra up north past the white dragon's territory. So Partune you might be right after all…"

Partune puffs out his broad chest and smiles. Yewdrone continues, "Garsa, I think that your history hall might help me. Celestra was telling me about it on our walk here. She said it was the most amazing thing to see when you thought you had no family. Being an orphan destroys hopes and dreams. There is no one to shelter you from harsh truths or even harsher creatures."

They all nod and watch Yew start to explain how he ended up with Meoneal a few years back.

Lastra started thinking about her lost whelp. She always had a terrible fright that one day, Sarclaw would disappear. Drieston was always good at calming her nerves at night with the nightmares, but they never stopped. Looking over at Yewdrone, a certain instinct churned up inside. She felt maybe she could take care of the little whelp from now on. She knew it wasn't too healthy to place a heavy burden on her at this time, but her core tells her it's the right thing to do. If she's wrong, life will certainly show her otherwise.

Yew a young whelp, about fifteen, was truly a self-sufficient dragon, but many things like puberty and adulthood were far off in the future for him. Someone needed to at least watch over him until then. Lastra asked Yew if it would be okay if he stayed with her. Yew, looked up at Lastra and stopped chatting about the past. "Really Lastra, you would take me in? Wow, you don't know what this would mean to me. I've been all alone without family for so long I don't know if I can adjust, but I accept your offer! Thank you so much." Hiding his tears, he runs over to Lastra and hugs her. Lastra a little touched by this equally hides her tears as she buries her head in his small body. The two of them embrace and for the moment, feel whole. The group smiles and all look up at the sky. At that very moment, a meteor fell through the atmosphere. They all watched as it burnt its way across the night sky.

Chapter Twenty Seven

Avenging the Abused

Celestra is almost at Meoneal's cart and is well aware this will be no easy feat to complete. This deal is complicated and without getting seriously hurt, she must calculate every single move. It's time to use her skills in a different fashion. This time, Celestra is hunting a dark mind instead of a tasty buck. Ducking into a corner alley, she starts masking herself up to look like Garlochia. With the streets quieter, she proceeds much easier than earlier. "I can do this; I can make it through this alive. I've been through worse."

Without Celestra knowing, Tarmax is watching in his birth form, far in the distance. Dropping the bag of drogs, wine and the paper, Celestra pulls in her wings and rolls around in the light tan dust. Tarmax smiles at how cunning she is.

The two hybrids can move safer now that the night is quiet. Celestra tries to become the character she was earlier today. Tarmax watches in awe at how far she is going for just one whelp. Despite the manipulation involved with this situation, he realizes what a devoted and good-natured heart she has. She needs someone to show her the same. Someone who wouldn't abuse it or take advantage of it. A real male who was just as strong and loving she was.

Letting his mind wander too far, Tarmax almost forgets to keep watching her, so he turns to regain proper attention. Seeing Celestra approaching the cart jolts him straight back into his present objective: to protect her. Tarmax stares in wonder as she walks up to Meoneal with such feminine flair.

Her tail waved high, as her false royal pride, oozed out of her stride. "Well hello, my dashing saber, how the stars shine for us tonight. Now about that deal..." Meoneal looking up at

Celestra smiles and eyes her entire body. "Later hot paws, later... I would rather mosey over to those tall grasses for a while. That's gonna be our deal."

Meoneal panting at the sight of young fresh meat can't repress his desires any longer. The whole time Celestra's been gone, he's been crazed and eagerly waiting for this moment; especially without Yewdrone to keep him busy. "I think we should scamper over there and skip the formalities."

Growling low in disagreement seemed to be proper for Celestra, but not proper to another feline. He sees that as a form of flirting and lunges for her neck. Crawling out of his hold, she makes sure to spot an escape route before pushing the money onto him. Some of the tan dust falls away. "Well I would take you on your other offer but I am betrothed to a Prince, and he will know otherwise. Besides, here is a bag full of drogs, royal grulo and a parchment proving your endangered species rights. This should be enough compensation for what we discussed earlier today."

Meoneal for a moment stops to gaze over the wonderful things she has brought. Amazed she didn't lie, calms his calculating frame of mind. Still, his lust refuses to back down. "Thanks, gal, I am truly honored that the court recognizes my problem, but there is just one thing left, my real prize." Just like that, he picks her up by her nape and starts to run to the grasses.

Clawing at his stomach, she fights wildly to be freed. "How dare you! You, scummy saber! You will not succeed in ruining this deal!" Twisting out of his hold, but losing some fur, she darts to the grasses being nimbler than he. Tarmax freaking out snorts violently over what Meoneal was doing to her. Stomping his hooves to release some anger, he realizes he will need to intervene to save her hide. "Damn stupid cat..."

Celestra hiding in the thick grasses' fears for her life, in a way she's never known before. Panting from the struggle, she collects herself just enough to make the next move. Meoneal fast behind her speaks out, "Oh royal temptress, where are you hiding? I wish to serenade you with my growls. I will find that pretty rump of yours before you know it."

Meone snarls, as he scours the dirt for her scent. Celestra knows that there are two ways of getting out of this: fight or be taken. Both seem hopeless at this point. Seeing an opening in the grasses, she waits to see if he will approach. Listening hard for the sound of pads prodding, she tries hard not to panic. Taking this moment to change into her birth form, Celestra will fly straight up to escape. Just as she tries to run free, a set of claws sink into her rear pulling her down. "Got you my precious little lay, let's rock mother nature's roots out of the ground!" Pulling her forcefully underneath him, pain shoots throughout her legs to the point she almost falls to the ground.

Growling out in anger, Tarmax hears Celestra and panics. His hooves stomp back and forth as he throws his head. "What do I do? That dirty lion has his paws all over her! I can't take this!

That's it, I will defend her honor!" Tarmax feels a burn on his head growing. Instantly, he turns into a large black panther with wings and runs into the grasses.

Scenting out the two of them, he runs at full speed and throws up his claws and lands on Meoneal fiercely. Being much larger, he pulls him into the air straight off of Celestra.

She stares in amazement at this male panther defending her. - *This humiliating moment of weakness. Yeah, I'm such a strong warrior...*

Snarls and growls of male anger fill the night air. Disheveled, Celestra can only sit and wait, panting heavily in pain. She licks her badly bloodied fur and tries to calm herself down.

All around the streets, Meoneal and Tarmax's deafening howls of anger, echo across the grasses. All life twitches as they rip each other apart. Celestra tries to stay out of their way but they almost trample her. Old Meoneal, terrified at this gigantic panther with wings, fears for his life - and fights like it too.

Bleeding from many open wounds, the poor excuse for a saber has already lost his false tooth and the other one as well. Panting through a bloody jaw, Meoneal tries to reason with this large panther. "Who are you, and why do you disturb things that do not concern you?"

Looking at Celestra's wounds, enrages Tarmax even further. His eyes get red and dark. "That is my Princess, my future mate, you were harassing and hurting! Do you think I would let her come here alone and trust you wouldn't try this you dirt wallowing lion?"

Seeing Celestra, Meoneal is astounded to see she too has wings and is no lioness at all. "Why the lies Princess? It wouldn't have changed this bag of money, but, it would have made for a better ban-"

Tarmax enraged, spit on the ground, moves in front of Celestra, and answers for her. "How dare you attempt to mate my partner against her will? That document and money are not deserving of a saber with such low quality."

Celestra seeing how much Meone really hurt her, can just stare in amazement. Meoneal for his old age still was quite strong.

Bleeding from her hind legs and her nape, was bad enough. Her claws also were so over-extended, she could barely walk. This startles Tarmax to such a degree, that his inner herding instinct, forces him to teach Meoneal a permanent lesson. Once and for all. Still, Celestra was the one who made the false move of coming on to the old geezer.

"Meoneal, understand that this is over. No more will you ever need to contact my fiancé or the courts. We will honor your extinction papers and the drogs in one case only: that you leave her alone, and never discuss it again. Know that you are always going to be watched and there is no way out of this. We will put you down if you attempt to breach this verbal contract. You are lucky you're escaping with no more than a few surface wounds.

As far as I am concerned, your legs should have been chewed off, and used as toothpicks with my next meal, but I hate the taste of street trash. Go now, before I change my mind you scourge of this splendid city."

Meone with head low, dripping blood grabs the sack and the document in his mouth. The royal grulo, he would come back for. Hardly walking and badly wounded, he ducks into the alley where Cerpiendra's parlor is located. The night surrounds him as he tries to gain composure.

Celestra terrified, but grateful it's over, looks to Tarmax, "Thank you so much, sir. May I ask your name? You seem so familiar, but I can't place your face." Celestra stares in amazement, and her heart links tightly to this valiant knight defending her honor. His blue eyes can be seen clearly in what's left of the starlight. "Don't you recognize me Celestra? I'm Tarmax. I was told to follow you if you were in need of protection. Please do not get mad, I wish not to offend you, but you really needed some help there. Are you okay? You seem badly hurt." Celestra stares at Tarmax amazed he can change into a panther as well.

"Geeze. This is a bit more than I can handle now. Please Tarmax, I will ask you one favor. I am very weak from the struggle, and that saber has some strong legs. Please, can you help me get up and back to the courts?" Stunned that this is all she asks for, after being through so much, Tarmax humbly obliges to help her home.

Changing into his dragon form, he flies her in his arms back to the courts. During the journey, Tarmax remembers when he was just a simple horse.

He realizes he could have died without ever knowing his powers. Thinking of this reminds him how much he should appreciate his genetics and for life, giving him this strong-willed and beautiful creature resting on his chest right now. Never knowing whether or not she will accept him is one thing. From this point on, he will wait for that answer with drive. He could never be with any other. This, he was for certain.

Tarmax's emotions exploded outward and stood strong for her through this terrible ordeal. If this is not a reason to look deeper into their connection, what would? Still, right now, the most important thing is to get her to safety and cleaned up.

Chapter Twenty Eight

Bruised at the Banquet

Bringing Celestra back into her room, Tarmax lays with her until she regains consciousness. Turning back into his panther form, he licks her tattered and wounded fur while purring. Curling around her, he thinks to himself how this must be love. This burning desire he feels to protect another creature and to make sure no harm is brought to them. He looks up at the night sky and sees the horizon starting to get lighter. A common thing his mother said to him was, "Love can do strange things to your heart Tarmax. It can raise you up and it can bring you down. The best thing to remember is that love is free. It cannot be caged. It's truly wild in nature and should be respected that way always." Tarmax closes his eyes, "Mother. I understand you now." His tears fall upon Celestra's face as she stirs awake, "Tarmax…"

Tarmax overjoyed answers her softly, "Yes Celestra?"

She starts to purr, feeling his large warm body surround her. "Stay…with me…" then she nods off again.

Eventually, the group went looking for them both and saw them sleeping in the room. Celestra hears them approach. As everyone crowds around her, she attempts to collect herself and tries to place what happened. Waking up fully now, Celestra thought she saw what seemed like blurs of shadows around her. Looking at the floor, she sees bloodstained cloth, and wonders where it was from. "Are you guys waiting for something? Whose blood is on those rags?" Startled at her response they all look to her wondering why she can't remember a thing. " Celestra, don't you remember what happened before? Meoneal attacked you and took you down."

As if she didn't hear him, she looks at the early morning sky and can tell that the banquet is almost over. "Well I remember part of it but I think shock kicked the rest of it from my memory. Why don't you guys go back to the banquet, I'll be fine."

They all discuss whether or not she's really okay. Tarmax in dragon form walks closer to Celestra and nudges her face with his hand. Startled he is showing her affection, she recoils and gives him an odd look. "Really, I'm okay, I know most of you aren't used to such ordeals, but understand this kind of interaction was a way of life for me. I will be fine. Please don't pamper me and miss the festivities. I will come back in a bit, just give me some time to clean up and rest a bit more." Garsa gently pulls her aside to talk for a bit and tells the others to go on ahead. Tarmax knows he really shouldn't let her actions bother him, but can't help feeling hurt. He lags behind the others while walking towards the banquet. "Celestra is definitely independent, but because of her pride, she really isn't. Someone will have to help her when all goes wrong...Right?" Tarmax sighs, these new emotions are starting to confuse him.

Walking into the hallway, Garsa sits for a second in silence before telling Celestra the update on the journey they will take in the morning. Celestra steals this as an opportunity to express herself. "Garsa, I'm sure unlike these other creatures, you have experienced such battles, if not stronger ones."

Garsa nods his head in agreement but doesn't respond. Celestra continues, "Well, then you know the only way to move on is to take your losses humbly." Garsa shakes his head affectionately at her and points to his bad eye. "This was a scar that could have been avoided, little warrior. You see I let my emotions cloud my thinking, and this is the result of it.

You let your guard down for only one moment and Meoneal took advantage of it. The best advice I can give you is: 'Do not let this good lifestyle make you soft. I may appear to be, but this is only when I trust my company."

Looking at her wounds, she realizes he was right. Meoneal is a shady, corrupt creature and she should have gone with someone to secure the deal. "I understand Garsa, that's something that will have to come with time."

Garsa touches Celestra's shoulder. "Celestra, soon we will set out for the white dragon despite you and Meoneal's encounter. Are you up for the quest?" Knowing she will say yes no matter what, he still asked to be polite. Celestra answers, "Yes Garsa." Looking over her badly wounded body he is amazed to see it's healing very quickly. Tarmax must have attended to her wounds and licked them clean.

Looking at her sad eyes, was the one thing he knew no one could heal. That was something Celestra has to handle herself. "Well, maybe you can learn from this and apply it to future lessons in life. I know you were a solo huntress, but it seems you may have to learn when to ask for help. It's an important responsibility to know when you cannot take the world on all by yourself."

Celestra stirs and walks over to the bathing pool to get some water. Lapping up the water, Celestra realizes Garsa is right. Despite her pride telling her otherwise. "Garsa, you are wise beyond your years, and for that, I know Uniqua would be accepting of you. Thank you for talking to me before going back."

Garsa laughs at Celestra and swats her head with his hand. She smiles back. He heads off to the others. A bit of cleaning and stretching will fix her up for sure.

She's missed most of the banquet. Just like Lu'barthrow, she hasn't been involved in such a fancy celebration before. Full royal treatment, festivities, and companions deserving of her. This brings a smile to her face that generates the pleasant sound of purring; even if there isn't much time left, she'll enjoy every minute.

Chapter Twenty Nine

The Dark Stranger

Tarmax is restless and his thoughts wander. *How could Celestra just shrug off what I did for her? Is her exterior that tough she refuses to recognize she needed help or was she just embarrassed?* Heading back to the banquet didn't seem as enthralling as it was before. Quite frankly Tarmax felt uncomfortable going. *I wonder if she just blanked out from the blood loss. I will admit she does heal incredibly fast. No need in harping on it, she seems okay, but it would've been nice to have received at least a thank you from her.*

Bothered, Tarmax walks to the banquet hall anyway. He won't admit it but he's just as scarred from that moment with Meoneal as she probably is. Also, what his heart was telling him about Celestra isn't helping either. Drained and tired, he walks slowly. In the mist of his travels, he decides to change back into a horse to ease his mind. "Mother, I wonder what you would think of all of this."

Plodding to the Ballroom, his hooves slightly drag over the dry ground beneath him. Clouds of dust swirl around his ankles like lost souls. The early morning sun reveals a deep level of concern on his face; his features worn with far away eyes. His life has changed so quickly, he cannot even begin to digest it all. *Could this be my destiny? Attempting to correct the imbalance between humans and dragons? Greggils, as these dragons call them. What does the word greggil mean anyhow? Neither creature due to their past can see the present situation clearly. Some humans aren't bad, and some dragons aren't good. How could they not see that after so much time has passed?* Tarmax softly speaks these things under his breath as he approaches the ballroom. Hanging around the entrance he sees Celestra. He wants so badly to talk with her, yet for now, is content just watching her.

Luckily for Tarmax, she pays no mind to anything around her. He desperately wishes to know if she remembers anything from before. Pulling her head up from grooming, she looks over to where Tarmax is standing. She is aware something is there, but his hiding place is secure for now. Curious, she perks her ears around in all directions and listens, while studying the air. Tarmax takes this chance to move a bit closer but fails to elude her keen senses. Smelling his presence, she lowers to the ground.

Damn...Celestra knows I'm here, but does she know it's me? She may not remember me as a horse. Maybe I can work this to my advantage.

Walking out from the brush, Tarmax trots along up to the entrance. Celestra watches him closely and wonders why he seems so familiar. "Hello there miss, are you waiting for a date to the ball?" Celestra studying Tarmax is still unaware it is him. "Well, honestly no, I didn't ask anyone, nor did they ask me." Smiling, Tarmax looks down at her and winks. "Well, that's perfect. I wasn't asked either. Let's go in together and enjoy the rest of this party; how about it?" Celestra seems uninterested but longed for some company. "Well okay, but what is your name, horse?"

Tarmax was smiling that Celestra still is unaware of who exactly he is. He bows on one leg. "The name is...Max, and what is yours?" Celestra seems a little more relaxed and answers accordingly. "My name is Celestra. It's nice to meet you, Max." Tail flicking in the light wind, Tarmax motions with his head towards the door. "Well nice to meet you too Celestra; shall we go in then?" She agrees and they walk through into the banquet.

Finally, inside, they are both astounded at how wonderful everything looks. The candles are lit, the band is playing, and the atmosphere is slow, relaxed, and enchanting. "Wow, I've never been to anything this lavish before, what about you Max?" Celestra asks. "Well no, I'm new to this city. I grew up on a farm down south." Celestra turns to him and stares into his eyes. "Do I know you from somewhere? Your voice is so familiar."

Tarmax chuckles and can feel that his true identity is going to be found out, "That all depends upon how you pair the body to the voice." Looking him over, she studies all his features well.

"Wait a minute… You're Tarmax! I forgot you are a horse too! How many things can *you* turn into?"

He laughs and explains why he is more at home as a horse, rather than all the other animals. Tarmax explains where he came from and how he lived with humans most of his life. Celestra listens intently never knowing his story. "So you mean to tell me you thought you were a common barn horse? Wow, that's funny. A trinity hybrid like *you* thinking he's common."

Feeling a little pride, he smiles wide at Celestra. Tarmax finds it funny, that dragons ended up teaching him, his true self. "Lord Cannor was all I knew, and because of this terrible wound that never healed, he was always so mean and bitter. It certainly was from a predatory-like animal. The marks were displayed there plain as day, but when I would ask the local animals what could have made it, they were stumped."

Puzzled by this, Celestra tries to remember, if any creatures she came into contact with could have left such a mark on a human, but nothing came to mind. "Tarmax, where did it happen? This could help me figure out what wild animal could have made it." He thinks back to when he heard Cannor talking about it. Thinking hard he remembers a field being spoken about when Cannor was a child. '*I was chasing this cute little cub with my friend Carmine in Fictine forest, but when she cornered it, it struck my arm incredibly hard. Instantly I was bleeding and I passed out from the attack...never thought such a small creature could do so much damage.*" Celestra shutters and is brought back to that day she herself was in a very similar situation. Two human cubs were chasing her and she had to defend herself. It all started to sync up quickly to the story Tarmax was telling.

Whether or not to tell Tarmax remained the only question. She realized how close the two of them were in proximity. *Imagine that.* She thinks. *Tarmax and I were raised very close to each other.* Tarmax continued to tell her the finer details of his relationship with his mother, and the nice family that took her in and how it seemed odd that the dragons think all humans are bad. Celestra presently distracted, notices that Drako, Garsa and Avalo, are talking over by the bar, so she looks at Tarmax and heads over to them. She would rather change the subject as quickly as possible to lighten up the mood.

Tarmax catches on to this and feels slighted. His nostrils flare as she starts to chat with the others. *Why does she keep us from being alone? Is she just nervous or am I that boring?* Tarmax joins in, but with a bit of reluctance. It's quite obvious by the way he drags one hoof before walking over to them.

The three dragons look quite nice in their smoking coats. Standing with goblets of grulo, they discuss the lighter things that make life so livable. They're all obviously very drunk. Laughing about the small dilemmas that seemed so big in the moment is a wonderful way to heal old wounds.

Celestra and Tarmax just watch the three in heavy discussion, enjoying their warm harmony. She realized that this wasn't their first drink of grulo this evening; so much for Garsa being the sober one.

Garsa sees the two of them from the corner of his eye. He nudges the others to include them in the discussions with a jab of his elbow. "So, are you two enjoying the party? Nice change from all the chaos we've experienced recently. We all must thank Raspier for organizing this. He is the royal planner after all." Garsa gives Tarmax a tap with his fist and then pats Celestra's head. He thinks to himself, *the two of them still seem tense from earlier today. Hope this party will loosen them up a bit. We have a long journey ahead of us all.*

Over to their right, they see Raspier with two female griffins attempting very hard to impress them. Avalo, the trickster that he is, brings up his hand and draws a line with his claw over Raspier's head. Garsa watching, half smiles but isn't too pleased with his actions. Raspier, a schooled gigolo, surely wants nothing to interrupt him. They see the streamers above his head break free, and fall on the two ladies entangling them slowly. Raspier instantly looks to Avalo and smiles. "Oh ladies, it seems you are in need of some help. Let me get that for you." Both of them seem very embarrassed and accept his help.

Raspier gently starts to unravel the streamers from both of them. Chuckling at the event he conjured up, Avalo grabs his tail in delight. Garsa stares him down. "Avalo, like that griffin needs any help with those two. Curb your magick please." Blowing off what Garsa said, he continues to meddle. Seeing the streamers undone on the floor he waves his hand in a half circle, then closes them very fast. The streamers tangle around Raspier's feet, and he falls right on top of the two ladies. Avalo can barely contain his laughter. This is becoming way too funny to hide.

Raspier now terribly embarrassed, tries to think about how to keep his dignity. Instead of seeing the ladies laugh at him out of pity, they laugh at how adorable the situation is. The two ladies wander off with Raspier, streamers still tangled around them all. Avalo shines his claws on his chest scales and laughs. "Now that's a thank you. Don't you all agree?" Avalo laughing hysterically slaps Garsa's back tearing from humor. Garsa finally smiles and laughs with them all. Raspier, however, would have gotten those ladies anyway. He surely didn't need magick's helping claw.

Watching the room quietly Celestra is pleased being an observer tonight. She sees everyone having a good time, except Tarmax. Something is eating him up inside. Walking over to the bar whelp, she asks for two goblets of grulo for them both. "Uh, could you put them in that basket? I'm not very good at holding one yet, let alone two." The whelp agrees and she brings it slowly over to Tarmax.

Placing the basket down carefully, she looks up at Tarmax, "Hey, I can't help but notice you seem very down. Is there anything you would like to talk about?"

Before accepting the drink, he turns into his dragon form. "Well that event with Meoneal, it's bothering me a bit. You weren't very gracious about the help I gave you and quite frankly, I'm offended. I stuck out my neck for you. Why act like it didn't happen?"

Celestra confused reacts poorly. She still cannot accept that he managed to change into a panther. She honestly did not recognize him. Upset that he cannot understand that she had no clue, who he was, made her mad. She's only now digesting what happened.

"I didn't know it was you, Tarmax... please, I'm hurt already. Why add to my pain?

I'm very sorry Tarmax; it all seemed like a blur, for it happened so fast. I'm not really good at saying thank you. My social graces are quite remedial. I might have died if it wasn't for your quick thinking."

Tarmax relaxes finally, getting a small amount of appreciation. She tries to recall the events before she passed out. Remembering Meoneal's claws digging into her back legs almost made her faint. The thought of that drooling street rat makes her stomach turn inside out.

Seeing Tarmax throw Meoneal down like that told her two things: Either he's a true warrior, or he's just completely nuts.

His royal story was also brilliant. "Tarmax, I remember now. You didn't have to go that far; an attack would have been enough. You showed true courage and respect. I have to ask though: What was it that helped you turn into your panther form? Was it a free-willed transformation?"

"Well, watching you getting abused by that muck dragging mule, churned something inside of me. Maybe *this* is how I transformed accordingly. Really, I don't know Celestra."

Stunned, she pauses, and she stares at Tarmax drinking his grulo, then at the drunken partygoers. Wondering why this emotion seemed different from all the rest was confusing, but oddly familiar. *Is this love? Is this the feeling I've been searching for and its right under my nose? So much pain and anguish I've gone through to ensure love exists and when it's finally in front of me, I'm left speechless?* Tears start to well up in Celestra's eyes, and her lower jaw starts to quiver. Anxiety riddled her mind in a way she has never felt before. Tarmax raises his eyebrows watching her, and can feel her emotions shifting into a darker void. Instinctually, he pulls her into him and holds her tight. The tears can't be held back any longer as she softly sobs into his dark scaly chest. The two despite being surrounded by so many, are alone in their moment.

Drako noticing the two hybrids, tries to direct the others attention away quickly. Garsa pretends to ignore them.

Celestra's sobbing continues as Tarmax engulfs her in a tight embrace, to shelter staring eyes from gazing at her. He swallows his doubt and picks her up, taking her away from the banquet. Celestra caught up in her emotions realizes that Tarmax is taking her somewhere, yet still cannot stop crying. Walking out of the banquet hall, Tarmax looks up to the sky and wonders why love in this crazy world has to be this hard. Only a few days ago, it was simple living. Yet he drove himself away from home to go explore the world. Seeing this crazy conflict between the dragons and humans leaves Tarmax feeling hollow inside. *This is all about us. Hybrids; yet do they really think about the truth? Maybe we're not supposed to be here after all, and that's simply it.*

Looking down to Celestra, he sees her true self beneath the stern and strong nature she showed from before. Her femininity shined outward, but was terribly weak, mistreated, and abused. Celestra looks up at Tarmax and wonders herself why this all was coming together in this way. In deep thought she thinks,

Am I losing my mind, or, am I losing my grip on the warrior? Nudging Tarmax with her head, He puts her down on the ground. "What's up Celestra, why are you so upset?" She looks up at him and shows a weak smile, this isn't going to be easy for her to say. "I think I'm falling in love with you, but I can't seem to handle it. I've been fighting for so long in this frame of mind, in this chaotic world, that love seems so alien to me." His eyes widen as Tarmax misses a beat in his heart.

He agrees this is an alien emotion. Yet, the difference is he desires it wholeheartedly and welcomes it. "I've never really had anything destroy my faith in love, so I have no trouble trusting this, but if you need time, I will give you as much as you need. You are worth it, and never let anyone else tell you otherwise."

Celestra being so open with her words, starts to fidget uncontrollably. Tarmax watches her with endearment and kisses her face. "Would you like to go back in, I promise we can keep this to ourselves for now. Is that okay with you?" She nods her head and starts to clean herself as to not look frayed for the others inside. "Don't worry Celestra. You look wonderful, let's go."

With that, they walk back in to mingle a bit more. Whether or not this was something real, these hybrids swallow their fear and prepare for the journey ahead of them. These two creatures were trying so hard to find their real lineage and always felt so alone in their search. Now educated and awake, they both feel even more alone than ever before.

Chapter Thirty

Griffins Dance of Fury

Raspier wandered off with the other two ladies drunk on grulo, yet didn't realize he was just as drunk himself. In the garden maze, they chase each other playfully, while flying up occasionally cheating to see where the others are located. Laughing, growls, and squawks echo throughout the chill of the morning sunshine. Their voices fade with the settling dew. "Wow, it's been so long since I've had this much fun with my own kind. This is an eternal delight!" Tientara and Balutra run circles around him in the maze and he just lets them think they're getting one over on him. "Sisters, sisters; so much fur and feathers with so little time; how will we accomplish all of our desires?"

The girls run around to the center where they start to dig a hole in the ground. Planning to trick him, they dig it deep enough just for his head to stick out. Covering it with large palm leaves, they await his arrival to that part of the maze. "Won't it be funny to see him fall up to his neck in dirt? The little clean freak that he is..." Balutra says to Tientara. "Well funny for a moment, I guess, but we must help him out after." Balutra's getting the idea that her sister actually likes this stuffy griffin, gives her a peck on the head. "Ouch! What was that for?" Balutra stares her sister down in disgust for not knowing. "That was for your emotions getting in the way of our humorous manipulation, you don't actually like this bird brain, do you?" Tientara lowers her head and scratches the earth with her front leg. "Well, yes I do actually. What are you going to do about it?"

Balutra laughs at her younger sister. She pushes her head into the bushes and then goes out to lead Raspier into the trap. Preening her head feathers, Tientara reminisces about the times she felt stronger and smarter than her sister. Trying to figure out how it all changed is too baffling.

"Such a low-level breeder that one. No care for how things turn out after the fall..." Hearing them running fast in the distance, she starts to worry. "Oh, I have to make this fall apart on her somehow, but how?"

Looking around for something to put at the bottom of the pit to launch someone back out, wasn't that hard. The canopies hanging above the benches here would be perfect. Quickly ripping them down, she sets it up into the hole, checking that it's tight enough to bounce a griffin just once. Taking another one down, she covers the hole and then scratches dirt on top to mask its presence. Then she takes the palm leaves and places them in front of the hole.

This should trick Balutra into jumping straight into it. Finishing just in time, she knows to wink at Raspier and puff out her chest feathers to make him stop short. This, in turn, will give him enough time to see Balutra fall into the trap.

Both come running like bolts of lightning with wings tightly held into their body. Laughing and snarling they approach the bend fast. Balutra winks at Tientara and prepares to jump over the palm leaves. Tientara winks and ruffles her head feathers at Raspier. He stops short to stare at Tientara.

She feels the ground give way beneath her feet. Yelping in confusion, she goes down into the pit and bounced over the adjacent thick, brush wall. Squawking in fear as to just where she will fall, Balutra haphazardly plummets to her fate. Raspier hysterically laughs and topples over. Balutra falls to the ground with a thump. "Tientara, you brat, you foiled my trick! Get over here!"

Tientara grabbing Raspier's neck pulls him to fly off before she can get back, "This way, come now, she won't be able to get up that quick, hurry!"

Flying to this little tree nook, they hide to avoid the steaming Balutra. "Not to interrupt your shenanigans here, but I am the head of the party. I need to return shortly. Oh, and by the way, that was quick to get rid of your sister. Man, what a nasty griffin."

Tientara laughs because that was what Balutra said about him.

"Look, she set that pit up for you. I changed it to throw her over the wall. I happen to like you and for a change, I won't have her ruin it." Raspier blushes from her forwardness, "Wow, what a noble creature you are, thank you, Tien, you are quite the catch yourself I must add. Your sister actually seems to be the runt of the litter, is this true?" Tientara smirks, and giggles softly. "Well yes, she was also picked on for her lion ears. If you look really hard, she buries them under her head feathers." Raspier wonders about this odd little family feud he's stumbled in on.

He asks himself if it's even worth his time to pursue her. Then as he brings his head around to look at her, he sees Tientara cleaning her fur, with a leg gracefully dangling in the air.

Her tail swishes rhythmically to his heartbeat in sync. Sitting upright now, his brow raises, as he thinks about how he could even question this. *She is perfect. A supreme genetic beauty, with humbleness and grace. Mother Nature carved this one from stone and took quite some time I imagine.*

The morning light silhouettes her outline and absolutely drives Raspier crazy. Tientara looks back to Raspier and blushes at him staring so intently. "Oh, I see you must have found something you like, your pupils are highly dilated, or did you just get some sunlight caught in your eyes." Purring she smiles. Raspier highly embarrassed that he was caught, fell right out of the tree, and humbly apologizes.

Well, she sees, I'm interested. Clearing his throat, he readies to ask her that timeless question. He climbs back up to talk with her.

When he tried to open his mouth, only air escaped. Standing there with his claw extended out, she waits for his speech. Softly she chuckles at his goofy display and wonders if he will even be able to say what he wants to.

Seeing him squirm, proves his humility. This Balutra was wrong about. It's equally rewarding to see that sometimes underneath the facade of elegance and esteem, a real creature lives and breathes.

Tientara realizes that some things deserve more than just a quick glance. Raspier finally gets up the nerve to say his speech as Tientara is perched very patiently. "Tien, well what I think I'm trying to get to here is that I think it would be nice to see you. Uh, well...Umm, you know...take you out and...Hmm..." Raspier, for the first time, is left speechless; no matter how hard he tries the words won't come.

Tien feels him, hard. Without giving it one chance for it to choke his lungs, she flies down and rubs her head across his beak. Gently she starts to curl her body around his, entangling her tail into his own. Speechless still, Raspier is beginning to understand sometimes words aren't the right form of communication. No word can replace basic body language; especially when your heart is the one doing the talking. In the distance, they faintly hear her sister calling out for her, but they just let it fade with the stars.

One of Raspier's ravens, swoops past the two love birds, headed towards the commotion further into the courts. Down below him, he sees the drunken mass losing steam. It chuckles. Seems birds have a good sense of humor.

Celestra and Tarmax notice everything is winding down. They are scared some may have noticed their moments. They look around and see.

Garsa and Partune are in a challenging game of hurtly with old crystals. Lastra is playing with the small ones running around. Some are even sleeping in a pillow nook in the corner of the room. Drako was helping already with the clean-up, as Avalo, is staring out at the shifting morning sun.

A good number of the guests are still dancing at this point. They're all very drunk but are outnumbered by the guests collecting their young and belongings approaching the door.

The sun is almost fully up, if that's not a clue on how late it is, their dizzy headaches will be later.

Tarmax sees Avalo by the window and wonders why he seems so down and far away. Getting used to his cryptic mannerisms was enough, but to see him lost in his head shows that he too is just like the rest of them.

Celestra at the same time, was trying to piece together this strange change she felt inside. *I was so used to being alone. There was no one to answer to, no one to care for, only opponents to fight. It was a solitary life.*

Avalo, also catches Celestra's attention. Getting Tarmax, the two of them wander over to him wondering what's wrong. "Daydreams and dragon tails, that's all I have left..." They hear him mutter under his breath. Leaving their own dilemmas behind them, they go to tend to Avalo Ryu. Tarmax comes up behind him and swats him with his tail, hoping to get a good reaction. Avalo turns his head and affectionately stares him down. With a twist of his tail tip, Tarmax's nose twitches to spill out a sneeze. Clearing his throat, he backs off.

Celestra, can see through the veil, covering this old mystic. "Have you lost something Avalo? To be poetic, it seems your heart has left for another sea, and your body now floats helplessly in the currents. Why so down?"

Celestra hoping her words could trigger something from him, gets nothing.

Avalo just continues to stare out the window. "Should we leave you be, Avalo?" Tarmax asks.

He sighs, realizing these two aren't going to leave him alone. "No, you two just caught me reminiscing about a time when my heart was free from guilt. The moonlight earlier reminded me of a night with a very special lady, but that was a long time ago." Both Tarmax and Celestra are catching the spark floating around invading their minds tonight; love. With all this celebrating it's bound to be drawn up from the past. Celestra asks if he would like to talk about it. "Well I'll tell you this; I will have to see that blue-eyed memory soon, whether or not things can be resolved. There is a real reason for needing her aid. Just wish I'd held my promise to her so long ago. Things could have been different."

Understanding this is about the white dragon, both of them see that Avalo was once involved with her somehow. Just before Celestra and Tarmax could ask another question, a griffin crashes straight into the banquet table by the door.

"Tientara where are you! Crafty little sidewinder. I will rip this place apart to find you!" Balutra screams out.

Drako sees this griffin has a terrible rage disorder. Calmly walking in between, her and the rest of the party, he stands with his arms folded behind his back. Clearly displaying proper body language, "Is there a problem young lady? I would truly like it if you would lower your voice, for there are other people here enjoying themselves, and you are disturbing them. You shouldn't be in the courts anyway without invitation."

Eyes red with anger, Balutra headbutts him and thinks this will move him out of the way; however, Drako is incredibly strong and some little female griffin won't be the first to learn the way. He picks her up from the back of her neck, and holds her feet in his hands, preventing her from moving, "Look I asked nicely, now you've tried my patience. Who is this *Tientara* and why ruin *our* party? Obviously, she isn't here. Wait; I recognize you… You are one of the females who was talking with Raspier earlier. If he has done something to you to make you this upset, please understand you will get nowhere by being angry. Now *calmly* tell me what happened and *maybe* I will help you."

Balutra slowly calming down started to feel a little embarrassed, that she was subdued. She gives in only to get out of this faster, "I apologize, but my sister and Raspier tricked me into falling into a trap. She wanted him all to herself.

She ran off with him, and left me not even caring if I was hurt." Softly faking tears, she stiffens up and tries to make her lies believable. Drako seems concerned, but wary of this. Raspier has made some bad choices for mates but none this deviant and destructive. Whispering in the corner is Avalo, Tarmax, and Celestra. Drako calls them over to help in this situation. Now sitting on the ground released from Drako's grasp, Balutra hopes her story wins them over so she doesn't have to admit the truth in the matter. Avalo now driven away from his misery turns to her with his same old cryptic self; he's already brewing some trouble up.

Walking over to the dramatic griffin, Avalo continues to get closer and closer to her until Balutra is met by his muzzle pressed against her beak. Balutra gulps at the enormously radiant energy this dragon emanates, and she feels him rummaging through her head for the truth without permission. Quickly she knows to believe her own lie to make this work. All her thoughts revolve around her story and all the workings that would make it true. Drako stands with arms crossed. He knows no mind can escape Avalo's grasp; that is except for

Lu'barthrow. Drako sits for a second and looks about. He realizes that sneaky panther is still missing.

Chapter Thirty One

Lu'barthrow's Final Straw

Earlier in the night, Lu'barthrow was still pouting alone in the city ruins. He has been up to something dark despite his good soul. All light inside of him is blocked by rage and bitterness. The darkness engulfs his mind and heart like a virus. Grunting and swatting rubble next to the broken-down dwelling he stayed at so often, Lu'barthrow continues to let his anger sicken him. Enough time has passed that he feels compelled to check up on Meoneal. The old saber has no idea how he was tricked and sadly may never. It takes a real deviant mind to pull one over on Meone and Lu'barthrow would rather not know such a creature. "That prissy lioness stole that whelp from right under his muzzle."

He decides to go back to his cart. Lu'barthrow walks out of the ruins towards the street. Morning has arrived and it's time to find him. Even if Meone wishes to turn him away, he must try to help. Running back to Meoneal's cart he sees his old master quite wounded and badly limping. It was so shocking he stopped short. He had a feeling it had to do with that shady lioness. He can smell her scent lingering. It strangely seems familiar.

Calling out, he runs fast towards him. "Meoneal, are you alright? What happened to you?" Growling under his breath, he barely acknowledges him standing there. Instead, he continues to repair everything as best as he could. "Meoneal, did you hear me?"

Lu'barthrow, starts to worry about his affiliation with the courts. He wonders if Meoneal will take it out on him. Meoneal turns around and Lu'barthrow can see that both his teeth are missing. Dried blood still caked his bottom jaw. Limping from both back legs, he painfully picks up his herbs from the floor.

Seeing his slow pace, it's obvious he has been doing this for hours. "Here let me help you Meone, there is way too much stuff here." Realizing Meoneal is ignoring him he starts to help anyway. Instantly the saber turns and scratches Lu'barthrow away. "Get out of here black paw, you've done enough with your fancy stuck-up friends, leave me to my rubble that was once my livelihood, and let me keep the one last thing I have left, my *pride*!" Yet again Lu'barthrow continues this sick cycle between the two sides of society. Looking at Meoneal, he sees two separate personalities: The brutish master manipulator who can get out of anything, and then there is the old lion who wishes to just live and be left alone. One who has learned the horrors of reality and survived them all, yet still manages to have fun despite. Then in that moment Meoneal turns to him and sits staring intently at him. Watching his movements, he sees that his mask is off as well as his pride.

A softer side to Meoneal is creeping out of his tattered seams. An effortless and tired sigh spills out to ruffle his fur. "Lu'barthrow, you are one of the few who could see through me. You seem to read me better than I read myself. All my life I've only been running from the fate that has become this truth in front of you. There is no real secret to life; it's just a game of cat and mouse. Energy transfers and energy fades to the next. Sadness is the realization of this, and happiness is nothing more than a chemical in the brain. If this is the only thing you remember in life, you will succeed."

Meoneal knows he's beat, and it seems his importance in this world has faded. Walking away from his cart he feels life tug at his soul to repent for the last time. Refusing to give up his pride, he lets it choke his last few words, "Never think though that you can make it alone. That was my greatest mistake. That little whelp was my last attempt at having a family. I failed it seems."

With that moment now fading, Meoneal sinks to the ground, finally leaving this plane behind him. Lu'barthrow has no idea how to react, for his only real companion has just died due to the court's paws and claws.

If Meone had some more time to be shown the light, his soul might have been saved. Growls curl out from below Lu'barthrow's whiskers, and claws firmly dig the earth up from beneath him. Eyes straight and narrow, he knows he must avenge his death.

The warrior inside him has just been given his first assignment. Lu'barthrow's eyes gleam red with fury, as the hybrid gene takes over. Out of his fur, huge wings sprawl out, covered with black scales. His head shapes into the build of a dragon, yet with enormous curled horns. His body elongates into a stout black dragon yet mixed with horse genetics. Snorting and still full of rage, the beast inside pushes him to go; however, he drags Meoneal to the tall grasses first and starts to cover him in large stones. Growling out of fury, Lu'barthrow places the stones with care.

When finished, he dusts the sad pauper's grave with the proper herbs to protect his misguided soul, as he enters the after world. Now the time has come for Lu'barthrow to become his true design; in spirit, in body and in mind.

Lu'barthrow enraged starts the hunt for whomever did this to his dear old friend. The Sad thing is he doesn't know his own flesh and blood is responsible. Soon, everyone will learn Lu'barthrow's true inner pain.

Chapter Thirty Two

Griffin Family Feud

Raspier and Tien are cuddling, practically falling asleep on each other, when Raspier hears Drako calling him. Inner ears perked. they both pay close attention. "Who's that Raspi? Someone is calling you?"

Utterly embarrassed that he's been gone this long, now sobering up from the grulo, Raspier realizes something is wrong for Drako to be calling for him. "I wonder what he wants." As if life planned this out, Tien and Raspier hear Balutra calling for her, apparently putting on some overblown act.

"Oh sister… I'm worried about you." Tientara hisses out of frustration. It seems her sister has won over Raspier's friends with a wild story. "Geeze that griffin is rotten to the bone. I'm sure she has already deceived your friends by saying some outlandish version of what happened, knowing they will try to act accordingly."

Raspier, not looking forward to a feathery family feud, tries to soothe Tientara.

"I'm sure they can see through something like that, Avalo is the king of truth. Can't verbally stray him, nor mentally. He'll get to the bottom of all of this I'm sure." Tien laughs at Raspier due to his poor knowledge of her sister. "Well, he just met his nemesis, Balutra the backtracking skink." They both fly down to see Drako, Avalo, and Balutra standing outside the maze. "What is this I hear about tricking your sister, Tientara? I don't think that was very nice of you, she's terribly upset and barged into the party ballistic." Drako huffs out.

That's why her name is what it is...Balutra; the Ballistic Griffin; Hmph. Tien thinks.

Avalo turns to Tien and smiles. She feels something funny. *Is Avalo, poking around in my head?*

Making sure no one was looking at him, Avalo shakes his head softly at her, *"Yes"*. Tien smiles back in comfort.

Balutra, laying it on really thick, looks up at her sister with tears in her eyes. "Tien, why yet again do you wish to tease me and embarrass me in front of all these royal folks? I wasn't going to go for that griffin anyway, besides it seems he's already made his choice." She says faking more tears.

Tientara expects nothing less from her sister. Trying to make her out to be the bad guy. "Balutra, I have to ask, why bother these creatures during their party? Did you even consider if they wanted to get involved in the first place?" Knowing that statement could be taken the wrong way, she keeps an eye on Avalo, to see what he feels. He refrains from a physical acknowledgment but in Tientara's mind, she feels him watching. Raspier can't believe that someone could be this deviant and manipulative, and he stares down Balutra looking for her lion ears. Seeing that he's looking for them, Balutra firmly presses them into her head. *That should remind you what you are; a genetic misprint.* Raspier thinks.

Drako understands the situation, so he decides to leave it between Tientara and Balutra. Motioning to Raspier to go back, he tells Avalo to stay behind and keep the peace in the shadows. Nodding his head, he fades into the background. Raspier looks to Tien and knows to walk away. Anything else, will anger her sister. "Drako and I are going back to the party to clean up, I will see you later. Tientara, you know where to meet me."

Balutra surprised they aren't staying, panics. Walking back over to Drako she nudges his arm with her beak. "Aren't you going to help me?" Drako turns to her with a cold and bothered look. "We did find your sister, and the rest is not our business." With that, the sisters stared at each other full of rage.

Drako walks away, feeling the tension between Tientara and Balutra. Raspier frazzled, looks over at him.

"Thanks…I needed backup." He smiles and they calmly walk back to what's left of the party. Some family feuds should stay in the family.

Chapter Thirty Three

Love Finally Free

Celestra and Tarmax stayed behind to help out with the clean-up and to convince the night owls it was time to go home. "I'm fine, don't bother me, please...just leave me alone." An old drunken tortoise mutters out slurred. Looking up at Celestra he sees two instead of one. "Wow, twins, you must be a lot of fun; 'Hick-up'..." Grumbling with a low brow, she stares at this pathetic excuse for an animal. "Look, sir, you have to go home now, the banquet is over." Stumbling as he tries to get up, the tortoise ends up flipping onto his back. "Now that's not nice... moving so fast I fall over, and why are you two upside-down?"

Celestra sighs at him, trying to lift him to his green feet. He's much too heavy for her.

"Man, grr, you're very uh, strong sir, come on help me get you up, I am no slave to drunken fools." The tortoise bends his head around to look at her. "Why such sticks in the mud girls, there is no need, besides there is two of you, can't you both cooperate?"

Frustrated this tortoise is taking up so much of her energy, she decides to get Tarmax. He's presently watching all of this, snickering.

"I don't think this is that funny, Tar. Can you please help me get this guy out of here?" Remembering back to how that raven just watched him laughing, he gives in and picks the drunken tortoise up from his back.

"Thank you, guys. ::Hiccup:: Apparently, these two prissy cats aren't as strong as the both of you." Laughing hysterically at this drunken mad tortoise with double vision, he tells him to go straight home, hoping he will listen. Judging by his frame of mind, he might not even remember where home is.

Celestra finishes up with the drunken guests on her side of the ballroom, as Tarmax has a few left on his. Finally, the two of them can relax for a while... or so they think.

Not really fixating on the emotional moment they shared earlier, Celestra has managed to center herself again. She starts to pick up a few loose things to put in a lost and found crate. Feeling Tarmax watching her, she stops what she's doing.

"I notice when you look at me like that, it sends this tickle throughout my body, not sure why it is or what it does, but I'm trying to clean here. It's very distracting." He sends her an engaging glance in return. "Oh, really, distracting huh? Well, what if I was to do this then." Instantly he turns into his panther form and rolls onto his back. "Better your highness?" Smiling and blushing she can no longer ignore that growing tickle. Her body heat rises and she begins to stalk him slowly from behind the table she was standing by. Growling softly, she creeps along the floor perfectly in rhythm to his heartbeat, as if not to make a noise he could decipher. Tarmax still getting used his feline form, is terrible at stalking properly. Feeling confident, he lets her surround him in tight circles like he was the prey. Giggling to himself, he finally sees how wonderful flirting can be. Taking this slow will be much more worth it. Tarmax plays this game of cat and mouse eagerly.

She feels her heart practically beat out of her chest, as she gets closer and closer. Then as if both were prepped in the matter, she lunges onto him, and instinctually they begin rubbing necks and heads. Purrs and growls resonated throughout the ballroom. The sunlight peaks through a thin line above the mountains in the distance.

Quietly in the kitchen, Garsa leaves before it gets serious, for these two definitely will be the predecessors of the great Garlock himself. The hybrid race never had such a good pairing since

Bardone and Celestaria. These were Celestra and Lu'barthrow's parents. Only right that she would keep the genetic line improving. Tarmax's parents are still unknown, and maybe in the midst of searching for Uniqua, Celestaria, and Sarclaw, all of their whereabouts will be revealed. There is a future for these hybrids and it seems already written into history.

Celestra and Tarmax play fight together like night meeting day. Paws pulling, snarls of joy spit out in between licks of passion. Tarmax has never experienced such bliss before, let alone known what real love is. Celestra has only seen the darker side of love. Lust was her only interaction from those stray felines in her area, let alone none of them was even her kind.

"This is so incredible, and we're just courting. Tarmax you are quite the gentleman I must say." She says between pawing his back in play. The two of them lie together in heavenly rapture by the intensity of their touch. Knowing the others will be back soon, they realize they need to cut it out. "Uh, Tarmax, could we just keep this between us? Cause, well I'm not really sure what I'm doing in the first place..." Tarmax tilts his head to the side and affectionately stares at her for a moment.

"Anything you desire, Celestra. When Drako found you, Partune, in turn, found me. You've helped me in more ways than I can ever explain. To this, I hope we can build a future together, but I will keep my distance." With that, he grabs a tiger lily from the vase and snaps the stem off in his mouth. Turning into his dragon form, he places it, behind her ear. Realizing, he's ignoring his left brain by being more romantic, Celestra beams with delight.

Apparently, I've found my match....

Tarmax and her walk outside before taking a nap to watch the sunrise. Seeing the rays of red, gold and blue dart in and out of the clouds fuels their peaceful souls.

The colors looked like ribbons. Slowly, they weaved in and out of the dawning day. This puts a pure smile on Celestra's face. She is happy without a question. This is because, for one day in her life, she saw the sunrise knowing where she came from. Her spirit is in the sunrise, and it is at peace. Now with Tarmax by her side, she feels no matter the battle, no matter the feat needed to master, they will be together helping each other.

He turns to gaze at his love, lit, by the colors of morning. Her eyes are sparkling in every color imaginable. They glow with a light that renders all sunrises before, incomplete. The two enjoy their company before finally curling up with each other in Tarmax's room.

Raspier and Drako, had already slipped into bed. Raspier obviously has forgotten to visit Tien. Knowing today is the quest outside of the city limits, they all try to get some sleep before starting the long road ahead. They will be traveling the great northern trail to the white dragon. All dream of the new discoveries that lie, on their road ahead.

Chapter Thirty Four

Tracking the Run Away

Chirps of birds, echo, throughout the dry leaves of the trees. Animals surrounding the city are preparing for the harsh weather. Their instincts triggered them, to store food and fat. The greggils move faster to build this castle more than ever with Lord Cannor gone. None knowing why he has disappeared; the level of nervousness grows within their gossip.

Trea'sten, Cannor's right-hand man, tries to direct the men as best as he can, running Cannor's directions over in his head. "That crazy man, I wonder where he ran off to with all this work to be done. Tis a better thing though; I can help the men get their needed rest to work properly. He works them in the wrong way, to where they need to drop for two days without opening their eyes."

Surveying the group of men, Trea'sten sees they're much happier with him as their master. Men work harder when they're taken care of. He hopes it's possible they can finish the bulk of the work by late fall. By winter, they certainly will need shelter with a roof.

Heading back to the manor, Trea'sten goes to pick up a few items the men requested. Looking around for them, he sees a note by the stables. Written incredibly fast, he looked puzzled over it for a moment. The name it clearly intended for is Trea'sten's, but making out the scribbled words after was impossible. "This looks like Cannor's writing but it's so distressed, I'm not sure what it says." Instead of wasting time on figuring it out, Trea'sten gives up.

Giving it one last look, he tilts his head to one side, letting his sandy colored hair flop, in his eyes in front of his glasses. "Hmph, well if it was so important, he would have written it better. This is of no help to me now." Seeing that he couldn't use the letter, he threw it out next to the stables. Lord Cannor will not be pleased, but he brought it upon himself.

On the adjacent fence to where the old stable muck was, a raven still on the lookout by orders of Raspier sees Trea'sten throw the letter. Wondering if it could be of any help to the dragons back at the city, he waits for him to leave before he picks it up. Grabbing it, he immediately heads back to Raspier.

Still in pursuit of his lost horse, Lord Cannor approaches a small lake. There were signs that animals were there recently. Jumping off his horse, he inspects the surrounding area. Seeing the scratch marks in the dirt were from a bear and a horse, he thought the worst. Upon further inspection, he saw traces of fresh blood, about a day or two old. Figuring that it belonged to Tarmax, he quickly mounted his horse to follow his trail further. Seeing the tracks kick into a full gallop, he wonders how hurt he could be going at that speed. "What are you up to, Tarmax?"

The plains in front of Cannor are quite long and the afternoon approaches quickly. He packed just enough food for two days and hopes he will find his renegade horse before nightfall.

Chapter Thirty Five

The Unknown Hybrid

Celestra and Tarmax unravel from their tightly knit ball, stretch out and almost forgot in their sleepy state that today was the journey. Surprised no one woke them up, they frantically get ready to find the others and set out.

"Where the heck *are* they? I can't see anyone around anywhere." Tarmax looks at Celestra, "Neither do I. Do you think they would have left without us?" Celestra yawns and stretches out with muscles twitching. "No, they can't because I heard Lu'barthrow saying that they need at least one hybrid to speak with the white dragon."

Celestra stops for a moment, realizing she hasn't seen Lu'barthrow since early yesterday evening. He mustn't be doing well. Just then, Lastra pokes her head in through their window. "Hello lovebirds, ready for the journey? We've been waiting on you two, so, get with it. We let you sleep a bit later since you two cleaned up the ballroom last night." Both blushing at her comment, they agree and follow her.

Walking along with Lastra and Tarmax, Celestra feels a pull in her heart, about lying to her own brother. *It would have been worse trying to free Yewdrone as myself. Besides, Lu'barthrow is a trickster as well. Now meeting him, I could never leave him behind. Yet he always seems to want his space.*

Looking over at Lastra, she wants to ask her where Yewdrone is, but is wary. Surely, he's with the others, and probably asking to go on the journey despite his youth. He seems just as stubborn and prideful as Lu'barthrow.

Watching Tarmax chat up a storm with Lastra, was refreshing. He in is dragon form gracefully walking, certainly was a pleasant distraction. *I still feel with him by my side anything is possible. We can accomplish whatever we put our minds to...* Celestra begins to realize how powerful love is. This was a gift being able to watch it grow and blossom. Tarmax looks over to her and throws her a sentimental look.

As the three walk towards the courts, neither realize a bizarre creature is relentlessly charging towards them.

Coming up from behind, in a surprise attack, it pins Tarmax to the ground by his throat with its immense horns. The ladies scream out in fear. "Where is Garsa, take me to him you filthy hybrid." Twisting out from its hold, Tarmax quickly jumps up, grabs it by the horns, flipping it onto its back.

"Who do you think you are, you nasty beast, and why should I tell you anything with an attitude like that?" While Tarmax firmly holds it down, Lastra comes up from behind and grabs its hindquarters. Celestra instantly runs to an old cart to tear off some rope to tie him down. With the two of them holding the grunting animal, Celestra catches her breath and ties up his feet to keep him from attacking again. "I will get loose and you'll all be very sorry." The beast snorts out of rage. Tarmax laughs at his hostility, "*Who* are you?" Angrily it spits at Tarmax before speaking. "Why do you ask me such a stupid question Tarmax?"

Stunned it knew his name, Tarmax wonders how he could possibly know this being. He hasn't been here for that long to gain a new enemy. Tarmax looks deep into his red eyes and tries to link the inner knowledge of his name to his own. Slowly a stir inside him starts to tell him that this is a hybrid. "I'll ask again nicely: Who *are* you... hybrid?"

Intrigued he can sense his own kind, he laughs. "Well, you're so good at sensing things... figure it out yourself, Tarmax." Celestra and Lastra stand around the beast stunned over his rage. Wondering what on earth could have triggered it, was what bothered them. Tarmax catches his breath and stares deeply into his eyes again. He begins to see a cart and that Meoneal character very weak. Seemingly cleaning and tidying up the shambled cart, the saber seems quite lethargic. Looking deeper Tarmax sees he is viewing the situation through the eyes of this unknown hybrid.

Standing closer to Meoneal, he starts to talk to him, yet Tarmax cannot make out what he is saying. This cart seller seemed raw, without any harshness, and something pure about him touches Tarmax. At that moment Meoneal drops and breathes his last breath.

Tarmax shutters because he knows he is the reason this old saber has died. Judging by the appearance of its face, he was apparently very close to him. Feeling terrible that Meoneal was dead, Tarmax is put into a troubling situation. Rage was still overwhelming the hybrid, while the three of them were perplexed what to do. Tarmax tells Celestra and Lastra to go meet with the others. Celestra obviously objects and looks puzzled at Tarmax, "Why Tar? What will you do with him?" Pulling her to the side, he explains that Meoneal is dead and that it was from when he had to defend her. "This hybrid knew him." Celestra understands the honor he must uphold.

Nodding her head, she walks back with Lastra. "I wonder who that hybrid is. His voice seems so familiar, but I can't place it." She tells Celestra.

Celestra's skin crawls knowing she is the reason Meoneal is dead. Worried her lie has gone too far, she cringes.

Lastra equally worried looks to the little panther. "Celestra, you do know Tarmax is much bigger in his other form, right?" Celestra agrees but knows from experience, wrath overpowers any size. That pattern of rage seemed very familiar for it matched hers. Still confused, Celestra attempts to figure it out while walking back to the others. Her mind refuses to let it go.

With all this hostility brewing, Lastra feels better if she grabs Celestra to fly back to the others.

Celestra can fly herself, but shows no objection. Dragons are faster, and she's already exhausted.

Approaching the courts, the group was a bit restless. They finally land in the main square. "What took you guys so long?" Partune says. "Hey, where's Tarmax? Is everything okay?" Lastra and Celestra attempt to explain the situation as best as possible.

Their told, Tarmax feels obligated to honor the death of Meoneal, by letting the creature fight him. Avalo showing interest in this hybrid starts to ask a few questions about it. Lastra and Celestra, describe it as best as they can, while noticing Avalo's face deepening in thought. "You all start your journey. I will meet up with you later. I think it would be best if I tend to this situation since it does involve hybrids..." Garsa nods at his old friend.

He motions to the rest to start walking towards the north gate. Looking back at Avalo, he smiles. "May the first dragon stay by your side. I know you are good with hybrids but this one seems to have lost it totally. Be careful." He smirks, shaking his head low at his friend. Slanting his eyes at Garsa, he turns and flies towards the two male hybrids. Garsa sighs and watches him fly off.

Most are uncomfortable leaving without Avalo and Tarmax, but the ones who know Avalo, are aware he has handled much worse situations. He will without a doubt make sure these two will not kill each other along with him. So they start heading for the white dragon's city of 'corns, and the whereabouts of their lost companions.

Celestra's heart hurts with a pain never felt before, and slowly as she walks tears trickle out from her eyes. "I wish you a steadfast claw, and may your noble heart protect you above all, Tarmax."

Somewhere in her thoughts, Celestra begins to think that this innocent emotional connection could possibly be all in her mind. Slowly Celestra begins to doubt her love. How could something start so quickly yet become as strong as an oak tree, in no time? Turning one last time to look down the city street, she sets her heart free for the journey ahead, praying Tarmax will join up with them later.

Avalo sees Tarmax restraining this strange animal. Eyeing this combination between a panther, a horse, and a winged dragon, he attempts to figure out what it looked like before this mutation. Seeing these different species combined, he imagines it's some sort of trinity hybrid, to have the capabilities to perform this level of transformation. Yet upon a closer investigation, he sees that he's not seasoned in transforming, like himself, yet even newer to it. "I have to tell you something unknown hybrid that you won't like very much." The hybrid picks his restrained head up and stares at Tarmax. "Oh, try me Tarmax; too much has already happened for me to care any longer." Tarmax bows, and humbly explains. "You see your friend Meoneal attacked my…friend, and almost took her against her will. I was sent to protect her and make sure she was not harassed. What kind of creature would go back on his word, and then attack the very spirit trying to make peace?"

Tarmax sees the unknown hybrid breathing heavy, seeing smoke, billow out from its nostrils. "Keep talking Tarmax, you fool! I desire to hear how you mangled my master!"

The hybrids eyes grow darker and even more filled with rage. Tarmax holds his stance and with control, continues.

"Well, I couldn't stand to watch him shredding through her. So, I attacked. I jumped him in panther form..." The hybrid laughs, "You, a panther Tarmax; now I've got to see that!"

Pausing, Tarmax waits to see if there would be any further interruptions,

"The fight was equal, and I think that his wounds ended up being fatal because of his age. That saber lion was no easy match. My companion was badly injured by Meoneal, and it was a deserved attack to save her. He took her without permission."

Lu'barthrow was calm only for a second and then became enraged all over again. "May I ask the female's name, no, better yet, I'll tell it to you...It was Garlochia; that court brat!" Tarmax sees this is going to get even more complicated. *No need in telling him Celestra's real name...*

The strange hybrid enraged growls and tries to free itself again from the restraints. "That little court tramp got what she deserved. A little roughness to remind her she cannot bully creatures with her royalty. Too bad he didn't knock her up, for she would have to raise those cubs knowing the price of lies. She practically stole his helper in exchange for a fake document, some grulo, and a few measly drogs. Damn brat should have been killed instead of Meoneal!" The creature spat to disgrace her further. The two hybrids stare each other down, but Tarmax controls his anger.

Lu'barthrow can't take it anymore. "Grr, let me out of this and fight for the honor to still live. If you have any honor, you common barn horse."

Feeling the pain on that low comment, he unties the creature to fight. Instantly the enraged hybrid swipes its claws at Tarmax but misses. Knowing they need to change into matching forms of strength, he tries to arrange a moment where they can at least pause.

"Look, I defended a friend, and it in turn, created havoc for you. So out of respect for your connection with Meoneal, let's fight the hybrid way, if you are familiar with that. If not, I will tell you about it." The creature seems to be itching at the chance to fight the killer of Meoneal.

"So, the great trinity hybrid, is my master's killer. How should I make you pay?"

"Lu'barthrow, why such hostility for me, this Meoneal character meant this much to you?"

Stopping in his tracks, Lu'barthrow realizes he lost his cover. "Well, you're not as stupid as you look horse. Congratulations for seeing past my facade of horns, claws, and might. I too am a trinity, but Avalo decided to keep it from me. I am beginning to see that they all kept me down because they were jealous of my abilities.

Meoneal was the only creature I had, that showed me reality. Now, he is gone, because of some ridiculous trick to free a whelp, that knew no better." Tarmax truly feels bad for him, as it seems his trust in life is destroyed, *but why on earth could he not see that it was Meoneal that poisoned his mind?* Lu'barthrow and Tarmax change to their horse forms, and interestingly enough, they look very similar. Lu'barthrow is slightly smaller though and all in black. Locked dead on, they stare at each other emotionless like statues.

Manes blowing in the wind, and hooves dragging through the dirt, they await the point of battle. Lu'barthrow trembles with anxiety, and desires so to watch Tarmax bleed to death, as poor Meoneal had.

In an instant, Lu'barthrow runs and headbutts Tarmax, with such force it throws him backward. "Rage will get you nowhere when your mind is poisoned by it," Tarmax grunts out. Running past him, he jumps off the side of the building to throw a stronger headbutt at his side knocking Lu'barthrow over.

Kicking up quickly, he retorts, "So you lived your whole miserable life as a horse, how does that make this an equal fight? You are less of a hybrid of honor then most think, but I can conquer you despite." Fully charging at Tarmax, Lu'barthrow runs up to him stopping short just before his face. Tarmax didn't budge one inch, instead snorts in laughter. "Why do you think I will get as angry as you? Don't you see I'm aware that I've harmed you? Besides, fighting out of anger will only bring broken legs." Lu'barthrow now puzzled by Tarmax's calmness even in the midst of a serious opponent, stops his mind from raging.

Tarmax notices he has his attention. "Quite frankly Lu'barthrow, I must add, your trinity form is really interesting. It seems to be a combination of a horse, a dragon, and a panther. Would you mind changing again?" Hoping that he can trick Lu'barthrow out of his rage, he continues to remain mellow.

"I suppose so Tarmax, we don't seem to be getting anywhere with this battle anyway. I'm sure I can rip out your throat either way. Ah, to think, finally, I am a fully transformable hybrid; a trinity hybrid. Strong, intelligent and dashing quite frankly. Grandfather would be proud. You know Tarmax; I really don't give you enough credit. Here you are amongst new creatures, a new way of life, the fresh realization you are a hybrid, and now the resulted death of a mere cart seller from his own greedy acts. I should really care less about that muck licker, but for some reason, it feels great to finally get my anger out, and right now, you are my target."

Tarmax realizing Lu'barthrow is actually talking himself out of fighting, he decides not to interrupt him. Hoping he will smarten up over this whole thing, Tarmax just listens with baited breath. He can see his eyes turning from red to green, ever so slowly.

Lu'barthrow speaks, "Something told to me once comes to mind. You can't make it in this world alone, no matter how you strive. This despite Meoneal's death shows me something more than he was worth. All of you blindly trusted me, even when I was deliberately pushing you away, plotting how to turn things around and ruin your connections. Then it came down to you and your honor. Even though you ended up being the killer of Meoneal, you stand here ready to fight because of my respect for him. I must say, it really seems dishonorable for me to continue this debauchery. You really are noble Tarmax. Despite how much I want to hate you, I just cannot." Lowering his head Lu'barthrow finally feels how his bitterness has almost robbed him of true friends."

"Hey, nothing personal, but did Avalo tell you what to say?" Tarmax stirred a bit from the comment, looks perplexed, "Uh, why would you say that?" Lu'barthrow points with his muzzle to the corner across from where they are standing.

"I know you can't see him, but he's been standing there the whole time. I know he cannot penetrate my head, but he sure as hell can get through yours, nothing personal though."

Tarmax laughs and calls out to Avalo to see if it's just a joke. Apparently, Lu'barthrow was correct.

"Well, well Lu'barthrow, you never fail to impress me with your abilities. In fact, for your information, I didn't tell you about your genes because of your rage disorder. It would have caused more damage to you and to other as I can already see. That needs to be taken care of before you can advance. A bitter soul only ends up destroying himself. " Turning back to his panther form, he crouches lower into the ground to show his humbleness, something he's finally growing used to, but slowly.

"Well, shall we go meet up with the others now that this dispute has been settled?" Avalo urges. Tarmax looks to Lu'barthrow, hoping he's calm down now. He is fully aware that killing Meoneal was a hard blow for him. It would have been like someone killing his surrogate mother. This may leave a silent scar on Tarmax, but it was also just the trick to show him that not everything in life was so clean cut.

Nothing was black and white. There were only shades of grey. Lu'barthrow and Tarmax just sit for a second and absorb the meaning in this moment. They've both experienced much change and pain. Ironically. it all had to do with one creature, Celestra. If neither of them had met her, who knows what they would have known. Much is gained, much is lost. By resolving their differences, both see it's time to move on. Tarmax and Lu'barthrow have found their inner resolve.

Following up on the north pass, the three remain silent. The shuffle of their slow walk, beats out the rhythm of consciousness. The turn of seasons has begun, as these young hybrids have learned. Change is the only thing that stays the same. Still, Tarmax did not reveal Celestra's name as the lioness. It would only complicate things. At the moment, he was too tired to care. Avalo however, was quick to catch the whole disturbance in his head. It will not forgotten.

Chapter Thirty Six

Tarmax's Last Stand

The raven flies as fast as he can, to alert them of the message he'd found, by Cannor's barn. Little does the raven know he will pass Lord Cannor, almost at the second lake, where Tarmax passed in pursuit of the city. Continuing onward, the raven fades quickly into the horizon. Lord Cannor galloping up to the lake sees his horse is terribly exhausted. The horse shivers sweating in the cold wind. Stopping, he lets his horse drink and eat.

While wiping down the sweat from the horses back, he remembers something. Something he'd almost forgotten about up until now. Because he is so near to the city, Cannor has this sense of restlessness. The wall to the city produces an effect on greggils that causes them to turn completely around, or create internal distractions of the mind, so irritating, they cannot help but wander off in another direction. Cannor being so stubborn denies this feeling as long as he can.

Slowly he regresses back to his childhood, as he chews his jerky and fresh bread.

When Cannor was young, about seven, he was quite the little adventurer. Always looking for something to track or discover despite his father's harsh words of discontent. One day, he ran around to the stable hand's house in the far right of his father's land, to pick up the worker's daughter Carmine.

He and the little red-haired freckled-faced girl, were dear friends. Often, they would play together. Once they had run off to the edge of Shackle River, west of his father's castle, and saw a tree had fallen.

They happily crossed it.

Their eyes lit up with wonder over this new find. Instantly they split up, to see if there was anything they hadn't found before. Carmine had found some interesting bugs under a rock and was studying them closely. Cannor, whose first name is actually Prudence, saw something white, jump out from the tall grasses in front of him. Running over to it, he calls for Carmine to check it out with him. Both of them come to find a small white panther hiding in the grass. Terrified, the creature runs but Cannor and Carmine were right on its tail. They chased it across the entire area until it was finally exhausted and couldn't run any longer. Cornering it by a tree, Carmine approaches it. "It's so cute Prudence! We should bring it home and keep it as a pet!" She walks over closer and tries to touch it, but Cannor sees it's ready to attack and warns her to back up. Stubborn as a mule, Carmine refuses; the cub rears as Cannor jumps in front of Carmine to protect her. In one quick swipe, the cub scratches through Cannor's shirtsleeve and draws blood. Cannor falls to the ground screaming over the pain. Terrified, Carmine has no idea what to do, and out of fear runs for her father.

The cub frightened itself, freezes for just a moment seeing it has caused damage, and then instinctually runs. Poor Cannor just laid there with his head spinning. Pale-faced and weak, he soon lost all feeling in his arm. After a few moments, he passed out.

Waking up in his bedroom, he tries to move, but is sadly too weak. Seeing his parents hover around him, starts to make him nervous, but he stays calm. "Where is Carmine father? I want to see her." His father drops his look of concern, and shows an angered face.

"Son, you've been in a coma for a week. You must rest. Don't worry about her. Carmine and her father have been removed from my property. They no longer live with us here at Clarney Manor." Cannor looks up to his father and simply cries.

He's always so alone, and when Carmine's father was hired to aid with the stables, companionship had finally touched his life.

Looking up to his cold empty hearted father, he just turns his head, and buries his face into the billowy blankets.

Knowing his father's way is the only way, he gives up on the chance of ever seeing her again. "Look, son, she was dangerous, undereducated and a bad influence on you. This action was needed to protect you. Besides, you haven't been studying as much since they came to work for me. Please rest, we will start it up again, as soon as you heal." With that spoken, he leaves his only son, not caring about anything he would have to say. This man may be good to his own disciples and his kingdom, but what is a man when he treats his only son like a prisoner? Yet Prudence was the only one who really knew Darston Cannor. The stone heart, surrounded by love and admiration. Blood can flow around stone, but never within.

Cannor snaps out of his trip through memory lane, by the low squawking of a raven overhead. Watching it for a few moments, he notices it is fleeing from the same direction he was coming from. What could have startled it so? Surveying the land again, he sees he hasn't much time left for traveling. Mounting his horse, he readies to trek further North. He must shake out of this misery.

Oddly, depressing memories seem to get stronger the more north I head.

Before leaving, he studies the ground, inspecting the horse tracks left behind. "Tarmax if you survived this attack, where on God's green earth are you running to? Just like his master, never knows when to give up."

Turning back to his chosen course, he figures out that he can travel several more miles in daylight without another break. Knowing that his steed is headed in Tarmax's direction, he keeps steadfast to his course. "I'll find you horse if it's the last thing I do!"

The raven terribly exhausted, sees the city underneath him. Guessing by the daily chirps of fellow birds passing around, the party leaving for the white dragon has already left out the northern gate. Keeping to his speed, he sees them walking up the road. Swooping down, he skids into Tarmax's feet. Squawking loudly and flaring his wings in a show of concern, the raven tries to gain his attention. Dropping the letter at his feet, the raven pushes it into his foot and squawks for him to read it.

"I don't understand you raven. You're speaking too fast for me. Do you want me to read this?" It nods its head and pushes it further towards him. Tarmax changes into his dragon form and picks it up. Reading it, his face instantly turns to grave concern.

"Oh by hoof and tail, I think Cannor is on his way to find me! I must stop him before he gets to the city!" Raspier stares at Partune and ruffles out his neck feathers, "Stupid dragon, I told you this would cause trouble." Partune stares back at Raspier and snorts out a bit of fire.

Tarmax looks over to Raspier and tries to speak words of solace. "Raspier, I am well aware of the risk Partune took helping me. You all keep going on ahead and I'll head back to turn him from the city. I have a plan, to keep him from continuing on this course, so just keep moving forward. I am forever thankful Partune put his neck out to help me. Otherwise, I'd still think I was just a boring barn horse. This is my destiny. Please forgive him. If you must blame someone, then blame me."

"No, Tarmax, just do as you must. There is no blame here. Isn't that right Celestra?"

Feeling the cheap shot from Raspier, she and Partune both shuffle their feet uncomfortably. The group says their goodbyes, yet, Raspier retains his anger. He still thinks his old friend didn't plan his actions well enough, and here is the proof. Garsa throws Raspier a deep look to silence the arguing. "We always have choices and repercussions. In the end, the outcome can be met by all possibilities and still prove to bring misfortune. Good luck Tarmax. I know all will be well when you return."

Running in his dragon form, Tarmax takes flight to see where Cannor's present location is. Flying over the city, reaching the southern wall, he can see in the distance Cannor is about thirty-five miles from Drondia. The steed he was riding could just make this journey straight, without dropping. Rising higher into the clouds, to avoid being seen, Tarmax heads back to the lake where he hurt the bear with his horns. Knowing the trees on the other side of the lake will prove necessary to complete his plan, he lands at the far edge of Cannor's forest.

While Tarmax was hovering, he changes into his horse form and lands, with his feet aimed towards the lake. He wants to trick Cannor into thinking he drowned.

"Ah, finally where I can show the blessings of being a hybrid. Cannor won't have the slightest idea that I set him up."

Once in the lake, Tarmax changes back to his dragon form and flies straight upwards and shakes dry in midair. Returning to the spot he was once standing, Tarmax yet again changes back to his horse form. Neighing as loud as he could, he prays to catch Cannor's good hearing. He just hopes he'll turn around. *Come forth Lord Cannor, and taste your destiny. I am no longer your property. One day I will avenge you fully. Today is just the test to see if I can out do you.*

Tarmax can see in the distance that Cannor stopped dead in his tracks. He's ready to leave behind his past as a horse, and proudly walks into his new life as a hybrid. Now he must remain patient and wait for Cannor to arrive. Tarmax keeps neighing to help Cannor pinpoint his location. Faster and faster Cannor approaches as Tarmax watches his figure grow on the northern horizon. Chunks of sod fly out from the hoofs of his horse, as the poor steed pants and drools from being pushed too hard. Something Tarmax will never miss: being human transportation.

Almost giddy with anticipation, he plans to walk a bit, following his tracks backward exactly. Then, he will change and fly straight up to watch Cannor pass beneath him.

Tarmax can see Cannor getting closer.

Suspended, close above the trees, he sees Cannor approaching the mouth of the forest. Tarmax was holding some large rocks to drop into the lake, right before Cannor emerges. Hopefully, this will lead him to think he fell in the lake. Tarmax seeing Lord Cannor from the distance, heats up his brow even more.

Cannor screams out with fist in the air, "You cannot escape me now!"

Watching his plan in action, Tarmax smiles. "Perfect timing, so perfect you black-hearted twit, now it's my time to really be free!" Tarmax flies over the lake and drops the rocks into the water. Cannor hears the big splash and a horse neighing in the distance.

"You stupid creature. It sounds like you've gotten yourself into more trouble." Carefully throwing the smaller rocks, Tarmax counts down the steps Cannor makes to the lake. Finally the last stone was cast, and Cannor picks up speed thinking he was somehow caught by bramble under the water.

"Damn you, stupid horse. Now you've gone and drowned. What will I do with this? I finally find you, which proves I'm at least a good tracker, but now it's all in vain. Even if this is a trick, I will recuperate. Horses are usually great swimmers.

After a good night sleep, I'm sure this folly will be put to rest. If someone is trying to lead me away from finding Tarmax, God help them."

Cannor examines the water rippling and sees tiny bubbles escape from inside the center of the lake. All this travel and tracking has led him nowhere. Trotting around the area, he waits to leave as the last of the water settles. Tarmax laughs quietly above. He waits to leave until Cannor starts to head back to his half-built castle.

Cannor confused and very tired, heads back down south to see what the men have completed. Finally, Tarmax can fly back to the others without having to worry about his former master finding the city. His freedom has been secured for now. Still, he is fully aware, Cannor will not be pleased to be the one who goes without his desires fulfilled. Tarmax may never be really free from him, until, he is truly killed.

Chapter Thirty Seven

The Griffin Connection

Tientara still unaware there was a journey planned for sunrise, frantically looks for Raspier. She is longing to apologize for last night. Sadly this is a lost cause, for she has no idea he's already left on the quest to the white dragon. Hoping maybe he's still at the courts, Tientara runs to the gardens in front first. Seeing a yellow guard, she asks if he's seen Raspier. "Last I heard of them they were heading on some sort of quest out the northern gate, but *I* didn't tell you anything. You just seem so frantic, I'm sure it must be important." Tien sighs they've already left the city.

She heads over to the northern gate, hoping she can catch up with them. "I wonder what's so important to make them leave so secretly."

Tarmax flying overhead sees Tientara gazing out into space with a worried look. Curious why she seemed so flustered, he flies down to the entrance of the northern pass. Slowing down his wings, he lands a bit too close to Tien, and the wind knocks her down.

"Sorry Tientara, still getting used to these wings. So, may I ask why you are waiting here at the northern gate?" Tien looks up at him and explains that she still wished to talk to Raspier about the other night. Tarmax realizes that Raspier may have left because he didn't want to deal with female drama. *I do hope Raspier doesn't get mad I took her along.* Tarmax knows there are way too many strikes against him already. This may be the last straw. They both set off to reunite with the others, equally uncomfortable with the situation, but for completely separate reasons.

After flying for a bit, the two of them find the group resting on the path. Landing, Tarmax goes to greet them and is met by Raspier. He was incredibly frustrated, with his head feathers fully flared. Whispering into his ear, Raspier asks why he brought her along. "What's the big idea bringing her here? I didn't ask for her to come. I've had enough of those girls for one day." Tarmax not looking forward to being screamed at, tries to explain. "Well she needs to speak with you, and she seemed so upset over it. Look, just talk with her and maybe things can be resolved and she can go on her way." Raspier now furious Tarmax was organizing his love affairs, decides to talk to her, but only out of spite. Garsa and Drako can't help but notice. "That little player will never learn." Avalo watches and revels in the drama. "This could get interesting." Chuckling quietly, he settles in and materializes a snack and a full cup of grulo.

In the meantime, Celesta walks over to Tarmax. "So, did you lose Cannor? Actually, that's a stupid question. You wouldn't be here if you hadn't." Tarmax smiles and pulls her to the side to explain. "Oddly Celestra, I don't feel the slightest bit upset. My time to shine has finally come. That man will always be a threat to us. I feel it in my heart, but for now, we can just keep that between us, okay? I don't have the energy right now, or the heart to tell the others."

He looks up to the sky, and the sun seeps through his closed eyes. Times are growing strange, very quickly. Certainly, stranger days are sure to come. Tarmax goes to rub his head against Celestra's but she backs away. Confused as to why she seems so distant, he questions her with his eyes. She replies with a reserved voice. "Tarmax, you must understand I am not the kind of feline who settles down. I am the kind of lady who will fight battles and live off the land. I am no female who will simply bear kits to die of old age. I am a solitary animal who has never known that life. I will avenge, travel, fight for the good, and kill the wrong. My dinner table is Mother Nature's floor, and my bed is her grasses. I still don't know what you see in an old worn out warrior like me anyway. Look, there is a long journey ahead and we will need all of our wits to prevail. Let's not jeopardize our chances of survival right now okay? We can come back to this road when all is finally said and done. We are young explorers who need to fulfill a destiny..." Tarmax really can't find the words to tell Celestra why he desires her. Looking down at his dragon form, he feels his heart drop. "She may be right. How could either one of us start something now?" Lying down, he turns from Celestra and decides to let her do as she pleases. Besides, she is only the first female he's met, there will be others, right? Tarmax knows his heart does not agree with any of this, but he will not fight at this moment. "Guess we will just let time take its course." He whispers under his breath.

Celestra watches Tarmax curl up alone. She's so fearful of trusting anyone, that relationships have a hard time developing. Love does heal old wounds though. For her, apprehension seems to be the wisest action to convey the truth. Yet somehow, it didn't produce the desired result. *Why does he sulk? I just want to be free right now. If he really thinks about it, we barely know each other. It would have been foolish to jump into something right before a long journey. I wish he could see that. I wish he really could.*

As these two settle down for the evening, others are still restless. Tientara just sits, staring with sad eyes at Raspier. She wishes so much for him to understand her situation and her emotions. Raspier seeing her, sighs, "Tientara, I don't mean to be rude, but it's obvious you imposed yourself upon Tarmax's good nature. What do you want from me now that you are here?" Tientara stares at Raspier, growing a bit angered. "You mean to tell me that you're not the least bit happy to see me at all? I've been led to believe from our little folly last night that you were quite dedicated to me; is this wrong? Are you just some sort of joker looking to get a good treat from a naive girl? Hmph...The nerve of you...You stuffy over educated twit. I should just rip your feathers out of your head right here!"

Raspier fearing Tientara's rage might match that of her sisters, gradually backs up from her as she pushes forward. His nasty attitude seemed to wash away as soon as she started venting. "Uh...Tien...I wasn't...playing you...This is just an important journey and I couldn't waste any time chatting about things that could wait until I returned." Smiling at her with fear in his eyes, he prays she doesn't get any more heated. It might lead to him cleaning his wounds later.

Unfortunately, Raspier doesn't know how to talk to females unless he's flirting; this is obviously not going to end well. Tientara is disappointed so deeply by Raspier, she can't help but blow up, "Oh, so I'm *not* important enough to say you are leaving on a journey? Well, that's not what you said last night....

How about this, you liar! I'm going to prove that I will be worthy on this journey, not to you, but your friends. I will also show that I don't *need* you. I actually had genuine feelings. Sad to say it, but my sister was right about you. So take this you stuck up gigolo!" And with that, Tientara head butts Raspier so hard, he flies back and crashes into Lu'barthrow. Lu'barthrow gasps and tries hard to brush off the mishap. Quickly he runs a good enough distance away from this battle, "I'd rather my fur stay clean today you crazy griffins." Tien now steaming, lunges on top of Raspier and pins him down beak to beak. "Frightened now!?"

Raspier gulps and weakly smiles at her, "Gee you're strong dear..." Tien snorts in his face, "Dear!? *Dear*? You now call me *dear* but it's obvious you're just saying that to escape punishment. Ha, let's just see who you are you stuffy pigeon."

She releases him and pretends to walk away. Raspier gets up slowly and nervously starts to clean his tattered fur and feathers. He turns his back to her when finished and walks over to Partune. Tientara sees this and turns herself around. Kicking into a full out gallop her target is picked. Partune seeing her speeding towards Raspier, can't help but start laughing. Partune and Raspier turn to see the action. Head aimed for his rear, Tientara launches him way into the air. All of them watch as Raspier flies without using wings.

At this point, everyone paying attention was cracking up. Avalo's snack time quickly ended by him dropping everything and keeling over on his side laughing. Garsa and Drako try to keep their amusement subdued, but only can hold it for so long. Raspier gets up and humbly walks over to apologize, for being so rude. Rubbing his tail, he speaks softly to Tientara without meeting her gaze.

Garsa waits for the two of them to finish before walking over to talk to Tientara. Just to play with Raspier a bit, Garsa decides to keep her along, despite Raspier's opinion on the matter. "Tientara, I see you are full of determination. Your services will actually prove valuable to us on this journey, and quite frankly, I wonder why Raspier didn't invite you along in the first place." Raspier looks up at Garsa and his beak drops open in shock. Tientara walks over quite proudly and slowly shuts it for him. "Thank you Garsa. Glad at least *someone* appreciates me." As she gloats, Raspier realizes he has to stop fighting it. There is no way out of this. Tarmax smiles and laughs at all the commotion, yet doesn't expect kind treatment from Raspier for quite some time. Giving him a look, he tries to show his deepest apologies. Raspier just snorts and walks off, tail high.

Celestra and Lastra happen to like Tien, and are more than happy to have her on board. Anyone who can snuff Raspier like that is great to know. Despite all of this going on none of them are aware that there is a disturbance brewing far south.

Lord Cannor after a bit of time, found a shorter path back to his castle. He was there in a few hours. Sadly, this time he did not take a break and the horse was pushed too far. All it could do, after he dismounted, was to lie down and whinny out of exhaustion. Looking down at this sad mess, he can only sigh. "Damn horse, you are no comparison to the one I lost." It cannot keep up with him like Tarmax could. *That horse is going to be hard to replace.* There has been something strange going on the last few days, especially with the disappearance of Tarmax.

Knowing Trea'sten goes much too easy on his men while he is away, he prepares for a confrontation and some harsh words of reinforcement.

Now back up North, a few miles past the northern wall of Drondia, the group continues on their path. Lastra, Yewdrone, and Tientara were chatting. Celestra and Tarmax were at least being friendly. Avalo and Lu'barthrow were throwing theories around. Garsa and Drako were plotting their best route towards the white dragon. All while poor Raspier, was grunting with fully puffed head feathers, in the front with Partune. "Come on man, it's not like you to be so easy on females. What's really eating you up about Tientara being here on this journey? I know you too well. There's a deeper meaning somewhere and you're not fooling me at all. Fess up..."

Raspier appreciates his friend's humor, and loosens up a bit, "I really didn't want to tell her because I knew she would insist on coming. I fear for Tientara because she thinks she's a lot stronger than she really is. Garsa and the group have me all wrong. It's not that I just wanted to discard her; it's just that I worry about her safety. If I really wanted to, I could have stopped any of her angry stunts earlier. There's no need in hurting her. It's not like me to care Partune, you know that. It's just that she's so..."

Partune smiles at his old friend and nudges him with his elbow. "I think she's strong enough Raspier, look... She still kicked your tail, didn't she? Actually, to be honest, I think she will be fine. Tientara will prove valuable to us all. Just give her a chance." Raspier smiles at his friend's kind words; he might be right.

For about a day's length, the group keeps on their path with no more interruptions. Surveying the perimeter, they watch the dry grasses twitch in the breeze, and note the feel of their blades beneath their feet. The leaves are splendid in their autumn colors as they start to fall. To these travelers now, the land of the greggils is their home. All must be on guard, as they no longer have the protection of the city walls. Their journey is long and will certainly have further complications.

Chapter Thirty Eight

The Journey Really Begins

Garsa being the most seasoned traveller, knows the old stories and history better than most. He recalls some past knowledge about this part of the country. His teachers like Tiergon, the former leader of Drondia had taught Garsa much about the world's history to become a proper guardian. In addition, one of his pastimes was reading old books written by greggils lost in transit during the Draconian war. Garsa can read many languages. As the present leader of Drondia, it's imperative he can communicate with all walks of life.

Staring out into the marshlands, he recalls what he was taught about these lands. Realizing they've gained some needed downtime; he slowly falls into a deep lucid dream.

This north-eastern land, long ago, was what the greggils called New York. The most densely pack area was an island called Manhattan. The name "Manhattan" derives from the word Manna-hata, as written in the 1600's.

It was a bustling city by the shore, constructed of gigantic towers of glass, stone, and metal. Long stone roads, carried huge metal vehicles for transportation, then known as automobiles. Small townships surrounding the densely packed city could be seen for miles. Currency drove these greggils towards darkness and control. These immense populations, were mere cattle to the capitalistic overlords, of the twenty-first century.

The melting of the polar ice caps during the year 2065, flooded the lands, as well as most of their underground tunnels close to the shorelines. This smaller continent, now called Apropon Rar, has suffered many changes since the last greggil nuclear war.

The year now is 5026, almost 3000 years later. The opposing western coastline eventually detached itself, to form islands off the coast of Apropon Rar, with unknown inhabitants. A terrible earthquake separated the lands.

Many greggils refuse to leave their revitalized natural communities, to explore anything nowadays. They are too afraid of the consequences and smart enough to refrain from such curiosities like their forefathers. Now the last remnants of those populated eastern islands, are marshlands and bays on the far most eastern coast of Apropon Rar. It is also much colder in climate as the tectonic plates have shifted greatly.

To dive a bit deeper into this history, the greggils that colonized these lands were living in rather respectible harmony with each other. During the 16th century and onward, visitors from other lands sailed here to settle colonies. The greggils in this area were naive to the dangers around them. The invaders pushed them into smaller communities little by little, choking them out. As most happens with the law of chaos, they eventually needed the invading greggils in order to survive. There was no escape from the claws of technology, except extinction.

By the late 19th Century, these natives were no longer the keepers of these lands. The foreigners from over the great waters were breeding and overtaking the country incredibly fast. All greggils now look back and shed tears of shame for their ancestors. Fools tore down beautiful forests that stretched for miles. Destruction of their habitat was vast.

Hoarding is a popular squirrel trait that most greggils possessed. This type of greggil back in history was completely on overload, however. They were buying and selling everything. They would dig up minerals and crude oil for their machines. Harvesting anything they could from the environment, they started to think they owned nature. All of them had forgotten the proper way of life. All instead were taught to consume; the true birth of the word consumerism.

Commonly this continent as history tells us, was a melting pot of all greggil society from around the world. It had the right structure for mental growth and spiritual healing. The electricity within the earth was very strong during this time, and effected individuals all very differently. They were incredibly driven and tended to throw care to the wind.

This generation of greggils, had a rather short-lived rein. The creation of nuclear power was the moment they wrote their own downfall. Albert Einstein himself never had any part in its creation, yet is responsible for pushing the president of the United States during WWII to create their own atomic bombs. Indirectly, his act destroyed their future of overseeing Gaia.

There were many before him that learned to harness the power of the planet. Benjamin Franklin during the eighteenth century was a greggil of heightened enlightenment. His contributions to science and community were vast. Primarily, his discovery of electrical conductivity was the largest. He also was quite an inventor. Another later contemporary, from across the great waters, Alessandro Volta had created a device that could store electricity; back then known as the battery. Later in history, these ancient greggils named the derived unit of electrical potential, the volt.

Nikola Tesla and Albert Einstein were the most noted of the greggils during the twentieth century. There is an ancient story, that when Albert Einstein was questioned, "How does it feel to be the smartest greggil alive?" he replied, "I don't know, you'll have to ask Nikola Tesla." Nikola was able to use alternating current electricity with an astonishing ease. He could screw glass objects with a thin wire inside, into the ground and saw them light up. He had discovered that the earth itself was in fact, a giant battery, thus negating the need for storage devices. Greggils looking to control this electricity didn't like the idea of free energy.

Tesla had tapped into an ancient knowledge, predating the great flood of Gaia. The greggils prior to this catastrophe were highly advanced in forms of technology and mathematics. Some were of the good and some were only greedy. This seems to be how the great flood occurred according to tradition. A calamity caused by them destroyed the great islands and much of the world. Some mystery schools and private groups preserved these teachings but much was lost forever like these older races of greggils. Only the dark greggils of greed carried on with the schooling as was their design. It seems the post great flood greggils, changed their own history to keep rule over others. They wanted the power or wanted the original history removed from the well-known timeline for unknown reasons.

Garsa ponders about the theories that these pre-flood greggils, were not a pure species. They may have been hybrids in fact. This would make complete sense as to why they were highly innovative and intelligent. Some even say they still exist today, hidden away deep in the earth. Some old dragons swear on the first scale, that they were mixed with reptilian genetics. There is still no evidence of this, and Garsa refuses to even entertain the thought. The greggils known today, are certainly dim-witted in comparison to their ancestors. Sadly, this was due to the breeding population that was saved from the nuclear fallout.

Within his lucid dream, Garsa remembers more on this rather entertaining walk through greggil history. Tesla had discovered, electricity flowed freely from Gaia herself. The planet is a powerful battery that can send electricity to any point in the world, with the right tools. Those tools were commonly crystalline and metal in nature.

Let us fast forward returning to the greggil-dominated world, the near end of the twentieth century. Albert Einstein had his eye on the universe as a whole, most commonly for the better of greggil society. His theory, however, was becoming more of a threat to the planets' safety. He constantly voted against the use of it in warfare. After his death, some realized the greatness he had provided for humankind. Many also realized his theory led to one of the greatest destructive devices the greggils have ever known. Nuclear weapons were the very technology Einstein wished never came to fruition.

Towards the end of the year 2020, many greggils had witnessed the immense destruction of nuclear weapons. Now they felt the same as Einstein. They had to prevent their use in warfare. The creation of a new form of combat was almost complete. In underground tunnels and habitats across the country, genetic sciences were developing literally underneath the common greggils above. These projects consisted of hundreds of scientists, doctors, and animals from all over the world. Knowing they couldn't outfight them by warfare, they turned to genetic enhancement. During that time, this country was the United States of America, a part of the continent North America. This country was the dominant world power, despite being so young.

There was a perfect storm churning across these lands back then. Chinese and North Korean greggils were two of the large countries still holding on to communism. Russia was now a strong force in the world and constantly proved that they have risen above the American world government. Islamic nations were fighting America and longed to see their power greatly reduced. Still, the United States, had their claws in everything. Even the powers that fought against them.

Europe as a whole most of the time, went along with America to keep the peace as best as they could. To Europe, America was a stepson that way outgrew their britches. Always ducking out on responsibilities, yet will throw the first punch anytime their lies were uncovered. Yet to America, their Parliament was antiquated and losing steam quickly. This is why the UK was losing control as a world power.

America was the strongest country in the world. Yet, as the strongest nation, you have many enemies. The government could have heeded the warnings, but felt they were more intelligent; this was a bad mistake. Time was finally running out for this dominant ruler of the greggils. They were not the only race in history to use mind over heart. Just like the ancient greggil Romans, the Egyptians, and the Atlanteans, their fate was sealed in ignorance.

The European Parliament had higher sights in mind and was no longer taking a back seat to their rebel kin. Yet their overall population wanted the power back for themselves, each their own country. The Islamic nations were chipping away at the American control a little at a time and would not relent. Communist countries were starting to notice the need for stronger borders and were turning inward to protect themselves. Russia continued to push forward as a stronger nation with highly publicized morals. They would not back down to the worldwide American militia. The American government was only concerned with keeping their oil-backed currency strong and their military presence around the world. They needed their investors to remain interested in them. They were so close to unveiling their secret weapon, and nothing was going to stop them. This would keep them safe as the top world power. Sadly, for America, the pendulum of existence was swinging into its next direction. Their time here ruling over Gaia was through.

The idea of invention and ownership had made most of the American society a shell of their true existence. Spirituality has fallen in importance steadily over centuries and left these greggils without the inner light to be one with Gaia. Religion was one of the main reasons for this. They built a dark claustrophobic world where they caged nature and themselves. Their focus was on self-indulgence and capitalism, which was the real cause of their obliteration. None of these greggils understood the destructiveness of such acts and over hundreds of years, eventually succumbed to the same demise as the old ancient greggil societies. A heart that beats without the light of Gaia will only fall into the darkness of greed. The American overlords were falling apart internally because they had lost sight of their true goal, Gaia's preservation.

The American military was so obsessed with finding spies and people against them, that they destroyed the very idea they founded their nation on, freedom. Privacy became a privilege rather than an American right. Freedom of speech, the right to clean air, water, and food also lost importance, yet not to the common greggils trying to survive. This government, strong armed its society, in fear of losing control of Gaia's true energy source. Slowly the common greggils started to fight back against their own government. They protested the chemically altered foods and seeds. They stopped using everyday products because of toxins. The lies that were piling up quickly with modern medicine, their economy and health care also turned most to natural means of healing. The light was starting to reach their hearts. Yet their overall intelligence, year after year, fell drastically when compared to other countries.

Those were very strange times, in deed. The early twenty-first century greggils commonly saw flying crafts or lights in the sky that did not make sense to them. They started to feel as if creatures from other planets were watching them; calling them aliens. Disturbing dead hybrid creatures were washing ashore now for decades. Antarctica was a cold continent back then and rumored to have lush green lands deep within the center of the ice. The older order of dragons, claim, that is where the ancients went to in hiding. The fabled lost Atlantis from the pre-great flood times. The greggil public felt there were alien crafts and a civilization beneath the glaciers. The elite greggils of the world were constantly hiding the truth about it from the public. This would not be so simple to do anymore, as the connection to Gaia and the public, was finally widening.

The common greggil started thinking differently from what the media was telling them. Gaia, had opened their heart to the power she possessed inside of her. This communication sent via radio waves or other forms would flash pictures with sound into their dwellings. Commonly used to sway or push the public into directions they would not generally entertain.

Many were brainwashed by this and were completely ignorant of its true purpose. Of course, there were no such things as hostile aliens at this time. The world government started the hoax of an attack in the early 1950's. Sometimes the top greggils in power, used floating crafts to cause panic. This heighten the threat of an alien invasion and would give them more control over "Space", as they called it. Generally, it kept running for many generations and the public believed up until their last nuclear war.

All this false "news" was used to distract the mass from their experiments, going on underground, far from prying eyes. It was hidden technology and forbidden sciences. Greggils started to alter the genetic code of lifeforms on this planet. Gaia was not pleased with this. Sometimes, these poor creatures, would escape, only to die on the surface. These, however, were true living and breathing animal hybrids.

The powerful greggils during this time kept the true origins of their kind and its history under tight lock and key. They only gave the public what they felt they could handle. Yet there were greggils awakening to the inner light of Gaia and were starting to question the validity of many things. Places like Plum Island and incidents like the Montauk Project, the Manhattan Project, or the Philadelphia Experiment, were all surfacing in secret studies, leaving these awakened greggils quaking in their boots.

There was an attack coming from over the great waters. Too distracted by their own country and its collapsing ways, they American elite, and the poor souls below them, never saw it coming.

The natural lay lines of the earth were shifting at a much faster pace during these times. This was due to greggils building wherever they wanted, not in line with Gaia's electrical grid. Undereducated, these new generations of greggils were not aware they were going to flip the poles because of this. They ruined the carefully laid temples and lay lines, that acted as a protective grid, built thousands of years before the great flood.

These greggils of the twenty-first century were the ones who finally destroyed the very workings of nature on the planet.

One cold winter's day, there was an attack barrelling towards the United States of America. It was a nuclear weapon of mass destruction. Somehow, involved in their own inner turmoil and civil unrest, the government failed to catch this. Rumor has it their sensors which could tell approaching danger, were compromised. Cursing their gods, they sent out their own counterattack in an attempt to even out the odds of such impending death. If they were to be wiped out, so would their enemies as well. All that remained of these greggils were the scattered few who hid inside the fallout shelters in the great cities across the world. They were smart enough to realize that possessions were of little importance now if they wanted to survive. The modern world they had come to know so well was about to be destroyed. Yet humanity did survive. This was just the death of consumerism.

Torrential chemical rain poured down on the lands and killed anything it touched. Deforestation, deformities, and cancers of all kinds plagued anything living on the surface. Plants and water became too poisoned to consume and lost all living properties. The oceans were no more than a death pool of rotting bodies for miles, filled with trash and chemicals from dark sciences. Death loomed everywhere for thousands of years. Nothing on the ground was without torture.

Now the greggils that were able to get underground before the blast were the only survivors of the nuclear holocaust. Some even traveled far from overseas with protective ships and suits. They did not wish to destroy lands they desired to take over, but there was no other way to stop this insane new world order. So this nuclear cleansing was the only option left that would bring their desired outcome. Greggils of that time had very little connection to their mother Gaia, and could not fathom peace.

Those same underground tunnels, once used for government projects and secret experiments became homes for communities.

Their technological life that they had built up over hundreds of years was destroyed in a heartbeat and obliterated. Huddled together frightened and knowing little about how to survive without their comforts and luxuries, this new generation of greggils swore to denounce technology and to revert to living off the land.

The melting pot had begun. This catastrophic act worked to consolidate the different breeds of greggils back into two single versions of the species, as we know today.

In this year 5026, their ancient city ruins are the marshlands and waters of greggil failure, the reminder that extinction is always drawing closer to them. The hybrids are the only other reminder left from that century. The greggils out of bitterness feel that if they can wipe them out altogether, they can quell their inner regret for what they did to the world. Sadly, Gaia has no say in this except with the defense of her dragon overseers. We swore to attend to them and make sure they too can exist in peace. Yes, hybrids are a by-product of war, but they became very creative and helpful children of nature.

Forever, this plain is the graveyard for the original cultivators and wise native inhabitants, who once roamed this territory, now a mere memory in the minds of these modern greggils. For now, they only exist in folklore and stories, but physically resemble them so much in today's times. Most are brownish-red skinned, with long black hair. Yet, there are a few "Elites", still running around and ruining everything.

Coming out of the lucid dream, Garsa will always remember the tragic history of this land, simply because it shows what to expect for the future. His teachers before him knew the importance of passing on the truth. Hiding it, would only make history repeat itself.

Shivering, Garsa feels the energy from the surrounding area seems altered. He shakes it off and sighs quietly. *I will have to find more research on those ancient pre-flood greggils. Something doesn't sit right with me.*

Chapter Thirty Nine

The Assumption of Ignorance

In the morning of their second day, the group walked along in silence for a while. They all seemed to carry an air of sadness and pain. Garsa thought it could be due to the negative energy left behind, from the greggils timeless war. Anything can be possible. As they push on through the fields outside the northern gate, something kept them from socializing. As time progressed, he became certain it was an outside force affecting them.

One possibility is that a droge troll is nearby. Bombarding travelers with thoughts of depression and pessimism, they hunt these pour souls and draw them closer to their lake. Once drowning, the troll has a nice easy meal. These creatures are ancient by trade, and certainly magickal, but were warped by the nuclear war thousands of years ago. *By tooth and claw, if one is in the vicinity I shall not be overcome by its sway. If only I could see ahead to prevent these disasters...* Avalo starts to notice Garsa's concern but remains silent.

Turning to see the rest of the crew almost in the same frame of mind, proves his assumption was correct. A droge troll must be around here somewhere. Still fighting the pull of its magick, he demands everyone to stop. Garsa looks around in midair for some sort of glistening lake. Seeing one to his northeast, he lands and makes everyone shake out their negative moods. "Snap out of it! These thoughts are not your own! They are conjured up by a droge troll. They're nasty little things. See that lake all the way over there? He is luring you to take refuge there so he can simply catch you like a blind deer, in other words...A free meal."

The group confused for a moment, tries to imagine a simple troll having that much power over them. Lu'barthrow found it easy to block the magick's hold. He knows much better than to gloat or comment on the subject, thankfully. They all look closer at the lake and see that this tiny island is harboring a small troll. He doesn't look very menacing, and is actually on the thin side.

Avalo pulls Garsa over to talk a bit, and tries to think up a good plan, to disarm the droge. While the rest of them are waiting, Avalo and Garsa chat about their plan to hustle out some local gossip and news on the greggils. It's been a while since the both of them have had a challenge, and tricking a troll into spilling the beans, isn't exactly bad karma.

Avalo walks back over to the rest of them and tries to explain more about droge trolls. They listen carefully and keep raising each other's spirits. Drako turns to Avalo, "So how are we retrieving this information?"

Avalo slowly curls up his mouth to show a deviant smile. Teeth bare and eyes slit, he laughs softly. "Well, as you know I love pranks, so we'll just trick this little fellow into thinking I'm his next meal. We're far enough away that he cannot detect our presence. I'll pose as the miserable one who finds my fate. No troll can overcome my magick, but I can overcome theirs. Then we'll use Lu'barthrow to stalk him in the lake reeds, and pounce at just the right time. Catching him, he'll bring him out on to the bank, and his power will start to decrease. Any troll out of it's lake is like a dragon without fire; they become powerless. So, do you think you can handle this job Lu'barthrow?"

He picks his head up and smiles. "Sure, it's a piece of cake Avalo. Just tell me what to do, and we'll launch this operation of 'Droge Domination' immediately."

The group knows to stay back on this one, and let the master and his pupil handle it. Garsa explains a few more details on the droge trolls while Avalo and Lu'barthrow are off to rustle some information out of him. Avalo is to play the role of the depressed creature held by the troll's magick.

Garsa out of the corner of his eye, can see Avalo slump over and sigh in discontentment and chuckles, *such a good actor that one; Never will grow up. It might just kill him to even ponder the thought.*

The troll very hungry, sees Avalo lurching towards his vacant lakeside retreat, *Oh goody. A meal and quite a big one! This has to be the most I've gotten to eat in three months. That Carthine was terrible the other day, too stringy and tough.* Quickly scampering into place, the troll begins to conjure up, the perfect method of capture for this blue hearted beast. "What a catch, a dragon carcass could last me for days. Good eatin's sure in order."

Lu'barthrow out of sight, slinks toward the other side of the lake. He quietly crawls into position. Peering through the dense reeds, he sees the troll right in front of him, about three dragon-lengths away. Lu'barthrow is downwind from the troll. *If I use my newly discovered wings, I'm sure to catch him in midair.*

Finding a tree to settle down by, Tarmax and Celestra sit and talk. Lastra is chatting about better days, while Partune builds a small windmill from reeds and sticks for Yewdrone. Drako and Garsa cannot resist; they watch with baited breath for the outcome.

As everyone's attention is occupied elsewhere, Celestra stares into Tarmax's eyes, to try to see deeper. There were swirls of crystal blue and light green that were so distracting. Carefully following his heartbeat with each breath, she thinks, *such pretty eyes.* Shaking her head, she drops the thought quickly, "Tarmax, May I ask you something?" She nudges him with her head. Tarmax affectionately looks back at her, "Sure, what is it?"

Celestra obviously uncomfortable, sighs before talking, "Well, did you ever think you would find a mate?" Tarmax a bit shocked at her question, looks back at her, "Beg your pardon,

Celestra?" A bit embarrassed, Celestra corrects herself, "I was referring to when you were a horse."

Tarmax chuckles. "If you mean to ask if I have ever had someone special in my life, the answer is yes. Her name was Willow."

You could almost see Celestra's heart fall out of her chest. Quickly, she picks herself back up and stays alert. Tarmax figured she would react this way.

"Willow was a horse that Cannor bought to possibly produce offspring. He figured that I was a good charger to breed out. Life for me was very simple. I know you can understand our differences in upbringing. Yet, to answer your question, I cannot deny, she was absolutely a stunning horse."

Celestra slowly, crouches down lower to the ground, as her tail softly swished, back and forth. Tarmax reading her emotions continues, "...Now, we would trot around the fields in the back of the stables and play small tricks on the stable hands, but all in jest. She was very nice to be around. No stress. I started to fall for her heavily and desired to stay. Remember Celestra, that as the animal I was raised to be, there were no long-term relationships, just mating. Yet I did feel as if I desired more than that. Apparently, Willow did too, which I found out from this old barn cat, I spent much of my time with.

Frauwser, a rickety old tomcat, that Cannor kept around to kill the mice and rats, would always spread rumors or start trouble. He had access to all of the stables and knew a lot for a simple domesticated cat. One morning before Cannor came to take me out for a ride, Frauwser came over to my stall. He did his usual once over for rats and other scurrying rodents. Yet this day, he had an air of secrecy to him.

Munching on my oats, I watched him without letting on. Frauwser jumps up on the saddle table to get eye to eye. "Hey Tarmax. Did you know that Willow, takes to you more than you think? I know cause, I chat with her and the other mares, while on the hunt. Shall I passss any words to her today while I waltz by her stall?'

I watched Frauwser curl his orange jagged tail around as he scratched into the stable walls. I could only blush at the news. 'Well, if you like, tell her that mating isn't just what's on my mind. I...I feel something more than that.'

Nervous to be talking like this, let alone to some stray cat, I quickly got back to my business, so the other horses wouldn't sense my mood change. Frauwser showed me a crooked smile and sneezed in laughter. 'You horses are all alike. Follow mother to the grave, never swaying from the well-worn path. I shall tell your little filly of your words. Should I also tell her, you're too afraid to tell her yourself?'

Now Celestra, you would imagine at this point I was very displeased. Stomping my hoof, I told Frauwser, 'I am not afraid of being myself, my mother taught me better than that!' Frauwser gazed upon me sternly. Looking me in the eye, he said one thing before hopping off to his daily hunt.

'If I was just an average cat, I might say you were a common horse. Yet, I know that is not what you are, as I am trained to know better. Remember Tarmax, skin is merely skin. A soul is something different altogether. So remember, cats that chase their tails get nowhere!' Then the old tomcat jumped down to kill a rat, walking by the wall."

Celestra thinks for a second, about what Tarmax said. Looking up at him, she smiles: "He was a very deep cat...Something to consider."

Tarmax finally realized what Frauwser meant. To all there at the stables, he was a simple horse, but in actuality, he was a hybrid. Frauwser apparently could tell this.

"You cannot teach a cat to hunt when they think they are the mouse...

That cat knew much more than he led on to..."

Celestra warm's back up to Tarmax and they enjoy each other's company. Truly, she knows in her heart, she's the one with the issues. Yet still, it is growing obvious that denying her emotions for him will not be easy. She honestly cares about him, and these little moments certainly prove it.

Garsa walks over to them, "Sorry to interrupt your heavy discussion, but this is important. Trolls like these are a grand issue to travelers and full knowledge of them is imperative." Tarmax almost welcomes the distraction. He wasn't in the mood to completely answer Celestra's questions in the first place. Willow was a sore subject with him, and getting Celestra's emotions involved with it, would not make it any easier. Tarmax happily listens to Garsa's words as Celestra sneers at the distraction.

Garsa explains each step carefully, in hopes they can avoid these creatures in the future. "You see how Avalo has already set himself up? He is sitting by the lake and slumping over like he's still under its control. Lu'barthrow is hidden over there beyond the troll's vision and will pounce when the time is appropriate."

Avalo mutters words of sorrow and splashes the pretty water with his claws. "I wish I was stronger like my brother. He always wins the fights and I'm left to look up to him. I never win anything except last place." The troll, waiting with an empty belly, finally sees his opening to hop closer to Avalo. "Hey there lonely traveler...Is there anything I can help you with?" Avalo looks up at the troll and weakly smiles.

Keeping the mood just right, he looks up with sad eyes. "Not if you can make me instantly a winner." The troll smiles ear to ear in delight. "Well, actually I can. Did I overhear you say you're always finishing last? Well, you definitely walked up to the right lake my friend. I'm a wishing troll and I can grant you anything you desire." Avalo plays along and lifts his head up curious about his offer. "Oh yeah, do you think you could really make me a winner for a change?" The troll lifts his hands and swirls them in opposite directions above his grey stringy, dirty hair. "If I am a troll who knows no sinners, make this dragon a sure shot winner!" Avalo looks above his head and sees medallions land around his neck. "Wow, what are these for?" The troll sees he is a bit weighted down by the medallions and starts to get a bit closer. He already has a great plan to get his meal waterlogged.

"The meanings of those five medallions are as follows: One for your humbleness, one for your patience, one for your intelligence, one for your soft nature, and the largest one is for being brave enough to get that trophy, from over there." The troll points to a rock out in the water over to where Lu'barthrow was hiding. "Oh no, I couldn't troll, I can't swim. Please take this one back for I do not deserve it. Besides, that's too far out into the lake and I am scared I'll end up hurting myself."

The troll smiles and bows to Avalo. "First off, my name is Seffaunt. Second, what if I told you I could make those stones bigger with my magick? Would you walk across them?" Avalo continuing with this well-played act, tried to pretend to be a bit motivated. "Well, I guess so. I need to actually accomplish the feat in order to wear the last medal Seffaunt. You know what? I will do it!"

Lu'barthrow readies to snatch up the troll as Avalo begins to hop along the stones. Each step of the way, the troll jumps on his own materialized stone. Thinking he has Avalo bagged, he will make the last stone disappear after he picks the trophy up. "Okay, you've got one more left. Think you can do it?" Avalo readies to jump and winks at Lu'barthrow hiding in the reeds. Lu'barthrow flies out and catches the troll midair, and brings him to the bank where the others are hiding out.

The troll bashes Lu'barthrow with his little hands but cannot break free. "Put me down you overgrown furball, I'll turn you into a newt and slurp you down!" Lu'barthrow tightens his teeth around the troll's neck and makes him shriek out in pain. "Shut up or I'll eat you dirty troll, despite how sour you'll taste." Dropping him on his head, Partune quickly picks him up and restrains him by his arms. "What is the meaning of all of this? Who *are* you creatures?"

Garsa walks sternly up to the troll and bends down to get eye to eye with him. Snorting some smoke straight into his face, he enjoys watching his discomfort. "Well for starters, I am Garsa Yean, the leader of Drondia, the dragon city. I would like to scratch your eyes out for trying to eat my friend here. Nasty little troll, I have but one request to gain back your freedom. Tell us the news you've heard from the local area or my friend here will happily mistake you for a comfortable seat."

Seffaunt squiggling inside Partune's grasp bends down and bites his arm. Partune howls and grabs him by the feet and violently shakes the troll. Small coins, bones, and sand topple out from his pockets. "Grr... that hurt you little water rat. Now you can dangle like a worm on a hook."

Seffaunt crosses his arms and refuses to talk. Garsa blows a blast of fire over him to change his mind. His body now badly singed, Seffaunt's confidence shrinks. Clothing still burning with embers, he shutters.

Garsa starts to laugh, "Anyone up for barbequed troll? I heard after you cook them alive, they taste better." The panicked troll screams and finally gives up. "Okay, fine you win, but you sure drive a hard bargain dragon. Look, this whole area is overrun with Carthines. The greggils apparently took over their old territory, south-west of here, Roden Forest. They had nowhere else to go. The Caverns of Mor up ahead, are all they have left.

To try to win back their lands they waged war on the greggils. In the end, both sides were able to compromise despite the terrible bloodshed. The Carthine's gained ownership to the Caverns of Mor in exchange. This would only happen if they joined forces with the greggils and their desire to destroy all hybrids and dragons. They agreed happily for land.

That stupid carthine I ate the other day, would not shut up about this. Now put me down you tree stump!" Garsa nods at Partune to shake Seffaunt again, until he talks more. "You guys are ruthless! You do realize I'm slowly dying out of that lake, don't you?! Soon I'll just be dust in these big oafs' hands..." Garsa snorts fire again and stares the troll down. "I can wait, can you? Start talking midget."

Seffaunt huffs in frustration. "Okay, but please no more fire! There will be nothing left of my body to answer questions. All of this I heard from some weird painted Carthine I ate yesterday. He looked like your male panther hybrid over there, but badly done up. He even shaved down his teeth. Oh did I ever thank the high old troll king; he was so easy to eat, I didn't even have to use my magick. He was already depressed."

The troll laughs while being held upside down. He still enjoys the memory of his last meal's issues. Partune stretches his body with both hands to remind him just where he was. "Ouch! Okay! Back on topic...You see if you want to pass the caverns, you will need to befriend the Carthines. Yet this will be very hard since you're a group of dragons and hybrids."

Raspier snorts and raises his beak to the troll. Tientara angered, slaps him with her front foot to make him halt.

The troll now has blood rushing to his head and gets a bit dizzy, but tries to keep talking. "The Carthines are relatively dimwitted. They depend more on brawn than brains, just watch out for their Prince. He is the opposite and *very* intelligent. You can outwit him though. It will take some careful planning.

The general of war is the real physical threat. Make sure your three hybrids here are in Gaia's natural form. Remind them to conceal their stars or they'll give themselves away. That is all I know so please let me go, so I can at least live to tell the day I was caught!"

Garsa thanked the troll for his cooperation but he shrugged him off. Swimming back into the water the troll grumbled in defeat. "Stupid dragons...don't know what they're getting into with that white female hybrid. The general will be sure to have her any way he can. The Prince will desire to lock her up like an expensive treasure. Good riddance to bad company I always say. What do I care? I'm just a troll, right?"

Seffaunt walking up onto a stone, slowly kicks a pebble. It bounces off a reed and splashes back into the water, disturbing some fish. "Hey, if I could have been a bear, I would be happier but, *this* is my role here on Gaia. I have no choice in the matter really..." He finally gets back to his island and curls up for a nap completely exhausted. The lake begins to glow again with that same illuminating sparkle, waiting for the next victim of the altered depression.

The group was now walking towards the Caverns of Mor. Celestra was thinking about what Garsa had said to her back at the city gate. He is kind and loving to those who deserved it. Never to those who disobey the laws of Gaia. Silently she walks, respecting Garsa a bit more after the event. For once, like when she was with Uniqua, she feels protected.

Tarmax was highly amused over the troll but now had his old life on his mind. Something told him he had to return to the barn. All of them need to know that there is more to life beyond the fences. He also wanted to thank his strange colleague Frauwser, for his assistance.

Well, she's not mine anymore, that Willow. He never finished telling Celestra the story. Tarmax always dreamed of life outside the stables. Repeatedly, he found himself daydreaming about living out there. This greatly concerned Willow.

Back then, she once said to him, "Tarmax, it seems your attention lately is not here with me. Is there something out there calling you?" Tarmax turned to her and rubbed her neck with his head. "Well, not anything prettier than you Willow. I cannot deny the idea of being on my own is calling me. I desire to be wild and to feel the free air running through my mane. It's growing stronger."

Willow grew continuously more irritated that her mate wanted to leave the barn to face possible death. They fought about it constantly. Despite her threats, he ran off without ever saying goodbye. *She probably knew it was going to happen sooner or later. I do miss her; I hope she can forgive me.* Tarmax distraught, caught up in his past, continued walking.

Drako, Partune, Lu'barthrow, Avalo, and Garsa were all laughing over the troll. "I'll turn you into a newt and slurp you down. Ha! That's funny. Sure did a number on him huh?" Lu'barthrow continues to boast his triumph, while Garsa suddenly feels a little bit more alive. He has not let loose like that in quite some time. Frankly, it felt good. Partune rubs his bite wound. Somehow, he was the only one who ended up hurting.

Chapter Forty

In Walks Garabolo

Lord Cannor down south, was making sure his workers were still on track. Trea'sten was yet to be found. Cannor quite angered, but calmly, asks a worker adjacent to him where Trea'sten was. "I believe he's in the back Lord, around the other side of the castle."

Cannor snaps back at the man, "Work harder, for the snow is coming soon. There are only two months to build the main roof. Now get out of my way, lowly worker. I have to find your irresponsible nobleman." Pushing the worker aside with his horse, he trots away.

He eventually finds Trea'sten mending a workers' broken arm. "There you go Fenton. I hope that will hold you over until you see your wife later. I'm no doctor, but hey, it's secure."

Cannor furious dismounts his horse and walks over to Trea'sten and Fenton. "What is the meaning of this?! Can't this dirty ox take care of himself? You know this will cost him his day of rest. Now, go pick up that log and bring it to the woodworkers over there. Make haste if you want to feed your family for the winter, rat!" Fenton in great pain, starts to pull the log across the dirt, like a dog pulling an ox cart. You can almost hear the sinew in his arm snapping, as he moved forward painfully.

Garabolo walks up and takes it from his weak arms. "Drop it, Fenton, don't do such a preposterous feat with that arm, go home to your wife, I'll handle this."

Garabolo whistles out for his horse, a white mare called Willow. "Come, dear, take Fenton home. You know where it is." Fenton with some help from Garabolo nervously mounts the horse just well enough to get on. It was only three miles to his homestead. Garabolo slaps her rear and sends her off flying, "Ride steadfast!"

Cannor stares in amazement at Garabolo. He directly disobeyed his orders, which makes him a traitor. Sending his laborer home when personally he felt he could work for longer. "What is the meaning of this Garabolo? Do you want to be fired and starve this winter as well as this man?" Garabolo stands up and towers over him nearly two feet. "Look, *sir*, that man was badly injured because he is overworked and underfed. He has not had sleep in days. I will take his penalty... whatever stated. But you must remember: to harm these men means you go through *me* first."

Cannor grumbles under his breath at Garabolo's hero complex. *Why protect these lowly men... why? He could lose his job and starve just like the rest of them.* Yet his size and intelligence frightened Cannor. This is why the men voted Garabolo their representation for rights under his rule. No matter the build in Apropon Rar, all working people have the law behind them to elect their own representation of choice. Cannor always despised this and now more than ever.

He remembers back a few nights ago where Trea'sten and he were playing a game of poker. Still upset over losing that white mare, he mumbles to himself. *What a drunken fool I was...Losing my horse to that beast of a man.*

The game of poker between Trea'sten and Cannor seemed like child's play to the large man. Walking over to the two of them, he sits down at the table. Cannor grunted at the site of Garabolo but eagerly desired to beat him. Trea'sten dealt him into the game nervously, and, nobody spoke a word.

As a man of the woods, Garabolo was a tracker, a bounty hunter and a trail guide, whatever he could do to make money for his family. His most profitable years were during the

Draconian wars. In these peaceful times, he had no choice but to join Cannor's building team. There was very little work out there. Rumors flew around the build site that Garabolo had remained a scout for the people of Dar Tochchu, still is to this day. Cannor was not oblivious to this gossip. He watched this man from across the table with a deep silent rage.

Garabolo, a studious man of royal blood was smart enough to hide it. Winning something valuable out of the deal was more of the challenge. "Cannor, I've had my eye on that pretty little white filly you have, let's say if I win this hand, I can have her." Cannor looks up at Garabolo and stares blankly at him in disgust. Trea'sten nervous rearranges his glasses and keeps dealing. Plotting out when his own small stable would be complete, Garabolo hoped Cannor would take the deal.

Two traits Cannor possessed showed his humanity: His honor to uphold any agreement and his memory while drunk. So in his present inebriated stupor, he agreed to the deal. Alcohol here certainly seemed to be the great equalizer. Garabolo was quite aware of this and kept his cup filled much to Trea'sten's dismay.

Garabolo needless to say, won the poker game. He probably could have with his hands tied behind his back. Trea'sten was terrified somehow this would end up being his fault, but he handed over the reins, without uttering a single word. The air was thick with discomfort. Cannor's brain was starting to hurt. He had no option but to pass Willow over to Garabolo. A deal was a deal. Rubbing his drunken face, he gags a bit, knowing he needs to eat something soon. He manages to mutter out, "Damn Tarmax, where have you gone?"

Garabolo, still a bit concerned about Tarmax's whereabouts', offers to hunt him down, but Lord Cannor refuses. Garabolo instead, wishes them a good evening and trots off with Willow, leaving them both behind in a cluster of dust. Cannor, drunk, tries to walk home, still angry and full of rage, with Trea'sten following close behind.

As Garabolo rides, he thinks about the offer to search for Tarmax. Rarely will he speak of his business around Cannor, or his workers. When talking with the stable hands earlier, he learned Tarmax had went missing. *Cannor would surely believe I'm the cause... that I wanted two horses out of the deal instead of one.* He kicked Willow into a full forced gallop home. Dirt flicked up with her heels as she whinnied forward.

Now aware of this large man's intelligence, Cannor will no longer take any chances. Angered over this, he stews in silence. Deep inside of him, he questions Garabolo's worth as a worker. Poor, tired Trea'sten sits in the hallway, overexerted from dragging him home to the manor. Halfway back, Cannor dropped and he had to pick him up. Turning into his room, he wishes his lord a good night and heads home. Rubbing his tired head, he wonders how he ended up involved with this creep, as he walks home.

The next day, Lord Cannor refused to let Garabolo out of sight. Incredibly paranoid, Cannor took Trea'sten to the side, "...Watch him. He whispers into Trea'sten's ear. "I am going to return to my stables. I wish to see work actually done when I return. There has been too much commotion going on around here. This castle must be finished in two months! Get Garabolo to organize the men and create a new plan for faster work in these shorter days."

Trea'sten sluggishly agrees and goes to converse with Garabolo about Cannor's orders. Not unlike Garabolo, Trea'sten's every move will be watched. Just in case Cannor decides to traitor him out too. He may be a faithful servant of Lord Cannor, but he is no fool.

Chapter Forty One

Meeting the Carthines

The next day, the group was walking at a faster pace. They can see the caverns up ahead, but start to get weary. Garsa stops everyone, by a collection of trees. He explains how they will handle greeting these Carthines. "Look everyone, we heard from the troll, that Carthines are working with the greggils. Yet, I'm sure none of them have seen a single Griffon. So please keep this all-in mind. In addition, they require a boost in ego, so make sure to treat them with respect, no matter what they say. Hybrids, go cover your stars and transform as instructed. We will have none of you worn as pelts anytime soon."

Avalo figures out how to make this a safe passage. He sees an opportunity to use the Griffins to their advantage. They will pretend to be transporting prisoners to the white dragon. Drako concerned, this is a bit risky, consults Garsa, "You think they'll buy it?" Garsa with shrugging shoulders replies, "I'm not sure, but what other options do we have at the moment? Fighting or running will only bring death."

Drako looks to Garsa, "Well, let's decide the best way to do this, and tell the others."

They get to work planning their moves to escape the Carthine's wrath. Despite their procrastination, the group centers themselves, for whatever may be coming ahead. They realize, there is much they can learn about this society of warmongering creatures.

They toughen up, and head out towards, the Caverns of Mor.

About an hour passes, and they had not seen one sign of a Carthine. Garsa was not going to assume, they could just waltz through their territory, without being seen. Sadly, in the distance, Lastra sees something running towards them.

Raspier takes this opportunity to fly up and get a better view, "It's three big cats. One has a thick brown mane running the course of its spine, and it looks incredibly strong. Actually, I see why. It's three quarters the size of Garsa!" They all gulp their last free breaths.

One of the Carthines screams out a warning, "Guards! Come quickly, we have intruders!"

The large, dark maned cat, calls out for backup and then, skids short just shy of where they are standing. Raspier instantly protects the group by jumping in front of them. Tientara follows suit, and they both open their wings to shield them. The Carthine puzzled at Raspier and Tien, studies them closely. Seeing both hawk and lion together confused him. Raspier immediately asks, "Who are you...*Cat*?

"I am Raspier. This is my partner, Tientara. These are prisoners, headed to the white dragon for prosecution. We demand, that you let us pass. Let us speak with your leader immediately to be granted safe passage."

The Carthine snaps, "I am the leader next to the king. I am his son, Prince Zertarx. We will see if you can pass through our territory. Yet first, you must tell me *what* you are. You seem to be a different kind of hybrid, but none I have seen before..."

Raspier and Tientara look up at the Prince for a moment, and try to word this correctly. They are of Mother Nature's old magick. Snobbishly laughing, they wait a bit, before answering, to add to their false personalities.

"We are griffins. Mother Nature's hunters, trackers, and messengers. The Ancient Odin is our god. His ravens are our servants. As we have explained already, these are prisoners of the white dragons', and we must continue, before the early snow. The afternoon sun is getting lower, as you can see. Making a pact, with you and your tribe, is very important to the holy Lady, Sorrokine Arou."

The Carthine Prince was exactly how the troll described, except the size. Something he conveniently forgot to tell them. He was large. Garsa never remembered them being so big, but it was a long time ago when he last saw one.

Avalo glances at Garsa and nods. He's keeping a keen eye out, to make a run for it. Celestra, behind Tarmax, tries to hide, hot headed. What she really wants to do, is to rip through this overgrown barn cat, and show him just, *'who will pass'*.

This stalemate moment only lasted for a short while. Prince Zertarx tries to scan over the gang behind the two griffin's wingspan, but they are well blocked. "The white dragon has specific orders of privacy, and she is no creature to anger or *disobey,* Carthine... *Mark my words.* "

Prince Zertarx, is losing his patience with Raspier and growls to prove it. "Raspier, come with me, if you still wish for the ability to fly, otherwise, I will gladly tear each feather out from your wings, one by one, and make your partner watch."

Raspier twitches but stands tall. Tientara takes this time, to show Raspier, how to handle this properly. "Strong and noble Prince, how may we assist in making this easy for you as well as ourselves?" Prince Zertarx sneers at the sight of a female guard but answers her question. "By coming to the meeting cavern and discussing whether or not we believe your story, or if these are real prisoners of the white dragon."

Just as they relax their wings, the Prince sees Celestra. "This pale bella you have here, what business does *she* have with Sorrokine? She surely cannot be a prisoner? Why is this female *white*, are not all panthers black, spotted or tan? From my studies this is considered rare. She is an... *albino*." Raspier not quick enough to respond, watched the Prince give an order to his men to take Celestra to the holding pens.

Raspier puts his wings around Celestra to show resistance. "Prince, you must understand this creature, odd or not, has no business, actually as a prisoner, but she is a chosen child of the white dragon. You mustn't keep her against her will, for her powers are great. Forcing her to be imprisoned will only generate more anger from the white dragon."

Somehow, Celestra's physique kept him from hearing Raspier. He motioned to the guards and they without care ripped her out from behind his wings. "My other guards here will show you to your...*quarters*. I will retrieve you later. We are finished here; guards seize them!" The Prince personally took Celestra to her pen, while the others headed off to their "so-called" quarters.

The guard nipped painfully, at their feet and tails, making them move quicker than desired. Lastra whispers to Garsa, "This is a disaster... What are we to do now?" Garsa nods in agreement but fears presently nothing can be done. So, they push onward, towards the center cavern, while Celestra and the Prince, headed in the other direction.

Chapter Forty Two

The Dragon of Doubt

Little did anyone know, but in the midst of confusion, Avalo managed to sneak away. He succeeded in completing his backup plan. Darting in and out, he spotted some thick trees he could hide behind. Exhausted, he pants until he regains composure. The old red mystic, quickly falls right onto his rump.

Claws on his head, he breathes heavy. "So, let me get this straight. Garsa and the rest of them are now prisoners of the Carthines. Hmmm, well not much here to work with. If I could conjure up proof of the white dragon, I might be able to stage a string of events to trick these pinheaded cats. Maybe, I can find a way to release them all."

As Avalo grumbles over the present dilemma, a small bunny hops over to him. It sniffs him carefully, as if it's never seen a dragon before. Sighing, with his head in his hand, Avalo peers down to the small rabbit. "Do I look irresponsible? Do I look like a failure? It wasn't too far from reality, when I was at that troll lake..." The rabbit just looks up at him twitching its nose.

Avalo continues to confess. "Could she even care about me, when so much time has passed?" The rabbit moves a bit closer, nibbling on some yellowed clovers.

"You're just a little rabbit, how could you help me?" It stares at Avalo, and twitches its pink nose. Not running, not moving, no fear. It just sits and watches him. Avalo bends down to pet the rabbit, and it stands upward to reach his hand. Smiling at the innocence this small mammal possessed, made him think back to his life on the streets.

Tiergon, the leader before Garsa's time, ended up taking Avalo under his wing. Something told him he was perfect for training and rehabilitating hybrids. Tiergon was looking for a young dragon to take care of the unicorns as well. A promising young dragon with no ties.

At the time, there was no in-house mystic, nor any general training for hybrids. Times in Drondia were changing. No longer was it only a habitat for dragons. Now, it was a sanctuary for all intelligent creatures, looking for relief from the war in the south. Tiergon knew, that training new leaders for the 'corns and the hybrids, would be a large undertaking. Avalo, an orphan at the time, was wild by nature. He commonly roamed around the royal courts, looking for food.

One day, when Tiergon, was heading a heated group of dragons, a small red whelp, ran out from under the table. At the last second, the guard made him fall and drop everything. He had stolen from them all. This dragon was a young Avalo.

A stern unmovable dragon walked up to him, as the guard held him tight. "Who are you little whelp? Have you no manners? Why are you taking things that do not belong to you?

A tall dragon walked up to him, "I'm Tiergon, leader of Drondia. I order you to return these items immediately!" Avalo had no choice, but to do as he was told. Apologizing to Tiergon's company, he handed back the items.

Most of the dragons were curious, why a whelp would need to steal in the first place. Tiergon asks him if his parents knew where he was, concerned for his welfare.

"I'm sorry sir, I don't have parents. They abandoned me at birth, and I've been living off the streets to survive."

Tiergon was surprised at this answer, but understood why he was stealing. The little whelp had no other choice. Every creature, has the drive to survive. Realizing he needed a dragon that had no roots to become his new mystic, he came up with a plan to school the young dragon and put him on a better path. This was very convenient. A student ended up finding him. Trying not to look as stern, he asks him some questions, "Whelp, do you know your name?" Avalo looks up at this towering dragon and shook his head yes. "My name is Avalo Ryu."

Tiergon wondered why an orphan of common dragon blood was given a middle name. Ryu was a foreign name very common beyond the great waters. Usually, that's only reserved for royalty or given under heroic conditions in adulthood, not birth. He figured Avalo was a gift from the Dakinis and should not question. Still, couldn't he have received a sturdier character for the job, instead of a thieving orphan whelp? His instincts told him despite is concern, that this was the dragon for the job.

Tiergon told his company they would meet up later and apologized for the interruption, but this little whelp had some learning to do. Avalo now terribly frightened he was caught stealing, trembled. Not only was that bad enough, but he ended up thieving belongings from the leader of dragon city himself. *What will he do with me?* Shivering from the thoughts, Avalo walked with Tiergon down the hall passing the kitchen.

Passing in silence, Avalo had no idea really what he'll do. They both walked without conversation. Coming up to a large room with books, Tiergon points all around slowly opening up his hand into an arc. Gazing upon all this literature, overwhelmed Avalo, but equally alarmed him. *Am I to read all these pages? Maybe memorize them, or my punishment is to reorganize them all?* Tiergon saw his curiosity for the books. He was certain Avalo could grow up right, with careful schooling and become the next mystic. It was the fear he couldn't see sadly.

The city hasn't had a mystic helping hybrids for millennia, and the closest one they had was Tiergon. He had spent time with Curlothier, the last mystic when Tiergon was a young whelp, but never took it on as dedicated.

"Avalo Ryu, how would you feel if I were to tell you, you can stay with me here in the royal estate?" Avalo stared back up at Tiergon amazed it wasn't a form of punishment that uttered out from his mouth.

Staring at the large orange dragon, Avalo felt so small. His back had so many spikes; nothing could pierce through those scales. Not even steel. Avalo was amazed that this gift of training was being offered to him. He could finally be off the streets and fed well for a change. Avalo figured Tiergon had other plans for him. "Do you wish to make me a guard sir?" Tiergon laughed, "Well I see you are a bit perceptive little whelp. You are almost correct. I wish to teach you the ways of the mystics, and in turn, put you in charge of rehabilitating and teaching hybrids." Avalo's mouth opened wide and couldn't believe what his ears were hearing. *Does this strong intelligent dragon leader think I'm the future mystic for Drondia? How could this be?*

Avalo looks back up at Tiergon and smiles. "I'm glad to join the team, sir. When do I start?" Tiergon reaches down and shook the whelp's hand. "First thing is to remember we do not steal little mystic. We *earn* our keep here." Avalo blushes and puts his head down smiling.

Coming out of the walk down memory lane, Avalo realizes time is not on his side. Shaking his head out, he must think fast how to save everyone, before this gets worse.

Now inside the Caverns of Mor, Celestra and Prince Zertarx were already at one of the holding pens, "So just what kind of panther *are* you? I've never seen such a beautiful coat. Pure white like the snow. Why does the *white dragon* think you are a *magick* child?" Celestra not briefed on this line of Raspier's lie, quickly thinks up a logical answer for the large Prince. "Uh, well, I was given a rite of passage by one of her representatives and now I'm leading these prisoners with General Raspier and Sergeant Tientara. It's very pressing matters we get to her on time, she hates when people are late."

"You haven't answered my other question pretty bella, why are you white? Are you an albino?" Celestra goes with this lie. "Yes; I'm an albino panther, which means my pigment wasn't programmed into my genetic coding." The Prince, who apparently was a learned cat, comprehended this. "Wow, a real live albino, never thought I'd ever see one in my life. You will certainly be entertaining... Well, I must go off to speak with my father about the whole lot of you, for prisoners must be always recorded in his journal."

Celestra realizing the slip, comments. "Hey, I thought you said we weren't prisoners..." The Prince obviously being seen through, gives her no chance to explain. "Listen fluffy little bella, first off, we are a warrior race, which means any creature entering our territory, is guilty until proven innocent by the King. Second, we are out of bellas, due to the greggil wars. They fight much better than males when it comes down to tactical maneuvers; however, they are not as...strong. In other words, you may be a perfect bella for furthering the reproduction of our kind. Sleep well; a guard will bring you your first meal by morning. Oh, and on second thought, I recommended you don't sleep, because our guards are terribly frustrated and may desire to...uh...*meet you*. Good day bella." Celestra cringes over the thought. Sadly now, without a doubt, she can see they most certainly were prisoners.

Tarmax was worried about Celestra's wellbeing. He figured all these Carthines were just as restless as the Prince. Sitting in their so-called quarters, Tarmax admits to himself they *are* in no way guests. Garsa and Partune were discussing the same thing and they all agree.

Lu'barthrow seemed preoccupied with Celestra as well as Tarmax. Garsa understood this was perfectly normal for the two. Trying to lighten the mood, he starts to bring them together. "Hey, we are all alive and no harm has come to us as of now.... Right? That's much better than we expected, so there will be a way out of here. We just need to keep spirits high, okay?" Yewdrone looked around the cell. He was carefully making a full circle counting the number of heads as Lastra took notice of his behavior, "What are you doing Yew?" Yewdrone stopped and started to snicker. "You guys know what? Something is very funny here..." No one was really in the mood for humor so they just rolled their eyes at the little dragon. "What?" They all say. Yewdrone softly giggles, "Look who's not here!"

Yewdrone starts laughing as they take a look for themselves. Garsa realized what the whelp was pointing out. Avalo wasn't with them. "By stars and teeth, that sly old dragon did get away! Now, this changes everything!" Where the others were expecting Avalo to be scheming out a fine-toothed plan to retrieve them all from prison, he was actually sitting, sulking over past mistakes.

He was lost in his memories with the little bunny sitting in his lap, petting it softly. The play in his mind was at the second act when he first met Sorrokine Arou, the white dragon.

Remembering back, he recalls her sparkling iridescent scales just like his own. They were smooth, wide and short. Light lavender spikes lined her spine, leading down to a four-pronged tail tip. Small needles cascaded down her snout, with a short-spiraled horn in the center. These made a triangle with the two rear pointing horns, coming out of her brow. Her curves, her muscle lines, the small way that her silhouette danced across the ground when they would fly low – this all made him melt. "What a superb dragon. She was perfect in every way."

Poor Avalo was lost in a sea of emotions over his past love. He felt her hate for him must exist still even after 35 years.

Sorrokine Arou was an elite dragon, kept under restrictive schooling by her parents. Sadly, she wasn't very street smart. She knew her parents did not approve of her frolicking with such a low bloodline. They had tried many times to set her up with this purple dragon from the high north. Frukschtein was a pompous and shallow stocky brute with perfect genes. Dragons from the north are infamously known for overzealous personalities as well as being presumptuous and conceited. This was common for a dragon from the city of King Deetstro Trea himself. One thing you can say about them, is they sure hate greggils. They will out-right char them on the spot, and then chomp them down as a tasty snack. Sorrokine truly had no interest in courting a half twit from the royal north. Avalo had charm and intelligence but most of all, heart. Many had more faith in the rebel side of the south and Drondia City at that time. This was exactly what drew Sorrokine to Avalo in the first place.

Avalo had become very skilled in mysticism at this point. Tiergon's and Curlothier's training had advanced him greatly in his training. Sorrokine and Avalo used to study together often. One day after Curlothier's class, they met up for a quick bite to eat. Sitting down in the dining room of the royal academy, they discuss the lessons from the day. Avalo, having mating on his mind, wanted to get a bit more personal. So, he convinced her to take a walk to the west gate. Avalo told Sorrokine he wanted to show her a new method of levitation that he was taught. Before he could even finish his statement, Frukschtein walked passed.

He growled quietly at the sight of the two of them talking. He felt that Sorrokine wasn't being smart in hanging around an orphan from the streets. Despite Frukschtein being rotten to the core, he was certainly cunning. Avalo just sneered as they passed him. Frukschtein just lifted his tail high and ignored Avalo, winking at Sorrokine slyly.

Knowing night would be coming soon, Avalo wanted to woo Sorrokine and prove that his affections towards her were genuine. Sorrokine was impressed that Avalo was taking studying much more seriously. "That dragon can change for the better. My folks will see. They'll see he is meant for greatness."

Sorrokine was pondering the justification of doing a levitation spell by the river during sunset. As Avalo walked up, she realized he had other things on his mind. Growing a bit more aware of his feelings, Sorrokine at first wasn't sure how to handle it. Deepening her connection meant many other problems outside her life with Avalo. Sorrokine wanted to make sure his future was stable first; that *he* was stable. Watching this young dragon attempt a difficult spell just to prove his worth was indeed amusing. Their surroundings were silent except the chirps of mule deer, crickets, and the rustle of leaves from the wind. The sun setting in vibrant shades of purple and red, laid a beautiful hue on their bodies.

Tiergon only saw Sorrokine as a distraction for Avalo. He was too close to finishing up his schooling, to have it all destroyed by hormones. He was always trying to prove to the dragon collective that Avalo, was the new city mystic. Avalo always seemed to mess everything up at just the right moment. Their faith in him was often lost quickly. Where he was to perform a big transformation display for the collective, he ended up turning their seats into snakes. Where he was to do a large job on recalculating the history books under the gun, he fell asleep and knocked them even further out of order. Always missing the right moment, he just passed through life by the scales of his tail. Tiergon saw this exuberant energy with the promise of future refinement; however, he was careless and forgetful most of the time. The question that loomed in Tiergon's mind was whether or not Avalo will be able to grow up and take on responsibilities. The only thing Tiergon could do was wait.

The collective was growing impatient with Tiergon, and his choice to nurture such a wild card. This was also bringing down Sorrokine's reputation quickly. This aggravated her royal bloodline funding schooling. It was growing even more apparent that this was a job for more developed dragons…especially ones without a love interest. Tiergon had one chance left to show them all that these two dragons were written in the sands of time. They were the real chosen ones to uphold their job as leaders.

It was the young fire breathers' last day of finals. Sorrokine ran to the main lobby of Drondia's academy. She was rushing for no reason because it was early; however, Avalo as per usual, overslept. Sorrokine went through her finals and the collective were pleased with her results. Coming out of the academy, she noted that he still wasn't here. Sorrokine equally growing tired of his irresponsibility, telepathically threw him from his bed, with violent words of disapproval. "Get up you lazy dragon or you'll fail! This time it's your life!"

Avalo awoke and madly rushed to the lobby of the academy. Tiergon relaxed, once he saw Avalo quickly run through the doors. He knew at this point; he was on his own. Pushing him into the room, the collective only growled in disapproval Avalo made it on time. It was blatantly obvious they didn't accept him. Avalo passed Sorrokine and winked at her, but seemingly a bit frustrated, she turned away.

Inside, the collective watched sternly, ready to fail him and sadly prove Tiergon wrong. In the far back, Garsa another student of Tiergon's at the time, watched from the shadows. Avalo takes the stage and starts explaining to the collective what he had planned for them. Grunts and sighs came from the judging table.

Trying to remember his presentation on how he will collect certain objects by levitation and telekinesis was hard enough. Their negative energy wasn't helping the matter. he was to make a stable plaster, without the use of his hands. In front of him on the table, was limestone powder, water, tar, and stones. In the far-right corner, there was an open hole in a thick wall he had to patch in under two minutes. There were two torches on the wall that also needed to be lit without touch. Avalo did the entire final exam in less than two minutes and the collective was blown away. Verunith whispered to Curlothier, "How could a slacking orphan, be so thorough and exact, in such little time?"

The collective was astonished simply because none of them could do such a test in the time allotted. Tiergon fainted from the stress, and Garsa caught the heavy dragon before he clocked his head on the ground. Shortly after, Avalo raced through the halls straight to the outside garden to find Sorrokine. She seemed so distant, so indifferent to him, it made him quite nervous. "Uh...Sorrokine, are you mad at me?"

She turns her head up to him and couldn't stay mad at such a good-hearted male, no matter how irresponsible he was. "No Avalo, I'm glad you blew the scales off the collective, I knew you would." Avalo still confused as to why she was so absent of emotion, went to nudge her in appreciation of her support, but she pulled away. "Look Avalo, if I didn't telepathically wake you up, we wouldn't be sitting here like this. Why can't you show some responsibility?" Avalo was puzzled why she wanted such silly things out of a young dragon. He tried to explain his actions, but she cut him off. "I know we are young, but we are different from the rest of dragon society. We each have an incredibly important job that will require our life's dedication, and you show no drive. This worries me, for it tells my heart that you will not be able to take care of me or my future whelps."

His heart broke over the words so he turned his face away from hers. "Can I ask you one more thing? Will you walk to Sow River with me? I wanted to give you something Larcatch gave me if we both passed the finals. I've felt you were the one to wear it since the moment I laid eyes on your beautiful face." Sorrokine now feeling guilted into this, had no choice. So they walked.

Heading out the east gate, the sun was warming their faces on that chilly early spring morning. Silence sewed both their mouths shut as bird songs replaced their words. No glances, no expressions, just a steady walking gate to the river. This was very different from their special visits from times before.

Avalo deeply desired for her to be his partner. He understood though she would have to leave soon with the group of anicorns and unicorns for the Northwest Territory above the Sands of McFlout. That's where her future will continue. His was here in the dragon city. Maybe he could at least convince her to take the necklace that Larcatch gave him. To take a piece of his heart with her up north.

The calm river flowed in its usual pattern like all things in life, but there will always be those souls who need to buck the system. Avalo was no stranger to this; neither was Frukschtein. The young mystics weren't aware of the runoff creeping up fast from the mountains. A certainly nasty dragon misdirected the flow. Soon this entire area would be flooded.

Avalo terrified walks with Sorrokine hoping he has one more chance of giving his heart to her. Reaching the river, he sits her down and seems to be thinking hard about what he'll say. Feeling a bit bad, Sorrokine just patiently waits. Just when she believes he's going to be all sweet and nice, Avalo turns around and starts to wrestle. "Okay little lady, you got to fight me to get this necklace. Can you do it?"

Roughhousing wasn't exactly what Sorrokine thought he had planned, but refused to back down from a challenge. Lunging straight for each other, they roll around a bit biting and scratching. Avalo starts to pull out his magick and makes a dip in the ground to trip her. Falling down on top of her he pins her down and growls in her face, "Oh, has the mighty Princess been pinned by the straggly orphan whelp? Oh to shame, what will the collective think of this?"

Steam rising from her nose she growls back and uses her tail to tap him on the shoulder. Stupidly thinking there is actually someone there, Avalo turns around. Sorrokine then uses her back legs to launch him high into the air. Catching flight, he swoops down and throws her almost head first into the river. She managed to escape it quickly and begins to laugh.

Absorbed deeply in play, they couldn't hear the approaching floodwaters. A deer in the background calls out about the danger, but they cannot hear. Frukschtein smiles in the distance, knowing all too well his meddling scheme has worked. Continuing in their play, the water slowly rose around their ankles.

Avalo launches another move, but Sorrokine falls too deep this time. "Why on Gaia, would you do that! The river is swelling!" He attempts to save her with all his young heart. Frantically flapping his wings, he doesn't have the strength to pick her up. They fall into the water, only to be swept down the river.

"Sorrokine, stay with me!" She gasps for air, as water starts to make its way into her nostrils. They held onto each other for dear life, as they flew straight towards a large boulder in the middle of the river. "You stupid dragon, how could you let this happen to me! I can't take you anymore! You really are a threat to my life!"

"Sorro', this really isn't the place to discuss this right now, concentrate on getting out!" The waters start to overpower their grip, and their claws drag along the rock, making deep lines in the stone. Out of nowhere, Frukschtein swoops down above them. "I see you two young dragons decided to ignore the warning about the river. Not so smart."

Avalo handles yet another situation badly. Looking up to the laughing dragon, he ignorantly retaliates against his mockeries. "If you're only going to stand there and make fun of us, why don't you just leave?"

Frukschtein astonished this young dragon has the nerve to push him away, when they obviously needed help, takes advantage of the situation. Showing no concern, Frukschtein flies off to leave them to their fate.

At this moment, Sorrokine gives up on the idea of ever getting deeply involved with Avalo. This dragon completely lacks true common sense. End of story. Letting go of the rock and Avalo, she swims downstream, trying as hard as she can to stay afloat. Avalo panics and starts to swim after Sorrokine. He manages to grab her despite the roaring rapids. They both begin to sink, as he cannot understand the combined weight they share. Sorrokine furious bites into his arm and he lets go. One thing nature surely gave Sorrokine was an impressive set of teeth. "Leave me alone you wretched creature! I want nothing to do with you and your black cloud of disaster!"

After some time, they were both thrown ashore. Avalo coughed as he pulled himself up. He sees Sorrokine motionless on the sand. "By the great dragon please be alive!" Running towards her he kneels at her body trying not to panic. Not only has she lost her fire, but no breath leaves her nostrils. He pushes on her chest and prays she'll kick out of it. "You're a fighter. Please awaken Sorrokine…"

Soon enough, she spits up the water keeping her from breathing, and turns onto her side. Barely conscious she laid there for at least an hour before waking. Avalo just sat there with tears welling in his eyes as he petted her softly. When she awoke, he was curled on top of her.

She slashed him with her claws and pushed away. "You...Stupid...Dragon...You almost killed us both! Then you deny the obvious help that the Dakinis sent to us with your youthful pride! I must find who that dragon was.

Bah, be gone with you and your affections. Loving you would be like loving a greggil skinning my hide." She crawls over to a tree to prop herself up and tries to walk. Her legs quiver more and more until she falls. Now on all fours, she humbly walks away trying to imagine how she will get to the city from here alone.

"Wait! Sorrokine, let me help you back. I'll carry you the whole way, you can trust me." She turns to his face and stops. Staring him down, she goes to burn him but nothing comes out. "Great! Now my fire is knocked out you buffoon. Just leave me alone!"

Seeing Sorrokine walk away from him, his heart began to crumble. He has botched everything up in the worst of ways. Not with his finals, not with the collective, but he failed the only dragon that truly loved him. As she slowly walks away, Avalo hears wings in the distance, a few pairs of them.

Looking up, he sees what appears to be three fast-moving white clouds. Sorrokine knows who is approaching just by the sound alone. "Arito, Shalti, Trastla, Thank the heavens you've come to rescue me! You must have heard my cries in the distance, you faithful 'corns."

Hatred was an alien emotion to 'corns, yet they almost felt this, seeing their newest master, injured. The three quickly stood, on their two hind legs. This made a trinity triangle. They placed their horns together above her.

A huge white circle of light, enveloped her entire body. Instantly she lost consciousness and started to soak up their light. Color came back to her face and she began to awaken. The three anicorns back up neighing loudly to wake her further. Sorrokine rose and was surprised that it worked. Turning to them, she hugged their necks and congratulated them on fine-tuning their healing spell. "Let's go, we are finished here."

At that moment, the anicorns looked to Avalo with sadness. They knew they must leave him weak as their master gave no orders to help him. So Avalo laid on the bank still bleeding and winded, yet defeated.

Walking along the side of the river, Avalo hangs his head in great shame. He retraced their steps to see if he could find the necklace Larcatch gave him. She was his favorite hybrid. He often was mothered by her. When Avalo misbehaved, she would set him straight in two shakes of a dragon's tail. Hoping he would come across the key soon, he scans the ground looking for anything silver in the sand. When he was just about to give up, he finally sees it gleaming from the corner of his eye. "I'll thank the Dakinis for this one later."

Now feeling a bit better he found the necklace, Avalo starts the slow journey back to the city.

Sorrokine finally arrives with her students. Tiergon was waiting for her. Displeased she left without Avalo, he stared Sorrokine down. "Why did you leave him behind? Have I taught you *nothing?*" Sorrokine furious Tiergon scolds her for this, tries to explain what happened. Tiergon understands why she is so mad afterward, but not why she would leave him to fend for himself injured.

"You could have had the anicorns help him Sorro'. This is not good to show them pre-meditated selection when it comes to healing." Sorrokine looks at Tiergon with stern eyes. "Look, I am done with him. I have to take the 'corns to the northwest territory tomorrow and I must rest. Go get his babysitter if you need him rescued. Remember, he may be older, but he is no genius. He's a reckless dimwitted dragon. Good *day* sir!"

In the background, Frukschtein waits to catch up with her, obviously very proud his plan worked.

Tiergon was happy that Avalo passed his collective final. He will now be able to finish the training in his hybrid classes. Yet Tiergon was troubled that he failed the most important test. Proving he can be responsible for another soul. He worried mentally he was still too immature. *Avalo may not have royal blood in him after all,* Tiergon thinks. *Otherwise, these traits would have been present by now.* Seeing that Sorrokine left Avalo behind in this state, shows that she failed just the same. They were both too young to understand this kind of accountability. Maybe the dragon collective was right after all.

As he usually does, Tiergon sent for Larcatch to come and tend to Avalo. Now a mother with her own kits and whelps, she really had no spare time to tend to the reluctant dragon. Bardone was showing trinity traits and needed more of her attention. He sent out one of the griffin ravens with his message to retrieve Larcatch from her den.

Avalo had almost reached the southern gate, when Larcatch stopped him dead in his tracks. "Have you no sense of duty young one? It's not proper for the future caretaker of the hybrids, to be constantly reprimanded *by* a hybrid.

I should crack your tail in two for that stunt you pulled out by the Sow River. You were educated enough to know that this is the time of year the meltwaters can overflow the river. Shame on you! Also, I see you've let down Sorrokine for the last time. She has no desire to even see you again. Take this advice: Return to the city. Apologize to Sorrokine. To keep personal respect, you should be as humble as possible. Next, take your much-needed spirit journey. It's way overdue. Call the corners inside yourself and see how you can fix this dilemma. Honestly, I'm not sure of your success rate. For that kind of magick my whelp, is beyond even the Dakinis control."

Avalo hung his head low, for yet again Larcatch is right. He has truly messed things up. "I just don't know how to act...I'm like a horse running with a blindfold on. I wish I could change. Tiergon believes me to be the one, yet I cannot will myself to hasten my maturity like Sorrokine has."

Avalo stares unhappily back at Larcatch. Frustrated, she snorts a fire streak straight over his head. "Did you even hear a word I said?" Avalo quickly answers, "Yes Ma'am.", knowing her temper. "Now Avalo, understand I have my own young to take care of and they consume most of my time. Especially Bardone, he's a little trinity I just feel it. You, however, will always be *my* surrogate son.

Calikon and I have our hands full right now. I saw a greggil dragon around the den. This is the last time I am doing this. Meet back up with me in three days when you feel you have completed your journey. I plan to move my family a day later than that. We will discuss your right of passage and what you've learned."

Avalo in tears at this point, hugs Larcatch tightly, and without hesitation, curls his neck around her. She knows this is finally his time to show his true potential, or she is gone...

Avalo snaps out of his daydreaming, and noticed the air smelled sour. Something is going on around him. He might be past the point he can help. Looking down to the bunny, he places it back to the ground and thanked it. "You have reminded me, dragons are always innocent whelps at heart little friend, and for that, I give you this:"

In front of the rabbit, Avalo conjures up a thick patch of fresh growing clovers with tasty flowers. The bunny overwhelmed with joy, begins eating them. Avalo now feels the disturbance growing and knows he must act quickly. He cannot fail them, for that means he also will fail himself.

Chapter Forty Three

Where are you Drazbart?

Checking in on the others, we see the Carthine King Certalk, sitting humbly on his thrown. A stoic creature of old war creed, he is by blood and teeth alone. This cat truly lives by his tribe's code. As he sits, King Certalk stares out at his right paw cat, Drazbart. "Has nobility in this clan not been achieved by battle scars over kind deeds? Has not many a Carthine warrior shed their blood for this title, even died for the honor, Drazbart?"

He approaches nervously, "Uh, yes my King." Certalk puffs out his strong chest, and bares his yellowed teeth. "Ah, well, why can we not overcome these greggils and their petty war against the dragons? Why must we now hunt hybrids as well?" Drazbart not sure whether or not to answer, looks up quite uneasy.

The King obviously hungry from his thoughtful demands, yells at the small carthine. "Drazbart, fetch me a few deer legs. Would you? *Quickly*!"

Drazbart runs off to the hunters so he can pass the order along. As he's walking, he remembers back to his younger years as a kit with his parents. Even at a very young age, he was fully aware of the separation between the Carthines. Drazbart's parents were renegades against the war. Normal life was just a dream for Drazbart as a kit. Other Carthines refused to mock fight with him for two main reasons: First, he wasn't accepted enough to fit in. Second, his parents refused to let Drazbart participate in any folly or fighting. If this meant he was to play alone, then he had to.

The group his parents belonged to was 'The power without power'. PWP, for short. They begged the King for change. It was a new world where logic could save thousands, but the King refused. Brute strength and war, shall always keep the old code alive and prosperous. – This was the King's motto.

Drazbart, an indentured servant to the King, began his life-long dedication, at the ripe age of ten. Groge, the General of War, had caught his parents stealing battle plans from his office. Drazbart was fully aware of the punishment for such a crime. In a last-ditch effort, he begged the King not to kill his parents. In exchange for their lives, he would become the king's assistant, but without freedom. The King's slave, was his title.

His parents begged Drazbart, to let them die honorably. He, unlike other Carthines, had a heart. Drazbart couldn't believe that any harm would come to them. Sadly, his parents *were* right. They were tortured and killed later that night for their crimes. Drazbart's heart broke like a sheet of ice hitting the ground.

These memories haunt him to this day. He tries to shake them free, to continue onward.

Skidding into the hunter's den, he begs them to kill three deer for the King, but only gets laughter in return. "Oh, the King's puppet is begging for deer? Ha, we're on break little cat, so go tell your King he can wait!"

Drazbart offers, to let them stay the night in the Oct Bella's room. Immediately they ready for the hunt. Drazbart knowing she will not be pleased taking care of three hunters in one night, will expect something in return. The Oct bella is the last female alive out of the Carthines, simply because she bears the chosen coloring; pale tan. The King and the Prince had her raised in the castle with the lap of luxuries, but her return payment would be to make sure the race continued.

Knowing this would generate more of her breed, and it would keep the males happy, she didn't mind all that much. She was always well fed with the finest of comforts.

Females cannot hold high positions in the Carthine's world, for males consider them less intelligent. In actuality, they are much smarter. Bella's are used in battle just as much as the males. They maintain greater speeds and were better at maneuvering. In a true war clan, all participate to defend their territory. There are no exceptions besides those with cub.

During the greggil war, it was not breeding season, so sadly all had to fight for their territory. The Oct bella was the only one not captured. She will remain in the caverns for proper protection. Her name was quite suited to her looks, Sandtrala. There were rumors she was to become the Prince's mate before the war, but many things changed after that.

Drazbart walks up to her door and rings the second hanging bell. This lets her know that it was a royal guard on duty, not just a fellow in waiting.

Sandtrala, opens the door and rolls her eyes at Drazbart. Knowing it's another request he's going to ask of her, she sighs. "Hello Drazzy, what favors do you come to ask of me now?" Drazbart ashamed he has to gamble her gifts, to have the king fed, lowers his head. Without even hearing what he has to say, she picks his face up with her nose and smiles. "I *know* Drazbart...I know...It's just as hard for me too. So...How many are there this time; four, five?"

Drazbart holds up three toes. "Three hunters your sweetness, they wouldn't kill otherwise." Sandtrala understands, and preps herself for the guards before they return with their kills. "Look, it's okay Drazbart. I forgive you."

She pats him on the head and turns to close the door. Drazbart leaves her to her privacy, and heads back to the king.

- For whatever that was worth.

No emotion in his actions, empty as far as dreams go, Drazbart pushes on towards the door to the king's royal room.

Still, something told him inside he had a greater destiny, beyond this battle of blood and beauty.

For now, he must do what he can to survive. Sandtrala was right, for there is no logic resisting and losing your life - like the renegades.

Walking into the King's quarters, he feels a tug at his heartstrings. Something is pulling him towards the other corridor. Ears turning in all directions, the little Carthine smells the air to see if anyone is around. The pull gets stronger as he approaches the holding pens. *Someone has a very strong inner light in there.* Creeping up to the mouth of the cavern, he looks down the lonely walkway.

Scattering spiders and scarabs, litter the floor like busy greggils in their cluttered markets. "That positive energy is so strong! Where is it coming from?"

The little Carthine starts to run. He desperately wants to see the face that holds this inner fire. Skidding short in front of the last pen, he hears crying from inside. "What in the world is a bella doing in *here*?" Peeking through a hole, he sees Celestra.

He's overwhelmingly smitten, just like the rest of those jerks he serves. Taking a moment to center himself, he thinks on how awful this must be for her. She's small like him, and her fur is pure white. What he can't seem to understand is why she's locked away in here. He was to see the King and tell him that his meal would arrive shortly. Yet here he was, drawn to her.

Lost in thought, Drazbart's mind began to wander. *Streamline and soft, her curves were like a river bend in Spring. This snowy bella couldn't be on trial. She is way too innocent.*

Pushing on the door, with his paws to reach the hole, he doesn't realize the space between the lock and the frame is rather loose. The door slams forward to knock him backward and startles Celestra. "Who's there? I hear you moving around..."

Drazbart hears her voice and instantly falls in love. Her beauty leaves him speechless. *Wow, what an accent, what a voice. She speaks and my heart misses a beat.*

Celestra can only stare up at the small hole in the door, waiting for her brute to plunder her. Drazbart jumps up again and sees her glaring into his eyes, yet something throws them completely off their guard. Both freeze in the moment, and lock into each other's souls.

A large voice boomed inside their heads, saying:

"SPEAK NOW!"

Instantly Celestra and Drazbart, are mentally transferred to another dimension. She is fully aware of what this place is, but the Carthine apparently has no clue. These are the sacred planes. Not sure who conjured up such a meditation, Celestra stays alert and follows through. Trembling, Drazbart looks up at Celestra and holds his gaze, fearful to turn away. "Who *are* you bella? How did you enchant me so? Just... where are we?"

Seeing he is of no real harm at this point, she wants to explain. Celestra walks up to him and sits closer. Examining her surroundings, she sees somehow this Carthine has the gift of visions like herself. Still staring into each other's eyes, both are locked in a trance. Celestra tries to guide him worried he might lose his mind. "Well, for starters, what's *your* name? I have provided my own, so please, be polite."

Drazbart calming down a bit, looks back to Celestra. "I am the right scribe to the Carthine King."

Celestra was surprised. *How could such a small cat, have that kind of power?* "Well this may be hard for you to swallow Drazbart, but you have conjured up a sacred space for us. This is the *other* realm, the subconscious plane. This is a form of *meditation,* the world inside of our minds. Frankly, I'm not sure whether to thank you or be *wary* of you. *Any* creature not aware of his own gifts, is always more dangerous than one, who *is* mindful."

Drazbart was completely confused and honestly, not sure whether or not to believe her. "So you mean to tell me I have this *gift of visions*? How come it never showed itself before?"

Celestra understands that he's completely ignorant of magick. Drazbart doesn't exactly live in a spiritually charged community. So she tries to explain all of this in a digestible format. "Drazbart, the only world you know right now is the middle world. Then there are two more sub-planes. The upper world and the lower world. Some creatures have the ability to exist in all three. Have you ever had a feeling you are half-awake? As if your soul was detached from your body? These are all forms of mental visions. Do you understand?"

Drazbart shakes his head yes. "So, if I understand you correctly, there are other worlds I cannot see unless I am placed in this trance? I can apparently, reach these worlds, by adjusting my energy and performing this act called *Meditation?*" Celestra senses that he was absorbing what she explained to him, so she continues. "I would tell you my real identity, but it must remain hidden. As far as you know, I am a simple panther. You received an education on your gifts, and I'll as payment, keep my truths unknown. Drazbart, please help me and my friends escape. Please help us…"

This tiny panther's voice of reason and kind heart, deeply touched him. "You see Celestra, I am a servant to the King and I have no freedom.

The odd thing, is the King has already sent out a messenger to the white dragon, to ask for assistance with the greggil war. We Carthines usually keep to ourselves.

This deal we made with the greggils, is creating a deep hatred for dragons and hybrids alike. Our clan was brainwashed to think they were responsible. These nasty upright creatures swore this was the truth, and my clan believe it one hundred percent. The King sent out an altered soldier, to appear like a mock hybrid. He placed the warrior on a very light diet, and had two of his four fangs shaved down to make him look like a hybrid. They even painted a star on his forehead and shaved his fluffy tail. The poor Carthine marched out to meet his doom with honor. Dumb, in my opinion.

As I perceived, he was tortured and eaten by a troll the next day. Stupid cat went the wrong way after we carefully taught him the map for days. Maybe if you can assure the King your connection with the white dragon is pure, he might use all of you as messengers instead of losing another Carthine warrior. Between you and I Celestra, I think the Prince will have some ideas about you. He has taken a fancy to rare felines that can be interbred, so be fairly warned. Also, if a very large and muscular Carthine by the name of Groge ever comes to your pen, be firm. Don't let him push you around.

If you put up a good fight, and do not waiver, he will back down. Groge has a deep respect for strong females. You'll know that one instantly. He has a huge scar on his eye, can't miss it." Celestra thanked Drazbart for his help, and he thanked her. A deep connection was now made.

Hearing Drazbart run away, Celestra settles down and ponders how odd it was for her to meet him. He obviously had powers hidden deep within his soul. Not really knowing the real intentions Drazbart had, Celestra prays she wasn't wrong in trusting this vision. A connection to the sacred planes is not common amongst strangers. This is where she must keep a positive attitude and push forward with her decision wholeheartedly.

Celestra thinks instantly about her companions in their own cells. *The only one who probably could reach me now is Lu'barthrow, but it always scares him that I can do this to him...oh well, sorry Lu'barthrow...this time it's necessary!*

Giggling softly to herself, she prepares by chanting his name. "Lu'barthrow, blood brother, find my voice. Find my voice heart brother. Find my voice..." Chanting repeatedly, Celestra feels her spirit lighten. Making her way through the energy that surrounds her, otherwise known as the ether, she finds Lu'barthrow's energy. Releasing her spirit, she looks at her meditating body and smirks. *It's always so interesting to look at yourself from a third-party view.*

Slowly walking out of her pen, Celestra looks down the hallway. It seemed rather long and dark. She feels there is a fork somewhere ahead leading to other cells. The air is cooler and smells of living creatures. She looks around the bend and smells the air again. Lu'barthrow's energy grows stronger as she walks further along the trail. Looking down the tunnel, Celestra sees a soft glow up ahead, and feels a cool breeze. Sniffing the air, she can smell her friends just up ahead somewhere.

Excited, she starts to run. Celestra sees a large circular room. Stopping short abruptly, she can hardly make anything out. So, she sits and adjusts her eyes. All across the walls are inscriptions in another language, unfamiliar and blue. Looking at the ceiling, she sees white stones inside wooden beams. In the middle, was a large red crystal. It was a ruby. In the center of the large round table, was an immense quartz stone. Celestra's hackles rise and she softly growls...*There is ancient energy here. The Carthines did not build this. Quite frankly, I do not think they have any idea what it really is. I **must** remember this room...*

Celestra shakes out of it, and centers herself. Continuing on her spirit path, she smells the air again. She sensed there were two tunnels further along. She was startled by the discovery of that ancient room. *I will never forget that power. It was electric!* Calming down, she concentrates on Lu'barthrow's energy. She instantly feels his anger and almost falls over...

- That cat is a regular lightning bolt of power. I know I am on the right track...

Celestra runs in the shadows along the tunnel wall and finds the holding pens. Trying to keep her spirits up, she walks to the cell she thinks they may be in. Shadows engulf the entire area. Luckily, Garsa and Partune were talking rather loudly. Perking her ears towards them, she listens in. Now joined by Drako, they are discussing escape routes to the white dragon.

In the dim light, Lastra and Yewdrone were discussing healing recipes and herbs. Raspier and Tientara were taking a nap on each other, while Tarmax and Lu'barthrow, just stare out blankly into nothing. She tries to figure out why they're in such a deep trance-like state. *We're alive and well...Why would they worry? We'll get out of this.* She tries harder to concentrate but feels herself slipping out of spirit.

Celestra sits down in between both her brother, and her fancy. She decides quickly, to channel their energy. She touches the both of their shoulders once with her nose. "Uh, Lu'barthrow, if you're feeling scared, I guess I don't mind the cuddling..." Lu'barthrow stares at Tarmax confused. "I didn't touch you, but I certainly felt someone touch me...What's going on here?" As Celestra figured, Lu'barthrow starts to panic. He lets out a low defensive growl while sinking to the ground. "There is a spiritual intruder amongst us, I can feel it! Back up everyone... Someone or something is trying to take our minds..."

Tarmax figured that Lu'barthrow pulled this stunt to get out of his moment of weakness. Garsa looks up and oddly, also feels a presence. Lastra's feelers stand tall and alert. She smiles and glances over at Tarmax. Whispering in his ear, she tells him what she thinks. "I know who it is and it's definitely *no one* here to hurt us...Catch my drift Tarmax?"

He instantly feels that Celestra is with them. Tarmax starts to laugh. "Hey Lu'barthrow, that's no intruder, It's Celestra! I feel her!" Lu'barthrow stops huffing, and calms down a bit. Sniffing the air, he realizes there is a faint trace of her scent. "...*Hey, Celestra...*is that *you*?"

Celestra speaks, but tries to be soothing... *Lu'barthrow heart brother, they're right, I'm projecting and your energy helped me find you. You must speak aloud what I am telling you. There is a new development that might help us.* Lu'barthrow does as his sister asks, and will speak for her.

Listen closely. This small Carthine by the name of Drazbart, ended up tracking down my energy from somewhere in the caverns. He is very gifted in the ways of visions, and when he gazed into my eyes, he threw us into a sacred place to talk. I will advise you, that, he is the King's servant and unfortunately indentured due to his renegade parents. He warned me of two Carthines in particular.

The Prince enjoys collecting rare females, which is why he favors me. The second is the general of war, Groge. Apparently, if a female is weak, he does as he wishes. Yet he backs down to physical strength. If I defend myself and show more power than he does, I will be able to save my hide. Remember that if he comes your way. Ironically the troll was right with this information. Use Lastra and Tientara if necessary. He cannot be missed, by his eye scar.

I hope this bond created between Drazbart and I, can help us escape. He may bear hybrid blood within him, but Avalo will be a better judge of that...

Celestra wondered where Avalo was. He was not in the cell with them. This was a good twist. Understanding the obvious truth, she starts to laugh. "Why are you laughing, what's so funny?" Lu'barthrow asks. Celestra concentrates. *Haven't you noticed someone is missing from here?*

"Yeah, we found out from Yew. That sly old dragon. He managed to get away. Serendipity strikes again, and this time in our favor. Go now Celestra, and save your energy because I'm sure Avalo will try to find you. The rest of us will simply wait for you two to make a plan. Be strong...We will get out of here alive." Lu'barthrow tells her.

Celestra starts heading back towards her pen. Walking through the dark tunnels a second time, she thinks about how strange it was to bond with a Carthine. Especially one that has such a strong gift in sub-planing. Also, that strange room with the crystals.

There is ancient knowledge hidden inside there...

Something internally told Celestra, that Drazbart had a deeper destiny. She almost felt a little smitten with his reaction towards her. Strolling back down the tunnel to her pen, she tries to concentrate more on the issues at hand, rather than a visionary love-struck Carthine. Settling back into her body, she wiggles her toes, to realign her spirit. This was the longest Celestra had projected in quite some time. The city made her soft. They were right though. She should save her energy for when Avalo finds her. She decided to take a nap to recharge. There was too much at stake here for her now to be off her game.

Chapter Forty Four

Living in the Shadow of a Prince

Prince Zertarx was walking towards Groge's office, when he heard loud talking from a distance. The two voices belonged to Drumbler and Groge. The Prince was certain of this. The two of them were *always* together. All battles fought side by side. They may be shady, but they uphold the law ferociously and sternly. The Prince listens in on their conversation without being noticed.

"Drumbler, we will need another option to send our message to the white dragon. I refuse to lose another warrior by happenstance. It's bad enough the last one was eaten by a troll. We made him look like a prissy hybrid. Poor cat starved himself almost to death only to find it waiting for him. Just all wrong..."

Zertarx sees Drumbler nod his head. Groge continues talking. "If we are lucky, the king will give us another chance to retrieve our imprisoned bellas. We can attack the greggils this time in an ambush and win our old lands back as a result. The Prince is sure to thwart our plans. He says our population can't *handle* any more losses; bah. I say he has no warrior blood in him at all. Quite frankly, he acts like those soft-pawed renegades, and the King just doesn't see it yet."

Drumbler continues to listen realizing his General is venting. Clearing his throat, he offers a distraction from his complaints. "Well Sir, why don't I tell the warriors to adjust the catapults. They've recently built them up and had them fine-tuned. This way if an attack is launched, we are ready for anything." Groge agrees and sends him off to tell the warriors of their new assignment.

The door opens quickly and the Prince just misses it smacking him in the face. Quickly he jumps up on two legs and avoids the crushing weight. Drumbler runs off, so Zertarx has his chance to work on Groge now. Waiting a bit of time before he walks in, Prince Zertarx ponders what to say to put Groge in his place. He feels this big cat doesn't deserve to be General, even if just for a moment.

Strolling in, Zertarx sees Groge gazing at a gift the king gave him when he was younger. The General, comes nose to nose with it. Staring at it in great sorrow, he backs up angrily and slaps it off the table with a heavy paw. Growling, he mutters low words of discontent over his loss of affection from the King. He treated Groge like his *own son.* That was before the birth of Prince Zertarx of course. Sadly, this is when it all came to an end.

The King was so honored to produce such a rarity, a dark maned rogue Carthine. He spent much time perfecting his son's teachings and training. Groge became the General of war and at first, didn't see the change in treatment. To the King, there was no question of who was more important. Zertarx was of his own true fur and blood. Groge over time grew violently jealous of this and constantly tried to set up the Prince. He wanted to prove he was the better Carthine. The Prince, however, became fully aware of the foul play and always outsmarted him. As of today, this is still the same situation between the two.

Sitting at the foot of the table, Groge now seems to be contemplating further schemes to secure his position as general. Muttering odd things, it seems this cat has lost his mind completely. Zertarx walks in, as Groge's back is turned.

"I see you're hard at work general..."

Groge quickly turns around to see Zertarx standing in the doorway. "Good day Prince. What brings you *my* way?" Zertarx keeps a stern face and pauses a bit before answering. "In my father's best interests, I wish to now observe your meetings. Due to his poor health, the court is on high alert. We still need to free our bellas and retake our lands to properly prosper. When is your next meeting?"

Groge looks up at Zertarx and sneers but answers with an honest tone. "Tomorrow morning. Drumbler is alerting the men to configure their new fire catapults and informing them how to perfect their attack methods."

"Good." Zertarx smiles, "Then we're all settled. I'm off to tend to my father. General, keep me posted." Zertarx walks out with a wide grin. He cannot wait to remove him from rank. *Quite frankly, he won't even be a part of the royal army, after I'm done with him.*

That spineless little brat. He'll surely exile me after the King's death, unless he's stopped. Drumbler and I have much to talk about... Groge glances over the broken heirloom and tries to grasp the past is just that. The clan now seems more like renegades. They are turning against war like ways. "I will not have our clan turn soft paw! Our future race will be isolated from nature if we do not handle this correctly. We will deteriorate just like those damn greggils! The poor King has no idea what will become of his clan. This *is* my burden! I must restore the old code and save our future kin."

Groge truly believes in the superstitions against progressing towards technology and logic. It's been proven by the huge catastrophe the greggils succumbed to. Allowing deformed genes to prosper in their species only made them weaker as a whole. The pity for the disabled slowly poisoned their natural course of evolution.

Greggils refused to leave 'one of the pack' to die. Instead, they genetically rescued them. Added more skin here, took away from there. Not smart enough? Then take a pill. Not fast enough? Then implant these bionic joints. All in all, they began painting a pretty picture of denial on top of the front door of extinction. Humans enveloped themselves in this plastic and metal world.

This slowly suffocated and engulfed, the last wild bits of Gaia. Eons passed and they soon forgot what it meant to be an animal of nature. Instead, they drowned their instincts with their machines and their currency. Lost in a pool of illusion, they were helpless against themselves and became their own worst nightmare.

When the third world war came, all was lost. Their little plastic habitats, their square and rectangle stone mountains, their machines, their metal luminescent trees, and most certainly those worthless forms of paper currency. Humans belong to nature. They are not above it. All greggils live by this statement today. Groge remembers seeing it on a castle wall at their last battle.

"Bah, the Prince has no idea what it is really like out there. He has no idea how harsh and realistic our termination surely would be, as a renegade clan. Other clans haven't been heard from in a long time. I wonder why…Hmph." Lost for a proper plan in action, Groge remembers the addition of new prisoners from earlier today. Figuring that the Prince's next move would be to visit them, he decides to retrieve Drumbler to discuss what to do next.

Chapter Forty Five

Drazbart's Plan

Celestra is at a loss for what to do, so she just lies down in her dirty pen and tries to hold it together. Keeping her warrior mode awakened and alert, she still believes Avalo will find her. As luck would have it, he was already sneaking around inside the caverns. For some reason, there were also no Carthines present in this area. He plans to take full advantage of this. Once deeper in the caves, he notices some corridors had tall depressions within the walls to hide. *These guard posts are very handy. I can push back into them and become flush with the wall if a Carthine passes. Let's just hope they don't smell me first.*

Up ahead there are two tunnels. The first, leads further down into a larger opening, based on the light shining through. The other appears to be a long corridor. Avalo sensed strongly that there was a room ahead that even he shouldn't enter. *Stupid Carthines...You have no idea what that ancient technology really is. Thank the first dragon for that!*

He keeps lurking in the shadows further into the caverns. *I know I felt an energy exchange before in this area and its trail seems to lead down to the right.* Slowly creeping around the fork, he tries not to be seen. Smelling the mold and dampness hanging around the caverns, it throws off his scent trail. Seeing up ahead, Avalo can make out a line of cells. Crawling carefully past the door as to not disturb other prisoners, he makes his way down sniffing for Celestra's scent. *Ah, she's in the last one...good I'll just...*

He hears movement in the distance. Figuring this was a Carthine guard, Avalo quickly looks for a place to hide. Seeing a deep depression to his right, he runs for it and backs in on all fours. Keeping his head low, he breathes softly as to not reveal his location. *Hmm, wonder how I will deal with this situation?*

Didn't even get the chance to tell Celestra I was here. Into the room skids a small straggly Carthine. Out of breath, he lunges up and places his paws on the door, peering into Celestra's cell. The door slams and breaks her meditation. "Pssst, Celestra, I'm here..."

Avalo realizes this is his only chance to save her. So, he quickly jumps forward pinning the Carthine onto his back. "Oof...Hey... You big oaf. What are you doing?" Avalo rolls belly up and restrains the Carthine in his arms. "You will not hurt her! I will not have it you dirty squirt!"

Celestra props herself up to look out on what's going on. Her little blue eye, peers out of the hole. "Is that Avalo and *Drazbart*? Are you *both* out there?" Avalo looks up puzzled that she knows this Carthine. He stares at Drazbart for a second. "Uh, Celestra...You know this Chipmunk?"

Celestra, giddy with joy, squeezed her muzzle through the hole, in the top of the gate to talk. "Avalo! Thank the heavens you're here! I see you've met Drazbart, he's been helping me in here."

Obviously, Celestra couldn't see the situation, or she would have spotted Avalo strangling him. Drazbart choking and growling under his restraint tries to say, *"Let go...can't breathe..."*

Avalo stunned for a second, blushes in embarrassment. Setting him down, he pants for air on the floor sprawled out on his stomach. Avalo retorts. "Uh...Yes. Nice fellow he is. Celestra, might I ask, how you manage to befriend a *Carthine* so quickly?"

Celestra finally jumped up to where she can see, but wasn't happy to see what was going on. "Hey! Why is he on the floor like that? What did you do to him?" Avalo seeing Celestra is upset, carefully explains, "Well I really didn't think any of these cats would be, well you know...helpful to our situation. I was only trying to protect you Celestra..." Celestra smiles and laughs at his nervousness. "You'll always be a little whelp in trouble won't you Avalo."

Drazbart straightening up after the ordeal, tries to regain his dignity. Remembering why he came to talk to Celestra in the first place, he sneers at the red dragon. "If you don't mind *Avalo*, I have some urgent news to tell Celestra involving you and your friends." Avalo puts his head lower and waves him forward to talk. Drazbart jumps up and speaks to Celestra through the peephole.

"I just came back from the Prince. I've been informed he wishes to visit you all to explain what will become of your group. Especially *you* Celestra. Apparently, the Prince still desires to make you his own. This can be useful since your real identity remains unknown. Your friends are worthless to the clan. They may just be left to rot in their cells.

My idea is to convince the King to use you all as messengers to the white dragon. We've already lost many Carthines to the war.

This could be a viable option. The two that will need the most work, is the General and the Prince. The King will be my job. He is very easy to persuade when the preservation of his clan is guaranteed. The Prince is not as difficult to trick as the General is. My tactic will be, that those two are always at war for the King's attention. This means they are always distracted.

This is the plan: I will make a meeting later with both the King and his son, but General Groge will probably visit you all shortly to intimidate and push you around a bit. His words may be fierce, but Groge cannot act without royal consent. I thought about how your two griffins are personal transporters of the white dragon, and wish to use this to our advantage. They must report to her with the so-called, prisoners. The King will have to release you all realizing he has free messengers. Despite the stubborn nature of both Zertarx and Groge, this will be a better option for our race. Leave this part all up to me.

Since most Carthines are superstitious when it comes to magick, I need help conjuring up something that would scare them both deeply. It will be an easy act of persuasion to complete for a mystic. Who would be good for this Celestra?"

She smiles through the small hole after Drazbart leaped down, "Sounds good Drazbart. Avalo will be perfect for this." Drazbart turns and looks Avalo over quickly. "Avalo, I will need you to visit General Groge's room and attempt to conjure up an apparition of the Queen Carthine. He had a deep love and respect for her, yet she sadly died during the Prince's birth. This is not a well-known fact, so use it wisely. I am sure Celestra would only pick someone capable. So, this shouldn't be that hard for you. Can you handle it?" Avalo huffs and just ignores his comment.

Drazbart sees he is offended, continues without caring.

"Celestra, what I need of you is to remember this carefully: When Groge comes to check on you, he will be very nasty and cruel unless you are gruff and show strength. Just fight him as well as you can to get rid of him. He will back down and lose interest. So save the theatrics and drama for the Prince later on. When you *do* see the Prince, please shake violently and try to 'connect' to the white dragon and preach her words of discontent. I am fully aware of your mental capabilities, so do your best Celestra. Apparently, you've unlocked my own inner gifts and for that alone, I've decided that I should help you all escape.

Once the Prince is disturbed over your white dragon speech, he will then hear about Groge seeing an apparition, if all goes right. I'm certain he'll start to think he's lost his mind. Finally, if I am successful in swaying the King to let me travel with you as a scout, we all might be granted freedom.

Avalo, when Groge returns to his den, this is when you should launch our plan. The Prince at this time will start out to check on Celestra and your friends. Mind you, he will not be aware Groge has already done so. This is when Celestra, you channel the white dragon. After this, threaten the Prince to release you all or there will be severe consequences. The Prince is a learned cat and will not believe this right away until seeing Groge. All in all, this might create more trouble than it's worth, or it will help us escape with our hides intact.

I will check up on Avalo later tonight by the first guard's cavern. Avalo, at that time, you must leave for Groge's den and we will launch the second half of the plan. If all goes in order, we can get this done before noon tomorrow. Good luck and I pray to the first paw we succeed."

Avalo was astonished this small underfed Carthine had such wonderful leadership skills. *He could just be using us to foil our escape, but I will let this all take its course. Something tells me this cat has a brain and a heart.*

He turns to Drazbart before they left, "One question Drazbart. Was that energy exchange I felt before between you and Celestra? This would certainly explain why the two of you are so...*acquainted.*" Drazbart nods his head and looks up at Celestra. "She opened me up to my vision gift. I was drawn to her pen all the way from the King's quarters to then be rewarded with what she called a *planing* vision. This without a doubt told me to trust her explicitly. My parents raised me to know better. I will help her in any way I can. Her open soul is too beautiful to deny.

My apologies, but I must be off to the King now. His 'before bed snack' should be served soon, and there will be *hell* to pay if I am late. I will meet you later on tonight, Avalo. Thank you for your services. Hopefully, we will complete this without much trouble." They all prepare for the madness about to unfurl around them, and separate with little sound.

At this time outside the Cavern of Mor, Drumbler as per usual is throwing his power around. He sends the warriors running in all directions fine-tuning their catapults. "I said faster runts! You'd all be rugs by now!" Drumbler huffs angrily at how weak the last of these Carthines are. Not aware of Groge approaching, he continues to push the cats harder, making small amounts of improvement.

"You! Set that cord taught! No loose launches cats!" As General Groge gets closer, he sees how well Drumbler works the warriors. Groge sees this Carthine is on the right road to the top. He certainly is a cat that is working towards strengthening their race.

"Hey Drumbler, take a break. You've worked them and yourself hard enough. I have an idea about the prisoners. I heard from the guards that they've captured a *white bella* and quite frankly I hear she's a tiny diamond! I am interested in visiting her and having some fun. Her companions are in the holding pens further inside. They were a group off to the white dragon, or so they said to prevent imprisonment. The Prince *would* end up believing this after enough persuasion. We should go and discover the truth for ourselves before he sees them. What do you think? Are you up for some trouble?" Drumbler smiles and headbutts his dear friend, "Cats fall out!" Drumbler orders are met with relief. The Carthine's warriors head quickly into the night. Happy with today's training, Drumbler looks at Groge with a dark smile, "Let's go Groge."

Back in the throne room, the King's stomach was growling. Looking around for Drazbart he doesn't see him anywhere. He glanced towards the hunters' door and decided to retrieve them himself. Dusk was already approaching and he was… ravenous. Getting up from his throne, he nudges the swinging doors open to see the hunters relaxing. Utterly astonished they were still in the caverns; he roars at them to get their attention. Small stones fall from the ceiling and hit most of them in the head. Poor Drazbart even conned them to hunt with the promise of Sandtrala, yet they didn't uphold their part of the bargain. "What is the meaning of this? Lazy wretches get out and hunt for my meal! Am I *not* important enough to you? Go now before I decide to eat you all instead!"

The three hunters scatter straight out their forest exit. They left behind a collection of hurtly stones and some grulo. "What lazy freeloading beasts. They are starting to remind me of those dirty greggils. I will have Drazbart do something about them *if* he ever shows up."

As per usual, Drazbart scampers through the entrance to his lair, and screeches to a halt upon the nicely polished floors. Almost slamming straight into the King's haunches, he scratches through the top coat of the tiles to prevent a collision. Smiling looking up at the old but still impressive Carthine, his heart skips a beat for a second. Quickly, he gulps down his lost breath.

"I see you're late again Drazbart. This is becoming a habit against my wishes. Never mind that, the hunters have been slacking off. I had to snap them back into gear myself sadly. Do you deal with this *often*?" Drazbart nods his head yes, hoping in no way, this would turn into his fault. "Well then Drazbart, you should have alerted me of this. I am the King afterall. I'll get their hides moving. Now that dinner is taken care of, the Prince and I will be having a small meeting on the condition of our clan. There is another one later tonight including Groge about the prisoners. I will need you to scribe our actions and decisions down for future reference. Please be on time. If you are late, I may just have *Groge* deal with you instead."

Drazbart swallows his breath for a second time and obliges to the Kings simple requests.

The King lets Drazbart off easy, "I will be preparing for the first meeting in about two star turns, so, you have a bit of free time. Please let the Prince know about the meeting. Good night Drazbart." Drazbart huffs but knows if he hurries, he can alert the Prince of the meeting and then try to find Avalo. He already figures the general is off to see Celestra with Drumbler, so there is no time to waste. To his astonishment, Groge already wants a meeting on the prisoners and is a bit worried why.

Avalo awaits the return of Drazbart patiently, but cannot help feeling he's wasting valuable time by just sitting around. Gazing back and forth, he sees no sign of the stringy Carthine. Sighing out a bit of smoke, he tries to keep himself busy by levitating stones and placing them on top of each other to create a tower.

The night's cold wind, climbs straight up the spines on his back. Shivering a bit, he ends up knocking down the stones. "Hmm, winter is on the way earlier this year." Out of the corner of his right eye, Avalo sees two dark figures walking back from the warrior post. Figuring this is not 'good company', he backs up against the caverns outside wall, and hides to see who it may be.

Making sure his whole body including his tail and feet are consumed by the shadows, Avalo stares out to see these nightly travelers. "Wonder what the white bella really looks like, because you know, rumors that travel fast are *always* exaggerated…" Drumbler tells General Groge.

"Drum, I agree, but for the Prince to place her in her own holding pen, she must be at least *unique*. The one thing the Prince has, is good taste."

Drumbler laughs and nods his head.

"Hey, before we head over to that bella, want to have a few drinks of grulo? I have some on the side from the last batch made, and hell…it makes everything more fun." Groge at first seemed a bit wary of the idea, but gives in without a fight. "Sure Drum, don't mind if we do." Both stop off at Drumbler's den to share some drink.

Avalo watching these two, shakes his head in disgust. *This will come in handy later surely.* Avalo still sees no sign of Drazbart. *Now he is definitely late. Where is that runt?*

Drazbart runs down the hall towards the Prince's room. Praying he still has some time left to get to Avalo before the first meeting, he pushes harder than his body will allow. Slowing down to catch his breath, he walks into the royal son's quarters, panting profusely. "Drazbart, are you okay? You look terrible! How may I assist you?" Drazbart coughs, before being able to even utter a hello. Some spit falls to the ground from his tongue. The Prince perplexed by this display, stops his studying to walk over to him. "Sir, pardon my appearance... but your father has issued two meetings. One is in about a star turn and the other later tonight. I as well have other business to handle, ergo the reason for my exhausted nature. Pardon, I must be off. I will see you there your Clawness."

The Prince cocks his head at Drazbart's dedication and smirks. "See you later Draz'." Prince Zertarx watches Drazbart jet out of his swinging doors and laughs. "That little guy has one hell of a will. Somewhat respectable, I admit." Looking over his studies on greggil technology and mathematics, he contemplates their crazy theories.

"These underground tunnels they called 'subways' are rather interesting. Seems they would move humans back and forth by use of electricity and these objects called cable cars. The humans built them underneath the buildings above. Seems like a nice theory with layering to save space. What a quicker form of transport. Hmm, I wonder though why they would think this would *ever* be safe? Obviously, any other warlike race would destroy this system, to stop their daily activities. Greggils are so interesting, yet *so* stupid." The Prince closes his old textbook on American technology, and peers out from the upper window in his cavern. "The stars aren't quite there yet. I should take a walk for a bit to clear my mind."

The Prince may be in for an odd surprise. Prince Zertarx strolls through the damp caverns and remembers their old forest territory. He has strong feelings towards his cubhood hideaways and the thin chilly streams, "These caverns are a mere shadow of that warm forest floor." His heart hurt for the future kin who will be born in these dark tunnels. "They will never know that joy I was raised in..."

Walking outside, he was startled by two shadows sneaking about the prisoner caverns. Prince Zertarx lowers himself to the ground, his ears pinned back, and rear claws digging directly into the dirt. He awaits them to pass him before making a single move.

"I think it's this way, no; the other way. Well, wait a minute...do you hear something?" One of the shadows jets back into the darkness, leaving the other helplessly alone, "Hey where did you go? *Pssst*; I think something is here *watching* us."

Wandering dangerously close to the Prince, the invader has no choice but to freeze. It can't hear anything but it senses something is practically on top of him. Prince Zertarx waits for it to utter just one word to lock on his target. Sadly, this creature is very under-educated. It speaks out loud.

"Where are you?" The creature softly whispers, but it's too late, the Prince launches his large muscular body directly on top of it and helplessly it yelps out in fear of being caught, "Toodrum...*run*!"

The Prince pins it to the ground and sinks his thick fangs into its neck making sure to draw blood. "Do you wish to struggle or shall I tear out your throat now?!" The creature timidly says, "*No...*" As the Prince lets up from his bite, the bleeding creature shows it would rather die than get caught and imprisoned by bolting towards the warrior's field. "Hey stop! Stop now! Or I will hunt you until morning light when you will be dead from blood loss!"

Running straight into the darkness, the Prince almost catches up to the dark creature getting away from his grip. To his right he sees Groge and Drumbler waddling out of Drumbler's den obviously drunk off grulo. In that one moment, Zertarx trips and tumbles forward into a mesh net.

Wondering why the warriors didn't put their equipment away, he attempts to untangle himself, but it seems it's already too late - the trespassers are far gone.

"Oh father, this you will not be pleased with." Looking up to the sky, he sees he has a bit of time left to clean up and get to the first meeting. Yet despite this strange ordeal plaguing his mind, another began to bother him. "Why were Drumbler and Groge out this late? Have they not completed training with the warriors about five star turns ago? This shows me they're up to something and I'm sure grulo is involved."

Zertarx finally untangles himself and glances over to the first guard cavern, sensing something other than feline was waiting there in the shadows. "What is going on here? I will not have such mutiny brewing inside the land of my clan!" Zertarx walks calmly back towards the royal caverns and thinks about whether or not to alert the King of said activities. He's starting to dislike the fall of honor around here lately.

Prior to this, Drazbart had set out into the night, trying his hardest to make this plan happen. Knowing the Prince would find some way to keep himself occupied until the meeting, he figured he had time to meet up with Avalo. Slowly creeping around every bend, as to not be seen, he made his way from the royal chambers towards the guard caverns. Stopping to chew at an itch, he saw two dark catlike creatures stirring in the night. Watching them closely, he saw they were renegade Carthines, but from another clan. Their size and coloring were a bit different, probably due to the climate in this part of Apropon Rar. "I haven't heard of any other clans in years. Where are they coming from?"

Drazbart concerned watched them as they scurried about in search of something. He knew there wasn't any time to waste however, if he desires to speak with Avalo. He starts to walk towards the guard caverns when he heard Drumbler and Groge waltzing about. Stopping dead in his tracks, he saw them at the door of Drumbler's den. Drazbart realized if these two catch up with the renegades, it will destroy everything. The night watch stands will be lit and all put on high alert. So, he crept past them instead to the guard caverns, leaving the random acts of chaos to unwind themselves.

Celestra is sitting wondering how the others are holding up since her last visit. Realizing this is not how they planned to spend the first day of their journey, she only hopes they can escape unscathed. Obviously, with them working together, release and freedom are possible, despite the present hardships. Avalo should be waiting for Drazbart or meeting with him now. The Prince, should be off to his first meeting shortly, and finally, General Groge is almost at Celestra's holding pen. She remembers to remain in her primal thought pattern.

To stay as *wild* as she naturally is. Celestra makes sure to dust her star off, so she bares no mark of the hybrid. That surely, would seal their fate. Slowly, sinking back into her feral attitude, Celestra recalls something Uniqua had told her as a young cub:

"Now little warrior, know this during your daily romps in the woods. Sometimes others will expect you to react in a certain way, while others will never assume your actions. Some would rather see you as a stupid animal. Use this to your advantage... Being wild is a freedom most tame creatures never get to experience. In these parts, you never really come into much contact with domesticated animals. For quite some time, this education will be useless. It is truly an important key to survival though. Never let on to any of your weaknesses or your strengths; always remain a mystery in the face of adversity."

Celestra understood why this was an important lesson. Now held captive, possibly facing death or lifelong torture from an alien clan, this is her time to shine. Growling softly and holding stance, she speaks. "Uniqua, I will *not* fail you..."

Shortly after setting herself up for confrontation, she hears the pads of two cats approaching. Oddly, their feet are spastic and out of rhythm. Almost as if they were drunk. She listens carefully, and memorized the beat of their feet.

Her heart tries to stay steady, yet desires to race, as they get closer. Will these creatures rip her apart and leave her to bleed? Will they tear through her body out of primal rage? All Celestra can prepare for is the unexpected. Slinking back to the far-right corner of her pen, she prepares for them to enter. The jingle of keys can be heard; also, laughter outside of the door. "Here kitty, *kitty*, kitty...Want to come out and *play*?"

The door opens and Celestra is faced with a grand dilemma. Should she run for it? Should she maul them without concern? Or should she wait and see what happens...

She chooses to wait. Looking up at these huge cats, she certainly was intimidated, but Celestra doesn't move a muscle. "My, *my*... aren't you a *beau-ti-ful* bella! The Prince is *surely* to keep you...but I may desire a *sample* first..." Celestra watches without speaking, knowing things will go much smoother, if she stays in her wild mindset.

"So, do you have a name snowy little bella?"

All Celestra does is act like a wild creature. She growls back and stares ferociously. Celestra lowers herself to the ground readying an attack. Tail swaying erratically back and forth, she bares her teeth. Her claws now extended and her hackles were high and proud. Groge and Drumbler look at each other wondering if she understands their native language. "Well then, *cat* got your tongue? I may have a remedy for that *little bella*."0

Groge starts to circle her as she pushes further against the wall. She starts to raise a paw in defense slowly. He walks closer with his head hung low, while staring her down. "Why so defensive? I certainly want nothing more than to talk with you." Instead of retorting, Celestra lunges out, and scratches deep enough to draw blood.

Groge enthralled with his new toy, starts to get excited. "Ooh, now I see, you want to play, *don't* you?" Groge pushes her back against the wall with his head and slashes her right back. Celestra turns quickly around and sinks her teeth directly into his throat. Blood starts to pour from his neck. She hit his jugular in one shot.

With direct force, she trips the big lug as he tries to free himself, knocking him onto his side. Twisting Groge's neck skin into a quarter turn, she pins him with her claws, digging deep into his body. The blood flows faster now. Growling, Celestra waits for him to attempt to move. Then she could just rip his throat out in one fatal move. Groge is astonished that this small feline has such control and training. She's taking down a creature twice her size without any fear.

Celestra at that moment realizes Drazbart was right. Groge starts to back down.

Bleeding from many places, Groge signals to Drumbler to bite the nape of her neck to have her release. Celestra refuses to let go despite. Instead, she bites harder and starts to twist her jaw, making Groge scream out in pain. "Ouch!! Damn those little needle teeth! You *dear*, are ferocious beyond many of my own *warrior's* abilities. Let me go and trust I shall not hurt you, neither will officer Drumbler here."

Celestra decides after a few more turns to let go. She releases his neck and Groge's skin twists back to its rightful place – Slowly mind you. It all was rather painful.

A red pool has collected upon the floor. She happily licks his blood off her muzzle while staring him down. Groge twitches from the sharp skin correction, but realigns himself and cracks his neck back into place. Drumbler releases Celestra, impressed, wondering who taught her to be such a strong warrior.

She continues to remain silent. Both think she is unable to communicate at this point and is truly feral. Hopefully, this will work in her favor. Groge backs up and quietly attends to his wounds, while Drumbler just gazes at Celestra in wild amusement.

After some time, Celestra is still in the same position. Groge proudly walks up to her. Keeping her ground, she refuses to show any change in personality. She will not let him knock her down. Staring deeply into her eyes, he starts to feel he may have met his female counterpart.

"So, will you *still* not speak? I'm fondly curious about the name of this little bella that can stand up to me. Speak strong warrior and tell me really what you and your friends are doing traveling through our lands." Celestra wonders if she can use this to her advantage and remains silent.

Drumbler was growing frustrated with the display of brawn and bitter silence. He nudges Groge. "Sir, don't forget we shouldn't be seen here. We should make this brief."

Groge stops for a second and turns to his friend. He smiles and nudges him back. "That's why I made you high officer, Drumbler. You're always on top of things. Well, it seems this little *warrior kitty* refuses to talk. Much to my disliking, yes, but she has earned her privacy. I will be back to discuss things with you later, so expect my presence again. Hope you happily lap up that bloody pool on the floor. You've earned that meal." With that, the two of them prepare to leave and take her mystery with them.

After the door shuts, Celestra drops to the ground panting. *What strange creatures these Carthines are...*

Going back earlier into the evening, we find Drazbart petrified thinking of all the ways the King will have him killed for this escape plan. Finally evading the obstructions in his path, he makes it to Avalo. "*Pssst*, Avalo are you there?" Sadly, he looks up to see him being held by two rogue renegade Carthines in a gigantic net. With his mouth gaping open, Drazbart just stares. The cats gaze back at him and begin to growl. "What is your make *Carthine*? Are you on our side or the *corrupt* King's?"

Drazbart has one chance to say something effective. Staring at these highly impressive cats is quite overwhelming and Avalo is now in their possession. He's just too nervous to answer their question. Weakly looking over at Avalo, he sees him wink at him. *That dragon has something up his claws.* Drazbart was right. He let Avalo make the next move and simply froze.

"Now obviously you two must be proud renegades, yes?" Avalo asks them. They turn to him, wondering why he was asking such a thing. "Yes, we are part of an underground control unit. Under careful orders by our leader, we were to capture anything we could. There were two strong Carthines roaming about, but they seemed preoccupied and much too strong for us to take. Why do you ask such questions *dragon*?" Avalo angered just smiles. Spinning his two pointer claws, he removes the net and uncurls his scrunched-up body. "Ah, now that's much better. Wouldn't you say kitties?" One of the renegade Carthines terrified jumps backward at the sight of magick. Avalo continues to harass the guards, "*Now*…the reason I asked this is that my friends and I were traveling through this territory and Prince Zertarx decided to take us in as prisoners for trespassing. We need to change this time line a bit…"

One of the Carthines groans, apparently from a wound. "I've heard of his impressive intelligence for tactical aggression and that he is admired for it. We know the Prince is on our side. It is only a matter of time until he admits it."

Avalo looks at the Carthine's paw. Poor thing had some deep cuts. He leans in for a closer look, but the Carthine backs away in fear. "Now, is that any way to treat someone who wishes to help you? You have already held me against my will in a net, which mind you, I didn't like. So, at the very least, you should give me a chance to show you something." Drazbart stares at Avalo amazed at his ways of persuasion. Defying all laws of chaos, he managed to convince them he is not a threat. Now he has a chance to speak freely to these Carthines.

"Uh, excuse me? I have some information you may wish to hear. Freezia and Jasberous were my parents. I took on the role as the King's assistant to save their lives against their wishes, but sadly I was informed shortly after my ordeal, that they were killed anyway." The two Carthines stare at him wildly. "Those renegade heroes were *your* parents? We're terribly sorry for all of this. I think this mission is a total failure. We must get back to our base before our leader wonders what is going on. We offer our apologies to you and your heroic parents. *Drazbart* was it?"

Avalo confused at the information he just heard, wonders what is really going on with these cats. "Well before you go, let me tend to that wound...uh...What was your name again?" The renegade cat speaks up. "Beluvium. The name is Beluvium. This is Toodrum." Toodrum smiles as best as a Carthine can smile. Avalo smiles back, "Ah, well thank you Beluvium. I am Avalo. A pleasure to make your acquaintance. Here, now stay still and I will tend to that wound."

Slowly chanting old Draconian verses, Avalo performs a collective spell to heal the violently shredded paw on Beluvium. Within seconds he was as good as new. Both Renegades look up at this gentle giant and seemingly change their idea of dragons. "Not quite like the *demon creatures* you were taught about, huh? Well, why don't you two go now and change that *bad* reputation for me. Hmmm? This is all I ask for payment." Both run off leaving many questions unanswered between them all.

"Well, Avalo you seem to surprise me every time we meet. I have a small amount of time left, so listen carefully. Groge and Drumbler are just about to leave for Celestra's pen, but you mustn't follow. Make sure to stay put and begin to set up his den for the apparition. I will be in the first meeting with the Prince and the King so it's necessary I leave now. Meet me back by the cavern square when you are finished with your next mission. It's great you managed to escape, for none of this would have been possible with you behind bars. The cavern square is behind the prisoner's caverns, and we'll work on contacting Celestra from that point on. Good luck, but not like you *need* it."

Drazbart runs off. Avalo waits for the drunken Carthines, to waddle out from their den, to start this weird, haphazard apparition.

As all energy circles around themselves, the story meets like a snake biting its tail. Beluvium and Toodrum are slowly slipping out of the clan's territory trying not to stir up anyone's attention. But sadly, the Prince at this time, is heading out for a walk. "Psst, I think it's this way, no. That way... to the left..." Beluvium whispers to Toodrum. Toodrum looks up and can make out a faint figure in the darkness, "Beluvium...Don't move. There is *something* out there." Beluvium didn't hear him. "What? Where *are* you?"

The Prince is onto Beluvium in a heartbeat. He panics while fear wells up in his eyes, "Toodrum, *Run!*" The Prince sinks his teeth deeper into his throat and tells him there is no use. He will not get away.

Beluvium barely conscious from the strangling bite, tries his hardest to break free. Somehow, he managed to escape from the Prince's jaws and made a run for it.

Beluvium bolts straight for the warrior's field without looking back. The two are astonished the Prince trips into the net, left out from them capturing Avalo before. Thankfully, they realize they can escape with their lives this time.

At this point, Avalo has managed to sneak into Groge's den. He still feels something is watching him. Making sure to match the shadows, he slips on by into Groge's den. Looking around, he notices simple personal items. Some war memorabilia, some old crude weapons and that's about it. *This is not a very elaborate living space. Groge isn't a dragon after all.* Seeing a small nook by the bed, he walks over to take a closer look. "Hmm, there is a crawlspace in here, I wonder if I could fit..." After some contortions and squeezing, Avalo manages to fit into the crawl space. With a twist of his claw, he throws a veil of darkness over it to complete the illusion, "Ah...Now to wait for this Groge to return. Hopefully, it is soon. It's quite uncomfortable in here."

Now, Drazbart can walk to his next destination at a calmer pace. So, as he enters the royal room, he sees Prince Zertarx frazzled speaking with the King. Nervous the Prince is keen on his actions, he keeps calm, but worries the Prince has found him out. Seeing the King's expression made him relax. It seems the Prince was complaining about finding intruders that managed to run off. There was much at stake here tonight and any small thing could break it to pieces. Scribing down everything they discuss, Drazbart falls back into his normal routine as a court stenographer.

Poor Celestra was not too pleased with this 'friendly' guard visit. Licking her fur to calm her nerves, she wonders how all of this managed to escalate into such a mess. Her inner soul softly tells her that in time these moments will only become memories. Memories of a time she was being tested for a greater good.

Now that Celestra knows of her history, and her species' right to exist on Gaia, this all doesn't come as a surprise. In addition, where had her master's silver ring gone to, and who was that black panther wearing it in her dream? She has not forgotten any of this. Questions only seem to raise more questions and never any answers. Celestra realizes that she must be patient. This was not one of her greatest qualities. Right now, all that she needs is a message from Drazbart or Avalo, but that is some time away. So, she tends to her wounds and takes another small nap. What else can she do anyway?

Following a night guard towards the other jail cells, we find the rest of Celestra's group in a sad state. Tarmax in his horse form, just swats the metal gate with his tail in a sour mood. Drako and Garsa are discussing better trails to the white dragon. Partune and Raspier are chatting about past times together at the academy, and how many nasty tricks they pulled on their professors. Lastra, Tientara, and Yewdrone are quietly chatting about herbs. Yet Lu'barthrow, sulking in the corner seems to be deeply lost in thought. All others are far from his mind, but one. The mere thought of Celestra alone in that cell, makes him pound on the hard rock wall. "This isn't supposed to be this way! How could we let them take Celestra without a fight? She could have been with us. Where we could still protect her."

Lu'barthrow runs straight for the cell door and attempts to bash through it with his head. Repeatedly, he rams into the bars attempting to loosen them from their place. Blood starts to roll down his forehead and the group starts to get worried. Partune couldn't bear to watch this any longer, and grabs him. Restraining his legs, Partune just nearly misses Lu'barthrow's claws, flailing about. Tarmax walks up to him and smacks Lu'barthrow with his front foot. "Look, I myself should be doing the same thing, but it won't help her, nor will it help us. It will draw too much attention. Celestra, from which I have learned, is quite capable of fending for herself and maybe better than some of us. Relax and save your energy. Please before you hurt yourself anymore. She's learned a lot since Meoneal."

Tarmax realizes he said something that he should have questioned but missed. The issue with Meoneal was nothing to let slip out like that, only some of the others knew that Celestra was responsible. Thank heavens Lu'barthrow in his anxiety-ridden state didn't hear what he said, however, Garsa caught every word. *His face was terrifying...*

Garsa walks towards them. He looks at Lu'barthrow and waits fully for him to calm down before asking Partune to let him go. Lu'barthrow's head raises, and shows embarrassment. Garsa simply smiles and tells Partune to put him down. Fur tattered and panting heavily, Lu'barthrow just attempts to relax by lying down on the cool earth floor. He starts to clean the blood away from his head with his paw. "I'm sorry guys. I think it's just starting to get to me that we're stuck in here." They all just nod and equally share the thought.

Tarmax may seem calm but has the same fears about Celestra. After all, he was the one that saved her from Meoneal. These Carthines are at least twice his size and much stronger. The odds are slim to none that she will survive an attack from one of them. Still, his barnyard teachings apply well now: *If left powerless against it, do not worry. If an answer is to come, only a clear head will receive it.*

Tarmax lies down on the ground and tries to regain his composure. Looking around he noticed the rest of the group was working hard to do the same. They all prepare for sleep. Inching closer to each other, they huddle to stay warm. It has almost been a full day inside this Carthine prison. Tomorrow will definitely feel much longer if Avalo fails at breaking them out.

To be continued...

INDEX

Knorvein (Norveen)- the Icy Kingdom of the Purple Dragons– King Deetstro Trea

Kuit Forest – South of Tangolir Mountain Pass, West of Parscers Plains

Nessadra Forest - Forest North of King Cannor's Castle

Ocro – the lands of the far North - Astrof Mystics

Orlegon Sea – North West Sea Shoreline

Pittiney Lake- Droge troll's home

Port Numbis Liee - Stragguion Shores, Count Orpinious' Father is Leader; very wealthy port

Roden Forest - Carthine's old territory; Southwest Apropon Rar Lord Cannor's new castle

Royal Estate - Sky Kingdom's Elite Long Ears

Sands of McFlout – Strange and haunted Desert east of Durken Territory

Shackle River -Stream Cannor and Carmine played by as small children, Bliart Manor

Sky Kingdom - Long ear's kingdom; Matriarch Niyo Lentruio

Sow River – From Tangolir Mountain Pass and forks into Shackle River past Castle Clarney

Tangolir Mountains – Controlled & Tolled by Dar Tochchu, Dar Tochchu Mountain Pass

Tarmax Lake – Where Tarmax encounters the bear

Toc Lake - NW of Werras Lake, Feeds Jonibye Stream

Tressdresua Hills - Count Grestrada, South Apropon Rar, Unified with King Cannor

Werras Lake – North West of the Caverns of Mor, feeds Jonibye stream

List of Characters and Items:

Alpha - First gen of underground hybrids; Guin Tunnels

Alvon - Bardone's kit jaguar cub

Arac de Lout - Leader of seamen mystics, meeting stone leader

Arito - Anicorn

Avalo Ryu - Red Mystic Dragon for Drondia city of Dragons

Bardone - Celestra's father Trinity Dragon/Panther/Horse hybrid

Behestra Grenich - Leader of the Night Walkers; Anicorn; City of 'corns

Beluvium - Renegade Rogue Carthine

Beta - Second gen of underground hybrids; Guin Tunnels

Bibonion/Fuore - Huassen's Guards Killed

Bortho - Rider/Rouge Tracker for Huassen has hybrid dog/Astrof Collective

Brandledorgh - Hybrid Elder - Lion/Buck/Alligator; Guin Tunnels

Calikon - Celestra's Grandfather Panther/Horse

Cappibovine - Large rodent like cows/Used like horses and cows

Carmine - Cannor's Girl Childhood Friend

Carthine King - Certalk, the King of all the Carthines, Caverns of Mor

Celestaria - Celestra's mother, Unicorn/White Panther Hybrid

Celestra - Main Character, White Panther Hybrid, Raised in Fictine Forest

Celticar - Wolf/lion/Rhino guard for underworld; Guin Tunnels

Cetera - Third gen underground; Guin Tunnels

Chassie - Celticar's sister; Guin Tunnels

Commoricu - Jackrabbit tortoise hybrid of the Guard; Guin

Tunnels

Curlothier – Last dragon mystic/taught Tiergon – Star Collective member

Dar Vestuin – Overseas on Fyuion Island In charge of fourth human Meeting stone

Darshan – Dorcore's Son

Darston Cannor – High king of Apropon Rar – Prudence's Father – Clarney Castle

Delphi – Fourth generation; Guin Tunnels

Dojen – Asian Guard Dragon, Couscon Manor

Dorcore – Greggil's Dragon – Was brainwashed during Draconian War

Seffaunt – Droge troll

Drako – Next Dragon leader of Drondia

Drazbart – Kings Right-hand man, indentured servant Carthines

Dreather Grouse – Large colorful pheasant/ground bird

Drieston – Lastra's dragon mate who disappeared with Sarclaw her whelp

Drog – Coin/Currency for Apropon Rar's Humans

Dromino – Guard at Dar Tochchu Mountain Pass/Tangolir Mountains

Dynacis – Bardone's kit jaguar cub

Ernesto – Hyena Hybrid; run away from Guin Tunnels; shore clan

Fali – Hybrid in Durken Territory – Durken/Dolphin/Eagle; lives with Durkens

Fatuu – Slow Durken guard – dropped on his head at birth.

Fenton – Hurt worker Trea'sten helped

Foyo Falcon – Long ear son of Teya Falcon. Leader of the long ears for peace

Freezia – Drazbart's Renegade Mom

Frauwser - Barn cat/Tarmax's friend at Bliart Manor

Frukschtein – Dragon Prince from the Icy North with Dragon King Deetstro Trea

Galeiour - Main messenger for Hernshire

Garabolo - Trapper/Bounty Hunter/works for Lord Cannor

Garlochia - Celestra's Alias lion name; fake Princess title

Garlock - Celestra's White great grandpa

Garsa Yean - Leader of Drondia City/Black with one eye missing

Goiyan - Hybrid Mystic Asian Dragon (Apprentice) Couscon Manor

Grass Glider - Small raptor-like plains dinosaur.

Grendel - Top hybrid of the Underground – Bear/Black Unicorn/Dragon; Guin Tunnels

Groge - Carthine General of war, Caverns of Mor

Grulo - Dark Red Wine

Harmen Lyu - Leader of the Lost City of Hybrids

Heighton - Bortho's eldest son

Hesstrues - Dead Carthine Queen

Hurtly – Dragon board game played with crystals.

Ingpou - Hybrid underworld Guardian Panda/Elephant/Gorilla; Guin Tunnels

Jasberous - Drazbart's Renegade Father

Kiento - Scholar Ancient One - Dragon of Couscon Manor

Kiliro Vinasta - Leader of the Day Walkers; Anicorn; City of 'corns

King Back - Carthine Male Rogue

King Deetstro Trea - King of the Dragons in the icy north, lands of Knorvein

Larcatch - Celestra's Grandmother Dragon/Horse

Lashton - The youngest of Bortho's sons

Lastra - Water/Air Dragon, friends with Drako and Partune

Lilly - Trea'sten's Wife

Lord Dojhee (Doe-he) – Old Lord of Durkens
Lord Prudence Cannor of Bliart Manor – Son of King Darston Cannor
Loresen - Bortho's hybrid - Horse/Dog/Phoenix
Lu'barthrow - Celestra's brother
Lyant - Black anicorn healing specialist in the city of 'corns
Master Loreja - Master Dragon for Couscon
Master Trungpa Maitreya – Master of Couscon Manor
Marendo - Runaway hybrid from Guin Tunnels; Shore Clan
Majin - Tarmax's Long Ear Name
Maybelle - Bortho's beautiful wife
Meoneal- Saber Lion Street Vendor in Drondia city of Dragons
Michamo - Fox Rune reader/Star Collective member
Nari - Top scientist that created the sky world trinity hybrid, Sky Kingdom
Nastruvio - Bardone's hybrid kit
Nathan - Bortho's second eldest son
Neiges - Leader of Ocro and the meeting stone for the Astrof Collective
Nichi Partu - Anicorn Top Guard for Sorrokine Arou, Historian; City of 'corns
Niyo Lentruio - The Long Ears' Matriarch
Northern Separation - Dragons who want to kill all humans; work with long ears
Niyo Triuli - Upper World Guard of Release; Part of the Long Ears for Peace
Oct Bella - Carthine Female rogue light tan fur
Officer Drumbler - guard and friend to General Groge of the Carthines
Partune - Tracker Dragon for Drondia
Pourdries - Bliart Guard for Cannor

Quarx Dieyon - Retired professor from Drondia City; resides in the Durken Territory.

Raspier - Griffin/Historian for Drondia

Reesta - Head Lab Anicorn (DNA Research) at the City of 'corns.

Reibyrous - Shamanic Chakra Healer - wolf hybrid at Sorrokine Arou's city of the 'corns

Rogue - Male Black Back Carthine

Rubos - Rabbit/Buffalo/Penguin hybrid from the Delphi generation; Guin Tunnels

Sandtrala - Tan Oct Bella Carthine

Sarclaw - Lastra's missing whelp

Sattva Kien - Asian Guard Dragon Couscon Manor

Shalti – Anicorn

Spartan - Yewdrone's Grass Glider

Stralima Vou - Garsa Yean's whelphood love

Sureena - Bardone's kit jaguar cub

Tarmax - Bliart Manor – Lord Cannor's Horse – Trinity Hybrid

Teya Falcon - Long ear that wanted peace on Apropon Rar, helped build Durken Territory

Tharrow - Top hybrid of the Underground – Leopard/Antelope/Honey badger; Guin Tunnels

Tiergon - Old Leader of Dragon City

Toodrum - Renegade Carthine

Trali - Librarian Anicorn in Sorrokine's City of 'corns

Trastla – Anicorn

Trea'sten - Lord Cannor's right-hand man/ Blonde and thin with glasses

Trochilu - From Underground Hybrid tale– Wolfhound, War charger horse, Phoenix

Uniqua – **(Ooo-nee-cuwaa)** – Celestra's cubhood master. Brown and white bear.

Urisis - Bortho's Third eldest son

Vercon - General of war/Dar Tochchu

Veruda - Bardone's Jaguar mate

Verunith - Dragon of the Star Collective

Wenion - The first hybrid who set foot underground; Guin Tunnels

White Dragon - Sorrokine Arou

Willow - Tarmax's old horse mate at Bliart Manor — Lord Cannor's Horse lost to Garabolo

Yaster - Character in Tarmax's Mother's story

Yewdrone - Orphan Purple Whelp living with Meoneal the Cart Seller

Younger Vrillion - Right man to Chief Huassen of Dar Tochchu

Zertarx - Rouge back Prince of Carthines